PUSHKIN PRESS

Praise for
The Rabbit Back Literature Society

'Unnerving, enigmatic… Hints of *Let the Right One In* and
Haruki Murakami's elliptical early science fiction novels
flavour a creepy tale about mutating books, buried secrets and
ghostly encounters'

James Lovegrove, *Financial Times*

'Wonderfully knotty… a very grown-up fantasy masquerading
as quirky fable. Unexpected, thrilling and absurd'

Catherine Taylor, *Sunday Telegraph*

'Mixes the small-town surrealism of *Twin Peaks* with the
clandestine-society theme of Donna Tartt's *The Secret History*'

The List

'Charming and intriguing, switching from playful to creepy
to heartfelt and back again'

Bookbag

'Odd, strange and beautifully written'

Books, Bones & Buffy

'A novel about big questions… wonderful characters…
amazing'

TQR Stories

'Thoughtful, intelligent, and at times playful, this story about Ella and her encounters with the Rabbit Back Literature Society will leave you smiling, and at times scratching your head in wonder at the imagination of the author... marvellous'

Ginger Nuts of Horror

'Strangely magical... a wonderful and unusual story'
The Stardust Reader

'An intriguing exploration of how stories can define us, and what it means if reality doesn't measure up'
Follow the Thread

'*The Rabbit Back Literature Society* is a lobster pot of a book... an exquisite balance of suspense, precision-engineered structure and darkly playful humour... fascinating. And fun'
5-star review, *SFX*

'Charming, chilling and gripping from its very first page'
Bizarre

SECRET PASSAGES IN A HILLSIDE TOWN

PASI ILMARI JÄÄSKELÄINEN

Translated from the Finnish by Lola Rogers

WITHDRAWN

PUSHKIN PRESS

Pushkin Press
71–75 Shelton Street
London, WC2H 9JQ

Original text © 2010 Pasi Ilmari Jääskeläinen
Secret Passages in a Hillside Town first published in Finland
as Harjukaupungin salakäytävät by Atena Kustannus.
Published by agreement with the Kontext Agency.

English translation © Lola Rogers 2017

First published by Pushkin Press in 2017

F **I**
L **I**

This work has been published with the financial assistance
of FILI–Finnish Literature Exchange

1 3 5 7 9 8 6 4 2

ISBN 13 978 1 78227 337 0

All rights reserved.
No part of this publication may be reproduced, stored in a
retrieval system or transmitted in any form or by any means, electronic,
mechanical, photocopying, recording or otherwise, without prior
permission in writing from Pushkin Press

Designed and typeset by M Rules, London

Printed and bound by
CPI Group (UK) Ltd, Croydon, CRO 4YY

www.pushkinpress.com

SECRET PASSAGES
IN A HILLSIDE
TOWN

PART ONE

1

Publisher Olli Suominen spent the rainy days of autumn buying umbrellas and forgetting them all around Jyväskylä. He also accidentally joined a film club.

The club was screening twenty films that winter. In early September they showed François Truffaut's *Jules and Jim*, which made an impression on Olli. After he saw it he amused himself by looking for women who reminded him of Jeanne Moreau—on the street, at his publishing house and at meetings of the parish council. In the meantime he lost umbrellas—three of them on the worst day.

In October Olli was in his office munching on an apple, fell asleep in the middle of a bite and dreamt until he was awakened by the sound of the telephone. It was a call about a book fair he was planning to attend. Outside the window he could dimly see the rain-drenched park around the old church and the people scurrying through it. After the phone call he ate the rest of the apple and tried to recapture his dream. All he could muster was a trace of melancholy, a feeling that had lingered in his mind over the past several mornings.

This mood came to a head that evening when he saw Clément's *Forbidden Games*. An orphan girl and a farm boy befriend each other in wartime France and create a grave-yard for animals. At the conclusion of the film they are separated. Olli tried to fight it, but in the end he let the tears come.

At home later that night, Olli's wife, Aino Suominen, a schoolteacher and mother, wondered at his red eyes. Olli blamed it on the wind that had hit him as he came up Harju Ridge.

Joining the film club was a consequence of joining Facebook. Other consequences would follow. Later, at the point when things had gone terribly wrong, a memory popped into Olli's mind:

He's with his Grandpa Suominen, the notary, on the shore of Tuomiojärvi, throwing rocks into the lake. The wind is driving splashing waves over the open water towards the boats in the distance. There's a shiver in the air, although it's only July or August. The school holidays are dwindling and summer is curling up into a grey lump, like a spider Olli once accidentally killed in his father's office.

Grandpa stares at the rings of ripples on the water. His tie is flapping in the wind. He's been quiet all day. Now he smiles, points at the stones in the little boy Olli's hand, and says: "There is no act so small that it can't have larger consequences."

Olli drops the stones and turns to look at his grandfather, and there the memory ends.

Olli ended up on Facebook the previous summer after receiving an email from a colleague in Berlin:

Check out my Facebook profile. I set up a Facebook profile with my pictures, videos and events and I want to add you as a friend so you can see it. First, you need to join Facebook! Once you join, you can also create your own profile. Thanks, Dieter.

4

In the publishing field one must be accessible, so Olli signed up for the service and spent half the workday fiddling with his profile.

He disregarded the vampire games, opinion polls, childish quizzes and virtual gardens. He had no interest in writing trivial messages on his acquaintances' walls or sending them little pictures that were supposed to be some sort of gift. He would use Facebook to attend to business matters. As a phone book and communication tool for the Internet age it was excellent.

At the end of September Olli received a Facebook invitation from the film club. The message said that the club was meeting in the basement of a video store on Kauppakatu. He had met the man who ran the video store several times. The man had served for years as a pastor of a small district of the parish, then received an inheritance, left his job, quit the church and opened the video store.

He had told Olli that he'd lost his faith but found God again through classic movies.

Olli didn't have any time for movies. But out of habit he marked the date and address on his calendar. Then, when the day arrived, he went to the place, thinking that it was some important meeting to do with the parish council.

The seats in the darkened room were filling up. Footsteps. Rustling. Then silence. Olli could hear the breathing of the other people in the room, and the drip of water from his umbrella on the floor. He realized his mistake and started to get up, but then a light spread over the screen and sound flooded the room.

La Dolce Vita was beginning.

*

On 14th February, Valentine's Day, Olli got a new Facebook friend. The message said:

Greta added you as a friend on Facebook. We need to confirm that you know Greta in order for you to be friends on Facebook.

The link led to a fuzzy profile photo.

Olli already had 324 Facebook friends, and a poor memory for names and faces. In addition to his activities in publishing and the parish council, he belonged to a number of committees and organizations. Theoretically, he knew hundreds, if not thousands of people, although many of them looked alike to him. He wasn't sure if all the people he had accepted as friends were people he knew. So it was under-standable that he didn't recognize his first great love when she found him on the Internet.

He added Greta to his crowd of Facebook friends.

April was a busy month. Olli found himself doing a slapdash job with the children's book projects. The guilt gave him indigestion, and it was worse during meetings.

The rest of the group pretended not to notice. Their Western mores of politeness demanded that they ignore everyday unlovely phenomena like pimples, rashes, natural bodily odours and the sounds associated with the digestive tract. At one point the rumbling got so loud that there was a pause in the talk and everyone turned to stare at him, then looked away, shocked at their own tactlessness, and Olli was mortified. He covered his face with his hand, pretending to massage his forehead.

He had been waking up at night with attacks of melancholy. He had been dozing off during the day. One day on his lunch hour he fell asleep at his desk. When he woke up he had a craving for pears. He got up, intending to go to the Mr Delicious fruit stand.

Then there was a knock on the door. It was Maiju Karikko, the house editor, with a stack of manuscripts in her hand. Olli sighed and lowered his bum back into his chair.

Maiju was a businesslike woman, bland and blonde and taller than Olli in her high heels, though Olli was rather tall, like all the men in his family. Maiju walked across the room, settled in the chair across from him, laid the papers on his desk and picked up the manuscript on top.

Olli looked at her hands. She wore her fingernails short, without nail polish. Her fingers were long and thin. Olli, on the other hand, had hands like shovels. "Hands like an educated lumberjack," his mother had lamented, years ago. "The Creator must have run out of matching parts."

But Olli liked his hands. He thought they had a delicate power. Aino had once thought so, too.

"The new Emma Bunny," Maiju said. "Came in the mail."

"That's book number fifteen, isn't it?" Olli said, touching his forehead. "Well, they have sold well since she won the Finlandia Junior Prize."

Olli sank into his thoughts. Maiju mumbled something, then leant towards him and said, "*I have a fanny and you have a wee wee...* What do you think?"

Olli started to cough.

Olli Suominen travelled extensively for his business and

met women everywhere he went. Many of them offered themselves to him. But he didn't feel a temptation to enter into any erotic adventures. In fact the thought of getting to know an unfamiliar body with all its idiosyncrasies and imperfections made him feel anxious. His sexual fantasies always focused on his wife's body, which he had come to know inside and out, making the experience pleasantly straightforward.

Olli stared at Maiju without speaking.

"OK," she sighed, seeing his discomfort, but not understanding its cause. "It's only a working title. We'll probably have to polish it a bit. In any case, it's an introductory sex-education book for preschoolers, and that has to be clear in the title."

Olli relaxed and lost himself in staring at a photo on his office wall.

It was a photo of him, taken in that very office, a black-and-white portrait of Olli Suominen, Publisher, in authoritative mode. He wore a grave expression and an upright posture. Olli had a similar photo at home, not of himself but of his paternal grandfather, the notary Mauno Suominen, whom Olli strongly resembled. The similarity had been reinforced when Olli started wearing horn-rimmed glasses and relaxed but stylishly continental suits, just as his grandfather had worn in his day.

Olli wondered what his grandfather would have thought of this children's book.

In addition to writing, Amanda Vuolle was an accomplished watercolourist, and had illustrated the book herself. Maiju showed him two of the illustrations, in which a girl

8

bunny first shows her private parts to a boy kitten, and the boy kitten then shows his private parts to the girl bunny. The author's misty style oozed with sweetness.

Maiju read aloud from the manuscript:

"'I have a fanny, and you have a wee-wee,' Emma Bunny said to Karl Kitten, and kissed him on the cheek. 'I am a girl and you are a boy. Do you like me? I like you. When we grow up, we can get married and have children together.'"

Olli wanted to say something publisher-like, but nothing came to mind. His bum searched for a more comfortable position in his chair. The back of his hand wiped his mouth. His chest felt tight. His nose twitched. He struggled to tamp down the surge of emotion this bunny–kitten love story had evoked in him.

Maiju looked at him. Olli pretended to be clearing his throat.

"We decided at our September meeting that I should commission an educational book from Amanda," Maiju said. "So here it is. Yeah, it sounds odd, but it's well executed and I think it's a sure hit."

Olli nodded, got up, walked behind her, took off his glasses and wiped his eyes on his sleeve.

At the end of the workday, Olli stood in front of the large, many-paned window of his office and looked out, pressing his cheek against the stone wall, his fingers resting on the windowsill. The old glass warped blisters into the wintry cityscape and stretched and twisted the lights and the people passing.

He couldn't see the sky in the dark of 5 p.m., but it was no

9

doubt cloudy. Olli wondered if it was about to snow or sleet. He decided to take his umbrella, just in case.

He shot a glance into each office as he left, hoping not to attract anyone's attention. He had dinner waiting for him at home.

Seija, who handled the finances and served as Maiju's assistant, had left for the day. In the third room he passed he saw Antero, their young publicity agent. He had neat blonde hair and immaculate clothing: a white shirt, narrow tie and suit trousers. He was working on a book ad for Helsinki's largest newspaper, and it had to be ready in the morning.

There was an opened cup of yogurt on his desk, the cover licked clean and carefully folded. Every time Antero licked the cover of his yogurt his Adam's apple bobbed up and down. His thyroid cartilage was larger than average. Sometimes it irritated Olli. It was hard to watch, and harder not to watch.

When Antero noticed Olli in the doorway he pointed at him and mouthed the words *Don't forget the flowers.* Antero didn't wear a ring. Olli did. He remembered that he had asked Antero for this reminder. He thanked him, and said, "You may have saved my marriage."

Olli went down the stairs, stopped when he got to the street, and paused a moment before starting off. The asphalt was icy. It would be easy to fall and break a bone. He'd had better soles put on his shoes, but he still needed to be careful.

He proceeded with cautious steps, his arms spread slightly, not caring that he looked a bit ridiculous. Once he was safely across he walked onto the ice-free pedestrianized street and gave silent thanks to the city engineer who had thought to circulate the district's heating water under some of the streets, at least.

Jyväskylä's town centre was small, basically just a few square blocks. Every evening it was jammed with people getting off work, stressed and hungry. They mingled with the school kids loitering on Compass Square or in front of the Forum shopping centre.

Sometimes there was the occasional street musician along the way. Today there was a ragged accordionist on the corner playing *The Umbrellas of Cherbourg*. Olli dropped two euros in his accordion case. The playing intensified. The accordionist wanted to give him his money's worth.

The crowds of people made Olli nervous. Too many faces. Every few steps he raised a hand or nodded in greeting. He met a constant stream of familiar faces—acquaintances from the many organizations he belonged to, or just people who seemed to know him, people he ought to recognize. There were too many of them. Their names and connections were a mystery. His head felt strained. His cheeks quickly tired from this rapid smiling, even if it didn't use all two hundred muscles.

Olli crossed the Forum to the flower kiosk and bought a bouquet of yellow roses.

Aino was wearing a yellow dress the first time they met, in a nightclub popular with students. The place had been too crowded and Olli's friends had decided to continue to another bar. Olli had looked around, chuckling at his mates as he emptied his pint, when suddenly the light in the room had changed somehow, and the sight of a girl came hurtling at him through the dimness.

He still remembered that moment.

A girl in a yellow dress on the other side of the restaurant, chatting with friends. She touches them, laughs and gestures, stands out from her surroundings like a brimstone butterfly alighting on a highway.

Olli finds himself walking across the room. He makes some insignificant remark, and she answers. Two hours later he says, more to himself than to the girl, whose name is Aino, "It's weird, but I feel like I've always known you…"

They're sitting at a corner table. Olli's hand rests lightly on Aino's, as if he wants to hold on to her so she can't get away—not yet, maybe not ever—but it isn't too possessive, not at that moment. Her face opens up more and more with each minute that passes. Olli enjoys her warm expression, its sincerity. "It's like I was always meant to know you," he says, then regrets it, because Aino is startled, grows serious, withdraws, tilts her head and examines him, looks long and deep.

Olli's smile freezes. She's going to get up and leave, he thinks.

But the girl nods, takes hold of his hand and smiles, as if she's just got to the bottom of an important question.

Olli walked past the compass inlaid in the pavement on Compass Square and headed towards the yellow facade of the Lyceum.

The cold wind slapped at his coat-tails and toppled three bicycles, which fell at his feet. He jumped out of the way, teetered, then righted himself and corrected his stride, in a complicated series of steps that brought him to the other side of the street and made two schoolgirls burst into giggles.

As he reached the corner, he yawned. His eyes closed for a moment. When he opened them again he nearly stumbled over a cocker spaniel that had appeared in front of him. Stepping around the dog, he found himself crossing against a red light, and a car nearly hit him. The horn blared. Olli strode to the opposite kerb, angry and embarrassed, looking back over his shoulder, and ran into a stocky fellow who had just stepped out of the school building.

The man took Olli by the arm to keep him from falling.

"You seem to be in quite a hurry, Mr Suominen," the man said. It was the principal, who was also a member of the school board. Olli took a breath and apologized. The men shook hands in a show of mutual respect. *Like two honoured city leaders who each in his own way and of one accord uphold the civic culture of this, the Athens of Finland*—that was how one of the jokers at the Jyväskylä Club once put it. "You might have spoilt your fine bouquet," the principal continued. "What's the occasion? Is today your wife's birthday?"

Olli told him it was his anniversary. The principal congratulated him. Olli thought about dinner, which was probably already on the table, his wife and son picking up their cutlery at that moment.

The principal lifted his chin, gave Olli a serious look, and said in mock sternness, "Mr Suominen, I hope you have bought your club membership."

Olli shrugged, smiled, and said, "I've been very busy…"

The principal laughed. It was the same old joke every time Olli saw a member of the Jyväskylä Club. The last time had been two weeks earlier when the principal invited him to the club for a meal and a cognac with the higher-ups of the city.

While he was there it was explained to him, once again, that club membership was not only an honour but a civic and social responsibility, and that he shouldn't put it off any longer. With all hesitation drowned in a snifter of Delamain, Olli had promised to take care of the matter at the first opportunity. The next morning, however, it hadn't felt quite so urgent.

The two men wished each other a pleasant evening and parted. As Olli continued on his way he noticed that the pavement in front of the school was well gritted, and for that he was happy.

The Suominen's house was in Mäki-Matti, a verdant residential area on the far side of Harju Ridge. There were three possible routes home from the publishing house. The easiest and safest was also the dullest. That was the route Olli took, because he wanted to be home before Aino and his son got up from the table. He crossed the market square and walked down Harjukatu along the lower slope of the Ridge.

Harju Ridge was Jyväskylä's most important landmark. If you stood at the summit and looked south-east, you could see over the city streets as far as the lake and beyond. Olli passed the new school annexe, a red-brick colossus where teenagers studied for university entrance or for a profession. It looked like a prison. The sign in front read "MUNICIPAL–REGIONAL EDUCATION DISTRICT". It sounded ugly and bureaucratic to him, and brought a scowl to his face.

Boys in billed caps and girls dressed in black were standing at the bus stop. Olli strode past with his brow furrowed.

He didn't like the walk home from here. It lacked all atmosphere. Jyväskylä nowadays had too many out-sized structures that tired the eye; oppressive, purposeless spaces; roads and tracks laid in the wrong places; buildings with no personalities; erasures of history.

In cities like Paris or Budapest, your senses opened to take in experiences, but Jyväskylä nurtured dullness. Olli had spent the best summers of his childhood in Jyväskylä, but the city in his memories was more beautiful, larger, magical.

He turned left at the corner of the school. On his right was a car park, and beyond it a small city park—although it was really just a paved square. It looked like it had fallen randomly where it lay. There was a flea market there on Saturdays. Most other days it was full of skateboarders practising tricks. It had several step-like structures, a fountain and a massive signpost that marked the distance and direction to Jyväskylä's various sister cities: DEBRECEN. ESBJERG. ESKILSTUNA. FJARÐABYGGÐ. YAROSLAVL. POTSDAM. POZNAŃ. STAVANGER. MUDANJIANG. Presumably there was in each of these cities a sign that pointed to Jyväskylä. Olli found the thought depressing.

At last reaching the end of the long school building, he came to the first houses of Mäki-Matti. The Ridge with its street lamps, footpaths and benches rose up on his left. Runners and dog walkers flitted by among the trees.

On the top of the Ridge was the observation tower stretching up to the sky like a prayer from the city fathers and mothers: *Our Father who art, perhaps, up there in heaven, do not forsake Jyväskylä, but give us this day our daily vision, mission and development strategy, and a little relief from budget deficits!*

Every summer Olli went at least once to the observation tower with Aino and the boy. They rode the elevator to the restaurant, bought bowls of ice cream with chocolate sauce and looked at the view: the downtown streets, the lake, the little people swarming around the stadium, the wooded suburbs that surrounded the city.

Olli thought about dinner. It was Tuesday. Potatoes and hamburger gravy.

They had lived at their present address for ten years. Before that they'd lived in a two-bedroom apartment, their first shared dwelling. When Olli was given the post of publisher and Aino got her job at the school they took out a loan and bought a house at the top of the Ridge.

It was an expensive house, but brighter and roomier than their apartment, and in a lovely neighbourhood. "Have we really earned a house like this?" Aino exclaimed with tears in her eyes the day they moved in, and Olli laughed at her childlike joy. They dashed from room to room, holding each other by the hand, and made love on the pile rug in the kitchen. Olli had bought the rug as a gift for Aino when she was living in a sublet room in a pensioner's house.

Seven years later a little boy just learning to walk had diarrhoea on that rug. As Olli carried the rug out to the bins Aino had said very sensibly, "That ratty thing. A family with kids needs a kitchen floor that's easy to clean."

As the years passed, the house revealed its little failings. Aino didn't mind them. And Olli tried not to think too much about them. A person should be positive.

For instance, the slope of the wood floor at the south end of the dining room didn't really bother him once they adjusted the legs on one side of the table. They could replace the floor later, once the boy was bigger and they'd paid off more of their home loan and Olli had the time to arrange it all. And if they didn't hang any shelves or pictures on the living-room wall, they didn't really notice that it leant in by about three centimetres.

Sometimes as Olli lay in bed waiting to fall asleep and listening to Aino snuffling in her dreams, the flaws in their house would circle in his mind like houseflies. It was a comfortable, pleasant house. Aino found it pleasant, anyway, and so did their son. Olli tried to. He just felt that when the place was built the horizontals weren't quite made horizontal, or the verticals vertical.

The builder seemed to have been missing his spirit level and measuring tape. Sometimes when Olli thought about this inattention to detail it made him so angry that he had to get out of bed and go to the kitchen for a glass of milk. The kitchen had been remodelled properly, and neatly. It was a sort of temple of clarity for Olli, where he could, on nights like these, regain his peace of mind.

The house had a little metal gate in front. When you went through the gate it squeaked open and slammed closed. In the yard were five currant bushes, three apple trees, a rowan and, at the moment, a metre of snow, with Aino's flowerbeds beneath them, waiting for the spring. A narrow path led to the front door. Olli came through the front door with the bundle of flowers under his arm, smelling the aroma of food. He hung his things on the coat rack, took off his fogged glasses and stuffed them in the breast pocket of his shirt, and went into the dining room.

Aino and the boy were eating potatoes and hamburger gravy. The cutlery jangled. Olli was late from the trip to the florist and the five minutes taken up by his chat with the principal.

Customary greetings were exchanged. Olli ruffled his son's hair and handed the flowers, tightly wrapped in paper against the cold, to Aino. Aino thanked him, smiled and laid the bouquet on the counter next to the pot of potatoes. "After dinner we can see what kind of pretty flowers Mommy got this time, Lauri. There's a surprise for Daddy too. But let's eat first."

Olli took out his glasses and polished them with a napkin, dished three warm potatoes and two ladles of gravy onto his plate, and sat down. The chair wobbled on the uneven floor so that one chair leg was always in the air, but it didn't bother him if he didn't think about it too much. There was rye bread and low-fat spread to put on it. Olli's blood pressure had been high for the past few years, and since he didn't have any extra weight he could lose, or a smoking habit he could quit, he had no choice but to eat more healthy food. There was a bowl of tomatoes sliced in half. Olli put two halves on the edge of his plate, well away from the gravy. Gravy and vegetables mustn't be allowed to mix.

Everyone had their own drink. The boy drank milk, Aino lactose-free buttermilk, and Olli mineral water. Sometimes he drank low-fat milk.

Aino told him about her day teaching Year 3. She had heard at the nursery school that their son wasn't taking his naps and that because of this he had thrown a tantrum when they were putting on their coats and hats.

"Aha," Olli said. "Is that so?"

The boy mumbled through a mouthful of potatoes. Forks

clinked against porcelain. Aino told the child to mix his gravy into his potatoes and reminded him that dessert was made for little boys who drank up all their milk. It sounded like a repurposed proverb to Olli, but Aino was a practical person, and not one to speak in proverbs.

"Your bones need calcium," she said soberly. "And milk has calcium in it."

The boy peered into his milk mug doubtfully.

Then Aino's attention turned to her husband. It was Olli's turn to give a summary of his day at the publishing house. He did so, and mentioned that he would have to go to Helsinki again in a couple of days, and wouldn't be home until about eleven. Oh, and there was a meeting of the film club tonight.

They watched the movie in the dark.

It was *To Die with the Blossoms*. Bold colours, veiled gazes. Tony Leung's character loves a sales clerk who looks like Maggie Cheung, but she's obsessed with her dead lover. *It's good to love the dead, because they live in yesterday, and yesterday will never leave us*, Tony Leung says. Then he strokes his moustache, lights a cigarette and burns the letter that would have revealed her dead lover's crooked past, and thus freed her from his grip.

The rainy city changes to a sunlit beach. The bright film screen lights up the room. Tony Leung steps out from a sea of umbrellas and follows a girl in a flower-print dress.

The saturated colour on the screen pressed Olli into his seat and quickened his breath. He rubbed his stubbled chin and glanced to left and right. There were about twenty people in the room. The purpose of the film club wasn't to get to know people; the point was to share the viewing experience, not the feelings it aroused. They showed up in the darkened hall to watch a film, then exited up the dim staircase.

End credits.

Olli and a couple of other viewers remained seated in the dark. A good film left a trace in the mind, like wine. You had to taste it before rushing back to your ordinary life.

When Olli finally got up, he saw a woman sitting near the doorway. He had noticed her before. A slender, delicate thing, gracefully gaunt. Flamboyant clothes. Like a movie star herself.

Olli still couldn't see her face. She had her back slightly turned, seemed to be looking for something in her bag. Today she was wearing a long skirt and a short-sleeved, pale-coloured blouse. Her hair was covered in a white scarf with a dark pattern on it. A lock of hair peeped out. A winter coat was hanging on the back of her seat.

Olli tucked his umbrella under his arm, straightened his tie and headed for the door. As he started up the stairs he noticed that the woman had an unlit cigarette in her mouth.

He stopped, hesitated a moment, walked back to her seat, and said, "There's no smoking in here, you know."

The woman gave no response at first.

Finally she said, without looking at him, "I'm not smoking."

"You've got a cigarette in your mouth, haven't you?" Olli said. He realized he sounded stupid and unsure, and regretted that he'd said anything.

"Sure. And I've got shoes on my feet, but I'm not walking."

Olli climbed up the stairs, embarrassed. It wasn't until he was out of the building that he realized he had just had a conversation out of an old American comedy.

He stepped into the courtyard under the black sky. There was a red Vespa parked next to the entrance. Olli stood looking at it. He ventured to touch it, ran his fingers over the red painted surface beaded with raindrops.

He heard voices approaching and hurried out of the gate onto the street.

Olli climbed up Harju Ridge.

The massive stone staircase had always appealed to him, but now it stiffened his feet and made him feel cold. It felt as if the chill of ten winters were stored in the stones. As he came to the crest of the hill and started down the other side a north wind struck him, freezing his glasses to his head and nearly stealing his hat.

When he got home, he was shivering. He hung his wool coat and fedora on the rack, took off his glasses, gloves and shoes, and went into the living room.

Aino was sitting on the sofa correcting tests. She was wearing loose green sweats. The television was showing a programme about the everyday life of a family. The children screamed and refused to do what their parents told them. A psychologist gave them some advice. The children's behaviour improved.

Aino was surrounded by a teacup, an open packet of Marie biscuits, a half-eaten apple, three children's books, a thick stack of test papers, a mark book, five pens, a packet of tissues, a bottle of lotion, wool socks, a phone, a wrapped present and a lot of biscuit crumbs.

Olli sat in a chair next to the television and looked at his wife benevolently.

Aino picked up the wrapped package, smiled, and handed it to him. "I almost forgot, because I had to put Lauri straight in the bath after dinner. Everything he had on had to go in the laundry. Plus I had to clean the kitchen floor—it was covered in crud. Luckily it's plastic. Anyway, happy anniversary."

Olli thanked her and started to open the package.

Aino turned down the sound on the television and watched his expression. "I don't know if you'll like it," she said. "I was walking by the shopping centre today before I went to pick up Lauri and I remembered our anniversary and I thought I should buy you something this year. I'm usually so busy that I don't have a moment to get to the shops so you have to go without any present…"

Obviously a book, Olli thought.

He was touched that Aino had bought him a book, but he braced himself for disappointment. He didn't want to hurt her feelings. She didn't really know his taste in books, didn't really know literature in general. For a teacher, she was surprisingly indifferent to the arts, or to anything cultural. She preferred kitsch of all sorts, and carried around a Hello Kitty pencil box without the slightest irony.

"Happy anniversary," she said again.

The wrapping paper fell to the floor. There was a picture of a pear on the cover of the book.

"Since you've been going to the film club, I thought…

It came out last summer and I heard that the first printing was sold out by Christmas. But it's in the shops again now. They've got a huge marketing campaign for it. Big best-seller. There was an ad for it on television yesterday and I thought you might like it…"

Over the top of the pear was the title: *A Guide to the Cinematic Life*. The author's name was Greta Kara. Olli opened the book. Aino had written across the title page in her familiar scrawl *For Olli from Aino on our anniversary*.

"I do like it," Olli said, happily surprised. He hugged his wife, who let out a chuckle and started watching the television again. Olli turned to the first page, which had a dedication:

For the love of my life, from the girl in the pear-print dress!

2

O N Thursday Olli was on the phone making arrangements for the book fair. Outside the window the old park was covered in snow. Inside was work that kept accumulating on desktops and computer screens. The work they already had was still for the most part unfinished. Olli could only spare an hour for working late today because he had a parish-council meeting at six o'clock.

At 5.55 he tore himself away from publishing and hurried to the parish house, just a few streets away. He stopped at the entrance and opened and closed his umbrella three times quickly to shake off the snow.

The swishing shadows made him think of a dream he'd had when he was elected to the parish council:

He's on his way into a meeting on a summer evening when he sees an angel ascending from the parish house roof into the air. Its wingbeats are so powerful that for a second the air is filled with feathers. The angel flies towards the Ridge and lands halfway up the Harju Steps, then points to its feet and gives Olli such a meaningful look that it frightens him, and he wakes up.

Olli looked up. There were no angels, just a lot of falling snow. He smiled and walked inside. In a place like Paris or Rome or Budapest, under the right circumstances, you might even believe in angels, but not in present-day Jyväskylä. The city had become a monument to dull ordinariness.

About forty people were gathered in the conference room. Greetings were exchanged. Olli talked with two recent appointees about cemetery maintenance and with three other members about the next meeting of the organizing committee. *Olli Suominen—sweating the details.* That had been his slogan in the parish elections.

During the opening hymn Olli started thinking about his umbrella, which he had left on the coat rack. It was the only one he had left. He had to remember to take it with him. He had forgotten his umbrella at the last meeting and he'd never seen it again. A brand-new one. Maybe somebody had pinched it.

Olli liked being part of things, but he got bored during the slow bits. While the others sang, he amused himself by putting his thoughts in the form of a prayer: *Merciful God, ruler of the universe, who art in heaven: would you mind making sure that the most absent-minded of your creations—publisher and parish-council member Olli Suominen, who sweats the details—remembers to take his umbrella with him when he leaves, because lately he's been spending altogether too much money on umbrellas?*

It crossed his mind that if he converted to Catholicism he wouldn't have to bother God himself about the umbrellas: he could ask for help from St Anthony, who was, according to at least one theologian, pertinent to Olli's umbrella problem. It seemed that Anthony of Padua had once lost his book of commentaries on the Psalms. Because of that deed he was proclaimed the patron saint of lost things. Which was the sort of saint Olli could definitely use.

When the hymn was over the pastor cast his pious gaze over the assembled and reminded them that people should be grateful for all the good they received because the Lord worked in mysterious ways and what the Lord giveth the Lord can taketh away and so on.

Olli dutifully began to feel grateful. After all, he had a steady job, in a position of responsibility that motivated him. He had his health, a family and a home whose faults really did seem to be starting to put the kibosh on his gratitude.

Olli forced his thoughts away from remodelling and found himself thinking that if the Lord taketh away all sorts of things, could he be the one who had taken the umbrellas?

As the pieties were nearing their end, Olli started to feel embarrassed at his childishness. He tried to get in a more businesslike frame of mind by thinking about his grandfather the notary and imagining the man scolding him, as he sometimes had when Olli was a child if he had done something inappropriate.

It was, after all, inappropriate to be disrespectful even in his mind when others took their devotions seriously. Notary Suominen had once said that you shouldn't allow your private thoughts any special dispensation just because others couldn't see them.

Olli genuinely liked the Church. It was a large, uncomplicated institution, which pleased him. He wasn't particularly religious, but he wasn't an atheist, either—he believed in God at least in theory, the same way that people believe in distant heavenly bodies, or in their own mortality, or in other things whose existence wasn't in dispute. But he also didn't let such beliefs disrupt his daily life.

The meeting was called to order and a quorum declared. The reasons for any appointees' absences were discussed and their proxies identified. The agenda was approved. When they started to choose who should inspect the minutes, Olli adjusted his tie and straightened his back so quickly that his vertebrae audibly crackled.

When such roles were being delegated, Olli was usually recommended, and was often chosen. His manner was one that inspired trust. It ran in his family. He was a reasonably intelligent and capable man, just as his grandfather had been. The result was that he was needed in many endeavours, and when duty called, he didn't like to refuse.

Aino sometimes tried to rein him in. "You're not the only person in Jyväskylä who can get things done."

Olli responded by quoting his notary grandpa: "A man has to carry out the tasks that fall to him with pride and humility. Otherwise someone somewhere might end up suffering in ways that he can't predict."

Olli was the first one chosen to inspect the minutes. The second chosen was Ritva Valkeinen, a mother of seven sitting a couple of rows ahead of him. She turned and nodded to Olli.

Olli had seen Marcel Carné's *Port of Shadows* at a meeting of the film club a couple of months earlier. Before Ritva Valkeinen turned back around her face lit up. She smiled at him, and for a couple of heartbeats she stopped being the God-fearing mother of a large family and looked very much like Nelly, the character played by Michèle Morgan.

When the meeting ended the group emptied out into the courtyard. The snowstorm had stopped and snowploughs were rumbling down the streets. Olli said his goodbyes, exchanged a few words of conversation, laughed at the others' quips, wished them a final good evening, crossed the street and started walking home. The snowy slope of the Ridge rose up on his right. Figures flitted through the shadows of the pines—joggers and dog walkers.

Olli gave a start when a black and white cocker spaniel came trotting down the hillside. It walked past him into the street, as if going to fetch something, then went back up the Ridge, kicking up snow as it went.

When Olli reached the Normal School he turned onto Oikokatu, then stopped in his tracks and shook his head.

The umbrella! That meant that…

He'd thought he had taken the umbrella off the coat rack, but now he wasn't sure. He retraced his steps to see if he had dropped it. He didn't see it anywhere on the street.

When he got back to the parish house, everyone had already left. The umbrella was locked inside. Well, he could pick it up tomorrow. Or maybe he should just buy another one. It wasn't a very good one anyway.

Besides, as Maiju had once said, buying umbrellas was sort of a hobby of his. Some people, like Maiju, buy shoes. And Olli was constantly buying new and better umbrellas.

On Friday morning Book Tower Publishing had its all-staff meeting. Afterwards Olli started his lunch hour with an ibuprofen and a walk down Puistokatu.

The linden trees along Puistokatu were dark and bare with winter. Looking at them gave Olli a heavy feeling. The gritted snow crunched under his feet. The darkness tired him. It was hard to believe that these were the same trees that cast their heady warmth and green glow over the street all summer. Now the only green was on the advertising banners that read *A Guide to the Cinematic Life*.

The ad drew Olli's thoughts to the book business. The staff had explained at the meeting that although the children's books were selling steadily and getting good reviews and winning prizes, increasing expenses and growing competition meant that the house needed to improve its sales figures. They couldn't leave the future of the business to what they made on Emma Bunny. Olli's task as publisher was to shift their emphasis to the non-fiction division and acquire a bestseller, or better yet, several. Otherwise they would need to undertake an overhaul and think up some new initiatives.

After the meeting Vilho Torni, the founder and lead shareholder of the company, had put a hand on Olli's shoulder and given him some fatherly guidance.

"Olli, you know better than I do that what sells nowadays are books in series for school-aged children. At the moment Book Tower doesn't really have any. Harry Potter, that's what the kids are eating up. When I was a kid I read boys' adventure series, and my son read the Famous Five. He always made sure to get every new Famous Five book as soon as it came out and have it on his shelf. Did you read Enid Blyton's books? No? A pity. You missed out. Unrealistic pulp quickly cranked out, but they're the reason I founded Book Tower. I wanted to offer children more picnics and secret passages and wholesome adventure, real escapism. But maybe animals showing each other their genitals will have to do, if that's what the people want…"

Olli knew the Famous Five books, of course. He just didn't want to think about them.

3

OLLI FREQUENTED THREE different umbrella shops. Two of his favourite shops were in the city centre, the third was halfway down Puistokatu.

He liked going to the shop on Puistokatu because it was the prettiest street in town. The name of the shop, Jyväskylä Umbrella, was painted on the glass door in small gilt letters. The shop space was more like a closet than a room and the narrow shopfront was hard to spot if you didn't know what you were looking for. No more than three normal-sized customers could fit in the shop with the seller present "as long as everybody is careful with their hygiene and doesn't mind being at close quarters", as the shopkeeper put it.

The shopkeeper was a woman with golden hair and sad spaniel eyes. Her name was Maura. Her age was hard to guess; she was a confusing blend of fifteen and fifty.

Maura had a habit of telling her regular customers anecdotes that were sad and sometimes harsh. But they would turn comic when she came to the climax of the story, put on a radiant, fake smile and took a couple of dancing steps.

Olli had once said to her that she was a real charmer. She replied, "Thanks, Mr Suominen. Actually I was voted the favourite girl in the class when I was at school."

"You must have been proud."

"Then the teacher scolded the class and told them that they had voted wrong, that the prize shouldn't go to me.

She decided the little statue of the smiling girl should go to a kid named Kirsi who had no sense of humour but always sat in the front row with her hand in the air and got tens on every test."

Olli stepped into Jyväskylä Umbrella. The clock ticked. Maura with the golden hair smiled from behind the counter, which was a metre and a half from the door. Her breath smelt like *salmiakki* liquorice. She said hello and asked if she could help him find anything. "Perhaps this reasonably priced, small, black one? They're three for the price of two today. It won't cost you too much money if you happen to lose it."

Olli smiled and browsed through the merchandise hung on the walls. "I was thinking of something of a higher quality this time," he said. "Something more special. An umbrella that can really protect you no matter what the weather. Maybe even an expensive one."

The woman took out a thick catalogue, set it on the counter, and started flipping through it.

"This has some interesting selections that I've been think-ing of giving a try in the shop. As you can see, they have aerodynamic umbrellas, flamenco umbrellas, a variety of art umbrellas, maps, ninjas, barometers. If you're looking for an umbrella that's good protection from the weather, would something like this interest you? It has to be ordered from abroad, though, and it can take months for delivery."

She laid her finger on a dome umbrella.

Under the photo was a description: *This umbrella is a classic Chantal Thomass design. A dome-shaped umbrella with a black pin-stripe fabric, edged with a wide border of fine black net with a black ribbon trim, reminiscent of stocking tops and garters.*

Olli stared at the photo, electrified. It was a style of umbrella quite different from what he was used to using, or seeing in the shops, but at the same time strangely familiar.

He tried to remember where he had seen one like it. In some movie? *The Umbrellas of Cherbourg? Singin' in the Rain?*

He told her he wanted the Chantal Thomass design, baffled by his own excitement.

4

E VERY SUNDAY, if it wasn't raining,the Suominen family would go for a walk. They would circle the Ridge, go to look at the anti-aircraft guns at the foot of the observation tower, and spend some time at the Mäki-Matti playground. The boy rode in the pram. Olli would push him up the hill and Aino would push him down the hill.

Once in a while, when Olli noticed that the light was just right, he would take pictures for the family photo album.

Sometimes Aino wanted to take the pictures, but Olli's SLR camera was too complicated for her. Even when Olli adjusted the settings so that all she had to do was point and click, her pictures were bad. She didn't have an eye for photography.

On their most recent walk, Olli had taken dozens of photos. He had brought the whole memory card in to be developed but only some of them ended up in the official family photo album.

When the pictures came back from the shop, Olli arranged them into two piles on the table in the living room. Successful photos were in the smaller pile, unsuccessful ones in the larger. Aino came in, picked a couple of photos out of the large pile and admired them.

Olli informed her that those were the photos he intended to throw out—the good photos were in the other stack.

Aino didn't see any difference between the good photos

and the bad photos. According to her, some of the so-called bad photos were better them many of the ones that Olli thought were the good ones.

Olli had patiently tried to explain what made a photo worthy of the album and what made for a bad photo—you had to be able to notice the lighting, the mood, the framing, the effect of the depth of field...

Aino had interrupted him and said that it was obvious he didn't know the first thing about family photos. Then she had scooped up the larger pile of pictures and announced that she was going to start her own album.

Olli pushed the pram. Snow had covered the street overnight, and it clung to the wheels. His hair grew moist under his fedora and his thick wool coat was stifling. He loosened his scarf, puffing like a horse.

The shouts of children echoed down from the west slope of the Ridge. They were sledding.

Aino wondered why in the world Olli hadn't dressed more sensibly. "You should have put on a tracksuit like me."

"I don't have one," Olli said.

"Yes, you do. I gave you a windproof one for Christmas. The blue one."

Olli remembered and knew he was in trouble. "That's right, you did. I wonder what happened to it."

"I would be happy to help, but unfortunately I don't know where it is now," Aino said. "I noticed in February that it was in the box where you put all your old clothes to drag out to the donation bin."

They continued walking. The happy shouts of the children

34

accentuated the tense silence. Aino's face twitched. They passed the playground without speaking.

There were four little boys and a girl stretching their heads over the playground fence and spitting on the ground. They looked up and stared at Olli expressionlessly.

One boy looked familiar, as did the girl with blonde hair flowing out from under her knitted cap. Olli waved at them with a friendly smile and the little girl whispered something to the others.

The children looked scornfully amused and Olli felt cold. Then he realized where he knew the boy from. He looked like a childhood picture Olli had of himself on a shelf at home. And the girl reminded him of a friend from years ago, who was of course a grown woman now.

When they reached the conservatory, Aino's mood changed. The tension disappeared, she forgot their quarrel, took a breath and started chirping about everything under the sun.

Sometimes Olli found this taxing. But at the moment it was a sign of forgiveness, and he accepted it gratefully. Olli didn't like quarrels. They made his blood pressure even higher than it already was and gave him a stiff neck.

Aino talked about the macaroni casserole waiting in the refrigerator, the apple pie she had baked for dessert, and how they should get home on time because there was a lot of laundry to do, and besides, she still had to go through her pupils' exercise books, make a call to a colleague, and prepare next week's lessons before tomorrow. Then she mentioned that she'd been awakened during the night by Olli's snoring, and he apologized. She told him that someone ought to change the bedding; it was quite dusty and the boy had been eating rye crispbreads in bed. Olli humbly promised to take care of it.

Aino wondered aloud when they had last cleaned. "But then when would we have had time, since you have your meetings and other goings-on in the evenings and I've got my work, too, plus taking care of Lauri..."

Olli made a quick budget calculation in his head and suggested that they hire a cleaner. He was still thinking about the blonde-haired girl he had known long ago.

The weather seemed to be getting colder. His breath was steaming and he didn't feel hot any more. In fact he felt chilled.

They came to the soccer field, surrounded by a chain-link fence. Olli touched his camera and scowled. It was hard to find picturesque places in Jyväskylä.

"A cleaner?" Aino's stride faltered for a moment. "That would be nice, of course, to not have to clean... But no. I don't want a stranger mixed up in our life."

Then she poked him in the ribs with her mitten and demanded, "Hey, have you read that book I gave you on our anniversary? Or did you toss it in the recycling bin?"

Olli told her that he had spent two evenings reading *A Guide to the Cinematic Life*. Aino was pleased. He added that he thought the book was very interesting.

Aino was delighted.

They were nearing the swimming hall now. Aino slowed down, grew serious and started to tell him about a dream. She'd had the same dream for two nights in a row, and thought it was caused by the cover of the book she'd bought him.

"I'm getting home from work, and I notice that a pear tree is growing in the garden. It's shading the house. You're inside the house, sitting and watching a video of *Casablanca* and eating a pear. I ask you to cut down the tree before it falls on the house. You turn to look at me and then I notice that you're crying. You cry so many tears that the house fills up with steam, until rain starts falling from the ceiling. This doesn't bother you, because you're sitting under an umbrella. When I woke up, I had to go downstairs and make sure we didn't have a leak or any water damage. I looked outside, too, to make sure there wasn't really any pear tree there."

The boy stirred himself in the pram and craned to look at Olli, until his hat sat crooked on his head. His smooth brow was furrowed.

"Daddy..."

"What?"

The boy concentrated intensely.

Finally he said: "Daddy, you shouldn't eat those pears. They're poison."

5

THE STAFF IN THE CONFERENCE ROOM of Book Tower Publishing were drinking coffee, munching on Marie biscuits and talking about *A Guide to the Cinematic Life*. The ceiling of the room was a high one, the ambience venerable.

They sat in ornate oak chairs hand-crafted before any of them were even born. The dark table was too large. There were interspersed empty chairs and everyone was far away from each other. Olli sat in his usual place at the head of the table. The window was open. A warm waft of air blew in, bringing a scent of spring. Maiju was at the other end of the table giving them a report of what she had learnt from an acquaintance at WSOY Publishing.

When Olli turned his head to the right, he was looking straight into the park. It was May. Now that winter was over, people were trying to learn to enjoy life again.

Children ran around, teenagers lolled on the grass. People sat on the benches eating ice cream from the kiosk in the park. An old couple strolled arm in arm wearing heavy coats; their bones still remembered the cold of winter. They passed a fat woman who was tossing breadcrumbs to the pigeons. Then the children ran up and chased the birds away, which gave the old couple a start, and the woman was left standing in the path in befuddlement.

In addition to Olli and Maiju, there was Antero, and grey-haired Seija. The rest of the staff were in Helsinki arranging a children's book event, to which Eduard Uspensky had been invited, thus making it worth their while for Book Tower to be on hand and visible.

There was always an intern present as well. These wards of the publishing house came and went. Just as they got to know one of them, a new one came to replace them.

The current intern was a blonde girl in a blue blouse. She was sitting in the corner looking neglected. "Please, have some coffee and biscuits," Olli said encouragingly. He pointed to the coffee pot and the plate of biscuits, which the regular staff were quickly emptying.

The girl shook her head and looked at the ceiling.

Olli peered at the intern over his horn-rimmed glasses. She had an interesting face. It had a certain refinement. The film club had recently watched *Vertigo*, and she reminded Olli of Kim Novak.

The girl shifted her gaze uncomfortably, the impression faded, and Olli continued listening to the discussion. They were still talking about *A Guide to the Cinematic Life*. Olli had left his copy on his desk. The others had also bought the book and were reading it at a fast clip. They were all in agreement that although the book seemed trivial at first, it quickly hooked you and made you think. And it was making its publisher a lot of money.

Antero said that as far as he was concerned it was mostly pseudo-philosophical pop silliness and the success of the book was proof of the book-buying public's poor taste. "But we should take advantage of it as well as we can," he added. "And people have a right to their bad taste. It's probably mentioned in the UN's Declaration of Human Rights."

Maiju said that the translation rights had already been sold to dozens of countries. WSOY was celebrating Greta Kara as their latest goose to lay a golden egg. "Apparently Kara is already writing another book," Maiju informed them. "She's writing it in an apartment in Montmartre, in Paris, provided for her by her French publisher, just so the media won't bother her. And she doesn't give any interviews. Supposedly. It's a good gimmick. Playing the mystery woman and letting the media's curiosity swell to bursting, the requests for interviews build up, until she finally gives in and, bang, suddenly she's on every channel and in every newspaper…"

Olli had heard enough. He stood up, waved his arms like he was swimming the butterfly stroke and roared, "Fine! Great! We don't need to worry that WSOY is going to fail for lack of sales! Roll another stone over my heart!"

Then he calmed down, tapped on the table and said, "Now can we talk about Book Tower business? Would that be all right?"

The Book Tower staff gave each other furtive looks. Mr Suominen didn't usually raise his voice. He was known as an extremely patient, deliberative and fatherly man.

Olli sat down and continued in a calm tone, "Speaking of best-sellers, how is the Emma Bunny book doing, Antero? Has there been much interest in the book or the author?"

"Surprisingly, no," the young man answered, without looking up from his cup, where he had dropped a biscuit.

Olli noticed that Seija, their grey-haired office and accounting manager, was following the discussion worriedly.

"Well, there will be a few articles, mostly the usual

children's book outlets," Antero continued. "Emma Bunny is a popular series, and I'm sure there will be reviews, and the 'let's play doctor' aspect of the new book will arouse some interest, but we might as well give up waiting for a media circus. Amanda Vuolle is no Greta Kara, and Emma Bunny is no *Guide to the Cinematic Life*. Which doesn't mean, of course, that the new Emma Bunny won't sell well enough, if Maiju can just think of a catchy name for it. *I Have a Fanny and You Have a Wee-Wee* isn't quite it…"

"Selling 'well enough' isn't good enough," Seija announced.

Everyone turned to look at her and Seija's cheeks reddened. Her faced tensed. "As I've explained before, we're not at any immediate crisis point. Nobody needs to start looking for a new job, at least not yet. But we need an increase in sales."

The conference room emptied and everyone went back to work on their own projects. Olli went into his office, sat on the edge of his desk and began thumbing through *A Guide to the Cinematic Life*. He started to tremble. He forced himself to relax. It was ridiculous to get so worked up about a book.

There was the picture of a pear on the cover. Olli read the author's name and whispered it three times aloud, first with disbelief, then tasting the words, as if saying a prayer. Then he opened the book. He examined the flap photo closely, close enough to smell the ink. It was a picture of Greta Kara.

The same photo was on his computer screen, open to a Facebook profile.

Lately Olli had been remembering his dreams more and more clearly, and waking up melancholy and restless. He already had 425 Facebook friends, but only one of them had been haunting him every night for the past several months.

View my friends (425).
        Greta Kara.

Olli thought for a moment, then moved his mouse.

Send Greta a message.

Click. A message box appeared on the screen.

Send Message.
To: Greta Kara
Subject:

Olli wiped his lips and wrote:

Subject: To the girl in the pear-print dress.
Message: Hello!

Olli lifted his fingers from the keyboard and stared at the screen for a long time before continuing.

6

Most of the time, life is a pear left in a glass bowl to rot while we eat potatoes day after day.

GRETA KARA,
A Guide to the Cinematic Life

The house is close to the river, at the edge of Tourula, his old summer neighbourhood. The trees and bushes hide it from passers-by. The window by the front door is broken. Inside the house is a fluttering sparrow.

Olli wipes sweat from his brow, sweat mixed with the dust from the dirt road. Climbs the stairs. Piano music from above. He recognizes the piece: Debussy's *Clair de lune*. It's beautiful. The door to the room is open. Inside is darkness.

He's winded. It's difficult to see. His pupils gradually dilate to adjust to the dark.

The piano player's fingers lift from the keys. It's quiet. Olli holds his breath and listens. Someone nearby is breathing quick breaths.

His nose is flooded with the scent of meadow flowers. The perfume is familiar. Thick curtains cover the windows. The light smoulders red; the day and the whole rest of the world are shut outside. Olli walks farther in. The floor creaks, the scent grows stronger, surrounds him.

A girl approaches him in the darkness. Olli closes his eyes, opens his mouth, breathes between his teeth and draws the smell onto his tongue.

"Why are you doing that?" the girl whispers in his ear.

"I'm tasting your scent," Olli answers.

He opens his eyes and turns. The girl's mouth is open. They breathe in the same air, and it takes turns inside each of them, growing hot. Olli looks at her lips and chin and neck and shoulders. He doesn't yet dare to meet her eyes, lest his heart beat too fast.

He touches her dress, with its pattern of pears, and lets his eyes move over it. He feels heat through the fabric.

He's terrified of the breath escaping from her reddened lips, scorching his skin, because it is palpable with a hunger greater than both of them.

7

GRETA KARA, THE AUTHOR, answered his message two days later:

Well, hello yourself, Olli! How delightful that you decided to write to me! And you remembered the pear-print dress, too! I'm flattered. I didn't know if you would remember it, or even me, any more. I'm sure you've met thousands of interesting people since you knew me, and it's been almost thirty years since we last saw each other.

Forgive me for the delay in responding. I've been very busy here in Paris. (I've had to spend some time in cafes, for instance, where the Années folles are becoming more and more palpable to me. Although Cocteau, Chagall, Miller, Beckett, Miró and the other big names who buzzed around here have of course been lying in the ground for a long time...)

You've probably heard that I wrote a book. It's been doing quite nicely. My French publisher loved it so much that he gave me an office to use in Tour Montparnasse, on the condition, of course, that he will get the French rights to my next book. Actually, he wants the rights to the whole series, but more about that later—it's still a secret! They even gave me a piano in my room; he knows I enjoy playing Debussy and Chopin to pull my thoughts together when I'm writing.

The view from here is worth mentioning. Can you believe I have a view of the Eiffel Tower? But I suppose that's not so exciting, now that it's become such a postcard cliché. And speaking of clichés: I confess that I went to Hollywood to write my first book, and I took one of those photos of myself standing at the foot of the "Hollywood" sign. Maybe I'll show it to you sometime—but I won't put it on the Internet.

How are you, Olli? According to your Facebook status, you live in Jyväskylä and you're married. Do you have any children? And, hey—is it true you're a publisher now? What kinds of book do you publish? Novels?

Let's keep in touch (when my busy schedule allows)!

Sincerely,

Greta K.

Olli started writing his answer.

After a couple of sentences, his eyes came to rest on the eyes of Olli Suominen, publisher and parish-council member, stiff in black and white, staring at him from the photo on the wall. The man in the photo had a career and a family to support and plenty more urgent things to do than bombard a beloved of his youth with messages.

With his cheeks burning, Olli closed his Facebook page, did a couple of hours of work, and left the office.

He had left his umbrella in a bookshop on his lunch hour, and now he needed one. It was raining so hard that water was flowing down Kauppakatu. Cars and bicycles splashed the people on the pavement. Olli's trouser legs were soaked, and he jumped back into the shelter of the building.

Finally, he ran across the street. His shoes slopped with water. His socks were drenched. He hurried to the next street for the shelter of the linden trees that lined the old church park.

The stone entrance of a bank offered safety. There were already three shivering old women there who greeted the parish councillor as they would a great gentleman. Olli answered their greeting heartily. They were flattered.

The next dash took him to the Forum shopping centre.

A passageway between the florist and the optician led to the inner courtyard. Teenagers were gathered against the wall watching the river of harried, middle-aged people flowing from work to the shops and from the shops to their homes. Two youngsters in black leather stood leaning against each other in the middle of the courtyard, oblivious to anything but each other, and the kiss they had abandoned themselves to. Olli remembered the film *The Wild One*, and Kathie's words to Johnny: *I wish I was going someplace. I wish you were going someplace. We could go together.*

Olli descended the steps, crossed the lower level and took the escalator to the basement shops, which included Jyväs-brella, the pearl of the Forum. Olli stepped inside and started looking at the umbrella selection.

The owner was pottering behind the counter—a large woman with black hair teased into a wild tangle who was always sweating, though she wore gauzy dresses and went around the shop barefoot.

The back wall of the shop was covered with a large poster of a seashore. After the first time he went in, Olli had a dream where the woman was part of the poster. She was standing at the edge of the water holding up her skirt and looking out to sea. In his dream, Olli had walked up to the poster and the woman had turned, stepped out of the picture into the shop, and started rearranging the umbrellas.

The shopkeeper recognized her regular customer and came to assist him with swinging steps. Sweat poured down her neck in branching streams that melted together again as they reached between her ample breasts.

The salty scent that surrounded her reminded Olli of a childhood trip to the Mediterranean shore. On the very first day of the trip the tide had carried his blue toy boat away. He cried over it for three days. He was only consoled when a local fisherman made up a story and his mother translated it: the boat belonged to the beautiful mermaids now, and whenever they played with it they would think about how much they loved the pale-haired Finnish boy who had sent it to them.

"Some weather we're having," the umbrella seller said hoarsely.

Olli nodded. Phrase number one. The woman was interesting, in a burlesque sort of way, but she never said anything original or surprising. Her eyes were peculiar, though. They sometimes made him think of a forest, other times of the Mediterranean, and when he looked into them he felt as if he were just about to remember something.

"Sure is raining today. Nice weather for an umbrella dealer, but not so great for everyone else," the woman laughed.

Phrase number two.

Olli decided that this time he was going to buy a perfectly ordinary, traditional black umbrella. He paid. As the woman gave his bank card back their hands touched and they looked each other in the eye a little longer than felt quite natural.

The woman's hands were hot and damp. Playfulness

flashed in her eyes. Olli remembered a dream from several nights before:

He steps into the umbrella shop. Aino and the boy are with him. Aino is wearing a ludicrously large sun hat and the boy has on a sailor suit. The shopkeeper is dancing and sweating. She twists and shakes her body, to make her flesh obey her, panting like a dying bear.

Olli can see that it's because of the pear-print dress. She has put it on although it's much too small for her. Now it's stuck and she's trying to dance her way out of it.

The dress is ripping a little more with each movement. Olli approaches her, apologizes for disturbing her and says that he's going to the beach with his family and that they need a parasol.

The woman shakes her head, fluffs her hair, smiles, dances over to him and gives him a noisy kiss on the cheek.

Just then, the dress rips open.

Her left breast pops out. It's enormous and white and it's splashing milk in every direction.

Olli's son laughs out loud and runs after the woman all around the shop trying to catch the drops of milk in his hands. Aino taps Olli on the arm, points to the woman's breast and shouts excitedly, "Sweetheart, that's the exact colour of white that I want for our bedroom walls! Look at it closely! Otherwise you'll forget when you go to the paint shop."

Water is pouring onto the floor. The poster of the seashore is leaking, and the sea is sloshing into motion. They're already standing in seawater up to their waists, and the umbrellas are drifting away.

Then a darker patch of blue flashes in the poster picture. It moves with the water and disappears under the surface. Olli mentions it to Aino, who nods, takes a breath, and dives after it.

Her sun hat is left bobbing on the surface of the water and floats away.

The bare-breasted woman dances until the fabric of her dress finally gives way and unpeels in strips.

She stops dancing. She's naked. Her green, surprisingly long pubic hairs flutter in the water like seaweed. They spread on the current through the shop and wrap themselves around Olli's legs.

The shreds of pear-printed fabric slither with the current out of the shop, hissing as they go.

Olli remembers his son, now. He doesn't see him anywhere. He looks into the woman's eyes and trembles.

The woman pulls him close to her. Her body is soft. Olli sinks into it and feels calmer. They kiss. They're both crying; she has lost all of her umbrellas, and Olli has lost his son.

Then she sighs, tells Olli to lower his head and puts one of her breasts in his mouth. Milk is flowing out of it. She whispers that it's salty like seawater, but it frees you of all sorrows.

Olli drinks.

She strokes his hair.

Olli can see that there is a menacing shadow approaching under the water. He tears himself away from the woman and makes as if to escape.

But the shadow is Aino. She rises to the surface and shakes the water from her hair. When she smiles, a gentle light radiates from her face.

Aino places a blue toy boat in Olli's hands and whispers, "Look what I found, darling. Don't let the mermaids take it away again. I had to make a dear sacrifice to St Anthony to get it back. But I have to go now. Our little boy is waiting all alone at the bottom of the sea."

Olli tries to take hold of his wife's hand, but she's already gone.

Four days later, Greta sent another message. It seemed her writing wasn't going well.

I've been spending a lot of time outdoors. The streets of Paris are filled with advertisements for my book. Yesterday I was walking on the Champs-Élysées and I saw five of them. People everywhere are reading it. I was in a cafe and a whole group of people at another table were in a heated discussion about it. They took the book's ideas very seriously, which is flattering, of course. They were all dressed cinematically and striving in general for a deep cinematic self—you could tell from their conversation. The magazines here are filled with articles about how to cinematicize your life. It's the newest fashion, a lifestyle that even has its own designated clubs now. I went to one yesterday. It had a rather strange, but exciting, atmosphere. I'm really happy that no one recognizes me from my author photos—otherwise I would never be left in peace.

A Guide to the Cinematic Life, *in other words, is selling amazingly well. I sent the first pages of my new book to my Finnish publisher. They didn't like them and suggested changes. I don't quite know what to think. It's depressing.*

Olli offered Greta the same fatherly advice he gave to his own authors when they lost their inspiration. Of course, this time he knew that it was more pastoral counselling than genuine practical guidance.

But he left it in the message. He thought for a moment, then started to answer the questions she had asked in her first message. Yes, he was married. They had a child, and a joint mortgage.

What should he say about Book Tower? They published mostly children's books but also some popular non-fiction, the kinds of things people bought as gifts, and read themselves.

Olli furrowed his brow and rubbed his chin. He sounded sterile and distant. He should write a bit more openly, more personally. They were old friends, after all.

As far as the children's books go, at the moment we have a bit of an oversupply and are actually trying to get rid of the most tired book series, and their authors, but we're always looking for interesting non-fiction to add to our list, so that we can keep afloat as a mid-sized publisher. That's actually the most worrisome item in my work life right now.

Olli read the last few lines several times.

He hoped they didn't give the impression that he was trying to persuade a successful author to change houses...

He tapped on his desk, tasted the words, squinted and decided to delete the last sentence, to avoid any misunderstanding.

But his hand slipped, and a mischievous finger hit the mouse button, and the message escaped without revision.

8

Two weeks later, Olli gathered the staff in the conference room. He filled his lungs with the venerable ambience and announced that, if all went according to plan, Greta Kara's next book would be published the following autumn by Book Tower Publishing. He added that the contract wasn't yet signed, so Antero shouldn't start issuing press releases just yet, but they would definitely be putting a contract together as soon as possible so that everything was settled and the marketing rumba could be set in motion.

There followed five seconds of silence, analysis of his facial expression, searching for any possibility of irony or misunderstanding.

The applause lasted so long that Olli eventually had to cut it off.

Later that day Maiju appeared at Olli's office door, perfumed and coiffed. She was wearing a white summer dress that showed off her long legs. Her fingernails were long now, and painted bright red. Her hair looked lighter.

"Don't you ever say goodnight?" she cooed, in English.

It took Olli by surprise.

"Hello?! Veronica Lake?" Maiju said huffily. *"The Blue Dahlia?* According to *The Cinematic Life,* Joyce Harwood is a character I can use to get in touch with my deep cinematic self…"

"Right. Was there something you wanted?"

"It's about Greta Kara's book… Who's going to edit it?"

"I am," Olli answered.

He was at that moment writing an email to the book-fair organizer. There was going to be plenty of work to do in Frankfurt. It wouldn't be easy to stand out from seventeen thousand other exhibitors from a hundred different countries. "Greta specifically requested it," he added. "We're old acquaintances, you see."

Maiju was speechless. "What kind of book is it exactly?" she finally said. Olli could see that she would have asked for more information about her boss's relationship with the famous author if she'd only dared.

Olli stopped writing, leant back in his chair and clasped his hands behind his neck. "Hopefully a book as successful as her first one," he said. "If it's money you're thinking about. It's going to be a sort of city guidebook. We're actually talking about doing a series of guidebooks. One for each city. At some point they could also be combined in one volume, once the concept is worked out."

Maiju gnawed at a fingernail. A deep groove appeared between her brows.

"OK. A city guide. I don't mean to be a drag, but hasn't that already been done to death? What does Greta Kara have to add to the guidebook market?"

"Well," Olli said, stretching. "The plan is to continue the filmic angle from her first book and adapt it to different cities of the world, large and small. That's how Greta described it. Have you read the part in *Cinematic Life* where she talks about the different degrees of cinematicness in different locations and how to judge them? It's a fun sort of mind game that was left a bit undeveloped, but it still has lots of potential. That's going to be the starting point for the guidebooks. Instead of discussing the usual city sights, she'll present the cinematic places, the kinds of places that haven't been much written about, places people usually don't know to look for. Magical, out-of-the-ordinary places where the atmosphere is especially concentrated, where life feels more meaningful. Greta and I have a working title of Magical City Guides, or Magical Travel Guides."

He could see the gears turning in Maiju's blonde head. "OK," she said slowly, her eyes glassy, her tongue clicking. Her face took on an expression that had a touch of pure sexual arousal in it. "Magical City Guides... It sounds unusual. Unusual in a sellable way. I can imagine buying a book like that for myself. And I would certainly buy it as a gift for someone who was planning to go to that place. Nice work, Olli. What cities will be covered? I suppose she'll start with Paris? There's hardly a place more magical than that. Or Rome?"

Olli shook his head. "Actually no," he said. "The first city she wants to cover is Jyväskylä, and its magical places."

Olli's announcement had been preceded by a two-week correspondence that was like two cats dancing around a hot bowl of oatmeal.

Greta had revealed that her publisher wasn't warming up to the idea of writing the first magical city guide about Jyväskylä, even if it was the place where she'd spent the first seventeen years of her life, and was thus important to her.

They tried to talk me into choosing Helsinki, or even Tampere, if the capital didn't inspire me for some reason. And the French publisher got even more nervous when he heard what it was I was writing. He promised that I could keep my room and my piano and my view of the Eiffel Tower for another year as long as I focus on large European cities as soon as I finished the book on Jyväskylä. It seems the potential magic of Jyväskylä is only of interest to Jyväskyläns. As far as France is concerned, Jyväskylä doesn't exist.

Olli answered that publishers, of course, have their own interests, and it was understandable that a publisher in Helsinki or Paris wouldn't share her interest in a small town in central Finland.

You're in a strong position at present because your first book is bringing in money. As a publisher myself, I understand your publisher, but don't make any compromises that don't feel right to you.

Greta responded:

The easiest, safest thing would probably be to give in to all their demands and forget my own whims and be a good girl and continue working with my present higher-ups. But you understand me better than anyone else in the world. You know that I'm loyal above all to my feelings and whims—what else does a person have! It's wonderful that you support me! Hopefully I won't burden you too much with my problems. You've got heaps of your own urgent publishing matters, especially now that you've got to find yourself some new non-fiction.

The next four messages dealt with everyday trivialities. Olli described his activities in the parish council and the publishing house, and briefly talked about his home, family and Sunday walks. He mentioned that he belonged to a film club and for that reason particularly enjoyed Greta's book, which he was reading as his schedule permitted, and sometimes on the sly during busy workdays. Greta, for her part, had described her own walks in Paris and reminisced about her time in Jyväskylä.

What I've been thinking about writing is mostly based on what I remember from twenty years ago. The old Tourula neighbourhood isn't there any more, and many places must have changed. It's clear that sooner or later I'll have to get to know Jyväskylä again and update my knowledge for the book.

Immediately after this came the pivotal message:

Olli, I just had the craziest idea! Or actually a really brilliant idea! How could I not have thought of it earlier?... What would you say if I offered my next book to your publishing house?

9

YOU LOSE FEWER UMBRELLAS in rainy weather, because you need your umbrella all the time. In June it rained constantly, so Olli only lost one, although it was one that had served him well for a long time.

It happened at Sokos department store. He had the umbrella under his arm, bought three shirts on the second floor, went downstairs with his shopping bag in his hand and walked through the cosmetics department, where pale sales assistants catered to customers amid clouds of perfume.

As he stepped out onto Kauppakatu he realized that he no longer had his starry-sky umbrella with him.

He went back inside and asked about the umbrella at the men's clothing department. The assistant looked under the counter and called someone. Then she said that unfortunately no umbrella had been found but if it was they would certainly call him.

Olli knew that no call would come. Missing umbrellas stay missing. He thanked the clerk and went to buy a new one. That night he dreamt that he went back to the store to look for it.

He peers between the shelves, enquires with the staff, eventually is crawling around on the floor. He has to find the umbrella. It's important. It must be here somewhere. He just has to look everywhere.

All around him are women's legs—thick, thin, bare, covered in stockings. The women are walking around him with their skirts rustling. They smell good. Each one has her own smell. No smell of sweat, just flowery scents, enchanting perfumes that can make a man forget his purpose if he's not careful.

The women cast suspicious glances at him. Some wonder aloud at the gentleman from the parish council creeping around on the floor, looking up parishioners' dresses to peek at their underwear. A high heel treads on his hand. There are angry hisses. He feels a kick to his backside. The women start to talk all at once about how degrading this must be for such a fine gentleman, speaking with mock sympathy, giggling. *A family man, crawling on the floor looking for an old umbrella. Can you imagine…*

Their teasing voices press down on him. There are several among them that he's thought of as his friends, but he knows the rules: if he wants to find the umbrella he has to debase himself and take whatever comes.

The scents grow strong, burning. Olli starts to feel faint. The flowery smells muddle his mind. It's hard to think, to remember, to act. He falls on his side, panting, can't make out his surroundings. Did he just come down the escalator? Did he already look here or not? What floor is he on? It's hard to see very far. The air is thick with clouds of perfume vapour and dark, flitting figures.

Then Olli sees, to his delight, the umbrella, on the floor in front of him. As he reaches to take hold of it a cocker spaniel appears out of the mist, snatches up the umbrella and runs away. Olli yells after it, but the dog doesn't listen.

He sits up, frightened. He's lost in the cosmetics department.

From somewhere far away he hears someone humming. A woman's voice. Beautiful, positively lilting. Gradually the hum turns into singing. Olli knows that he has to leave, to get as far away from here as he can.

So he's going to leave.

In just a minute.

But first he wants to hear the singing just a little longer. He can't make out the words, but he understands that the song is speaking to his spirit, asking him to stay a little longer, forever, to forget everything else. Now there are many singers. The song is alive and changing all the time and it holds his attention so that he won't notice the quick, rustling footsteps approaching through the clouds of perfume.

Then it grows quiet and Olli realizes the danger too late, and tries to get away.

But the saleswomen are already upon him. They look at him, smile ingratiatingly and whisper, *Hello. How may I help you?*

Olli tries to smile.

It would be so easy to fall for the sweet-smelling, carefully made-up women's faces, their hair, their breasts, to surrender to their services, just for a little while at first, and then forever. The only problem is that they seem to be part bird.

From under their fashionable skirts sharp-clawed bird's feet protrude, and although they're trying to hide the truth of their nature, Olli can see that they also have folded wings with slashing talons.

Every town has its own styles of businesses. There are large department stores, little speciality shops and market halls. Every place has its own unique atmosphere. In Paris's famous Lafayette department store, for example, one encounters refinement, history and decay—the ancient floors of the building slope and sway, making the shelves look as if they might fall over at any moment, although they've stood in the same spot for decades. It's a place with an enchanting, dreamlike magic, in all its frightfulness, a wonderful place for cinematic encounters.

Jyväskylä's analogue to the Lafayette is the Sokos department store, opened in 1962, which is not particularly historic as architecture, nor is it aesthetically dilapidated. But its magic is perceptible, particularly at the cosmetics counter, which has been tended for many years by saleswomen slender as birds who are charming but by all accounts chillingly cool when they are at their worst, and who have in years past been famous for their choosiness about their customers—many a simply dressed girl has not failed to notice that she doesn't receive the same level of service as wealthy ladies in furs.

The cosmetics department is filled with clouds of perfume that, combined with the well-groomed beauty of the saleswomen and the unreal atmosphere created by the lighting, can muddle the head of a man who happens to wander through. The Sokos cosmetics counter is its own sort of urban island of sirens, frightening in its magic, alluring and apt to elicit all sorts of desires.

GRETA KARA,
Magical City Guide Number One: Jyväskylä

The weather was rainy, but the sun was shining at Book Tower Publishing. Seija usually searched her account books for signs of catastrophe and chewed on her grey tresses, the others watching her the way seafarers watch a barometer. But now she was glowing. The whole staff thought that Greta Kara's next book would improve their finances and raise the company's profile, so the mood in the place had considerably improved.

The Suominens continued their Sunday walks.

Olli took pictures of their walks and sent them for developing. He didn't have to fight with Aino about the photos any more. They had come to an understanding: Olli chose the rare photos that he judged successful, in technical terms and in atmosphere, for the family album, and Aino put the rest in albums she bought at the discount store.

In a couple of weeks, she had filled four albums. Olli's expensive, leather-bound, exclusive album, on the other hand, had only five pages full.

The summer break started at the beginning of June, so Aino was on holiday and had started dreaming of travel again. Olli didn't know when he would have time for a break. He spoke tentatively of sometime in July or August. Aino grew resentful and reminded him that he had promised two years ago to take a long holiday and he'd said that the whole family could have a two-week trip to some golden beach. Olli assured her he would keep his promise, but perhaps not this summer, because he had so much work to do at the office.

Aino punished him by leafing through travel brochures and sighing audibly.

Because no such trip was in the offing and Olli couldn't get away from work, Aino invented ways to pass the days pleasantly with her son.

Every day when Olli came home from work, he saw Aino and the boy picnicking among the berry bushes in the garden. They read children's books, drank juice and binged on Marie biscuits. If it was raining, they would build a fort for shelter. Every day, Olli was invited to join them. The idea was attractive, in principle, and he could have taken some nice photos of such an activity, but once he had changed clothes he preferred to throw himself on the sofa for a nap and then relax in his office with Facebook.

Eventually Aino had had enough. She stamped her foot and said that Olli must have had the world's most boring childhood to have become such an absolute square as an adult.

Hurt, Olli replied that he had in fact gone on many more picnics as a child than Aino might imagine, and had marvellous adventures, but those days were long ago and now he was an adult and he preferred to eat his meals indoors instead of sitting in the grass with the insects.

Sometimes mother and son went into town to look at the shops and have a hamburger and a milkshake. Once when Olli came home in the evening he didn't recognize the boy because he'd been to the barber and bought some new clothes. He looked at the child, started polishing his glasses and said, *Who do we have here?* Then he sealed his fate by asking if they had any other guests in addition to this unknown child.

Three days of silent treatment followed.

Email whizzed back and forth between Olli and Greta's computers, sometimes on a daily basis. A publisher naturally has to keep in touch with a new star author. Greta sent reports on Paris cafes and the pastries she'd eaten. She wrote about her work on the Jyväskylä guide and promised to send the first samples soon, asking Olli to be gentle with his criticism.

Olli replied that he was eager to see the text and soothed her worries:

> *I think that the woman who wrote* A Guide to the Cinematic Life *can write about any subject in an interesting way. I'm still reading your book every day—like half the population, apparently. Have you seen Amazon? Your book is constantly at the top of their list, in spite of the religious criticisms—or maybe because of them.*
>
> *Right now I'm reading the part where you talk about the "cinematic self" that is just waiting to be found and to shine, and your examples are Chaplin's Little Tramp, Sophia Loren's mother figure in Ettore Scola's* A Special Day *(which we're just about to watch at the film club) and Ingrid Bergman's Ilsa in Curtiz's* Casablanca. *A silly, polemical, frivolous, annoying film—and absolutely enchanting!*
>
> *By the way, a couple of clergymen I know criticized your book vociferously when I told them you were moving to the Book Tower list of authors. When I read what you wrote about the moral heresy of Christianity, how the cinematic aesthetic raises the personal aesthetic to a higher norm, I completely understood why they were so indignant!*

It was an ordinary Sunday. It ended with Olli and Aino watching the ten o'clock news.

The clock ticked on the wall. The dishwasher churned and hummed in the kitchen.

Their son was asleep in his room. Aino said she hoped that the boy's cold didn't get so bad that they would have to take him to hospital during the night. Olli shared her hope and asked if they still had cough syrup in the medicine cabinet. Aino said there was still half a bottle.

The prime minister was talking. When he disappeared and the traffic report came on the screen, Aino started talking about their Sunday walk and a chance encounter they'd had. They had been walking up the Ridge when a red scooter had appeared alongside them. It was driven by the blonde woman with the scarf from the film club, who smiled at Olli, shot an odd look at Aino, and sped on her way.

Neither of them had made any comment about it. But now Aino asked if they knew each other, Olli and this scooter woman. Olli said he had exchanged a couple of words with her at the film club.

Aino started talking about the scooter, and finally announced that she wanted one. Olli looked at her in surprise and offered to buy her a scooter first thing tomorrow, if she liked. He asked if it mattered what colour it was. Aino asked if he was serious. Olli said he was. Aino said she was just kidding.

They stared at each other.

Then Aino said that they ought to buy their son a child's bicycle, with stabilizers wheels. And a helmet, of course. Olli sighed and promised to go to the bicycle shop tomorrow.

Aino leant into Olli's arms. Olli looked down the front of her shirt. She had nice breasts. They smelt like a rubber eraser. Olli stroked her thigh and asked if she might like to have sex. She said she was tired, but that he could get back to her about it tomorrow evening, if he was at home. Then the news ended. Aino said goodnight and went upstairs. Olli remained sitting on the sofa. There were only boring programmes, on every channel. He turned off the television, climbed the stairs, went into his office, sat down at the computer and opened Facebook.

He found Greta Kara in his list of friends and checked her status.

Greta Kara loves Jyväskylä!

10

I N T H E D R E A M, Olli is walking across a lawn.

The pale buildings of the rifle factory loom around him. Their narrow, three-storey structures look like headstones. On the other side of the buildings there are two roads: the car road that plunges towards the harbour, and beneath it the railway. A long train is clattering past. Olli enjoys the sound of it. He feels like singing, because he knows it's going to be a good day.

The sky is a deep blue. The grass under his feet is growing so quickly that he can hear the small sigh of it. Birds are burbling in the trees. Merry lizards are playing on the walls of the buildings, their songs only audible from very close by. The long, endless summer holidays are beginning, and soon his playmates, whom he has missed all winter, will be here.

But he doesn't see them now, or anyone else. He's alone.

He looks up. Maybe his grandmother, or his grandfather the notary, is watching him from a window. The windows are sooty black.

At the corner of one building is a fort made of blankets. It's usually full of laughing girls with bows in their hair. Now it's abandoned, and the hem of the blanket flutters in the wind, which is growing stronger and colder.

There's a doll lying on the lawn in front of the fort. It has a rough hole in its head with black air flowing out of it and seeping into the ground. A little distance away are other discarded things: a small red patent-leather shoe, a half-eaten sweet bun.

The bun is covered in insects. Olli can hear their rushing feet.

The light dims. The sun loses most of its brightness, as if someone has turned a dimmer switch. Olli feels nervous. Maybe the picnic won't amount to anything after all.

In the direction of town he sees a peculiar black pillar of cloud that swirls and dances, sending cars, trees and people flying through the air. He squints and for a moment he can see their mouths opened in shouts.

The tornado comes towards him, howling and humming like his mother's vacuum cleaner, uprooting everything in its path.

Olli runs to the door of a building. He has to push against it with all his strength to get it open. Then he's inside, and he starts up the stairs. His footsteps echo in the stone corridors. The roar of the cyclone still sounds close by.

His grandparents' apartment should be on the second floor. He can't find it. He climbs to the third floor, then the fourth and the fifth, but all the apartments seem to have vanished.

Olli holds on to the handrail. His chest feels tight. His lungs are wheezing so hard that the paint is coming off the walls of the stairwell.

Something has changed.

A moment ago he was a light, nimble boy. Now he has a large, heavy adult body that moves only with tremendous effort. Sweat seeps from his skin, soaks his clothes and trickles like a stream down the stairs. The sound of the dripping salt water echoes down the corridor.

Of course his grandma and grandpa don't live here any more. They're both dead and buried long ago. How could he have forgotten that?

He rubs his temples. Is he drunk, or having some kind of attack, so that he can't think or remember clearly? Or maybe this is a dream. That must be it: he's dreaming.

In any case he has to get out of this hallway; he can't stay here.

It's hard to move his feet. His bones creak and grind against each other when he tries to move. Bone dust sheds from his legs and makes him cough. The stairs are steep, but he has to go up; he can't go back down again.

He struggles, his kneecaps screeching, his feet covered in white dust from his bones. Eventually he wrenches his feet from stair to stair with his hands because it's the only way he can get them to move.

Finally he reaches the landing at the top. There's only one door on this floor.

It's open.

From the hallway he can see the only room in the apartment. No people. No furniture. Just a stack of newspapers in the middle of the floor. He picks up the paper on top. It's the Jyväskylä free tabloid, an issue from more than three decades ago. On the front page is a headline in large print: LOCAL FAMOUS FIVE UNCOVER BURGLARY RING!

There actually were a couple of stories written about them in the local paper. Olli didn't remember the articles being so prominent.

The other papers in the pile also have stories about the Famous Five of Tourula.

Famous Five Rescue Little Girls
From Assailant!

Famous Five Expose Arsonist!

Famous Five Find Lost Elderly Resident!

The darkness thickens. The letters and words won't stay in place, as often happens in dreams, but when Olli concentrates hard he can read what the articles say. They tell the heroic exploits of Tourula's Famous Five over several years. Everything that happened to them is there. Even things that he doesn't remember.

In the beginning it was all fun and excitement. His teenage years, his chance misfortunes, the sheer ordinariness that came with growing up hadn't yet spoilt it.

The first headline had their photograph below it.

The five of them, posed in front of the abandoned house. They were so small, adorable, innocent. In their own minds they had been big and worldly.

The house was where they found all the things the burglars had stolen from around Tourula: silverware, outboard motors, tape decks, Heikki Ojarinne's money stash, televisions, Aunt Anna's jewellery. The gang of kids had even rescued the Thesleff painting that the three men had stolen from Aunt Anna's house while she was picnicking on the lake shore with Olli, Karri and the Blomroos children.

The article told how "this latter-day Famous Five" spent their summer holidays making their detective dreams come true:

Taking the popular Famous Five adventure books as their model, the children gathered clues and made deductions—and just two days before school was to begin, these young defenders of justice found the burglars and their loot in an abandoned house in the old Tourula area of Jyväskylä.

The article marvelled at their cleverness:

Anne, the youngest of these remarkable children, is only ten years old, and Leo, the heroic senior member of the group, is twelve. Olli, Karri and Richard all turned eleven this summer.

The author pointed out that the children had been in real danger when the criminals, taken by surprise, had attempted to defend their cache with knives:

Things could have taken a terrible turn if not for the cool nerves of Leo Blomroos, star athlete at his school in Espoo, who told the other children to hide and made himself a decoy to lure the burglars. A furious chase ensued. When Leo judged that enough time had passed for his sister, brother, cousin and friend to reach safety, he made a dodge and managed to elude his pursuers. The other children summoned the police to the house, who arrived just in time to catch the wrongdoers red-handed and arrest them.

Olli puts the newspaper back on the stack. He knows he's dreaming, but he nevertheless decides to take the papers with him.

He hears a noise from the stairway.

A dog barking.

He steps outside into the hallway. The dog is a couple of floors below him. A black and white cocker spaniel, shambling up the stairs with ears hanging, his fur shedding mud and dirt onto the steps.

Timi.

Olli holds tight to the railing.

Timi has been in the secret passages for thirty years.

He disappeared. He simply didn't come back up with the rest of them.

No one knew what had happened to him. Memories of the secret passages faded quickly when you came back to the surface. Once you left them you could only recall them in bits and pieces.

He had waited for a long time for his dog to come back. When the summer ended he'd had to go home without Timi. For months afterwards every time the telephone rang he was sure that it was his grandma calling to say: *Guess who just showed up in the yard? It's that famous dog of yours. You and your dad had better come quick and get him.*

But Grandma didn't call. Autumn had turned to winter and Olli's father had come and sat down on the side of his bed and told him that it was time to give up hope and accept the truth.

Just as Olli is about to call Timi, the dog is gone and there are three children in his place: a pretty blonde girl and two boys. The Blomrooses. Olli was supposed to meet them in the yard. Only Karri is missing. The Famous Five of Tourula must be on their way to a picnic.

Olli faintly remembers that things haven't been particularly good between him and the Blomrooses lately. They seem to have been avoiding each other.

Not long ago he was on his way to meet Greta secretly, coming out of the shop with a pear soda and two Lola bars in a bag, and he ran into the Blomrooses.

They said hello and stopped for a moment, but couldn't think of anything to talk about.

After a tense silence, Anne scowled and said it was obvious that Greta had managed to ruin the Famous Five of Tourula. She said she thought it was Greta's fault that Karri was gone, and told Olli he ought to stay far away from "that crazy little bitch".

Olli mumbled something they could interpret as a promise if they wanted to.

Anne nodded, kissed him on the cheek and looked at him with a strange smile on her face.

Leo and Riku were trying to be relaxed, but they only managed to look nervous, gloomy and uncomfortable. Leo explained with his eyes downcast that they had been trying to find some secret passages on their own. "But we can't find them without Karri, of course," he said, digging his shoe into the dirt. "Karri's the one who led us to the openings and managed to get into one before we even realized it was an entrance…"

When the Blomrooses finally went into the store and Olli could be on his way, he sighed with relief.

Being with them had felt unbelievably oppressive, and it was sad. They had been best friends for so many summers. But like the pastor said at Grandpa Notary's funeral, there is a time for everything. The time for the Famous Five was over, and something else was beginning.

But their summer adventures had been good times.

Now, in his dream, Olli is upstairs at the rifle factory, and he remembers everything much better than he does when he's awake. The memories become clearer, and they upset him. He feels like he did as a child looking through swimming goggles in cloudy water.

The burglars were the Tourula Five's first case. Their adventures had begun three years earlier. Olli met the Blomroos siblings and their cousin Karri at the playground at Lounais Park. It was the 1970s. Olli had just turned eight. Grandma had bought him a birthday ice cream at the ice cream stand. Then they had walked to the park, and the Blomrooses and Karri were there with their Aunt Anna.

Olli and the Blomrooses happened to get on the carousel at the same time. They gave him a long look and asked him who he was and what he planned to do that summer. Olli told them that he lived in Koirakkala in the winter and was spending the summer with his grandparents in one of the buildings at the old rifle factory.

Karri leant back. He seemed to be deep in thought.

"He's always like that," Leo said. "Thinks his own thoughts and doesn't know what's going on around him. But he knows all the best places. Hey, you wanna go with us sometime and see? We actually need five members for the group…"

Riku kicked the carousel into motion. Anne laughed with her mouth open wide and Olli's hat flew off his head. When he grabbed hold of the carousel's metal handrail, his arm touched the girl's pale skin and their eyes met.

The girl winked at him, and it was at that moment that Olli's years-long, mostly one-sided crush on Anne Blomroos began.

The Blomrooses told him that their aunt Anna and cousin Karri lived in one of the wooden houses in Tourula and that they were guests there for the whole summer. They whispered among themselves for a moment, then invited Olli to come with them on a picnic the next day, and hopped off the carousel.

Olli, the Blomrooses and Karri started playing together, going on expeditions in Tourula and more distant parts of Jyväskylä, and eating Aunt Anna's lavish picnics. It was a small miracle that they all stayed thin.

The second Famous Five summer Karri led them into their first secret passageway.

They found the entrance on the side of a hill. Olli had brought his dog Timi with him to Jyväskylä, and without the dog they probably would have left it alone. The black opening didn't tempt any of them except Karri, who stared into it, mesmerized. They were about to continue on their way when Timi scented something, growled and crawled under the ground.

Of course they were scared. The thought of wriggling in after him was crazy. It might collapse, or they might get stuck and suffocate.

But they had to help Timi. And so the Tourula Five began their first exploration of Jyväskylä's secret passages in order to rescue Olli's dog.

That time they did find him and bring him back into the daylight.

There are a lot more secret passages than you would think. That's what Karri said once. But they're hard to find. According to Karri, nature tries to hide them, and the human brain isn't meant to notice them.

But now Olli is standing in the hallway of the apartment

house at the rifle factory, a child and an adult at the same time, watching the Blomrooses come up the stairs, searching his memories with a sense of foreboding.

Their steps echo menacingly down the hallway. Just a moment ago they were children; now they're teenagers. He can see on their faces that they're not on their way to a picnic. The time for picnics is over.

Olli goes inside the apartment, closes the door and gathers up the newspapers. If he leaves right now and runs down the stairs, maybe they won't even recognize him; he's an adult now, after all. Bigger, more muscular. If they do give him a problem, he can certainly handle the Blomrooses, even Leo.

He gathers his courage, ready to make a dash, but then someone whispers his name.

He turns and sees a door that wasn't there a moment ago. It's open. He hurries to the door and steps into a dark room. A dim figure is sitting on the edge of a bed. A candle illuminates the girl, who is wearing a dress with pears printed all over it. On the wall above the bed is a painting Olli has seen before. Thesleff's *Sleeping Girl*.

The *Sleeping Girl* used to be in a place of honour in Aunt Anna's living room. Even the children understood that it was a valuable painting, although Aunt Anna didn't make a fuss about it. Karri mentioned that he liked the painting and kept dropping hints until it was moved to his room. This amused Riku and Leo.

Karri showing any interest in the arts pleased Aunt Anna. She had made him take piano lessons for three years and was upset when the teacher eventually refused to continue, saying that the boy unfortunately didn't have an ounce of musicality.

So his interest in the painting gave her new hope. As she hung the picture in its new home, she couldn't resist teasing him a little: "You like the *Sleeping Girl*, do you, Karri? She is quite pretty, I must admit. Bosoms and everything…"

Leo, Riku and Aunt Anna laughed, and Olli laughed with them. Karri's eyes darkened. Anne didn't laugh; she touched Karri's arm.

Olli, who always watched Anne closely, saw the touch. He stopped laughing as jealousy tore at his gut. The beautiful Anne was in love with her skinny cousin.

It was only his love for Greta that freed Olli from his obsession with Anne. And there Greta sits on the bed, under the valuable painting, pleased that he has come.

She throws herself on the bed and beckons to him. Olli hardly dares look at her. He's ashamed. It feels criminal even to touch this tender figure in her pear dress now that he's become so big, so clumsy and middle-aged.

Luckily the candlelight is forgiving.

He sits down on the bed and lowers himself onto his back. Greta climbs on top of him, smiles and touches his face with her fingertips, wondering at the traces left by the years and laughing at his rough razor stubble. Her hair falls across his face and tickles him. She feels amazingly light, almost weightless. The green of the forest glows in her eyes.

She kisses him. Her hand presses between his legs, her lipsticked mouth smiling mischievously.

Olli trembles.

Then he closes his eyes and pushes his fingers into her golden hair.

11

OLLI SUOMINEN, publisher and member of the parish council, opened his eyes, threw off the blanket and realized he had just ejaculated into his striped pyjama bottoms.

He also noticed that he was no longer caressing the girl in the pear-print dress; he was in his bedroom, in a double bed, with a woman beside him who had at some point in his life become his wife.

He turned onto his side and stared at the sleeping woman's face, which was more familiar to him than his own. It was pretty, almost beautiful. The kind of face that was easy to remember, that felt familiar even when you saw it for the first time.

But now it was puckered up like an accordion and lying next to him.

As he had on many other mornings, Olli had the thought that the feeling of familiarity was an illusion. When people have lived together for years, they think they know each other through and through. In reality, the longer people are together, the more they become strangers to one another. At some point, people who were once in love get used to each other and they stop being curious, stop sharing any but the most commonplace thoughts, imagine that the other person will stay the same day in and day out. So they change without realizing it, become alien to each other.

It felt strange that the person sleeping beside him had given birth to his offspring. He remembered the hairy head, squeezed to a point, pushing out from between her legs, and the body that followed, equipped with a little weeny. He remembered the look on his wife's face when the newborn was laid on her chest, hungry and bewildered.

That child was asleep in the next room, his head nicely round now.

The woman smacked her lips when a strand of hair fell into her mouth.

Soon this person would get up and think it self-evident that the Suominen family's life would continue unchanged in this house where they had lived for years and would continue to live until death finally did them part. She would look at Olli, but see only the unchanged image of him she had already formed, would say the same ordinary things she always said, and he would of course give her his ordinary, equally unsurprising answers. They would both carry out their usual tasks and then in the evening come to this same bed to sleep and wait for another morning.

The thought of this horrified Olli, who at that moment felt torn loose from his life, didn't feel it to be a part of himself. It was as if some part of his mind had fallen away during the night.

He stared at the panels on the ceiling, which seemed to grimace at him, and finally grimaced back.

He dimly remembered reading a newspaper in his dream. In reality the articles about the Tourula Five had been considerably more modest.

79

The police were also assisted by five children who found the burglar's hideout by chance.

That was in the *Jyväskylä Lehti*. In the next issue there was a brief interview with the "junior detectives" who had helped the police. They were asked how it felt to be praised for their alertness. The grand group photo of them had gone unpublished because the space was needed for a meat market ad.

The article was published after summer was over. Grandma had asked the lady in the next apartment for an extra copy and sent it to Olli. There was also a fifty-markka bill with a picture of President Ståhlberg on it, and a note that read *Nicely done. With best wishes from Grandpa.*

Olli's mother and father had been amazed. They didn't know how to respond to the clipping or to Grandpa Suominen's congratulations. To them Olli was an unhappy boy who didn't get on with his teachers or classmates.

Olli was confused, too. He had started Year 5 and was living a grey routine of textbooks, boring classmates and dusty schoolrooms. When he held the article about the Tourula Five in his hand it was as if a piece of a summer dream had come sailing into his reality.

A couple of days later Leo had called him. The Blomrooses' mother had, it seemed, nearly burst with pride. She had written a letter to Enid Blyton's daughter Gillian Baverstock, who had had a standing request for any information about "real-life Famous Fives". Leo wasn't pleased about this.

"If you ask me, this lady Baverstock probably thinks my mom's a complete lunatic, and doesn't care a bit about what some Finn writes to her, no matter what it was we did," Leo said. "But anyway, see you next summer. We'll see what happens then."

Olli got up with a groan, threw his pyjama bottoms in the laundry hamper, washed, dressed, drank a cup of instant coffee and went to his computer. He had an uneasy feeling that drove him to look at his Facebook profile. He had collected 659 Facebook friends: acquaintances, colleagues, contacts in the publishing world...

As he was going through the list, which was arranged alphabetically by first name, he found three names from the past:

Anne Blomroos
Leo Blomroos
Richard Blomroos

He felt like he might be sick. There they were: the Blomrooses. Father a question mark, mother in banking and proud of her signed first edition of Enid Blyton from 1942. The names of her children were an homage to the great writer, and knowledge of Blyton's works had fallen on them as a sacred duty.

The Facebook photos showed middle-aged people, which shocked Olli more than finding them on his friends list. He realized that he had expected the other members of the Tourula Five to remain smooth-faced children.

Leo had been a muscular, athletic type whom Olli had admired and envied for his self-confidence. In the photo he was a puffy, ruddy man with a bald head. According to his profile, he was a car salesman. *Religious views: Ford forever.* Olli shook his head.

Richard, or Riku, as they always called him, was somewhat better preserved than his brother. Riku didn't give much information about himself, but he belonged to a Facebook group called "Tits and Beer".

And Anne. Beautiful little Anne. According to her profile her hobbies were yoga, golf, sailing, going to the gym, swimming, movies and collecting art. The only information about her profession was that she had a "leadership position in the business field". The photo showed a plump, bourgeois woman with blue eyes, blonde curls and freckles on her nose.

Olli had once thought Anne was the sweetest creature in the world with nothing but the most marvellous girlish thoughts in her lovely head. He used to think about her eyes and her freckles when he masturbated—particularly the freckles. Afterwards he was always wracked with guilt for soiling his angel with his lustful thoughts.

Then the awful things happened. When he looked at Anne's face now, a cold wind blew through his memories and the world flickered dimmer.

Olli didn't want to remember the Blomrooses or have anything to do with them.

Grandpa Notary once said, "Never poke at the past with a stick, because you never know what you'll stir up." Olli knew that his grandpa would have hated Facebook. Life was made up of meetings and partings. You get to know people, and then you forget most of them, often for good reasons. When you change locations, you change people, too, and that's a hidden blessing. But Facebook shrinks the distances between people with a couple of clicks and forces them to stay in touch forever. In that sense it's like something out of Dante's vision of hell.

Of course, he could remove the Blomrooses from his list with a few clicks. He could make them invisible on Facebook. Virtual world magic.

On the other hand, doing so might only draw their attention to him.

Olli wanted to be careful not to leave any trace on the Blomrooses' profiles. He hoped that the silence between him and them would remain unbroken.

At the film club they were watching F.W. Murnau's *Nosferatu*. Vampires were discussed in *A Guide to the Cinematic Life*:

Vampire movies offer a vantage point on life no other genre can. A vampire is an ambivalent creature, both hideous in his destructiveness and tragically beautiful. When we look into a vampire's eyes we see a person who is awakened to the emptiness of everyday life and aware that when that illusion is abandoned, all of us are alone, eternal outsiders. That is why he sees only emptiness when he looks in a mirror. It makes him a free being. He can be anyone at all.

When we accept this outsiderness and refuse to be one with our everyday image, we can surrender to life in a deep, cinematic way. This will, of course, terrify anyone who clings to the everyday, to the face in the mirror, unaware that the light of day, far from helping them to see the truth, actually dazzles them and prevents them from seeing it.

There had been more people than usual at the past few screenings. Maiju from the office was sitting in the front row. Olli waved at her. She didn't see him. Olli thought he saw Mrs Valkeinen, the conservative Lutheran mother from the parish council, come in. Maybe he was wrong, but he had seen her at the bookshop buying a copy of *A Guide to the Cinematic Life*.

Halfway through the movie, Olli fell asleep. In his dream, the girl in the pear-print dress was sitting in the seat next to him. She laid a hand on his thigh, bared her neck and asked him to bite her.

Two weeks later he received the first thirty pages of the *Magical City Guide* by email.

Greta wrote:

I hope and pray that you like it, because I've done my best, but if you don't then promise me you'll be honest. We both have to be proud of the book. We're doing this together.

Olli printed the pages, got in a comfortable position, and started to read. June was turning to July. Sunlight flooded the office. It splashed on the floor in a hot puddle. Olli remembered wading in puddles as a little boy in his bare feet with Grandpa Notary smiling down at him fondly. Olli whistled a little tune. The portrait of Olli Suominen, Publisher looked on with approval.

The Magical City Guides could be as big a hit as *Cinematic Life*. The focus on Jyväskylä would affect sales, but the concept had potential. If Greta wanted to write the first book about Jyväskylä, so what? It was her attachment to Jyväskylä that had led her to Book Tower Publishing.

Vilho Torni called and congratulated Olli on snapping Greta Kara up. They talked about the upcoming project. Torni advised him to turn the localness of the first book to marketing advantage however he could.

Olli suggested a collaboration with a travel agency. The *Magical City Guide* could be sold to tourists as a package with guided tours, and would, of course, be of interest to locals. Torni liked the idea.

Future Magical City Guides would deal with bigger, more internationally known cities, so their potential market would be considerably larger. Thus burnished, Vilho Torni thanked Olli again for the excellent recruitment. He stressed that it was Olli's job as publisher and Greta's personal editor to make sure that she was kept happy, and kept publishing through Book Tower in the future.

"I'm relying on you completely in this," Torni said, and ended the call.

Olli looked out the window at the old church park. He was secretly worried about the first book in the series. When he was a child, Jyväskylä was an interesting place. Not any more. There were fewer and fewer interesting places all the time. The old Reimari service station on the next block had even been torn down. And a couple of days ago when Olli was walking through the park he noticed that the old blue-bottomed fountain from his childhood was gone.

But Greta Kara believed she could find the magical side of the city and be able to write a whole book about it.

Olli tapped his fingers on the windowsill. Then he sighed, went to get some aspirin and told Maiju and Antero that he would be going out to read over the manuscript.

In A Guide to the Cinematic Life *I stated that some people are more naturally cinematic than others. They radiate meaningfulness particles that can momentarily elevate the cinematic level of those around them and thus enrich their experience of life.*

Places can also radiate meaningfulness particles. Some places, in other words, are cinematic, while others are marked by commonplace meaninglessness.

There are places—rooms, buildings, streets, landscapes, neighbourhoods, towns—whose unaesthetic ordinariness numbs a person so that they can't even imagine doing anything cinematic. But in other places it feels natural, if not unavoidable, to transcend the boundaries of the everyday self in our thoughts, speech and deeds. These are places with a particularly high concentration of meaningfulness particles.

These particules imaginaires, which are called M-particles, work in such a way that when they permeate a person's inner being, they activate the inner filmic self and temporarily increase one's cinematicness. In other words, they can raise the everyday above ethical normativity in both thought and deed, construct a character for the self purpose-built for its context, and manifest their own existence through cinematically aesthetic means. (This is described in greater detail in A Guide to the Cinematic Life.*)*

One example of such a magical place is Puistokatu, the

Jyväskylä street lined with linden trees that borders several city parks. It has one spot with particularly high levels of meaningfulness particles. Numerous natural elements combine there in ideal relation to one another and create an experience of cinematic meaningfulness.

You can find the right spot by following these directions:

Start on Kankaankatu with the cemetery on your left and Taulumäki Church on your right. Turn onto Puistokatu and walk south towards the centre of town. The wall of the cemetery will stay on your left. Walk on the left side of the street. Keep your gaze focused forward, but also be aware of the right side of the street. Stop when you see a building with a large Goodyear tyre advertisement painted on the side. Carefully adjust your position a couple of metres in different directions until you feel your experience of time, place and yourself begin to grow more concentrated.

Olli did as the guidebook said. The linden trees along Puistokatu cast their dappled shadows over him. But it was still hot.

The text of the book needed to be clarified, both in its ideas and their expression, Olli thought. And of course the whole theory of meaningfulness particles was entertaining but basically silly—though in a saleable way. Greta had, after all, introduced the idea in *A Guide to the Cinematic Life* and proved that her ideas could hit home with an audience.

According to Maiju, there was clearly an existing demand for Greta Kara's theory of meaningfulness particles and cinematic living. Maiju herself had started to adjust her life according to the teachings of the *Guide*, "just out of curiosity".

In addition to a new movie-star look, Maiju had dedicated

herself to a new way of talking. She had started to communicate in film quotes meant to create an artistic effect, and developed according to surprisingly thorough instructions.

The book covered numerous life situations:

Cinematic Ways to Get to Know Interesting People and Find
Unexpected Romance
How to Part Cinematically
How to Stay Together Cinematically
Cinematic Dress
Cinematic Dialogue
Cinematic Dining
Cinematic Travel
Cinematic Illness
Cinematic Revenge
Cinematic Death

Under these headings were discussion and analysis of movie characters, scenes and plots connected with each theme and explications of their aesthetics. The examples were followed by philosophically based methods intended to help the reader experience life as meaningful even in situations that were, on the face of it, banal.

A book about cinematicness naturally had copious illustrations. At the beginning of the chapter on revenge, for instance, there was a photo of Jeanne Moreau's character in Truffaut's film *The Bride Wore Black*. They had watched it at the film club in May. The pictures on the next page were taken from Jacques Becker's *Casque d'Or* and Sergio Leone's *Once Upon a Time in the West*.

The media had been enthusiastic about Greta Kara's theories. A couple of weeks ago one of the Finnish evening tabloids had published an article about *A Guide to the Cinematic Life* that rated Finnish celebrities according to their cinematicness. It was illustrated with a sketch of a "Kara-particle meter".

Olli grew impatient with the manuscript. The text explained that he should focus on being "exactly where he was", and let "the ambient meaningfulness particles" permeate him. He threw himself into it and followed the instructions even though it felt stupid.

Just as he was about to give up, something happened. Almost as if he just clicked into the right spot.

And then he wasn't looking at a streetscape full of linden trees.

He was looking at himself, looking through his being, deeper than he ever had, catching by surprise that formless creature that was himself, beneath his name, titles, situation, job and memories.

It bared its teeth, shrieked and bit him.

He fell down.

All of his thoughts are falling away into the cracks and crevices.

All that's left is a floating, spinning feeling, like the one he experienced years ago at the playground, on the carousel with the boy's head on top. The memory touches him, as cool as a beautiful girl's hand.

Then summer comes rolling down the street and smacks him to the ground.

He slides back into his skull.

The hot juice of the sun flows over the linden trees. The car tyre hums on the wall. The blue text of the advertisement burns into his retinas in capital letters.

Goodyear!

Brightness pours down in dappled, leafy drops. Darkness rises up from the ground; he breathes it in. He is part of a puzzle that assembles and disassembles itself again and again, thousands of times every second. And each time, the puzzle changes a little, though you can't see it happening.

For one second, he isn't there.

Then the meaningfulness particles delineate him and make him a part of the landscape.

As consciousness pours itself into his outlines, he sits up and notices people gathered around him.

12

*Magical places are dangerous. Meaningfulness particles can
awaken us to our existence. But when that happens, a person
can slip outside of the self.*

GRETA KARA,
Magical City Guide Number One: Jyväskylä

Greta sent pages every three days. They came as attachments
through ordinary email, which Greta described as too dull,
neutral and formal for personal messages. Those she sent
through Facebook. *So it will feel more like a real conversation.*

She didn't want to use chat, which Olli was glad of. *Its
urgent quality causes you to lose the nuances of the dialogue and always
leads to flat chitchat, or horrible excess.*

In her long and meandering messages, Greta recounted
her work in Paris. She also said she was planning to come and
update her conception of present day Jyväskylä.

*I've been to Jyväskylä a few times over the years to take care of
my affairs, but I haven't really had a chance to look at the place.
My information is from years ago, mostly from my childhood, so I
probably should renew my familiarity with my beloved hometown
and correct any dated ideas I have before the book is published.
Naturally I'm also terribly eager to meet with my publisher,
perhaps over dinner...*

As the manuscript grew into a book, Olli's doubts vanished. The book was going to be an event. It would be a smash hit, both in the media and with the book-buying public. There were all the readers who had loved *A Guide to the Cinematic Life* and would be interested in the *Magical City Guide*, not to mention the new audiences it would reach.

The book mapped Jyväskylä place by place, the way a guidebook should. Some places such as the carousel at Lounais Park with the boy's head on top, which she called a "dreamlike and even intoxicating experience", were already more or less familiar to Olli. Others were places he had never heard of. Apparently he didn't know his hometown as thoroughly as he had thought.

Olli continued to explore the places presented in the book.

As he wandered around Jyväskylä, he noticed to his amazement that some of the places really did have a particularly strong and even magical atmosphere. He also noticed that they more or less affected him in the way that the guidebook described: his thoughts quickened, his self-awareness grew stronger, his cautiousness and stiffness diminished, and in its place he felt an inclination to act spontaneously. But he didn't have any more "awakenings" powerful enough to make him "slip outside of the self", as the book warned. Besides which the weather had cooled, so there was no longer any danger of dehydrating and having embarrassing fainting spells in the street.

Olli didn't usually throw himself into conversation with random people he met in public. But in the places Greta listed as magical, it was remarkably easy to approach strangers. It was like being "at a dance where everyone is listening to the music of the M-particles and waiting for someone to invite them onto the dance floor", as *A Guide to the Cinematic Life* put it.

Many of the people he met seemed to have read the *Guide*. They looked like characters from a movie in one way or another, and there was something cinematically dramatic about the way they behaved.

For instance, as he was walking along the east bank of the river, where the path wound through the river valley past old overgrown stone foundations and then opened out on a peculiar view of a steam chimney, he met two women having a picnic.

The women are wearing pale-coloured, flounced dresses too fancy for a walk in the woods, their hair in long curls. They are sitting on a checked blanket drinking glasses of wine and eating chicken legs.

As Olli approaches, one of the women looks up at him and beckons for him to join them.

He accepts the invitation with a smile, sits down and lays the *City Guide* manuscript beside him on the blanket. One of the women, blonde and stylish, asks if he would like some wine. He answers with a line from the film *This Earth Is Mine*, which comes unexpectedly to mind: "The grape is the only fruit that God gave the sense to know what it was made for."

The women glance at each other, taken with this.

Olli notices that they are no longer young. Both have faces covered in fine wrinkles. But they are still just as lively and beautiful.

The dark-haired one, thinner and more angular than

her friend, smiles with delight, hands Olli an old book and says, "How fun that we were right about you; you're just as pleasant as you look! May we ask you to read some Christina Rossetti to us? We've been reading these poems to each other for fifteen years—in bed, at breakfast, on all our trips—and although we still love Christina as fervently as always, we're tired of hearing each other's voices. Perhaps a pleasant stranger can give our favourite poems new life, if it's not too much trouble…"

When Olli had read seven poems, it started to rain hard.

He stood up and opened his umbrella. The women didn't want to get wet, either. With excited shouts and laughter they packed up their things, yelled goodbye and ran to their Citroën waiting a short distance away on the road.

As they drove off, Olli realized he was holding not only the manuscript but also the book of poetry.

In addition to the umbrella and the manuscript, Olli had his camera with him. The book needed illustrations. He thought he might handle it himself and take at least some preliminary pictures. He tried to capture the atmosphere of the places, but failed.

The camera seemed unable to record M-particle radiation.

In addition to roads and streets, cities have their own footpaths, and those in Jyväskylä should definitely be explored. The density of M-particles varies on different paths, and at different points on each path. Earlier I described the west bank of the Touru River with its nature trail, constructed in 1995, when the river valley, once considered dangerous, was tamed and made more audience-friendly. But there are also paths on the east bank of the river. One of them starts at the corner just before the bridge and ends near the fence around the paper mill.

In summer, when the leaves on the trees obscure the uncinematic aspects of the surroundings, this path offers a couple of forest views rich in atmosphere. The view of Jyväskylä is best at a precise point, and can diminish with just a couple of steps as something banal comes into view.

A deepening of the life experience can be found halfway along the path at a point surrounded by trees, looking down the steep bluff towards the river (see map). If you suffer from slow continuum attachment, I recommend looking for these sorts of charged places. The mental aesthetic disturbance of slow continuum attachment is discussed more thoroughly in A Guide to the Cinematic Life. *It is a disorder that spoils life feeling and sensitivity to change and, if left unaddressed, can lead to complete numbness.*

Farther on, the path passes through meadows buzzing with insects. At that point memories of childhood viewings of The Wizard of Oz *and its fields of poppies may come to mind as the deep self charges itself with meaningfulness particles.*

Along the path on the east bank of the river rises the steam chimney of the paper mill. It isn't particularly romantic or pretty. But because the place combines natural and industrial elements in such a striking way, it has a certain dreamlike frisson, which I discuss in chapter 8.

It is also worth mentioning that there is an entrance to one of Jyväskylä's numerous secret passages in the vicinity of the steam chimney. (More information in Appendix 3.) Entering the

*passages should be avoided due to danger of collapse or getting
lost, as well as the high levels of M-particles.*

GRETA KARA,
Magical City Guide Number One: Jyväskylä

After looking around for two hours Olli called his office
and asked Maiju to check whether Greta Kara's documents
included an Appendix 3.

They didn't.

Olli searched the woods around the steam chimney not
knowing whether he thought he would really find anything or
was just trying to identify with the experience of enthusiastic
readers who might come to explore the area.

The place was strange to him and at the same time
puzzlingly familiar. This was where the edge of the old
neighbourhood of Tourula used to be, with its wooden houses
and gardens. This was where he had spent his childhood
summers with the Blomrooses and Karri. Somewhere nearby
was where the old house had been, the one that looked out
over the river, where he and Greta used to meet.

There was once an entire, living neighbourhood here.
But the city preferred to let the old buildings of Tourula fall
into decay, and then they were all torn down to make way
for new ones.

As he walked along, Olli searched for signs of the vanished
neighbourhood. The rifle-factory buildings on the other side
of the road had been preserved. In the north-east section, the
destruction was complete. The new Tourula wasn't a neighbourhood. It was an undefined, characterless area, like so
many others in Jyväskylä. In the old Tourula's place a road had

been built, a roundabout, asphalt, bus stops, shops, apartment houses, hamburger stands and extensions of the paper mill. All that was left of the old neighbourhood was a railing between the fenced-off nature park, the factory and the asphalted shopping area next to the road. There were also a couple of the old houses still hidden among the wooded meadows.

Olli looked up. Insects were gathering in swarms; it was going to rain soon. He walked along the path back to the bicycle trail, straightened his tie and opened his umbrella. Raindrops pattered on the taut fabric. A spike protruded from the edge of the umbrella. Olli touched it gingerly, like tending a wounded animal, and his face darkened.

He crossed the bridge. The Touru River ran muddy beneath it. The valley looked like it belonged on one of those travel posters: the trees reflected in the river, the delightful river road, the pleasing variety of elevation.

This view was mentioned in the guidebook. Its picturesqueness was unlike central Finland. It was easy to imagine he was in some foreign country, or even in a movie.

As he looked out over the landscape, Olli felt a longing that was difficult to define. It was the same feeling he had after a fascinating dream or a moving film. As if he had come close to something meaningful, but hadn't quite reached it. No doubt Greta Kara's meaningfulness particles were at this very moment whizzing through his brain and causing his restless feeling, Olli thought with amusement.

He walked down the wooden steps to the walking path, entering the landscape he had just seen from the bridge. In the winter wild ducks flocked near the bridge waiting to be fed. They were somewhere else now.

The road ran along the river, then rose up past the cemetery and arrived at the intersection with Puistokatu. The nature trail branched off the road and headed upstream.

Olli looked behind him. Someone was on the bridge looking down from where he had just been standing.

13

W HEN HE REACHED THE SCHOOL the rain stopped.
Olli closed his umbrella. The fabric tore a little more.
Then the metal parts of the contraption twisted and tangled
together and the tensile strength essential to its umbrellaness
vanished before his eyes. It looked more like the carcass of a
mechanical bird.

Olli glumly dropped the dead umbrella in a litter bin at
the hamburger stand and continued towards the nearest
umbrella shop.

As he walked he pondered the *Magical City Guide* manuscript. They probably should cut the references to secret
passages before it went to press. There was no point in confusing readers by bringing it up.

He did have a faint memory of the secret passage games
the Tourula Five used to play, which must have put the idea
of secret passages in Greta's head. He and Karri and the
Blomrooses had pretended to find entrances to secret passages in fittingly hidden spots around town and then spent
days wandering in them. They had encouraged each other to
invent everything a child's imagination could think up and
had been so caught up in their game that they saw and heard
non-existent things. The secret passages had been enchanted
and sometimes terrifying places.

The thought of the five of them excitedly rummaging
through the bushes, ditches and hollows put a wry smile on

Olli's face. He had to admit that nothing he'd experienced in recent years, not even sex, had been as thrilling as the secret passages of his childhood.

He decided to discuss it with Greta as soon as he could log on to Facebook. He hadn't asked for the author's phone number, and she hadn't offered it, since it was going so well on Facebook and email. That way they avoided those awkward moments that former lovers and childhood friends easily feel when they meet again and realize that they no longer see anything they recognize in each other.

Olli walked through the old church park and crossed the street at the bridal shop. The Pukkala rain-gear shop was between a sex shop and a women's clothing store. They sold raincoats, rain ponchos, rubber boots and quality umbrellas.

Olli went in and started to browse the umbrella selection, paying special attention to their construction. He didn't intend to give in and buy a cheap one that broke easily. It depressed him.

As always, there was music playing in the shop. The saleswoman played old tango records day in and day out, smoking in the back room, waiting for customers. There was a partly opened curtain hanging in the doorway. The woman was only visible in silhouette. She was surrounded by a cloud of tobacco smoke that escaped into the front of the shop. In any other place it would have been peculiar.

The saleswoman had reached middle age years before, but still dressed as she had in her youth, which had been sometime in the 1960s. Her nut-brown hair was pulled up in a banana clip to reveal her slim neck. Her dress had a black and white geometric pattern. It followed her slim, girlish figure and left her arms and back bare.

She watched the shop from her hiding place; only her eyes, lined in heavy black, moved. That suited Olli. He put off talking with her as long as possible.

In the bright light of the shop she was unambiguously ugly. Smoking had taken the natural colour from her face and far from hiding the lines in her skin her thick make-up accentuated them. From close up she was ordinary. But when she sat in the back room with her smoky silhouette falling on the curtain, the profile of her face and body had the lines of a Gustav Klimt.

The woman had made herself into a work of art in a way that was described in *A Guide to the Cinematic Life*.

Observe people in waiting rooms, on park benches, in train and bus stations. You'll notice that some of them disappear into washed-out meaninglessness, while others draw your attention and you can't stop looking at them and speculating about what it would be like to be a part of their lives and memories.

Cinematic people radiate M-particles in all situations. A person doesn't have to be young, beautiful or stylish—or even clean. Their hair and clothing are a part of the total impression, but it's more a question of the right sort of self-awareness, a deep realization of their own character.

That night Olli has a dream.

He is walking over the Tourula River bridge. He's wearing a fedora hat, a tie and nothing else but his striped pyjamas. There is a night-time festival going on in town. From one direction he hears orchestral music, from another a loud-speaker: SEE THE AMAZING HUMAN ODDITY! FOUND IN THE SECRET PASSAGEWAYS, BADLY BEATEN AND BATTERED, AND RESTORED TO HEALTH BY THE WORK OF TEN TOP SURGEONS! TODAY ONLY!

There are booths selling sausages and ice cream. A juggler on stilts strides by tossing not balls but dolls, and blowing into a paper kazoo.

A warm wind blows dandelion fluff. The air is thick with the downy seeds, and now and then it's difficult to see. When they touch the ground they take root and grow amazingly quickly. Here and there are glowing meadows of dandelions that the people walk through, shouting their delight. Olli is upset that he's left his camera at home.

There are crowds of people, all in nightgowns and pyjamas. There's nothing odd about that—you should wear night clothes at night.

The women's nightgowns are disconcertingly thin. Their bodies are works of art meant to be looked at and commented on. Like the other people, Olli admires their varied breasts, legs and hips, runs his fingers along the curves of their buttocks, muses aloud about the various aesthetic choices, as do the women themselves.

He laughs with joy and wonders why he so rarely goes out at night. Everything is so much freer than in the daytime, the people more open and sociable.

Then he notices a woman with a little boy beside her on a bicycle. She's wearing silk pyjamas with the top open. "Pardon me, ma'am, but you certainly have very sweet breasts," Olli says.

The woman lifts her breasts, thanks him for the compliment, says that is very kind of him but if he looks closer he'll notice that there is in fact much lacking in her breasts—lately they even have a rubbery smell.

Olli bends towards her and sniffs, and her breasts do indeed smell like rubber.

He looks closely at the woman, trying to get an impression of her face. There's something familiar about it, but the light is dim and the dandelion fluff is flying between them all the time.

"Excuse me, but do we know each other?" he finally asks.

The woman smiles sadly, shakes her head, and walks away, following the boy, who has already pedalled to the end of the block.

Olli is filled with anxiety. He shouldn't have let the woman and the little boy go.

He leans against a railing and notices that there's something wrong about the view from the bridge. Nothing is moving. The birds are frozen in the air. The river isn't flowing. The trees are lifeless cardboard. The distances are flattened.

The landscape is nothing but a big cardboard facade with a row of crows perched on the upper edge.

He shakes his head. He can't understand why this fake landscape hasn't been written about in the Central Finland or Greater Jyväskylä newspapers.

Olli is startled to see a golden-haired girl in a pear-print dress come into view from below the bridge. She looks up, waves a hand, and walks into the facade.

Olli tries to shout a warning.

But lines from the Christina Rossetti poem he was reading to the women at the picnic comes out of his mouth instead:

"Remember me when I am gone away, Gone far away into the silent land; When you can no more hold me by the hand, Nor I half turn to go yet turning stay."

He closes his mouth, holds his breath, and manages to swallow a couple of lines. They taste like pears. Then he tries to shout again, but more poetry comes out:

"Only remember me; you understand, It will be late to counsel then or pray. Yet if you should forget me for a while, And afterwards remember, do not grieve."

When the golden-haired girl in the pear-print dress is halfway up the hill she becomes two-dimensional and freezes, a part of the picture.

It's getting cold. Snow is falling and the wind is rising. Olli shivers in his pyjamas, sad at the girl's fate. The cardboard landscape sways in the wind. He hears an ominous cracking sound, as if the structure is giving way.

Then the landscape starts to fall.

People are shouting.

A rush of air sweeps over the bridge and tears at his clothes. His tie flies away with the wind.

As Olli looks at the fallen landscape, he realizes that it isn't a facade; it's a huge postcard. On the back, in large letters, is Olli's name and address and the message:

For the love of my life, from the girl in the pear-print dress.

14

*At the centre of all that exists sleeps our creator. We are not
made from dust and ribs. We are the images of God's dreams,
lighting up his eternal night.*

*The theologians are lost and the clergy and prophets are
leading us astray. The meaning of God is not to be found in
laws, commandments and holy scripture, but in classic films.
Open your eyes and look at the world and you will understand
that God is not a moralist, but an aesthete, the final critic. And
life is a movie.*

Greta Kara,
A Guide to the Cinematic Life

Olli awoke to a distant alarm. He sat up and looked around.
Aino lay with her legs sticking out from under the blanket,
her hair in her face.

Olli went downstairs to the lavatory and tinkled in the
pot. He remembered an ad for a natural remedy for prostate
trouble. His flow was still good, though. He had no cause for
worry, for the time being.

As he was washing his hands, the unofficial version
of publisher and parish-council member Olli Suominen
scowled from the mirror. It was a sort of rough approxima-
tion of the businesslike person most people knew. His hair
needed a trim. It was getting more grey in it. Hairs poked
out of his nose. Razor stubble made him look like a gangster.

The lines around his eyes were spreading like cracks in a marble statue. If Grandpa Notary was any indication, Olli would at least age gracefully. Grandpa went to his grave a charmer.

Before going back to bed he went to peek into his son's room.

The boy was snuffling under the covers. All that was visible was an ear. Olli bent to look more closely. The ear was beautifully shaped and flawless, a masterpiece of creation, or maybe evolution. When he looked at that ear, he believed in God, for a little while anyway.

Olli adjusted the blanket and tiptoed out of the room. He realized he didn't feel like sleeping, and went back downstairs. The house creaked and breathed as the night sucked the warmth out of the walls. Water murmured in the toilet. Something scratched in a corner. Did they have mice in the house?

There are all kinds of noises at night that you don't notice during the daytime. Olli didn't like them; they weren't meant to be heard. He ought to be asleep right now, like everyone else. He felt guilty, but he stayed up, sitting on the sofa.

The afternoon before he had sent Greta a message recommending that they remove the references to the secret passages, to avoid confusing readers unnecessarily.

An answer came half an hour later.

The message didn't take a position on the secret passages. Greta said she was in Jyväskylä and suggested that they meet the following day to discuss the manuscript and sign all the papers.

*

That Friday morning at the office passed slowly. They had agreed to meet at 2 p.m. in a restaurant downtown.

Olli was nervous. He couldn't concentrate on anything. He knew of course that there was nothing to be nervous about. A publisher was going to meet with a successful author who happened to be an old friend of his. They had once long ago been children and been in love, and now they were middle-aged, practical, reserved professionals. They would both behave in a way appropriate to their age and station. They might look at their shared past in amusement, with a touch of nostalgia, but the long-lost games of childhood would be kept in their proper perspective.

Everything would no doubt go in a businesslike manner, but Olli's mind kept coming up with alternative ways that the meeting might progress.

It was unavoidable, in a way, that his mind would eventually settle on a classic erotic fantasy, where one thing led to another and they ended up in a hotel room tearing each other's clothes off.

When he imagined the famous author Greta Kara in front of him on a hotel bed, naked and lustful, he felt ill. His head started to buzz and his stomach clenched. He took an aspirin and was washing it down with coffee when Maiju strode into the room without knocking.

The coffee ended up on Olli's shirt.

"Hang it all," he said.

Maiju stood in the middle of the floor.

Maiju had once been a pleasantly restrained person. Lately, though, she had adopted a chaotic flair, like something out of a Fellini movie. She burst into rooms without warning, was rash and boisterous, started needless arguments and accused her co-workers of insulting her. One older author who came to visit the offices had found himself in the middle of one of her cinematic exercises and was so taken aback that it sent him into heart palpitations.

The hot coffee burned. Olli expressed his displeasure at Maiju's behaviour and Maiju laughed, throwing her head back brazenly and answering him with a quote from *La Dolce Vita*:

"I am the first woman on the first day of creation. I am mother, sister, lover, friend, angel, devil, earth, home... But OK, I'll try to keep my life force in check, to please you. Fellini would be good for you, by the way, Olli. You ought to try it."

She was wearing a Fellini-style dress too showy for work. *A Guide to the Cinematic Life* discussed hundreds of different styles of dress categorized by director, genre and film. A couple of weeks earlier Maiju had enthused about finding a clothing shop where they sold cinematic attire for readers of the *Guide*.

"So here it is," Maiju said. "*Emma Bunny's Book about Boys and Girls*. Hot off the press. But you've got coffee in your lap. Do you need a tissue? Or should I go buy you a new shirt? I'm on my way to lunch. I can pick one up while I'm out."

Olli took his umbrella off the rack and went out himself. He wasn't going to get any work done until this meeting was over, anyway.

The drizzle was turning to a real rain. Olli opened his umbrella and headed to Halonen, where he always bought his clothes. He held the umbrella in front of him so that the spot of coffee on his shirt wouldn't show at a distance.

When he got to Compass Square he stopped. There was a pair of woman's legs in front of him, jutting out from under a skirt.

They didn't seem to want to go anywhere.

Olli tried to go around the legs, but then the person attached to them took hold of his umbrella and peeked under it.

"Is that you, Olli? It is, isn't it?"

Olli tried to give a logical reply, but his thoughts escaped from his mouth in every direction.

Afterwards he remembered explaining why his shirt was dirty and blurting that unfortunately he couldn't take Greta to dinner, urgent matters had come up, and they would have to take care of their business at the office.

And then the meeting was over and he was sitting at his desk in befuddlement.

Greta had just walked out of his office.

Olli only remembered her feet, clad in red high heels.

But at least the signatures on the contracts seemed to be in order.

15

GRETA CONTINUED WRITING. She sent new pages, and corrections whenever she noticed in her tour around Jyväskylä that places had changed, or disappeared altogether. The *Magical City Guide* was gradually growing into a complete book.

But the meeting fiasco put a damper on their Facebook conversations. The communication from Greta's side shrank to scant greetings.

Notary Suominen in his portrait looked down at his grandson disapprovingly. Olli considered punishing himself by skipping the film club meeting, but then went after all, to avoid Aino, who had been bombarding him with questions about summer travel. He had a publishing house to run and a future best-seller under production. He didn't know when he would have time for a holiday.

The film showing was Howard Hawks's *The Big Sleep*. There were a lot of dead bodies. Olli couldn't follow the plot. Apparently he wasn't the only one. The people around him looked befuddled. He concentrated on admiring Lauren Bacall's beauty and Humphrey Bogart's cool confidence.

When the film ended, the identity of the murderer was still a mystery to Olli. He was thinking about other things. He didn't need Philip Marlowe to tell him that Greta was seriously offended and that the fault lay with her editor, Olli Suominen.

Eventually he sent her a Facebook message explaining that he had felt ill on the day they were supposed to meet, and might have seemed "a little distant".

Greta didn't respond, but Olli kept trying. He had a responsibility as a publisher, which he was very conscious of. Greta Kara was important to Book Tower's future, an author he had to hold on to by any means necessary.

One night Olli was reading through *A Guide to the Cinematic Life* and Greta's new manuscript and pondering life. As he read, he wrote Greta a long message. It started with comments about publishing, but soon turned personal. He told her, for instance, that he suffered from slow continuum attachment and that his life was destined to stay the same to the very last:

I envy those who can live their lives the way you describe. What would it be like to be "Homo cinematicus", as you say in your book? But I depend on predictability. Change, new experiences, make me nervous. On the other hand, I also depend on being able to escape now and then to something new, to keep my life from becoming unbearable.

As soon as he sent the message, he regretted it. Having ascertained that he couldn't get it back, he made himself step away from the computer.

He walked through the house to the kitchen. At night, Aino's many mirrors multiplied the dark. Olli tried not to look at his reflection, but as he stopped to scratch he accidentally saw himself in the hallway mirror. A middle-aged man in pyjama bottoms looked out from the glass. In the dimness the hair on his chest made him look like a great ape. He still had some muscle, although the firm physique of his youth was history. He could stand to be a little slimmer around the tummy, too.

His stubbly face had a confused, surprised expression, which made him look stupid. He scowled to bring his features back under control.

He went into the kitchen and turned on the light. For a second he couldn't see anything. The kitchen had been completely remodelled a couple of years earlier, with money Aino inherited from her father. It was the only corner of the house without measuring errors or other imperfections, only eye-pleasing elements. Pale ceiling panels. Glass cupboard doors. Wood surfaces like dark chocolate. Four chairs around the table. A booster seat covered in food stains on one chair.

Olli opened the refrigerator. There was low-fat bologna, low-fat Gotler sausage, ground beef, tuna, meatballs, peanut butter, milk, yogurt, some strawberry compote that Aino had made, buttermilk, cucumbers, tomatoes, potatoes, carrots, eggs, cheese and low-fat frankfurters.

The peanut butter caught his interest.

When was the last time he'd eaten peanut butter? He opened the lid and the kitchen was filled with the thick, sweet scent of it. Peanut butter molecules slipped over the mucous membranes of his nose and sensory impulses raced down his neural pathways and entered his cerebral cortex. Lights went on in the darkest corners of his neural network. A recollection from years past began to crystallize in his mind.

*

They're lounging under an apple tree, feasting. Olli is enjoying Aunt Anna's fresh-baked French bread spread with a layer of peanut butter as thick as his finger. At home in Koirakkala he hardly ever gets to eat peanut butter. When he does, he has to spread it thin or his mother gets nervous.

Grass tickles the soles of his feet. The trunk of the tree feels rough against his back. Insects buzz around them. Bird sounds pierce the greenery.

This is Olli's seventh summer with the Tourula Five.

Leo and Riku are talking about television shows. Riku's favourite is *The Six Million Dollar Man*. Leo likes *Columbo* better. Anne thinks the best show is *Little House on the Prairie*. Riku makes a crude comment about Laura Ingalls's bum. The boys snigger. Anne mutters that she wishes she had Laura Ingalls as a sister instead of a brother who has a personality like that brat Nellie Oleson, and looks like her, too. Leo laughs. Riku doesn't. It makes Olli smile.

Even in the shade, it's hot. Silence falls. The Blomrooses don't feel like talking now. Olli closes his eyes, relaxes and lets his head rest against the tree.

He hears sounds:

The scratch of insects' legs on apple-tree bark.

The shush of water flowing inside the tree.

The hollow crack of its powerful slow growth.

There are noises coming up from the ground, too. The tree trunk magnifies them and transfers them directly to the bones of his skull and from there to his inner ear. When he lets his ears really tune in and listen, he can hear moles, grubs, beetles and earthworms moving through the soil.

Beneath the sounds of these small creatures, if he

concentrates hard, he can hear one more sound: the whisper of the secret passages.

His eyes open and green light falls from the branches.

Olli looks at the dozing Blomrooses.

Karri once said that the ground below Jyväskylä was full of secret passages. There are probably some here, too, right underneath them. In his mind's eye, Olli can see the roots of the apple tree hanging from a passageway ceiling.

His eyes close again. A dream is pulling at him, and bit by bit he wraps himself in its darkness. His heart is beating too hard. The sound of it is ringing through his head and making its way into the tree, spreading along the roots and underground into the secret passages.

Something deep in the earth wakes up and starts to listen.

His lost dog Timi?

No.

Something darker. It can hear him, is reaching towards him.

Olli breathes in rasping breaths, springs to his feet and throws himself away from the tree.

The Blomrooses rub their eyes and look at him in bewilderment. "Did a wasp sting you?" Riku asks, looking around.

Olli feels foolish. Startled by his own thoughts.

"No, but it tried to," he says.

He stands in the middle of the yard and the ordinary sounds of Tourula surround him. Someone is chopping wood. A small child squalls. Women talk over each other and laugh. A truck rumbles past. The Blomrooses bicker about something silly. Olli smiles.

Everything he has in Tourula makes him happy. The

Blomrooses, Aunt Anna, the garden, the grass, the flowers, the butterflies, the apple tree, the warmth and colour. Summer in Tourula is eternal, because when it starts to end he always leaves.

When he's with the Blomroos siblings and Karri, everything feels great. And not just great, but meaningful. Time isn't wasted on nothing, like it is in Koirakkala. In Tourula, every minute is spent in the best possible way.

The window creaks open. Aunt Anna calls them. They run into the house.

Aunt Anna is in the kitchen loading a picnic basket. Morning light is pouring through the windows, making her lemon-yellow dress glow. She is the Blomrooses' father's sister, a handsome, motherly woman. Olli can never stop looking at her breasts. The fabric of her dress is thin and the tips of her breasts show through, large and dark like the mint chocolates she sometimes gives them.

"Well, my faithful Five," Aunt Anna says with a smile in her voice.

Olli is charmed by her way of speaking to them in such a friendly, mischievous tone.

"It looks like you're all together and ready to go, as soon as that dreamy son of mine gets himself downstairs. I wonder what else I can supply for you. Here's your lunch. I did my best. I hope it tastes good. If you run out of food just come back for a refill. Would you please carry it, Leo? You're probably the strongest. Or have Riku and Olli been training over the winter?"

She puckers up her mouth and laughs until her breasts jiggle. The laugh infects the children, too.

The kitchen is full of wondrous aromas that wind their way through the room like the serpent in paradise. They come from the jams, cardamom buns, cakes, pies, rolls, meat pasties, marmalades, cookies and pastries that she endlessly prepares and packs into their picnic lunches.

Olli hopes and trusts that he will never forget the smell of Aunt Anna's kitchen.

The boys thank her for the picnic basket, nodding politely. Anne is sassy. "It seems like Aunt Anna's trying to fatten me up till I look like a pig," she says sulkily.

But you can see in her eyes that she's as excited about the picnic as the others. Her plaid skirt and short top show off the new shape of her body. She's grown over the past year, and she has breasts now. Her bottom is a "tight little package", as Riku said to Olli on the lake shore a couple of weeks ago when the others were out of earshot.

Anne's navel is showing. The skin of her belly makes Olli swallow. It's like white chocolate.

Then Anne makes a motion, turns her head and snaps Olli's gaze out of the air with the precision of a raptor.

Olli quavers. Anne's eyes narrow. A sly smile spreads over her lips. She is a beautiful, captivating girl. But she has a mean streak—Olli learnt that last summer. He arrived one morning at Aunt Anna's house with Timi. The door was locked. When Olli rang the bell, Anne came to open the door. She let Timi in, and then slammed the door shut in Olli's face.

Olli stood there confused for a second, then rang the bell again several times, and finally pounded on the door until the windows rattled. When the upstairs window opened, Olli backed off the porch onto the lawn. Anne had her hands wrapped tightly around Timi's throat. The dog was whining and struggling to get free. He couldn't breathe.

"Why didn't you let me in?" Olli asked.

Anne sighed. "Sorry, but we decided democratically that we didn't want to see you today. And Aunt Anna told us not to bang on the door because she has a headache. Come back tomorrow. Timi can spend the night here. We still like him. And he likes us. Don't you, Timi?"

The dog looked fearfully at the girl.

Olli's stomach clenched. "OK, I'll go. But let Timi come out first. He's my dog."

Anne thought for a moment. "Yeah, you can have him back. On one condition. Do you have any money?"

Olli searched his pockets. "I have five marks. Why?"

"Good," Anne said. "Go to the store and get us a Lola bar, a bag of liquorice drops and a bottle of Jaffa. We'll swap Timi for them. But hurry up. If we get tired of waiting for you the dog might fall out of the window."

The fixed smile on her face shocked him. She seemed to be completely serious. Olli felt sick to think that his best friends had turned against him and even Aunt Anna didn't care enough to defend him.

The dog yelped in Anne's tight grip.

Olli was just turning to go to the shop when the car pulled into the driveway. Aunt Anna, Karri, Leo and Riku got out carrying groceries and said hello to Olli.

"Have you still got a headache, Anne?" Aunt Anna asked when she saw the girl in the window.

Karri, Leo and Riku brought the bags up to the door.

"We bought you some aspirin, if you still need it," Aunt Anna said.

Anne smiled at Olli and fluffed Timi's fur as if nothing had happened.

Olli was relieved that he didn't have to wait to find out how long she would have kept teasing him that way. He wanted to believe that she wouldn't have really sent him running to the store, let alone done something to hurt Timi.

They were friends, weren't they?

Timi wasn't so trusting. He started avoiding Anne, though he was happy to wander Jyväskylä with the Famous Five. Then Timi disappeared into the secret passages, and never came back.

Sadness flickers through Olli's mind again.

He glances shyly at Anne, then meets Leo's eyes.

Leo winks at him and smiles. He knows that Olli has a crush on Anne. It's probably easy to see. Two summers ago he brought the subject up. "Don't worry, Olli. I won't say anything to the others. And I can understand it. Sis is pretty. She has a lot of admirers at home in Espoo. They fight over her. She's our sister so of course we love her, but… Well, I could tell you a couple of things sometime."

Olli wonders again what kinds of things he might have meant.

There's a creak in the hallway. Karri is standing on the stairs. He's wearing a large hooded sweatshirt that Aunt Anna has been trying to get in the laundry for a long time. You can't quite see his eyes under the hood. Karri has always been a watcher, a partial outsider even in his own gang of friends.

A shy boy, that's how Aunt Anna puts it. But lately Karri has started to seem odder than before, even hostile. Olli is worried that Karri might not want them to come and visit in the summer any more. The Blomrooses are his cousins, at least, but Olli is just a stranger they met in the park and invited for a visit. In fact Karri has never even invited him here; it was the Blomrooses, who often act as if this is their home instead of Karri's.

And what if Olli couldn't come here any more?

He has noticed Karri staring at him sometimes, as if he were about to say something unpleasant. Or wanted to hurt him. Olli hardly dares look him in the eye any more, for fear of annoying him.

The leader of the Tourula Five is Leo. Leo has muscles, smarts and authority. He's good-looking, and he knows what to do in all kinds of situations; even adults treat him as an equal.

But Leo has also said that when it comes down to it Karri is the one who actually *leads* them—a quiet boy who seemed silly to Olli at first, and is scary to him now. One time Riku started calling Karri an oddball behind his back, and Leo grabbed him by the back of the neck and reminded him that without Karri there would be no Tourula Five, just three bored Blomrooses spending summers with Olli and his grandparents at the rifle factory.

But it's time for the picnic now. Olli, Anne, Leo, Riku and Karri leave the house and walk through Tourula.

Tourula is made up of gardens, narrow dirt roads and alleys, cute little quietly decaying houses, woodsheds, privies and other outbuildings, shops, garages, service stations. A short distance to the north is the Jyväskylä bakery, and in the right weather the smell of its biscuits drifts on the wind.

Now and then they toss each other smiles of glee as they walk, happy in each other's company. Olli remembers how Timi used to run up to each one of them in turn and look into their eyes to make sure everything was all right.

Then Anne captures Olli's attention. He can't keep his eyes off her new body. She notices him watching her and apparently decides to allow it, because she smiles at him.

But at the same time, she looks back at Karri to make sure that he's noticed their little game. She's trying to make Karri jealous, Olli thinks.

Karri doesn't seem to care. Anne looks upset. Olli is amused.

The world is bathed in bright colours. Their steps are buoyed, carefree. Anything is possible, because everything exists just for them. Olli would like to run with the wind, climb trees, and shout his joy out loud. He controls himself, though, because he doesn't want to seem childish.

But nothing lasts forever. They've started talking in the dim of the evenings about how adulthood will eventually take hold of even them, and they'll become businessmen, doctors, engineers, fathers and mothers, boring grown-ups with rules and responsibilities. But the inevitable can still be put off. You just have to keep moving. Not stay too close to adults for too long, or pretty soon you'll start to think like them.

Aunt Anna once said, "Listen kids, once you're grown up, the days and the summers fly away from you, and there's not a single thing you can do about it." They know that, of course. Schoolchildren have summer holidays, but the shift workers at the paper mill and the plywood plant, just like the ones at the rifle factory, are always either at work or at home asleep, and they don't have time to do anything else.

There are railway workers here, too. One of them rides past them on a bicycle. His clothes are covered in dust. They know him as a gruff man who refuses to acknowledge anyone in Tourula except for other railway men.

To the Famous Five, the old man raises a hand and waves. They return the greeting politely.

Last summer at the Esso station they caught a robber who had stolen the railwayman's bike. As a reward the old man gave them his eternal gratitude and as proof of it arranged a tour of his workplace for them. They got to go in the train engine, where he gave them pear soda and Carnival biscuits.

Karri follows a few metres behind the rest of them, dragging his tennis shoes, raising a cloud of dust that the wind can't blow away.

They cross the little bridge and walk along the river upstream. The water flows quietly beside them. Leo, Anne, Riku and Olli stop when they come to a boat. Aunt Anna had a wooden boat here at one time. Last summer the Five used it to chart the river and the lake it feeds into. Then it disappeared, at the same time that Timi did—in fact it might have been on the same trip.

They've tried many times to work out the details together. The only thing they all agree on is that the day started with them setting out on a boat trip to find the river's source, and ended with them walking back to Tourula from somewhere on the other side of town. They were tired, dirty and distressed because Timi wasn't with them. None of them knew what had happened to him.

The next day they noticed that the boat wasn't in its usual place. They discussed whether someone might have taken it, or whether they had forgotten it somewhere. No one remembered returning the boat. Feeling guilty, they borrowed the neighbour's boat and searched the shores of the river and the lake, but Aunt Anna's boat was never found.

There are derelicts with liquor bottles sitting on the bank of the river. They're no trouble. They just ask passers-by for small change, with exaggerated politeness, and they never bother children.

Olli looks behind him. Karri has stopped on the bridge, staring into the water. The distance between them is growing. The others don't seem to notice.

Riku suggests that they eat their lunch now. Leo has more foresight and says they can eat later, when they've gone farther, maybe up to Taulumäki. They are on an expedition, after all, and explorers don't eat their lunches too early. When they find a good picnic spot they can eat and then Karri can lead them to the secret passages.

16

THE BUSINESSLIKE RESERVE of Greta's messages bothered Olli. He could read between the lines and he was
worried that Book Tower might not be the publisher for her
third book. "The furrows on your brow are getting deeper,"
Maiju commented at their weekly meeting.

Greta Kara was cool in her messages, but in his dreams
the girl in the pear-print dress was still passionate and
devoted, and the person Olli was in his sleep loved the girl
back, with all his heart. When at the moment of waking the
dream slipped back into the darkness between his synapses,
the feeling of loss felt like it could tear his ribcage open.

"What is it?" Aino gasped one morning. Olli must have
sobbed as he awoke. Aino stared at him aghast, trying to see
inside his head. Her sour breath wafted in his face and he
turned away. He couldn't talk to Aino until he got the dream
out of his head.

Plus he had to change his pyjama bottoms.

Aino pushed herself closer, like a reptile, opened her
mouth, touched his cheek with her fingertips, and sniffed at
him, her nostrils flaring.

Olli closed his eyes.

A moment before, the girl in the pear-print dress had been
in his arms. They had kissed, nibbled each other, cried and
whispered sweet nothings. He had licked her cheek and her
neck and tasted the salt on her skin. She had caressed, kissed,

sucked, bit him gently, all the while gazing at him with her green eyes until Olli came on her dress and she closed her eyes and whispered that she loved him.

Then something had changed.

They had looked at each other with the knowledge that something bad was going to happen. No time for goodbyes—the dream was torn away like a blanket and the girl was hurled into oblivion.

For several long minutes he was left shivering in the middle of a life he didn't recognize as his own.

That evening Olli decided to play with his son. It had been a while since they had last spent time together. He didn't mean to be a distant father; he was just very busy. But maybe they could do some wrestling today.

Olli walked from room to room, but he didn't see his son anywhere.

Aino was in the living room. She was sitting on the sofa, her hands in her lap, her back stiff. The television was off. Aino stared at the black screen. Olli picked the remote up off the sofa and turned the television on. There was a fun show about mongooses on the nature channel. Aino liked animals. Maybe this would cheer her up. There was still an hour before the news.

Olli asked about the boy. Aino didn't hear him, or didn't want to hear. He concentrated on the television programme. The mother mongoose's cubs were in constant danger and the show was steeped in drama. When Olli repeated his question, Aino said thinly, "Yeah, he's at the neighbour's playing."

Ten minutes later Olli was standing in the bathroom in

his pyjama bottoms doing his evening wash and brush. He didn't feel tired. He just wanted to sleep.

A couple of days later, and Olli was in the living room standing in front of the portrait of Notary Suominen. There really was a strong resemblance between them, him and the old notary. Guests often thought it was a portrait of Olli.

His grandfather's example had been an inspiration and an obligation ever since that resemblance was pointed out to him. The notary's expression in the picture was inscrutable. Olli liked to think that his grandfather was looking at him approvingly, but lately he hadn't deserved Notary Suominen's respect.

At Olli's graduation party, his mother had spread out the family photo albums for the guests to look at. Olli's aunt the doctor, his father's sister, whom the family hadn't seen since her father's funeral years before, was the one who compared the two photos and said that Olli and the notary resembled each other.

Everyone had nodded. It was thought to be a good omen for the graduate's future. As she left, Olli's aunt gave him a kiss on the cheek, hugged him and whispered, "Thank the Lord, Olli, I can see you have some of the Suominens' no-nonsense rectitude, which my brother, your poor father, doesn't seem to have inherited at all, for some reason."

Olli's father wasn't a particularly encouraging role model. Diabetes was eating away his feet and making him old before his time. In his final years he huddled in a wheelchair, sighing and constructing monologues that oozed with bitterness and injecting himself with insulin whenever he happened to remember to.

But at his graduation party, with the help of those two photographs, Olli broke free of his grim inheritance and turned his gaze towards his grandfather. Things became clearer. He would take his notary grandpa as his model and handle his affairs in such a way that no one ever need pity him or be ashamed of him.

And life had indeed gone smoothly, until that autumn when the girl in the pear-print dress appeared in his dreams. Olli touched his grandfather's portrait, took a breath and straightened his back until it cracked. He made a decision. He had built his life through a series of firm decisions up to this point, and that was how he would put things right. He fetched pen and paper, sat at the table and started to make notes. Solving a problem always starts with a thorough outline of what the problem is.

So. He had become estranged from his wife, his family and his life. Why? Because he was in love with someone else. Not any real person, but a succubus that had sprung from his memories.

That made things easier, in a way. There was no lover or illicit relationship to hold him. The problem was contained inside his head.

That meant that he had a *psychological problem*.

This realization made him feel faint. Olli turned on his computer and typed a search into Google: *psychological problem*. After correcting the spelling a couple of times, he hit enter.

One result was a text about the effect of mental-health problems on relationships.

A spouse's psychological problems can have an effect on the whole family. When a person has a mental illness it can touch the lives of every family member. Feelings of shame can be associated with mental-health difficulties, particularly in the early stages of the illness.

It was true: shame was pressing on his chest, squeezing his ribs so that it was difficult to breathe.

How to recover from this mental-health problem, to clear his head of this tenacious dream, which was beautiful, but was confusing his thoughts, his feelings, his whole life? He could turn to expert help. He could make a call. A doctor he knew wouldn't hesitate to help him or direct him to a specialist, a psychologist or psychiatrist. He could get a diagnosis and get help and everything could be all right. That's what people did in these situations.

Things have a way of working out, Notary Suominen used to say. Olli felt the same way, but he knew that before they worked out they might become unbearable and hard to handle.

Olli Suominen, mentally ill.

Now Mr Suominen, be a good boy and take your medicine and go back to sleep and that girl in the pear-print dress will stop haunting you in no time…

At the film club they had watched *One Flew Over the Cuckoo's Nest*. Olli didn't want to become a patient. He still had his faculties, after all. A survivor. A Suominen. Not like his father, who was weak. Surely for him milder methods would be enough. A few visits to a therapist and the right medication would no doubt help him get the contents of his head in order.

Olli decided to call the doctor at the first opportunity. First thing in the morning.

He postponed making the appointment, however, when he thought about how to explain the situation to Aino. Not that he wanted to keep the matter secret. He didn't like secrets.

At work, though, it would be best to keep his mental-health problems to himself. His employees didn't want to hear that their boss was teetering between sanity and mental illness. Their publishing projects would come to nothing if everyone was constantly expecting the publisher to have a nervous breakdown.

That day at work Olli went over the sales strategy for a book of popular psychology with Antero. He thought he would try to make a joke about Freudianism, but what came out of his mouth was a personal litany of wet dreams, romantic longings and deep melancholy. "I have a bit of a psychological problem, I guess," he said finally, trying to sound humorous but ending up sounding wretched.

Antero froze and stared at the floor.

Olli realized he had made a mistake. Now that he thought about it, he and Antero didn't really know each other very well. They just worked together.

That thought was followed by another: he didn't really have any friends. He had hundreds of acquaintances and colleagues, of course. He was constantly interacting with people and doing wonderful things with them. But when he thought about it, he realized he didn't have anyone to talk to about personal things like mental-health problems.

He explained, "Well, it's a very small problem I'm talking about. Like the flu, but in your mind. In here." Olli tapped his temple. "I just mean that it would be interesting to hear what sort of cryptic diagnosis one of these psychological theorists would think up for me if they got a look inside my skull."

Antero looked at Olli for a long time and said, "It's pretty simple. You're having a midlife crisis."

Olli must have looked sceptical, because Antero went and fetched a book from the shelf and read a section from it aloud. It was a book they had published a couple of years earlier titled *Ageing with Dignity*:

> *An awareness of the limits of his own life can make an ageing man cling to the fading shreds of his youth and take a sudden interest in the lost, golden age of his life. A fear of death will often drive him to behave inappropriately and cause embarrassment to himself and discomfort to those around him.*
>
> *Thousands of books and hundreds of films have been written about the ageing man's tragicomic struggles against the inevitable. It's best that a man familiarize himself with such works as he approaches middle age—if for no other reason than to avoid their most clichéd mistakes.*

As an example of the middle-aged man's methods of seeking out a vanished youth, the book mentioned taking up bungee jumping and other new hobbies, having a mania for exercise, exchanging a conservative style of dress for more youthful fashions such as piercings, tattoos or offbeat hairstyles, or changing spouses or professions.

A particularly classic symptom that was mentioned was throwing oneself into a relationship with a younger woman.

The book warned that some men stricken with a midlife

crisis abandon their families to begin a "May–December romance", burning their bridges behind them and almost invariably regretting it bitterly in the end. The author did have some consolation for the reader, however: if a man suffering from a midlife crisis kept a cool head and learnt to be content with his life as it was, the symptoms would eventually diminish and he would be able to age with dignity and avoid hurting anyone or bringing shame on himself.

So there was no need to get treatment. Olli was a textbook example of a midlife crisis. But in his case the May–December romance had showed up in dreams that reached back to his youth.

This was presumably good news.

And yet Olli felt dejected as he carried the copy of *Ageing with Dignity* home with him and embarked on accepting his life as it was.

17

THE FIRST THING OLLI DID was quit the film club.

Ageing with Dignity helped him to understand that romantic movies fed his obsession with the girl in the pear-print dress and alienated him from his daily activities and family life, exacerbating his midlife crisis.

After skipping the first movie night Olli stood in his living room and stared into the eyes of Olli Suominen, publisher and member of the parish council, reflected in the mirror. He examined his innermost self. When he had finished, he nodded approvingly and went to stand in front of the painting. He was delighted to realize that he was now able to face Grandpa Notary's portrait with his head held high.

He had things well in hand. He was going to overhaul his marriage, start being a better father, and remodel the parts of their home that most urgently needed remodelling.

He would replace the ceiling tiles in the bedroom. A carpenter could straighten out the floors and walls. The verticals would be made vertical and the horizontals horizontal and the house would finally become the house it should be. Aino could choose the new wallpaper. Maybe that would cheer her up—she had been so silent for the past few days.

Olli presented his ideas about the house to Aino. She had been sitting at the kitchen table all evening arranging photographs, which wasn't like her. Usually she cooked or played with her son. He was playing somewhere by himself now, or maybe he was at the neighbours' house.

"That's fine," Aino mumbled, not looking up from a photo of the boy sitting in the bathtub with his yellow rubber duck. When Olli put his hand on her shoulder, she flinched and turned to look at him.

It scared him. Her face was grey, there were dark circles under her eyes, and her hands were shaking.

He asked if she was coming down with something. Aino conceded that she was feeling rather weak. Seeing his worry, however, she smiled and said, "It'll be fine. I'll just take some aspirin. It's just woman troubles. You know. That remodel… Yeah, let's do that. Great idea."

Olli went to the computer and sent a request for bids to some contractors and a loan application to the bank.

At work he caused a brief panic when he announced that he would be leaving in a few days for a three-week holiday. Yes, three weeks. You heard right. No, the publishing house certainly wouldn't collapse while he was away, as long as everyone did their jobs.

The girl in the pear-print dress still haunted his dreams, but Olli was optimistic about the future. Everything would turn out all right now that he had begun rebuilding his life and recovering from his midlife crisis.

In the name of healing his marriage Olli delegated a couple of his most urgent priorities to Maiju and went home an hour earlier than usual.

The stone steps of Harju Ridge divided into two narrow stairways just before descending onto the street. Between them was a wedge-shaped space with a blue fountain, a couple of park benches, and an ice cream stand. As Olli was headed up the Ridge at this spot he saw one of Jyväskylä's many Grace Kellys, a woman at the kiosk buying ice cream for her three little boys. She was wearing sunglasses, shorts and a pale-coloured shirt, making an effort to look like she had just stepped out of *To Catch a Thief.*

A Guide to the Cinematic Life included a thorough discussion of all of Grace Kelly's film incarnations, right down to her clothes and hairstyles. She was a favourite among fans of cinematicness. Many who found something of Grace Kelly's timeless features in themselves decided at first to base their style on *To Catch a Thief* or *Dial M for Murder.* More advanced practitioners preferred the characters of Almodóvar or Wong Kar-wai.

The sons of the Grace Kelly clone launched toy sailboats in the fountain, their sails bright with sunlight, like an over-exposed scene from a movie.

Olli missed the film club. Maybe he should watch a video tonight. Perhaps *Casablanca.* Or, if *Ageing with Dignity* could be trusted, perhaps ordinary entertainment television would be better for a midlife crisis, he thought gloomily. A cheery quiz show or something.

The stairs Olli was climbing were mentioned in the *Magical City Guide* manuscript as the most photographed spot in Jyväskylä, and also as a very cinematic locale:

The Harju Steps, also known as Nero's Steps, were designed by Gunnar A. Wahlroos, and were constructed as a jobs relief project. The steps were named after city engineer Oskar Nero, although the work itself was overseen by city engineer J.E. Järvilehto in 1925. The M-particle levels on the steps vary from one day to the next, but even at their most ordinary they offer a fine vantage point on the great meetings and partings of life.

I am also aware of an entrance to a secret passageway located near the steps (see Appendix 3). It is difficult to spot, and entering the secret passages is not recommended to anyone, due to its many risks.

The *Magical City Guide* manuscript was coming together. Olli had added his comments and suggestions to the text. There were still the secret passages to be discussed. Then he could leave the manuscript with Greta to be polished, and go on holiday.

When Olli got home, the house was silent. He poured a glass of juice and went into the living room. The afternoon sun painted the room in shades of fruit juice. The trees and shrubs in the yard glowed outside the window. Through the hawthorn hedge he caught glimpses of the house next door, where his neighbour was walking back and forth in the yard wearing a red cap. A gas engine sputtered. The smell of freshly cut grass wafted through the window.

On the living-room table was the cheap photo album, and next to it was a pile of pictures.

He emptied his glass of juice and noticed that he was in a glum, cynical mood. He started looking through Aino's collection of photos. They were all poor pictures technically, taken over several years. The boy was in most of them. Olli himself didn't appear in any, and even Aino was only in a few of them, and always with her son.

In the earliest photos he was a button-eyed infant. The most recent ones were taken early that summer. When he was a baby he'd had Olli and Grandpa Notary's features. Now that he was five he looked more like his mother: a cute, instantly recognizable face.

As he looked through the photos, Olli decided to take the boy swimming. Aino could go, too, of course. Once they'd had a splash they could get some ice cream and lie on a towel in the sun and Olli could point out the hill and the ski jump on the other side of the lake. Maybe they could climb up Taulumäki. They could bring a picnic with them. And the camera. Aino could take some photos with Olli in them.

Olli went out to the garden, supposing Aino and the boy were picnicking there. When he didn't see them he went back inside, walked from room to room, wondering whether they were visiting someone or had gone into town.

He stopped in the bedroom doorway.

"Well? What is it?" Aino finally whispered.

Olli told her his idea of going swimming.

Aino laid her forearm over her face, heaving it there slowly, as if it were made of stone.

"Female problems again?" Olli said sympathetically. "Can I get you some water or an aspirin?"

"I already took one. Thanks for offering."

Olli asked where the boy was.

Aino said he was taking a nap, like her.

Olli went to peek in the boy's bedroom. The bed was empty. He went back to Aino and told her that the child wasn't in his bed.

"A nap at the neighbours'," Aino explained, without

looking at him. "Anyway Lauri has a sore throat. He can't go swimming today, and maybe not tomorrow, either. It was a nice idea, though. Some other time."

Olli went into his office and opened Facebook. He had a message from Greta Kara.

Hi, Olli. I'm still in Jyväskylä. Did you want to discuss the manuscript? Shall we meet today at 10 p.m. at the observation tower?

18

O LLI SPENT TWO HOURS on Facebook and sent a lot of messages about the Frankfurt Book Fair. When he went back downstairs he met Aino in the kitchen, sitting at the table eating Marie biscuits. She said the boy had come home from the neighbours', eaten dinner and gone to bed.

"He told me to tell Daddy goodnight and sweet dreams."

Olli said he wanted to read to the boy from a new Book Tower children's book just off the presses. It was called *A Day with Daddy*. In the book a kitten learns all about peoples of the world from his father while his mother is at home making fruit compote. But Aino shook her head.

"No. It's a nice idea, but he fell asleep as soon as his head hit the pillow. Some other time."

Olli shaved, took a shower, got dressed and flipped through the *Magical City Guide* manuscript one more time, adding more edits.

When he left with his briefcase in his hand, Aino was watching television.

On the western slope of Harju Ridge there was a summer theatre stage and behind it a narrow wooden staircase, which Olli climbed. The evening breeze rustled his clothes rather pleasantly. Halfway up the stairs, however, he had to stop and rest so he wouldn't sweat and spoil his clothes. Olli adjusted the knot in his tie. The last time he'd shown himself to Greta in a dirty shirt, and this time he had given special attention to how he was dressed. When the outside's taken care of it's easier to keep the inside under control.

He was wearing the jewel of his wardrobe, a high-quality Dolce & Gabbana suit made of thin virgin wool. Thus attired, Olli believed he could behave in a businesslike manner and not like an inmate off his meds the way he had the last time.

When he got to the top of the steps he turned left towards the observation tower with its neon clock. The Swedish city of Eskilstuna had presented it as a gift and installed it in the tower in 1953, when no one in Finland knew how to construct one, and they couldn't buy one from Sweden due to currency problems.

Olli had a habit of checking the time by this clock on his way to work. The clock had become familiar and beloved to him over the years; it sort of belonged to him.

It was five minutes to ten.

As he approached the observation tower, Olli looked up. He saw a person standing at the railing on the restaurant level. Possibly a woman. Perhaps the woman he was going to meet.

He passed the raised gun barrel in front of the tower entrance. It was a memorial to the bombings and the anti-aircraft guns that had protected Jyväskylä during the Winter War, and a regular stop on the Suominen family's Sunday walks.

Olli crossed the lobby to the elevator and rode up to the observation deck with a young couple.

Inside the restaurant a wedding party was gathered. The bride, radiant in white, was surrounded by champagne glasses. Olli walked out onto the terrace. Every outdoor table but one was empty. Next to the striped ice cream awning sat a slim woman. Her left hand was resting on the table; her right held a cigarette. She was looking down at the city. Her golden hair was pinned up. Her pale-green pear-print dress set Olli's heart pounding in his chest.

The manner in which she smoked her cigarette could only be described as reverent. Her slow motions were pure dance.

A Guide to the Cinematic Life had a whole chapter devoted to the art of smoking.

Thinking ordinarily, smoking is a vice that is hazardous to your health, and is thus limited, regulated and censured by society. In spite of that, or precisely because of that, it is also an indispensable part of the cinematic way of life.

What would the films of Wong Kar-wai, Godard, Truffaut or Kaurismäki be without scenes of smoking? How successful would Irving Rapper's melodrama Now, Voyager *have been if someone had cut the scenes where Paul Henreid lights two cigarettes and hands one to Bette Davis! It's easier to imagine Charlie Chaplin without a moustache than it is to imagine Humphrey Bogart, Tony Leung or Matti Pellonpää without cigarettes. A lit cigarette is an aesthetic element comparable to music, with a power of expression when used in dialogue that should not be underestimated. Like any tool, however, it takes practice to learn to use it correctly so that the effect created is the one intended.*

The following pages discuss various smoking techniques and situations, and examine how smoking can be used as an indicator of your persona and message.

(Smoking photo spread: Tony Leung in In the Mood for

Love. *Humphrey Bogart and Lauren Bacall in* The Big Sleep. *Bebe Daniels in* My Past. *Lauren Bacall in* Confidential Agent. *Ida Lupino in* Road House. *Bette Davis and Paul Henreid in* Now, Voyager.*)*

As he approached the table, Olli examined the woman's profile. He noticed now that from a certain angle she resembled the silhouette of the smoking umbrella vendor. If he could commission a painting of Greta Kara and hire any artist, living or dead, Gustav Klimt would have been the best choice.

Greta Kara didn't otherwise look familiar to him. Her hair was gold blonde, as he had thought—the same colour as Maura's at Jyväskylä Umbrella. Her dress also corresponded with his expectations. But in a crowd, he wouldn't have recognized her face. He dreamt about it every night, but now that he was actually seeing it, it was the face of a stranger. He was both saddened and relieved.

Now he was close enough to smell her perfume and trailing cigarette smoke. He was close enough to see her clearly. But he still hesitated, afraid he might be confusing her with someone else. Which was ridiculous. Who else could it be?

The woman was still looking at the view. That was how he knew that she was Greta. She wanted to punish him one last time. If it were someone he didn't know, she would have already glanced up to see who was approaching. Olli said hello.

The woman's head turned slowly.

Their eyes met.

"Olli."

A cloud of smoke escaped from between her lips.

She put out her cigarette in the ashtray and smiled. Olli sat down, leant his briefcase against a leg of the table and smiled back. It was hard to look her in the eye.

"A pleasant evening," Olli said.

"Yes," Greta answered. "A good evening to sit together and talk about books and cities. And a good place for it." She paused, then added dramatically, "The city is at our feet."

She smiled ironically. Olli sensed that she hadn't yet forgiven him for his earlier bungle. She was probably waiting to see how this meeting would go. Olli gathered his thoughts, ready to behave as he was expected to behave.

First of all he had to be an adult, dignified and self-confident, like the head of a publishing house, which was what he was.

Second, he should be a polite, friendly, respectful person; an editor who was meeting with a writer important to the firm, aware of his responsibility to make sure that she stayed with them, and aware that her sales could assure the daily bread of a large number of people.

Third, of course, was to be warm and attentive—they were, after all, old friends.

Olli remembered that they hadn't hugged, or even shaken hands. It left an uncomfortable distance between them. It was too late to correct it. The next natural moment for it would be when they parted.

They started to chat about this and that, without really saying much. Natural talk. Light.

Good.

That was how this thing should progress. They both had

their own lives, and new roles. This meeting was not between childhood friends and former lovers but between two middle-aged, sensible professionals.

At the same time, it was a tragic irony that he could never tell this woman about the dreams he'd been having for months, dreams that had thrown his whole life into disorder.

You know, last night you were sucking me off and I came in your mouth and you said you would love me forever. We clung to each other and vowed that if anything ever separated us we would find each other again. And if in the meantime one of us forgot what we once meant to each other, the other person would make him or her understand by any means necessary.

The door of the restaurant opened and three people came out onto the terrace to smoke and look at the view.

The tall man suggested they climb the tower. The short man was excited at the idea. The woman laughed and said, "Don't go up there. We can see well enough from here. Besides, I've been up there before. Going up again would show bad taste."

"Let's go anyway," the tall man said, putting a hand on the woman's shoulder. "Let's go without this guy. I promise I'll be a gentleman."

The woman took a flask out of her bag, uncorked it and sniffed the contents, smiling knowingly.

"What's in there?" the man asked.

"*Sulphuric acid,*" the woman said, her voice husky and dramatic. "*For the eyes of men who tell lies.*"

The short man laughed and poked the tall one in the ribs. "Did you catch that? She's turning into Catherine again. And you, I assume, are the unlucky Jim."

The man who would be Jim shook his head. "Whatever. I don't watch those old black-and-white French movies. Life is too short."

The woman smiled slyly, pulled the tall man by the arm to the railing and shouted, "*Jules, watch us!*"

The short man laughed. "Our Jules might not follow you so meekly if he had seen more old black-and-white French movies. At least he wouldn't get in your car until you had thrown that insane guide to life of yours in the trash."

Olli asked if Greta would like some coffee or wine or perhaps something to eat. Greta lit a cigarette, took a drag and said, "To tell you the truth, I feel like I've got mud in my stomach. I couldn't possibly get anything down until I've heard what you think of the manuscript."

"There's no reason to be nervous," Olli assured her. He opened his briefcase and took the printed manuscript out. "The first part looks good. I think it's going to be a fine book. Though it needs polishing, of course. Here are my comments. Don't be frightened. These are just my thoughts and ideas. Just suggestions that can, and should, be discussed. The main thing I've been thinking about are the references to secret passages."

Greta's brow furrowed. "Oh?"

"Don't you think they might be a bit confusing for readers?"

"Confusing?"

Greta looked at Olli with such amused disbelief that he felt confused.

He thought frantically, hiding his struggle behind a professional smile.

The whole time he was sitting there he tried to find something familiar in the face he had watched, caressed, kissed thirty years ago. But the face remained that of a stranger. Not that the years had changed Greta—they had taken a toll on his memory. He remembered many things wrongly, including the face of his beloved.

"Yes, confusing," Olli said. "It is a book of non-fiction, after all. A city guide. Everything but the secret passages is based on facts, a charming description of the city, which will help readers get to know Jyväskylä from a new angle. Why confuse them with this secret passage thing?"

Greta let her cigarette burn down between her index and middle fingers. She put it out, got up and went to look at Jyväskylä at dusk, where the lights were already coming on. She rested her left hand on the railing and lifted her right. She put her index finger to her lips.

The air had cooled. Olli went to stand next to her, thrust his hands in his pockets and waited for her answer.

Finally Greta closed her eyes, wiped her brow, and whispered. *"How can you stand here beside me and pretend not to remember? Not to know that my heart is breaking for you? That your face is the wonderful light burning in all this darkness?…"*

Olli stiffened.

Then he recognized the words. *"Wuthering Heights.* Heathcliff's lines. Played by Laurence Olivier. Directed by William Wyler in 1939. I saw it at the film club. Very good movie. But Merle Oberon's lines would suit you better."

Greta's mouth curled into a smile. "Did you know that they designed a new spotlight just for lighting Merle Oberon? She had been in a car accident in London and had scars on her face. Unfortunate for an actress. But the special lighting made it so that the scars didn't show in the film. The cinematographer who designed the light was her future husband. It was true love."

Then Greta turned and looked him in the eye and asked, "Have you forgotten Tourula?"

"Of course I haven't," Olli said.

A light blazed up in her sea-green eyes. Olli could see now that it was the same green that glowed in the eyes of the tousle-headed umbrella vendor.

"I do remember Tourula. The Tourula Five. Our game of secret passageways," Olli said. "But let's leave them out of *Magical City Guide*. It will be better without fairy tales."

Greta looked away, as if she heard distant music.

Olli didn't know what she expected of him. Before he could organize his thoughts, she took the manuscript, kissed Olli on the cheek and asked him to call her a taxi. "So. We'll think about it," she said, and shot him a strange look.

Olli's stomach hurt as they rode down in the elevator and exchanged a squeeze of the hand at the anti-aircraft gun. Greta's hand felt cool.

The taxi came.

Greta got in and rode away.

Olli walked home.

He ate some supper, brushed his teeth, went upstairs, put on his pyjamas and crawled into bed.

A disturbing feeling. Olli's eyes open. Adrenalin starts to seep into his body. He raises his head and sees that a painting has appeared on the bedroom wall.

The *Sleeping Girl.*

Olli looks for an explanation. Maybe Aino has bought a copy of the *Sleeping Girl* as a surprise for him. Quite a coincidence. She also bought *A Guide to the Cinematic Life* without knowing that her husband and the author were once lovers.

Then Olli thinks of a better explanation: he's dreaming. The girl in the pear-print dress herself steps out of the dark, takes his hand, pulls him up and leads him away.

His body follows hers as if weightless.

He looks behind him. The bedroom recedes. Aino is sitting on the edge of the bed swinging her feet and waving happily. She yells, "*See you later, dear! Have fun!*"

The soles of Olli's feet lightly touch a wood floor and he realizes he is in the room in the old house next to the Touru River. Their secret meeting place. There's the dusty piano and the bed.

Greta is still holding his hand. Olli can smell her perfume and the cigarette she just smoked. Every detail is precise and vivid.

"I couldn't wait any longer," Greta says. "Were you thinking you might not come?"

She flirts with him, circling him, touching and examining him, teasing, gathering impressions like seashells on the shore. The floorboards creak under her steps. Her dress rustles. Olli can see the pores on her face and the little cinnamon-coloured nuggets in the green of her eyes. Nothing could be more real. Her face and his feelings trace themselves into his consciousness as if the memories were drawn with a tattoo needle.

This time he will remember.

The girl stops and reaches her light, cool arms around the back of his neck. Olli's fingers travel up her spine and feel her vertebrae, her shoulder blades, the hollow at the nape of her neck. Joy ignites on her lips and spreads to her eyes. She presses her mouth against his throat. Olli closes his eyes. Her tongue is hot and wet. She presses tighter against him. Olli breathes through her hair. This is what gold smells like, he thinks.

Then someone begins to shriek like a seagull.

Olli.

Greta is biting him.

He struggles.

Her teeth sink deep into his throat. The darkness sways. Blood floods over his skin. Olli grabs the girl by the hair and tears her away from him. Her green eyes are full of tears, her mouth dark with blood.

"*Did I hurt you?*" she whispers. She has turned cold and sardonic. "*Forgive me, my love, but the pain you feel is but a hint of what I feel. Oh, yes, and give my regards to St Anthony.*"

The girl steps forward and pushes Olli. He topples onto his back.

The floor gives way.

He falls.

Olli sat up in bed. It felt like an angry gorilla was pounding at the inside of his ribcage. He felt his neck and stared at the bedroom wall.

No bite.

And no painting. Just the mirror.

He pressed his head into his pillow and tried to go back

to sleep. It was no use. Something wasn't right. He'd had an uneasy feeling for days. Now the feeling was stronger. There was something he wasn't noticing.

He was in bed alone.

He turned towards Aino's side of the bed, scrambled across and looked over the edge of the bed at the floor. There was nothing there but a pair of striped ankle socks.

He got up and went through the house, looking into every room at least three times.

Aino and the boy were clearly gone.

19

O LLI TRIED CALLING Aino's number, of course.
When he did, the *Turkish March* started to play in
the kitchen. He followed the sound, puzzled.

He thought he was reacting to the situation with calm
rationality—there was no cause for panic, after all—but the
pale, pyjamaed man he glimpsed in the mirrors told him
otherwise.

Olli found Aino's phone on top of the refrigerator. It was a
phone she'd bought around the time their son was born. Olli
had offered to buy her a new phone but she didn't want one,
since the old one still worked. The phone kept ringing. That
confused Olli, as did the message on the screen: *Olli calling*.

It took a moment for him to figure out how to make the
Mozart stop.

He walked around the kitchen thinking that he should do
something sensible. Clear this up.

No need to panic. At any moment Aino and the boy would
come clomping in and she would explain what happened and
Olli would wonder why he hadn't immediately realized what
was going on.

It would be best to wait in the kitchen. Olli made some
cocoa and sat at the table sipping it, staring at the empty
chairs. He tried not to worry, but worried anyway.

Give my regards to St Anthony.

Eventually the sun rose and reflected from the side of the

toaster. In all the houses in Mäki-Matti coffee was being made, papers fetched, breakfast cooked. Dogs were tugging at their masters' leashes, eager to get out to the street and take a crap. Children were waking up and running to wolf down their morning porridge. From somewhere nearby he heard the sound of a trampoline.

Olli's head hurt. It had fallen onto the table sometime during the night. Also on the table was an empty package of honey cereal. Olli hated that cereal, his son's favourite, but it had tasted good during the night, bowl after bowl. He took an aspirin, made some coffee and thought. It seemed his family was not here. His family was gone. But where? Why?

Maybe Aino's aunt or one of her sisters was seriously ill, had been in an accident or had actually died.

Olli considered this theory. Maybe news of it had come during the evening when he went out to meet Greta Kara. Then Aino had frantically called a taxi, taken the boy with her and gone to Joensuu, Helsinki or Lahti, depending on who it was who had come to harm. She had intended to call Olli from the taxi, but she had left her phone at home and didn't know his number from memory.

Olli called four numbers, without revealing the situation to Aino's family members. They were all fine.

Maybe she had left him a note. He searched the house for a message. He didn't find any.

He thought about the matter while he dressed and cleaned himself up. As he brushed his teeth he examined Aino's phone. He didn't find anything of interest in the numbers she had called. Her last call had been made several days earlier, to Olli. He remembered the call: she had asked him to buy the boy some new swimming trunks and a rubber ring, but Olli had forgotten.

He went through her saved numbers looking for clues. Acquaintances. Relatives. Fellow teachers. Most of the contacts were listed only by their first names, which meant nothing to him. *Anna; Anna-Liisa; Anne; Anu; Eeva; Eila; Emma; Emmi; Hair Salon; Hanna; Health Clinic; Irja; Jaana K; Jaana L; Kaisa K; Kaisa R; Kira; Kirsi; Liisa; Laura H; Laura N; Laura S; Mom; Noora E; Noora K; Olli; Paula; Principal; Riitta; Raili; Roosa; Secretary; Taxi; Teacher's Lounge.*

It occurred to Olli that he ought to have listened more closely when Aino talked about people.

He hesitated before reading her text messages, but decided that in an emergency like this it was all right to infringe on her privacy.

There was nothing in her messages that shed any light on the situation.

The next thing that occurred to him was that Aino might have left him. It didn't seem probable, or even possible, but on the other hand that sort of thing happened all the time. One person just got fed up and left, and the person who was left behind cried to everybody that they hadn't guessed a thing.

Olli didn't think Aino was the type of person who would leave her husband. But maybe he just didn't know his wife. After all, she didn't know him.

Aino and the boy's wardrobe didn't seem to have been emptied. One of the suitcases was missing. He didn't see her handbag around. The only toothbrush on the bathroom shelf was Olli's blue one. The red toothbrush and the dinosaur toothbrush were gone. Olli wasn't sure if that was a good thing or a bad thing.

He walked out to the yard.

It was going to be a beautiful day. The sky was dotted with fluffy clouds, some of them in weird shapes. The lawn was positively dripping with green. Bumblebees buzzed around him like fuzzy helicopters.

He looked at Aino's flower beds. He was surprised how many there were, and wondered if he should water them if it didn't rain within the next few days.

He went back in the house and watched television for twenty-four hours. The next morning he wondered if he should contact the police, and decided that he would eventually, but not now. Because at any moment the phone might ring or a taxi might pull up in front of the house, and everything would go back to normal again.

Olli called the publishing house and said he had started his summer holiday. Then he went into his home office and opened Facebook. *Facebook helps you connect and share with the people in your life*, the sign-in page said.

Olli had a new friend request. *Aino added you as a friend on Facebook. We need to confirm that you know Aino in order for you to be friends on Facebook.*

Olli accepted Aino's friend request and went to look at her page. There wasn't anything on it; it looked new. At the top of the page was the usual comment box. It said *Write something.*

Olli wrote: *Where are you?*

*

Aino had four other Facebook friends besides Olli. The first three were "mutual friends" of Olli's: Leo, Richard and Anne Blomroos.

Contrary to what Olli had by some peculiar logic instantly expected, Aino's fourth friend wasn't Greta.

Olli felt sick. His stomach clenched and black spots danced in front of his eyes. He had to go lie down on the sofa.

20

That Karri has been such a strange boy lately.

The breakfast table is set among the apple trees on a lawn still wet with dew. Olli and the Blomrooses are talking cheerfully. They're waiting for Karri to join them so they can leave on their expedition. They often have to wait for Karri these days. When Aunt Anna suddenly says out loud what Olli has been noticing since the beginning of the summer, everyone stops talking and Olli's cheeriness fades.

The sky over Tourula is misty and the sun is a dull ten-penni piece. The sparrows are chirping noisily in the trees and bushes. Then the neighbour's grey cat slips in under the fence and the birds go mum.

The silence that has fallen over the group gradually deepens until it's uncomfortable.

Riku is the first to break it and try to lighten the mood. With mock concern and a shake of his head he says sombrely that if you ask him Karri Kultanen has always been a strange boy. A laugh escapes from Leo.

Anne stiffens and looks at her brothers angrily.

"Karri is not strange, he's wonderful," she says in a voice that mixes cold control with a hot fury. Olli almost expects steam to come out of her nose. Anne smiles patronizingly. "He's so wonderful that not everyone can even understand him. While you two cretins are reading Tex Willer, the sports page and Riku's sticky old porno magazine, Karri is reading books. Real books. Classic novels and plays. Philosophy, medicine, art history. Biology. He thinks about things and he knows more than a lot of teachers do. He has his own ideas, which is more than I can say for you two fine gentlemen."

Then she turns to address Aunt Anna. "Don't worry about your son. Believe me, Karri is going to be something truly special. He's going to surprise all of us, me included— although I already believe in him."

Riku smiles teasingly and the usually serious Leo shakes his head pityingly. Anne meets their gaze without flinching, but can't hide the blush in her cheeks.

It upsets Olli to realize that he's still hopelessly infatuated with Anne, who obviously has feelings for Karri, although falling in love with her own cousin probably isn't quite normal.

Aunt Anna is lost in thought, staring emptily into the distance. Her usual liveliness is gone; she hardly seems like the old Aunt Anna. She looks like she's having some kind of attack. Olli and the Blomrooses look at each other in alarm. They feel as if they're sitting there with a dead person.

When Anne finally bends to touch her aunt's arm, Anna jumps and frightens them all.

The familiar, cheery smile returns to her face. She thanks Anne for her words and smiles until her eyes squint. "Well, we'll see how my Karri turns out. Maybe he will surprise us all."

The air is cool. Aunt Anna's large breasts stretch the fabric of her blouse so tight that the buttons look as if they might pop off, and, as always happens in cool weather, her nipples press hard and dark against the cloth. Olli certainly notices them—a person couldn't help noticing them unless he was "a hardened old homo" as Riku once said—but this time he can't take any interest in the Blomrooses' voluptuous aunt. He isn't even interested in the treats set out on the table, which Leo, Anne and Riku have started to eat.

He's busy worrying about Karri, about the future of the Five, and especially about his own place among them.

Karri has been strange for a long time. He's becoming even stranger. There are little things that only Olli notices. For instance, Karri often watches Olli, and sometimes the others too, from under his hood, as if he were planning something having to do with them. And although Karri has always been shy, his shyness has changed to withdrawal and poorly concealed hostility towards the other members of the Tourula Five—though he does still seem to think of Leo as a sort of big brother figure.

Olli has thought about this and decided that Karri may be planning to kick him out of Tourula and out of the group, or even planning to disband the Five altogether. Karri still comes with them on all their outings and takes them to the secret passages, but maybe he does it more out of duty and a desire to please Leo than from any enthusiasm.

Maybe Karri hasn't ever really accepted Olli. Now that he thinks about it, Karri has always treated him with a sort of edgy wariness.

Leo is still the leader of the Five and in a way Olli is under his protection. But Karri is the only permanent resident of their summer place. It's something they all have a habit of forgetting. The place that they think of as their own summer place is Aunt Anna and Karri's home in the winter, too. And besides, Karri is the only one who knows how to find the secret passages. So if Karri wants Olli out, he's out. In fact Karri has the power to end the whole thing.

The Blomrooses don't realize it, but the Tourula Five is in danger of breaking up.

The first crisis came when Timi disappeared. That was when they realized that a lot of bad things could happen in the secret passages. What happened to Timi could happen to any one of them.

This realization cast a shadow over their carefree adventures. That was why Anne was so serious after what happened to Timi, even though she had never liked the dog. They took a break for three weeks before they decided to go back to exploring the secret passages. What else could they do? Like Riku said, they weren't brave adventurers, they were hopeless passageway junkies. As long as there were secret passages to find they would keep going back to them, no matter what happened underground.

Karri has never been one to show his feelings or share his thoughts with other people. But once, when Timi had been gone for a week and Olli was sitting alone outside his grandparents' apartment at the rifle factory, Karri appeared beside him in his dirty sweatshirt.

He hesitated for a moment and then said, "Listen, I just wanted you to know… I've been looking for Timi every day ever since he disappeared. In the passages. I haven't found him. I'm sorry."

Olli thanked him. He waited for him to leave.

But Karri stepped closer, hesitantly took Olli's hand, and looked out from under his hood straight into Olli's eyes. It was disconcerting. Olli didn't know how to react. Afterwards he realized that Karri might have never looked him in the eye before, at least not from so close. Something about his eyes surprised Olli.

"I'm sorry about what happened to Timi," Karri said. "He was the best dog I've ever met."

Timi had certainly always liked Karri more than the other members of the Five—except for Olli, of course—and Karri had warmed to the dog.

Now it occurs to Olli that maybe Karri only put up with him because of Timi.

And now there is no Timi.

That can't be good.

The thought of future summers without the Tourula Five or Aunt Anna or the secret passages troubles Olli. At home in Koirakkala he doesn't have any friends. In Tourula, everything is different.

As Olli digs himself out of these thoughts of the approaching destruction of his paradise, Aunt Anna offers everyone boiled eggs, ham, toast, three kinds of rolls, raisin buns, apple marmalade, peanut butter, frosted cornflakes, tea and juice. Olli isn't hungry but he dutifully eats a roll.

Finally Karri comes out in his hood, grabs an egg from the table as deftly as a street thief, and goes back into the house.

The Blomrooses chatter among themselves as if nothing has happened.

Aunt Anna watches her son go.

Then she turns to look at Olli and her eyes are dark with tears.

*

When they finally go on their expedition, they walk through Tourula, cross the bridge over the river, and continue to Puistokatu. On the other side of the fence, a coffin is being carried through the cemetery. The bells ring in memory of the deceased.

As always, Karri follows a short distance behind the others. For a moment Olli forgets him completely and turns to look at the massive Goodyear tyre advertisement painted on the wall of a tall building. He has always liked that ad.

His glance meets Karri's. Something flashes in Karri's eyes that Olli can't quite name, and then it's gone and Karri looks away and his face closes up.

Olli runs to catch up with the Blomrooses and walks with them the rest of the way.

Summer's colours have faded like a painting left out in the rain. The washed-out greys of autumn are coming. The wind has turned cold. Olli is wearing a polo shirt and a denim jacket that he bought yesterday on a shopping trip with his grandmother, but he's still cold.

The Blomrooses don't notice the signs of summer ending. Olli likes them an awful lot, but they never notice things like that and it gives Olli a lonely feeling.

They pass the Taulumäki church and there is a wedding party celebrating in the churchyard. They cross the street and come to the sandy foot of Taulumäki Hill.

The north slope of the hill is high and steep. As they climb up, their shoes fill with sand and Anne almost falls and tumbles down the hillside. Olli grabs her hand just in time. She rewards him with a smile. Anne knows how to be nice when she wants to.

When they get to the top they climb up on the rocks to enjoy the view.

To the north-west is the lake, Tuomiojärvi. There's no one at the swimming area. Olli's not the only one who thinks summer is over. To the south-east is the city and the Orthodox church. Anne looks down at its gilded dome, her eyes glittering. "Just think if you could scrape all that gold off and keep it. That would make a lot of jewellery."

"Greedy little Anne," Leo says gently. "My sweet criminal sister. Leave the church alone. Stick to swiping candy from the store. Some things are too sacred even for you."

Anne grins.

The Blomrooses and Olli look at each other, fidgety and tense. Yesterday Leo asked Karri to try to find the entrance to the first secret passageway they ever found. The one that Timi crawled into without waiting for them. Karri promised to try. Olli forgets his doubts for a moment. Right now everything is like it was in the beginning. They all feel it. This is where it all began, the Tourula Five's secret passage adventures.

Leo, Anne and Riku think they know where the entrance is. They each go in different directions.

"It's over here, between these rocks," Leo says.

"No, it's over there under that juniper tree!" Riku announces. "I'm sure that's where it is."

"I think it's somewhere over here," Anne mumbles, peeping between some trees.

Karri goes his own way. Olli doesn't even try to find the entrance. Karri's the only one who can.

So Olli follows him, over roots, rocks and hollows, in the

shadows of the trees, careful not to disturb or annoy him, and Karri doesn't seem to mind. They look at each other and Karri even nods and gives him a friendly smile. At first Olli is puzzled and then happy—if there is something between them, it's been put aside at least for a little while.

Maybe everything will work out after all.

As he relaxes, the memory of the first time the Five found a secret passageway begins to grow clear in his mind.

21

THE FIRST SUMMER OF THE FIVE they were just getting to know each other.

They spent their days playing board games, hide and seek, and spin the bottle, or reading Enid Blyton books aloud—which was a lot of fun, though rather tame compared to their later adventures.

They went into the secret passages the second summer.

They had spent the first two days of holiday lazing about, playing old maid, sprawled on the lawn, until Aunt Anna had had enough. She came out of the house with a picnic basket.

"Kids," she said emphatically, "it's summer. You're on holiday. You're children. This is no way to spend your childhood. It's a waste. You would think you were as old as I am. Take this basket. Go on a picnic. Find a nice spot and stop hanging around here. There's a great big city waiting out there for you. Enjoy it. You can play cards when you're in the old folks' home. Don't come back here for the rest of the day."

They looked at her in surprise. She looked exasperated. "Go on!" she yelled, frightening them. "Have adventures! Go get lost somewhere. But find your way home before dark…"

Timi had been hiding for hours. Now he smelt the food and appeared again, sniffing the basket.

The kids sniffed at the contents of the basket, too. They were amazed at the abundance of food, and thanked Aunt Anna. She gave each of them a kiss on the cheek. Olli could smell perfume behind her ear. It smelt good. His mother never wore perfume.

After half an hour of consultation they decided to go to the burnt-out house. Olli had seen it from the car when his parents brought him to his grandparents' house. His description of the blackened boards, the belongings that had been dumped in the yard and the broken windows piqued everyone's interest.

Timi came with them. Olli's mother had made him swear to keep the dog on a leash, but he decided to trust the dog and let him go loose. He wanted to please Anne, who said that they were all on holiday, which meant they were free, so why shouldn't Timi be free, too? Freedom!

They wandered for a couple of hours, until everyone's feet ached and Olli admitted that he might not be quite sure where the burnt-out house was. Maybe it was in a totally different part of town.

Anne and Riku gave him murderous looks.

Karri didn't say anything, he just looked off into the distance, thinking his own thoughts.

Leo said that these things happen, and led them in the direction that looked right to him.

They ended up climbing a wooded hill, and found a swimming area on the other side. Later they learnt that the hill was called Taulumäki.

While the others sat down to enjoy their lunch, Karri explored the area. He paced about and said there was something peculiar about the place and that in some spots the feeling was particularly strong. He wanted to show it to them, couldn't even be bothered to eat something first. Timi sensed it, too, or perhaps he just sensed Karri's excitement. In any case he was jumping up and down around Karri and whining and barking, although Olli tried to order him to heel.

"That leaves more goodies for us," Riku said.

"Don't worry, Karri," Anne said. "I'll make sure we leave you some of everything."

Olli felt a twinge of jealousy. He had just got his leg positioned so that it touched Anne's pale leg. It was a hot day. Their legs were sweaty. Their sweat was intermingling. Olli didn't know why, but there was something exciting about it.

He glanced at Anne. She noticed him looking at her and gave him a crooked smile that told him she knew what he was thinking, but for some reason she was allowing him to do what he was doing.

Olli closed his eyes, enjoying the warmth and the touch and the fact that he was a member of the legendary Tourula Five, then he went back to eating his peanut butter sandwich with such concentration that he didn't even hear when Karri yelled to them or notice when the others got up and left.

A moment later, he became aware of noises in the undergrowth. Karri was explaining something excitedly. Timi was barking. Olli hurried to where the others were.

There was a dark hole in the ground. The Blomrooses and Karri were gathered around it. It wasn't easy to see the hole among the grass and roots. It just looked like a dark indentation in the dirt. But when you looked more closely you could see that it was a hole that reached deep into the ground.

"Some animal's burrow," Riku muttered. "Is this why you called us over here?"

Leo thought they should go back to the picnic basket

before the animal who lived here found it. Olli, Anne and Riku thought so, too.

"No," Karri said, so firmly that they were startled. He was lying on his belly on the ground with his face in the hole. "This isn't an animal's den. This is something completely different."

"How about we leave it alone, though," Leo said in his conciliating yet authoritative way. "Look at Timi. He's barking and staying away from it. There's something in there with sharp teeth. A badger or something. Maybe a fox. And if you keep spying on it it's going to bite your face off."

Anne said, "Come away from there, Karri…"

Karri sighed, looked at Timi, who seemed to have gone off his rocker, and withdrew from the hole.

"Maybe you're right."

He stood up and shrugged.

Them Timi sprinted past him.

Before anyone knew what was happening, the dog had crawled into the hole and disappeared.

They waited forever. Or for sixteen minutes, as Riku said later on when they talked over what had happened. "I know because I looked at my watch," he said. "It was still working then…"

They all squatted around the hole staring into the darkness, unable to speak, hardly even able to breathe. The sounds of the beach were from some other, happier world. A world where children didn't lose their dogs in a hole in the ground.

The day was growing brighter and hotter.

Timi stayed under the ground.

When you put your hand in the hole you could feel the unchanging coolness of the earth.

The horrified spell over them eased. They started to speak again. Their voices were shocked, solemn. They each peeped into the hole in turn. They shouted threats and promises and persuasions to the dog. Now and then they thought they might have heard a noise.

But there was only dark, impenetrable silence.

Olli was trembling. If Timi couldn't get back out, he would come to a cruel end underground. They couldn't do a thing to help him. The thought of it tore him up. But it would have been crazy even to think of going in after him. He might get stuck and suffocate and die. The burrow might collapse.

Olli wished he had kept the dog on a leash, regardless of what Anne said.

He tried not to cry. The others looked at him with the silent, fearful deference instinctively given to someone who's suffered a terrible loss.

Then Karri said that one of them had to try to help Timi. After all, he was one of the group, a friend to all of them, wasn't he?

Olli looked at Karri in amazement. Leo nodded and asked Karri what he thought they should do.

Karri said that one of them should go in after the dog— just a little way, so their feet were sticking out—and look to see what was really in there. It could be that Timi was just stuck not far under the surface. If they could get hold of his feet it might be easy to rescue him.

Before anyone had a chance to consider this suggestion,

Karri had already volunteered for the job and wriggled into the hole. It was bigger than the opening made it look. The rest of them squirmed uncomfortably. Anne kept telling Karri not to go too deep.

"All right, Karri. Stop now and tell us what you see," Leo commanded.

Karri was in the hole up to his waist and his answer was a faint mumble. Riku slapped him on the bum and told him to reach as far as he could and see if he could feel any furry dog's arse.

Leo growled at his brother.

Karri went in deeper. Now all that was visible of him were his shoes, which Olli and the Blomrooses stared at. Shouldn't he come back to the daylight now, while he still could? Anne started to get nervous. She worried that he might not be getting enough oxygen.

Leo agreed. He tried to grab Karri by the ankles, but just then the boy's feet disappeared into the hole.

Those left on the surface looked at each other stony-faced. Leo looked particularly pale and stunned.

They peeked into the hole, but they couldn't see or hear Karri. Riku's usual impish grin crumbled. He shot a look at Olli that seemed to say, *It's because of your dog, Olli, your stupid dog...*

Anne bent over, yelled into the hole and listened. Then she took a breath and, with stiff, robotic movements, wriggled into the darkness.

Olli looked at Leo and Riku, scared.

Riku whispered something that sounded like a curse.

They could see Leo crumbling. He was the biggest and strongest and most confident one in the group. He had always taken responsibility for the others. They thought of him as older than he was, but Leo was still a child—ten years old, just a year older than Olli, Karri and Riku. And now he had lost control of the situation. That had never happened before. His arms hung limp at his sides and he turned to Olli as if looking for help.

Olli felt sick.

Leo got down on his hands and knees and Olli and Riku stood frozen as he, too, crawled into the darkness.

He was stockier than the others and his shoulders tore the hole open wider.

Staying on the surface without Karri, Anne or Leo was a frightening thought. Even more frightening than the thought of dying underground.

Riku and Olli followed him in.

When they returned to the surface they were exhausted and disoriented. The bright light hurt their eyes. The fresh air stung their lungs.

They swayed for a moment in the sunlight, then walked a few metres away and collapsed in the tall grass. They didn't move or speak, just sighed, enjoying the warmth, the colours and sounds and all the other things above ground; they had been gone so long they had nearly forgotten them.

Gradually they started to see the trees and meadows. A little way off there was a walking path and people passing with towels over their shoulders, rubber rings under their arms, sandals slapping, ankles covered with sand. They were on their way home after a day of swimming.

Olli tried to think. He felt faint and sick to his stomach.

Something was licking his face. It was Timi. They really had found him, or maybe he had found them. Anyway, he had come back with them.

The dog was overjoyed. He gave a wet greeting to each of the Five in turn. Then he went back to Olli and lowered his snout onto his master's leg, his dark eyes filled with gratitude.

They had come out on a hillside that looked out over the city, several stone's throws from the place where they had crawled in. The sun was shining from a different direction now, lower in the sky. They had been under the ground for several hours.

Olli tried to remember what had happened, but his memories of it fled into the dark like mice.

Then he got hold of one memory: they were crawling through a tight tunnel single file, Karri first, and the others following, with Olli last. They could hear Timi's voice coming from somewhere, ahead of them or behind them, whining and panting. Olli's breath rasped in his throat. It was difficult to keep moving. His knees and elbows were torn open and he was running out of strength.

Finally Karri stopped. He said they couldn't go any farther; they were at a dead end. Riku started to sob. Olli was too tired to feel anything. He patted Riku on the back to remind him that there were others here, hoping that Riku would be ashamed and know that he should keep quiet.

Then there was a glimmer ahead. Karri had started to dig away the wall with his hands. Fresh air, and then light, started to flow into the passageway. Karri made an opening and they scrabbled through it into a bright, cave-like space.

*

When they had sufficiently recovered, they went back to look at where they had exited from the passageway. What they had thought was a cave was in fact a cellar with stone walls. It certainly was in an odd place, out here in the woods.

They found the remains of a building. Later Aunt Anna would tell them that it used to be a youth centre, but it had burnt to the ground fifteen years before when little boys were playing with matches there.

They noticed that they couldn't see the narrow opening any more. The stone wall had fallen over it. Maybe the whole passageway had collapsed.

They looked at each other, then walked away.

Riku tapped on his wristwatch and cursed. He'd got the watch as a birthday present and bragged that it was a "quality timepiece". Now it had stopped.

Riku looked accusingly at Timi. "Olli, just so you know, your dog has my permission to buy me a new watch. If it hadn't been for him we could have eaten our lunch without any problems and be lying around at Aunt Anna's right now."

Anne stopped brushing herself off and asked in a tight voice, "What happened in there? What do you all remember?"

They didn't say anything.

"Well, for heaven's sake, don't tell me that you can't remember anything either," she said. "I'm trying but I can't seem to think of a single thing that happened. Well, maybe something, but…it's just a hint of something that I can't explain."

Everyone tried their hardest to remember.

But it was soon clear that none of them remembered

anything that they could talk about in the light of day. Whenever they thought of something, they couldn't find words to express it.

That was five summers ago, and now they've decided to find the first entrance again.

They've searched for it before. The first time was right after they came up out of the passageway and went to get their picnic basket. They found the basket, but never found the entrance. They couldn't remember where it was, not even Karri. Timi didn't even want to look for it.

That time, of course, they were tired and confused and still very young. Now they're older and they won't give up so easily.

For the past few summers they've found new passages in other places, overcome their fears and gone inside them.

They quickly realized that the secret passages affect your thoughts, and especially your memory. Inside the tunnels things are distorted; they seem different from how they are above the ground. And time progresses differently, too: sometimes it slows down, sometimes it speeds up, and sometimes it stops altogether. Afterwards they remember different things, or they remember the same things but each in a different way. Some things they can't remember at all. Often after they come back to the surface, everything that happened inside the secret passages is cloaked in obscurity and all that's left is the feeling of bewilderment that the passages give a person.

Making sense of it afterwards is laborious but fascinating. Not once have they all been in agreement.

Leo's theory is that there are fumes and gases there

that muddle the functioning of the brain. It's a plausible explanation. It would explain why Karri is able to find the passages—because he has a nose for sniffing out the air that seeps from them.

Karri thinks that it's not just gasses. He believes that he's better at feeling the small atmospheric disturbances that the underground passages create.

As he walks behind Karri down the slope of Taulumäki, Olli believes him. He thinks he can feel alterations in the atmosphere at the same moment that Karri's demeanour turns tense, when he "gets the scent of a passageway", as they put it.

Karri stoops down, tosses aside some twigs and brush, and beckons Olli over.

There is definitely an opening, the same one they all crawled into after Timi five years ago. As he peers down into it, Olli can smell the peculiar scent of the passages, like a garden in autumn.

His hands turn cold, and he wants to run away. No sane person would crawl into the cold, dark ground. The hole exudes an indefinable menace.

But Olli knows that that is how the secret passages protect themselves against intruders. To get in, you have to empty your mind of thoughts.

He can hear the Blomrooses' voices far off. They're going in the wrong direction.

"Let's call the others," Olli says.

"Not yet," Karri answers. "First I want to show you something. Follow me."

Olli looks at Karri questioningly, but he's hiding under

his hood. Olli doesn't know what to think. He starts to feel nervous.

Karri starts into the tunnel. Olli can hear his sweatshirt rubbing against the walls, breaking off dirt and sand. They are all bigger than they were five years ago, and the opening seems narrower. Then the passageway widens and Karri's slim body slips smoothly into the darkness.

Olli doubts that Leo, tall and broad as he is, will be able to get in so easily.

Karri moves out of sight and Olli looks around. The day, though grey, feels pleasantly bright when he thinks of leaving it behind. He feels a need to take in the fresh air, to enjoy every breath.

Going into a passageway always feels the same. Like drowning. Going to sleep. Giving in. It's like trading the world and his ordinary life for a captivating dream.

Leo, Anne and Riku's voices recede. Karri is waiting for him in the dark. Olli hesitates.

It occurs to him that he shouldn't spoil his new denim jacket. He hangs it over a branch and pushes his way into the darkness. It's cold in the passageway at first, and it's difficult to breathe. But his body quickly adjusts.

22

THEY CRAWL ON HANDS AND KNEES through the dark, feeling their way.

A minute passes, or an hour. Underground, time has no meaning.

Sometimes it's hard to breathe, sometimes it's easier. For a while he can smell flowers, as if they were in a garden of exotic plants instead of under the ground. He feels heavy and light at the same time. His skin is tingling. His hands and feet don't feel like his own. His movements are slow, but smooth and in a strange way easy. Like diving through black water. But now and then he hits his head on the tunnel wall and then gravity reminds him of itself.

A couple of times he thinks he's lost Karri. He panics, then he hears and feels Karri again, moving ahead of him. He has to keep going forward. The passageway is too cramped to turn around. Stopping would mean death. But dying doesn't worry Olli; he just has to keep moving.

The surface of the earth, and the sun, are farther and farther away. Olli remembers that the original exit collapsed five years ago. So they'll have to find a place to turn around and go back the way they came, or find another way out. Assuming there is one.

Olli smiles in the dark. Not because he's happy, but because it feels soothing on his cheeks. The soothing feeling spreads from his face to his whole head as his thoughts follow the motions of his face. Things will happen the way they are meant to happen. There's no point in worrying. Karri must know where he's going. He's at Karri's mercy, so he might as well trust him as long as he has no reason to distrust him.

Life and death feel smaller in the passageways than they do above ground. That makes moving underground easier, but it's also one of the greatest dangers of the secret passages. Under the ground, it would be easy to forget yourself.

It's not completely dark down here. Olli can see something. Faint shapes. Karri's feet. His own hands. Fingers waved in front of his face. Or he might be imagining all this. Down here he can't be sure of anything.

He focuses on crawling.

Olli thinks he's lying in a bed. He's sinking into sleep, and he smiles. Grandpa Notary is standing in the doorway. *"Goodnight and sweet dreams, Olli. Did you have a good day? What did you get up to today?"*

"We went somewhere," Olli answers sleepily. *"Hey, I don't remember now. Let me sleep. I'm tired…"*

Something knocks against the top of Olli's head. He takes hold of it. It's a shoe. Karri's smelly shoe.

"Don't stop." Karri's voice is sharp. "Keep moving!"

Olli remembers where he is and latches on to the idea of moving. Crawling is all that matters. Here underground, there is nothing but crawling.

It would be easy to lose himself here. The world left on the surface is too far away to feel real. The Blomrooses, Tourula, his mother and father… they're all irrelevant. Meaningless.

But one thing is true here; there is one truth that they

can't forget even for a second. They must always remind each other of it: keep moving, keep crawling forward, otherwise the darkness will come and swallow you. It wants everything that comes here in its arms, wants everything for its own. It takes power to resist and return to the light.

It's been a minute, or hours, since Olli hung his jacket on a branch and crawled into the hole. Since then centuries full of thoughts whispered by the dead have flowed through his mind.

They've changed him.

He's different from the way he was when he crawled into that hole. The secret passages have purged him of all that he had accumulated around him. He no longer even remembers the name of the person he was before. The person who is here, crawling, is naked and nameless and weightless.

It crawls deep into the dark and smiles.

He's crawling. His name and all the other things do come to him every so often. They land on him like crows and make him heavy and slow.

Under the ground, he can see things. There are faint particles of light that sometimes gather around one thing or another and attach themselves to it. Then, for a moment, the invisible is visible, until the particles break off and continue on their way.

Olli sees all kinds of things.

Roots poking through the ceiling of the tunnel.

Underground intersections.

Passages stretching up and down and off to the sides.

And figures—barely real, furtive; small, large, fast, slow; perhaps animals, perhaps something else.

No need to worry, Karri whispers. *They'll stay away from us.*

Olli doesn't worry. He just keeps crawling.

He bumps into Karri.

Karri has stopped in front of some kind of door. It's small, like a little hatch. The light particles are attached to it. Olli doesn't remember it from the last time they were here. But maybe it was here—your memory plays tricks on you under the ground.

Karri tugs at the hatch. It's stuck. He has to wrench at it with all his strength. Stones fall down off the walls of the tunnel. For a moment it feels as if the passage will collapse. This doesn't really worry Olli.

Karri tells Olli to go through the door.

He goes through.

On the other side of the hatch, it's no less dark. But Olli senses that there is space around him now. The ceiling is high, the walls far apart. He stands up and walks farther in, his hands stretched out in front of him.

Karri is still in the doorway.

Then he asks Olli, "Can you see her?"

Olli doesn't understand. "Who am I supposed to see?" he asks, his voice amused.

The answer is so long in coming that Olli thinks Karri must have gone away and left him here alone.

"Do you see the girl? Look at *the girl*."

"It's dark in here," Olli protests. "I can't see anyone."

"Look hard and you'll see her," Karri whispers. His words hiss like insects. Olli starts to feel cold.

"Look at her hair," Karri says.

It's difficult to say which direction the voice is coming from. It sounds close by and far away. "Look how golden her hair is."

Olli opens his eyes as wide as he can. The darkness is deeper here than in the other passages. Then the particles of light come. They start to gather together and he does see something.

Hair.

A girl's curly hair.

Golden yellow.

Olli reaches his hand towards the light particles, then jerks it back with a start when he feels the strands of hair.

"And her lips," Karri's voice continues, tense and breathless. "Can you see them? Red lips. Soft and curving. Can you see them smiling at you?…"

Something red flickers in the blackness.

"And her eyes, Olli… What kind of eyes does she have?"

Olli meets the gaze of the stranger.

"Blue," he says, trembling. "No, green. I don't know. They make me think of the sea."

He's scared now.

"Do you think she has beautiful eyes?" Karri asks.

Olli whispers that he does. He is still staring into her green eyes. Then they disappear into the darkness they came from. There's a scratching and rustling. Someone or something is moving in the dark.

"What about my voice?"

The voice is soft and musical. It sounds like it belongs to the girl he just saw.

"Do you like my voice?"

Olli can't speak.

"Do you like *me*?"

Olli's heart pounds. "Where's Karri?" he asks.

"He went away," the girl says, and sounds amused.

Olli feels a touch on his cheek.

The girl is caressing him.

"Away?"

She steps closer. The light particles gather on her skin and hair and make her visible.

"Yes," she says rapturously, and kisses Olli on the cheek. "That poor, unfortunate boy finally left us all alone, and he's never coming back."

23

T̲HE LIVING ROOM̲ had always had its problems. But it was also bright and pleasant.

Now a darkness had settled in the corners and drained the life from the colours. Enough was enough. Olli felt a surge of energy, got up from the sofa, turned on the lights, and pulled open the curtains. Outside it was daytime. He looked at the trees and houses. The daylight came from a faraway land of ordinariness and clarity, where people didn't disappear from their homes.

He went back to the sofa. The room was still dim. The light didn't really illuminate it. Maybe the bulbs were wearing out, and the window was dirty. Or maybe over the years too much stuff had accumulated in the room and it was sucking up all the light.

Birds sat on the limbs of the trees peeping into the house. Olli realized that he didn't like birds. They were just little animals that zipped around through the air. And they were noisy. They sounded like an alarm from some electronic device.

Then he started to make an inventory of everything in the house. Many rooms: the hallway, the living room, the corner room, the kitchen; and upstairs two bedrooms and the office with the computer, and on it Facebook. In the rooms were chairs, tables, sofas, beds, shelves, cabinets, lamps, decorative objects, electronic devices, dishes, medicines, cleaning supplies, tools, food, clothing, flowers, mirrors and photo albums.

In the albums there were a lot of pictures of his wife and son. He had piled all the albums on the living-room table so that he could look at the photos whenever he liked. And he had looked at them, many times.

All in all, everything in the house was fine, except for the fact that the people pictured in the photographs were missing.

Olli decided to clean. He vacuumed half the living room. Then he stopped and stood staring at the birds perched in the trees, turned off the vacuum and went back to the sofa.

Olli was thinking.

He really would have preferred to sleep. But since Aino had vanished into Facebook, and the boy with her, he had to gather his thoughts and memories, arrange them, separate the fact from the dreams they were mixed up with. *The world is chaos*, Notary Suominen had once said. *A man's job is to bring order to it.*

The thought of Grandpa Notary made Olli straighten his spine. What would his grandpa have done in this situation? Olli furrowed his brow and sat up, then stood up and walked around, thinking about the office upstairs and the computer with his Facebook profile and all his Facebook friends—workmates and colleagues, the author Greta Kara, the Blomroos siblings, and now his own vanished wife, with her own Facebook friends, and among them, as Olli had discovered, was Karri Kultanen.

Karri?

Olli rubbed his temples and tried to make his thoughts progress more clearly.

The last time he had seen Karri Kultanen was about three decades ago. It was at the end of the Tourula Five's seventh summer. He remembered the day as if he were looking at it though the wrong end of a telescope. All of the Tourula Five were there. They had probably just come from one of their endless picnics. The Blomrooses were off somewhere and Olli and Karri were left alone. They had been looking for something, probably playing at searching for secret passages. Anyway they had been playing at something.

Then things had gone wrong. Maybe he and Karri had quarrelled. He didn't remember the reason. All he remembered was a surge of emotion. He sometimes had confused, surreal dreams connected with that day and its dramatic turn.

In the dreams there were always secret passages.

Anyway, he had run to his grandma and grandpa's house at the rifle factory and told them that he wanted to go home to Koirakkala.

Grandma had clucked over him and wanted to know why. Grandpa Notary had come out of his office and said, "Well, there's a time for everything and there is a certain wisdom in knowing when things are beginning and when they're ending." He had sensed that Olli didn't want to talk about it. Or maybe he just wasn't interested; maybe he just wanted to get rid of his moody grandson.

In any case, Grandpa had immediately called Koirakkala and informed them that the summer traveller was coming home. Olli's father must have tried to put it off because his grandpa's voice had turned sharp and he had said firmly that yes, the boy really was coming home, right now.

Olli stretched out on the sofa to sort through his thoughts, and fell asleep.

The passageway is dark and narrow. Olli is crawling forward. He's wearing his best suit. Dirt keeps pattering down on him. His knees and elbows are bloody. The fine Italian fabric of his coat and trousers is tearing, wearing through, getting filthy. Even the best tailor and dry cleaner couldn't save it now. But he has to keep crawling. He has forgotten something very important down here in the dark.

The passageway keeps pushing deeper and deeper. A great coldness radiates towards him. He sees a faint light ahead. Amid a swarm of light particles, there's a heap of clothing. A grey sweatshirt. That's what he came here for. He left it here years ago. Olli is relieved. Now he can go back to the daylight.

When he touches the sweatshirt, his hand touches something else, something solid. There's a person inside the clothes. A boy. Or the pale, withered ghost of a boy.

It turns. It whispers in a voice rasping with the soil of the passageways. "*Oh, it's you. So. I guess you know the reason I've been sitting here all these years…*"

Olli opens his eyes and realizes he's on the sofa. His clothes are damp with cold sweat.

There was a picture on Aino's profile now. It was a photo of Aino and the boy wading near the waterline on a deserted beach. In the background was the sea and an exotic point of land. The boy looked very happy. Aino was looking at the camera. There was panic in her eyes.

In the foreground was a man in a suit with his head cut off by the edge of the picture. A security guard, Olli thought. Or a keeper. The man's coat was open. The butt of a pistol peeked out from under it.

Where are you?

Olli's question had received an answer.

Hello, Olli. They're letting me answer your message. I don't know where we are. Somewhere warm, on the seashore. It might be an island. We were brought here by helicopter. We're going to change our location soon, from what I understand. We're all right, as long as we follow instructions. They tell me I should think of it as a luxury holiday, albeit an involuntary one. They apologized for their unorthodox actions, but they said that it has to do with some old story that you had a part in, and that you would no doubt understand the situation. You're supposed to help these people to correct some past error that you witnessed. Once it's taken care of, our forced holiday will be over and they'll let us go home.

Hopefully you can help them correct their problem, whatever it is.

It's very nice of you, by the way, to notice that I was gone. I don't think you noticed when our son was kidnapped two weeks ago. I'm sorry I didn't spell it out for you, but I was forbidden from telling anyone, including you. It seems that it was meant to be a lesson, as well as being practical in terms of the travel arrangements—they stole the child, and the mother dutifully followed. I eventually received instructions, left home while you were out meeting that author (I hope the meeting went well, dear, so that nothing bad happens to your publishing house) and the kidnappers—or "organizers" as they like me to call them— brought me to him. But don't be too worried. At least Lauri and I are together. We're being treated well and we'll be all right, as long as you do what's expected of you, provided you can spare the time from work for it.

:-)

Olli stared at the smile added to the bottom of the message.

Then he noticed that he had three new messages in his inbox.

They were from the Blomroos siblings.

PART TWO

24

WHEN AINO HAD BEEN MISSING for three days, Olli put down his book, got undressed, washed and put on pressed trousers, an Italian dress shirt, a tie and a pale-coloured jacket. He went to the living room and looked the portrait of Notary Suominen in the eye.

Deeds are a man's full-length mirror, the portrait reminded him.

Olli stepped out into the yard, stopped and waited for the vertigo to subside. He went over the instructions he had received. Then he walked through Mäki-Matti, cheerily greeting his neighbours. His greetings were returned. Someone asked the news and said to say hello to Aino. I certainly will, Olli answered. How's the boy? Fine, fine. Growing all the time. Having fun at the beach. They praised the weather and remarked that summer was, after all, a fleeting thing, and you ought to enjoy it just as long as you could.

Olli felt better. It was fun to pretend that everything was fine, to share a moment of the sunny, unchanged ordinariness that his neighbours still inhabited.

He climbed up Harju Ridge. When he got to the top of the Harju Steps he looked at the clock and thought that he should probably continue straight down the other side.

Start down the Ridge at exactly 1 p.m.

It was warm. The light over the city was dazzling. The rooftops glowed. The shadows on the steps and the cold rising up from the earth cooled him pleasantly. Olli prepared himself for the encounter. He put a smile on his face.

You will meet Greta on the steps, quite by accident. Your mission is to buy her an ice cream and make her look forward to your next meeting.

Olli could see that the girl from his dreams was coming up the stairs. The colours were so bright that it hurt his eyes, the outlines unnaturally sharp. For a moment he thought he could see the irises of her eyes from dozens of metres away. He felt dizzy again. His legs were shaking. What if he fell, tumbled down the stone steps and cracked his skull open? Would his family get to come home then, or would they end up dead, tossed in the ocean?

Olli looked into Greta's eyes as they approached each other. Her eyes sparkled. The surrounding foliage accentuated their greenness.

They met at a landing that looked like a little stone fort, halfway up the steps. Greta was wearing a sleeveless green dress and black pumps. She was the grown woman again, the successful author that the girl in the pear-print dress had become.

"Olli! What a pleasant surprise!"

"Greta," he sputtered.

His throat was dry. He didn't quite know what to do or what to say. He stood looking at her expectantly, nervous and embarrassed, a tight smile on his lips. They looked each other over. Greta laughed with a flirty tilt of her head.

"That's still my name. And now that we've remembered each other's name it must be time to dive into a little small talk. Beautiful weather today, isn't it? Where are you off to, Mr Suominen? To work again, I'll bet. Off to publish those autumn titles?"

No. I've come to meet you, so they don't kill my family, Olli thought, and said, "I'm on my way to the supermarket."

"Ah."

"To buy some liver casserole," he added, sounding reasonably natural.

"Oh," Greta said. "Do you like liver casserole?"

"No. But…"

They stared at each other.

"But your wife told you to get some?" Greta eventually said.

"Yes," Olli said. He was angry with himself. He shouldn't have brought his wife into this. It wouldn't advance his task. But it was too late to take it back. "The boy wants liver casserole," he said.

Greta smiled sadly. "Children like liver casserole because it has raisins in it. Even I used to like it, years ago."

"Time changes everything," Olli said with a smile.

Greta gazed into the distance and whispered pensively, "Everything changes, and nothing changes. A person, anyway, always stays the same."

Amid an electric silence, Greta sat down on the edge of one of the stone steps. Olli settled in beside her. When they looked at each other Olli could see how pale and transparent their safe roles as a publisher and successful author were; at that moment they were looking into the depths of thirty years past.

They felt embarrassed, as if they had both just realized they were naked.

Olli blushed and coughed uncomfortably.

Greta looked at her shoes. It was clear that she felt like running away.

Olli couldn't allow that. He had his instructions. He had to think of some snappy line to steer events in the right direction.

As they got up again, there was a flash of disappointment on Greta's face. She sighed like grass bending in the wind and mumbled, "So, I guess I…"

Just then their stone sanctum was invaded by a passing crowd of French tourists. The middle-aged woman leading the group was explaining the history of the steps, gesturing vigorously. Greta's voice was drowned out by a chatter of French as the tourists emitted admiring exclamations.

Your mission is to buy her an ice cream and make her look forward to your next meeting.

It was clear that Greta had hoped for more from this encounter. He had disappointed her every time. And he was doing it again.

Olli understood her disappointment. He had been behaving like a distant acquaintance who by chance also happened to be her publisher.

He couldn't think of anything to say. Words failed him.

And Greta was getting ready to leave.

If he failed at his task, his family would suffer.

Then Olli lifted his hands in the air like a praying Muslim, his palms towards the sky, surrendering to his inarticulateness. When there are no words, there are actions.

He looked Greta in the eye, stepped closer and took hold of her slender arm.

Her skin felt cool. Her startled, mint-scented breath brushed his face. Her surprise quickly changed to anger. Olli opened his mouth to explain himself before the situation became unsalvageable.

"Greta…"

Greta was waiting for him to say the right, conciliatory words, just as much as he was. An explosion was growing within the green of her eyes. Each failed encounter had built up the tension, and it was about to snap, one way or another.

Olli had spent the previous night reading the manuscript of the *Magical City Guide*. Now a passage from the book came into his mind.

And when it did, it activated the part of his brain where all good quotes come from.

Memento mori! Live like you still can, and live in such a way that when the time comes to give it all up, you will know that you have lived. Life is a divine dream, an unexpected gift, a film reel in a camera that's already running. Just as believers feel close to God when they are in a place like a cathedral, a temple or a mosque, so too, the cinematic possibilities of life are closer to us when we are in the magical places that this book is about. Under the influence of M-particles we can create ourselves anew, free ourselves from the slow continuum and learn to throw ourselves into the moment and surrender to the story that we are becoming at any given moment. So seek out cinematicness for your life in places where the M-particle radiation is strongest.

M-particles and the secret passages might show us that we're connected. Where there are M-particles there are often also secret passages, and vice versa. So beware, you visitors to magical places, for in the secret passages the M-particle radiation can be dangerously powerful, and for this reason the passages must be avoided if you do happen to find an entrance.

GRETA KARA,
Magical City Guide Number One: Jyväskylä,
INTRODUCTION

25

"I'M SORRY, but I can't let you leave," Olli whispers, not loosening his grip.

The French tourists climbing the steps look back at them in curiosity.

Greta's eyes widen and her nostrils flare. Then she relaxes and the angry shadows fade from her face. They stare at each other. Finally she asks with a child's wonder. "Why can't you?"

Olli gazes at her solemnly and says, "Because I have to buy you an ice cream. Otherwise something terrible will happen."

Greta's jaw drops slightly.

"I see," she coos. A new sharpness comes over her; a new game has begun. "All right. But only if you can guess what kind of ice cream I want. If you don't, I'm leaving and we'll never have anything more to do with each other. I'll even take my book to another publisher."

She says this with a smile. But Olli can see that she's serious and has horrified even herself with what she has said.

"Fine," Olli says, feigning confidence. He hasn't the slightest idea what Greta's favourite ice cream is, but he can play for time.

They start down the steps. At the bottom is an ice cream stand. They don't say a word, just glance at each other now and then, Greta trying to hide her fear that Olli won't remember, Olli trying not to look desperate. He has to calm down. His heart is pounding too fast; his ears are roaring so loud he can't hear.

He can't help but notice that the cinematic beauty of the woman beside him draws the attention of passers-by. This gives him pleasure, and a fatalistic calm. Whatever will be will be. Everything has its own meaning. He tries to focus on that. Don't think of what you've wagered in the middle of the game.

When they reach the street, Greta sits down on the edge of the blue fountain. Olli goes to the kiosk window and looks at Greta one more time. Underneath her smile she's like a frightened child.

Olli buys two ice cream cones, pays and turns around with the cones in his hands.

Greta's eyes sparkle with joy.

Olli answers her smile.

He needs to sit down too, so his legs won't fail him.

Just a moment earlier he was seeing in his mind's eye how this meeting could end in catastrophe. Greta, offended at Olli's forgetting, could leave him standing there at the bottom of the hill. The result: Book Tower would lose the author most important to its future, people would lose their jobs, the kidnappers would take revenge for his failure on Aino and his boy. Olli's life would be ruined.

Then he remembered something about Greta and ice cream. The closer they got to the bottom of the steps, the clearer it grew in his mind.

And when he stepped up to the ice cream stand, the memory finally opened up completely: he and the girl in the pear-print dress stop at a little kiosk at the corner of Puistokatu and Tellervonkatu, thirty years ago. They've come to buy ice cream. When they left the house Greta said she wanted a strawberry ice cream cone. She grabbed Olli's hand, looked deep into his eyes, and made him vow to remember forever that she never, ever ate any ice cream but strawberry.

Back then he never asked why strawberry, although he had wondered.

He asks now.

Greta demurs for a moment, but eventually says, "You must not remember it, but at the very beginning of our summer together I said I felt like having some ice cream. I didn't have any money. You had half a markka. Enough to get one ice cream cone at Hjelt's, which we ate together. It was strawberry, because they were out of everything else."

They go back up Harju Ridge and sit on a park bench near the steps looking out over the city. People are climbing up and down. Olli remembers something from the *Magical City Guide*:

> *M-particle levels on the steps vary from one day to the next, but even at their most ordinary the steps offer a fine view of the great meetings and partings of life.*

"So you're still not tired of this flavour?" Olli asks.

Greta licks her cone and shakes her head. "In Paris, Brazil, Hollywood… everywhere I've been I've only eaten strawberry. In Bombay I thought I would have to go without, but then I had Amul strawberry ice cream. I was rather weak at the time, and the ice cream helped me cope. I might have died without it. My friends there bought it for me when they found out what it meant to me."

Greta turns her face away, embarrassed. Her golden hair shines so brightly that it dazzles him.

"Oh, Olli," she whispers. "We have so much to talk about. More than we could possibly have time to say, or hear, even if we sat here talking for the rest of our lives. And we don't have… But never mind. You have to go to buy some liver casserole. I'm sure your family is expecting it."

She gets up, puts on her large movie-star sunglasses, thanks him for the ice cream, and walks away towards the city.

Your mission is to buy her an ice cream and make her look forward to your next meeting.

Olli is left sitting on the bench, thinking. They succeeded in eating ice cream, but will he succeed in the next part of his mission?

The order to meet Greta Kara "by accident" on the Harju Steps came from the Blomroos siblings. The three of them got carried away and each one sent their own separate message.

Richard Blomroos wrote:

Hey there, Olli. How are you? Good, I hope, even if your family is away at the moment "on holiday", if you don't mind the expression. I'm sorry about that. But I'm even more sorry about what we did to Greta thirty years ago. Of course, we were just stupid kids, but that doesn't absolve us of responsibility. We've thought a lot about what happened. We want to make it up to Greta, and to you. We took something important away from both of you.

 Your old pal,

  Richard B.

Leo Blomroos's message said:

Olli my friend, what happened to Greta late one summer is unforgivable. I wish I could blame Anne, who put us up to it. Or Richard, who never needed much encouragement to pull a prank, not even when he was older. (He's been to jail a couple of times, thanks to his poor judgement.) But as the leader of the Tourula Five, I'm the one who's ultimately responsible for everyone and everything, so I blame myself. I could have easily stopped them, but I didn't. That makes me the guiltiest of all. I'll be sorry for it for the rest of my days. I want to say that I'll never do anything like that again, but unfortunately I don't see any alternative right now, in spite of what my sense and my conscience tell me, but to go along with this thing, which I'm sure is causing you a great deal of stress. But it is an attempt of sorts to expiate our sins against that which we have broken. That means something, doesn't it? I hope you understand, my friend, but I realize that you probably hate all of us right now.

 Sincerely,

  Leo Blomroos.

The actual instructions, however, came from Anne, which didn't surprise Olli:

Hi Olli, dear old friend (take my word for it, I think of you often with fondness and nostalgia, although I'm sure you prefer not to think about me)—I know of course that this is all probably rather tough for you, but I hope that you're not too broken up to do what you have to do.

As you know, thirty years ago my brothers and I did a terrible thing. A criminal, traitorous, senseless thing for which there is no defence, not even the stupidity of youth or the jealousy that drove a young girl to desperate acts. Ever since then it has followed all of us, as it no doubt has our victim, Greta. There comes a time when such things must be settled, accounts balanced, sins atoned for. Due to unforeseen circumstances, it can't be put off any longer.

Olli darling, I'm so awfully sorry but now I have to boss you around. Tomorrow afternoon you must go to the top of the Harju Steps. Start walking down the steps at exactly one o'clock. You will meet Greta on the steps, quite by accident. Your mission is to buy her an ice cream and make her look forward to your next meeting.

Do not say anything about this message or mention me or my brothers. She doesn't want to hear anything about us. We did, after all, destroy her thirty years ago, in more ways than one. And don't say anything about your family being gone—there's no point in shocking her with such news. Make sure that she wants to see you again. You will receive further instructions later. And Olli, we will be aware of everything you do, so buddy, don't do anything rash if you don't want anybody to be hurt more than they already have been. That would break my heart.

You may be asking why Aino and your son have to be mixed up in this. We removed them specifically to protect them and to keep innocent bystanders out of this little opera of ours, which only pertains to those involved. For logistical reasons we first took the boy from your front yard, then invited your wife to where he was a little later on. You can rest assured that they will be treated well. You have my word on it. They are in fact quite comfy. I haven't the slightest desire to add to the weight of my sins—quite the contrary, if you do your part in this atonement project of ours, the whole affair will come to seem a great, exciting adventure to your family, travelling to the world's most pleasant and exotic locales! (Is it true, Olli, that your wife has never been any farther than Sweden? That situation has now been remedied!)

Of course, we also want to make it easier to do what needs to be done—if you don't want to do this for yourself and for Greta, do it for your family. Think of it however you like. But forget about moral considerations—you simply have no choice but to follow the script we've written for you. You and Greta had a beautiful love story; we understand that now. It's time your story had a beautiful ending.

With love from your friend,
    Anne.

26

T̲HE BLOMROOSES' LETTERS̲ made Olli sick. After he read them the first time he went and threw up, then he had diarrhoea. When he came back to the computer he almost deleted them. But then he printed them all, in two copies. He might need them later as evidence.

Olli sits on the bench, mulling over the encounter he's just had. His first mission.

It's still just as confusing, but at least he knows now what it's all about. And he's started to do something about it. It beats being in the dark, unable to act.

It is some consolation that as long as he follows the Blomrooses' "script", nothing bad will happen to Aino and the boy. The script is a good thing, ultimately, so he ought to stick to it. Because it has the plot twist that once Olli fulfils his role and helps the Blomrooses atone for their deeds, he'll get his family back and everything will go back to the way it was. *The End.*

Olli walks over to the steps and climbs back up to the top of the Ridge. The steps have been here for eighty years. At first he thinks about his feet, and then about everyone who has, like him, walked these steps, or will walk these steps in the decades to come. Or maybe centuries—where are stone steps like these going to go, even in a town that eats its own history?

The person he's known as—Olli Suominen, publisher and member of the parish council—is just one of innumerable people who will at some point in their lives find themselves trudging up the Harju Steps. Every one of them will carry with them dreams, worries, problems, plans, memories and sins that they think unique, meaningful, enduring. Every one will cling to life and be scared to death of change, which nevertheless must come to everyone, as sure as death.

The city at the bottom of the steps is changing all the time. The days, the seasons, the generations in succession. Only the Ridge and the steps remain the same.

According to *The Magical City Guide*, a cinematic life is best achieved at places like the Harju Steps:

In such places, the temporary phenomenon known as human life is put into perspective by time and by large physical elements, just as it is by the ocean, or a mountain. Paradoxically, the transience and fundamental meaninglessness of human life when seen juxtaposed with phenomena that reflect eternity can be the necessary starting point for cinematic meaningfulness.

Olli is struck with a fit of fatalism that makes him calmly smile. It's pointless to brood on it. Like everyone else who walks these steps, he has to accept his fate. No matter what happens, in the end no one will remember or care whether this strange episode had a sad or a happy ending. Until then, he'll play his role as well as he knows how, and then he'll either get his family back, or lose everything.

The thought feels cinematically liberating. He even feels a little spurt of joy as his body adjusts itself to better withstand the ordeal. When he gets home, he walks out to the recycling bin and tosses in *Ageing with Dignity*, with its warnings about endorphin and adrenalin addictions dangerous to the middle-aged:

> *Endorphins (endogenous morphine, or morphine that originates within the body) are peptides that present as opioids in the brain, pituitary and other parts of the nervous system. Endorphins bind to opioid receptors, and have a variety of effects including the reduction of pain. Adrenaline, or epinephrine, on the other hand, is a hormone secreted by the adrenal gland in times of stress. Adrenaline increases physical performance and feelings of well-being. It can accelerate heart function, expand the bronchial tubes and increase energy by altering the metabolism of sugar. It is clear that a middle-aged man who experiences endocrine and adrenaline cravings and intoxication can be susceptible to overestimating his abilities, and thus lose his sense of reality and rationality and make fatefully poor decisions.*

Walking past the observation tower Olli sees his reflection in the window and it amuses him. He looks like a character from an old movie. He thinks he understands now what he was reading about the deep cinematic self. Naturally he's still deeply worried, but at the same time part of him, surely his deep cinematic self, would seem to be feeling a sort of aesthetic pleasure that something has happened to break the ordinary routine of his life.

Intoxicated by this feeling of profound meaningfulness and fatalism, and perhaps also by his own endorphins, he descends the Harju Steps into Mäki-Matti. Dramatic music plays in his head. He senses his surroundings with uncharacteristic clarity.

As soon as Olli got home his anxiety returned. His stomach started to hurt. He felt faint. He crawled onto the sofa and whimpered like a sick dog.

It was slow continuum attachment again, getting him in its clutches:

> *Slow continuum attachment affects a person like gravity. It shoves a person's face into the dust of the everyday, the ashes of dreams. It persuades us to be content with our fate like a humble beast of burden and put aside the possibilities that every moment of life offers. The cinematic way of life is liberation from the slow continuum. Instead of unavoidable obligations, a person can learn to see all possibilities, even impossible ones, and live them out in a cinematic aesthetic spirit. All that's necessary is to dare to pick the pears hanging from the branches of life's tree and take a bite. Of course, that demands a lot—your whole life, in fact—but in the end it's nothing more than a choice.*

Olli pressed his trembling hands against his face and was afraid he would be squashed under the weight of the thoughts in his head, and lose himself in their seeping darkness.

When dusk fell he had recovered enough to go upstairs and read his new instructions on Facebook.

27

T HE OUTDOOR SEATING at the kiosk in the old church park was chosen as the stage for the next meeting.

The first week of August was restless and crowded in Jyväskylä. The mass event known as the Neste Oil Rally was happening. It attracted car-racing fans from around the world, and for a few days the city was full of people, cars and all sorts of vendors. During rally week Olli usually avoided the downtown area and took a taxi to and from work. He couldn't bear the crowds of drunken bar-goers who did bring money into the city but also pissed in the streets, disturbed the peace, broke bottles, littered and clogged traffic.

He didn't hear much talk about the races at the publishing office, although Maïju, in particular, secretly followed them with enthusiastic interest and was thrilled at the success of the Finnish drivers.

The trance-like passion that rally cars evoked in people had always baffled Olli. Even when they showed *American Graffiti* at the film club, it didn't give him an urge to buy a car of his own or lessen his scepticism about the pleasures of driving.

This year Olli had been planning to stay completely away from the central city for the duration of the races, but when his family was kidnapped he had to compromise many of his principles. So there he was, following the Facebook instructions and heading to the park, where he had orders to wait for Greta.

At your last meeting you gave her hope. Continue in the same manner. Walk with her through town hand in hand. Kiss her lightly so that you leave her dreaming, but without being too blatant. You have to leave her in suspense about your next meeting.

Olli's blood pressure was probably dangerously high, so he didn't measure it. He had eaten and slept poorly. His stomach was in knots. His back ached. His thoughts were muddled. He dressed his suffering body in the clothes of a casually stylish gentleman, examined the result in the mirror, took a taxi to the park, and sat at an empty table on the kiosk terrace.

As he had expected, people milled around him in a noisy mob. He stared at the table top and tried to shut the stress out of his mind. He was hot in his jacket but he couldn't bring himself to take it off. Time passed. He waited. People left. Other people took their places. Then they too left. Olli continued to sit. Someone sang a song in drunken German. The air was filled with the smell of beer and cigarettes. Taxis were lined up at the kerb like big, sleepy dogs. Now and then one of them awoke and crept away.

Olli drank three cups of coffee and a bottle of yellow Jaffa soda. The people at the next table were talking about the races the way soldiers in a movie talk about the war. Olli felt like punching them.

He started thinking about remodelling. There was a lot that needed to be fixed: the sloping floors, the ceiling panels in the bedroom, the slanting walls, the wallpaper. He made mental calculations of the labour, materials and expenses. His brow furrowed.

Then he remembered his wife and son, kidnapped and

taken on a forced holiday by the Blomrooses, and he sank into a gloom.

When a ripple of wind brushed against his face, gently probing it, sounds began to enter his ears. He looked around and noticed that the colours had brightened. It was as if someone had opened a hatch inside him.

It was hard not to worry about his kidnapped family, even if it was a beautiful summer day. But even the worst problems couldn't touch the creature that he was beneath his titles, tastes, obligations, responsibilities and memories. It smiled at him, carefree as a child.

It liked this spot.

The *Magic City Guide* describes the old church park thus:

This one-block park in central Jyväskylä contains a Gothic-style church built in 1880, a kiosk building, an old electrical switching station and a variety of monuments. The kiosk, built in 1954, radiates a particularly dense concentration of M-particles, which enrich the life feeling of people in its vicinity. The park is also a popular meeting place for lovers.

The scent of floral perfume awakens Olli from his thoughts. Someone is sitting beside him.

He hesitates a moment, then looks.

Greta Kara is drinking pink lemonade through a straw and smiling mischievously.

"If it isn't Mr Suominen," she says. "Taking some time out from the workday to enjoy the international ambience of rally week, I presume? I was walking by and saw you and called your name, but you didn't respond, although half the people in the park waved back at me. I've been sitting next to you for fifteen minutes waiting for you to notice me. Silly thing. A couple of minutes longer and I would have lit your trousers on fire. Now, don't you dare get angry with me, you little devil. You look as if you could bite my nose off."

Olli stifles a smile, looks at Greta blankly, and hears himself repeating a Burt Lancaster line from *Sweet Smell of Success*: "Bite you? I'd hate to take a bite outta you. You're a cookie full of arsenic."

For a moment Greta looks as if he's slapped her in the face. Then she recognizes the quote.

"Fiddle-dee-dee," she answers cheekily. "That's a quote from Scarlett O'Hara."

They look at each other. Olli's suppressed smile escapes and spreads to Greta, and it's very becoming on her.

They chat.

Greta talks about her happy life in Paris and the intoxication that came with the success of *A Guide to the Cinematic Life*. Her anecdotes reflect the charm, sharp wit and sensibility of their teller, her sometimes almost naive quality.

Olli talks of his own life in a vague way, avoiding any mention of his wife or son. When the conversation drifts too near to his family, Greta becomes uncomfortable and her face turns sad. Then Olli changes the subject and they settle on pondering life, art and other safe, abstract matters, but soon slip into talking about their own lives again when a good story or incident comes to mind.

The whole while they are both pretending. Greta pretends

that Olli doesn't have a family waiting for him in Mäki-Matti. And Olli acts the part of a man whose family is indeed waiting for him at home, as they are both aware, but pretends that they aren't, for reasons of convenience.

In spite of the difficulties this entails, the conversation progresses like a spring brook, branching and meandering in its search for a route, but never stopping.

Olli almost succeeds in forgetting that he's there as a victim of extortion. He allows himself to enjoy the conversation, and at the same time a part of him remains an observer, assessing the developing situation relative to his objective.

You and Greta had a beautiful love story; we understand that now. It's time your story had a beautiful ending.

A beautiful ending. But what sort? An ending like the one in Emma Bunny? *"Do you like me? I like you. When we grow up, we can get married and have children together."*

One thing Olli knows is that these meetings are just the beginning of the beautiful ending that Anne is demanding. Today they have orders to walk hand in hand and share a kiss. Next time they'll have to go further. The Blomrooses have decided to sacrifice Olli's marital fidelity and give Greta the gift of his love in compensation for the crime they committed as children.

Olli smiles at Greta's remarks, answers with his own, and tries to keep the conversation light, and his own grim thoughts hidden. It apparently isn't working because Greta reaches out and touches Olli's brow with the back of her hand.

"Do you feel all right? You don't seem to have a fever, at least. You look quite pale."

Olli remembers something he read in *A Guide to the Cinematic Life*:

> *A person's life doesn't consist of just one story but of many, some of them consecutive and others overlapping. While one story is a comedy, another may be a melodrama, or a thriller. It's important to recognize every incipient story's genre and let the deep cinematic self develop the right state of mind to supersede the slow continuum.*
>
> *The holy cinematic trinity is beauty, hope and pain. A beautiful story has a beautiful beginning and a beautiful ending. The illusion of happiness makes the beginning beautiful, but the ending draws its beauty from pain.*
>
> *In order to live with cinematic depth, you must surrender completely to the story that has become true at a given moment, even if it demands morally dubious behaviour or, as some would call it, sinfulness. Morality is one of the lower orders of aesthetics, and is ultimately subordinate to beauty. Morality changes—today's sin is tomorrow's beautiful dream—but the aesthetic is eternal. Even cruelty, betrayal and ruthlessness can, in some situations, be aesthetically justified and even unavoidable choices, and categorically avoiding them can lead to slow continuum attachment and the death of life feeling.*

Olli touches Greta's face and whispers, "I'm sorry. I'm just a little sleepy."

Greta answers, "Don't. Love means never having to say you're sorry."

Love. The word, carelessly tossed off, startles both of them.

Olli knows the quote. It's from *Love Story*. Some love story this is. He almost breaks character, but manages to pull himself together, nods with soldierly charm and genuinely believes in M-particles when a fitting line from Sergeant Bruce, in W.S. Van Dyke's *Rose Marie*, comes instantly to mind: "Well in that case… Your dream prince, reporting for duty!"

They get up and continue talking as they walk through town, listening to each other's voices, but not the words themselves. Their thoughts are trapped behind their words, and the unspoken seeps through between their sentences.

When they come to the compass embedded in the pavement at Compass Square, Olli's fingers feel their way down her arm and their hands join, as his instructions directed. It's pleasant walking down the warm street. Olli's step is light, and Greta moves with him, as sweetly as a dream, more gliding than walking.

The streets are full of racing fans, and of course people he knows from the parish council and publishing circles also walk past. Some of them slow down and turn to look at him. But Olli doesn't look at them. He gazes into the distance, smiling fixedly and squeezing Greta's hand so that he won't lose his hold from sheer weakness. This is no time to wonder what people are thinking when they see publisher and parish-council member Olli Suominen out and about with a pretty, golden-haired woman who is clearly not his wife. His wife, after all, is the one who could suffer if he started to hesitate or lose his nerve, and he wishes he could yell this at acquaintances who stare at him, overcome with righteous shock, but of course that, too, could cause Aino to come to harm. So he will just have to worry about his reputation later, if he's able to fix things such that it even matters.

Olli doesn't venture to look Greta in the eye until they reach Are Square, which is packed with people.

They've all come to look at the eighth wonder of the world, brought to town for the occasion: a rally car on a stage with a famous French driver sitting in it. Children peep at the car and the man from atop their daddies' shoulders; adults shove each other out of the way to get closer. Only two of the people present aren't looking at the car. They're looking at each other.

Greta opens the green of her eyes at Olli. No games now. No teasing.

Just complete openness, which is at the same time a question that shows her own vulnerability.

Olli looks deep into her and thinks that it would be easy to allow himself to sink so deep into that green that he forgot everything else.

They have left many things unsaid, but at that moment they stand facing each other, their souls bared, intertwined, although their bodies are not touching. This moment in a crowd is more intimate than a physical touch or nakedness could ever be.

Then Greta remembers that she has an errand to take care of and Olli says that he should get back to the office.

Before they each go their own way, they exchange a kiss. The touch of their lips is quick and light, an airy goodbye between friends that attracts no attention from anyone around them.

Olli crammed himself into a cab that had just dropped a passenger off in front of the pharmacy, and gave the driver his home address. It sounded strange and unfamiliar as he said it. He repeated it to make sure he hadn't got it wrong.

When he got home, he opened the refrigerator. He was looking for mineral water, but he got some juice instead. He felt like something sweet. The neighbours' lawn mower was yelling outside. He felt like his blood pressure was rising. He took off some clothes, went to the sofa, shut his eyes and forced his body to relax.

Sleep came quickly.

He dreamt about his family.

Olli is lying naked on a towel. Aino is on her own towel next to him. The whole family is spending a holiday on the lake shore at Tuomiojärvi.

His son is building a sandcastle. The towers are surprisingly tall and the whole structure is truly a masterpiece of sand architecture with unbelievably precise details.

Olli is proud of the boy. As the castle grows more and more fantastic, Olli's angst is also growing—he left the camera at home. Maybe he should go and get it and take as many photos as he can while he has the chance.

It's Sunday and there's no one else on the beach. They're all at church. The bells at Taulumäki Church are pealing. Aino sighs guiltily and mumbles that next time they should go to church, too, no matter how beautiful the weather is.

Olli reminds her that because he's in the parish council he's ineligible to go to the services when they're handing out tickets to heaven. "Unfortunately my position of trust prevents the two of you from getting into heaven as well, but somebody has to do this job. And spending eternity under the ground won't be so bad. Even God himself is there, at the intersections of all the secret passages, watching movies."

"Yes, that's what you always say," Aino sighs, and starts spreading suntan lotion on her legs. "And if that's what they said at the parish-council meeting then I guess it must be true."

The heat of the golden sand reaches their skin through the towels. Olli's towel is blue and Aino's is red. Olli wonders what it would be like to lie down with Aino on the red towel. The thought of it makes him feel aroused. Aino notices it and sits up. "Oh, no."

Olli looks at her questioningly.

Aino takes a syringe out of her beach bag. "Maybe we should paralyse that, just to be safe," she says, looking between Olli's legs and smiling uncomfortably. "You know what I mean. So nothing inappropriate happens. Since you are having your midlife crisis."

"No, thanks," Olli says.

"Are you sure?"

"Yes," Olli assures her. "Look, it's already shrinking again… You can hardly even see it now. No need for an injection."

Aino nods and lies back down again. The waves lap. Gulls float across the sky. The wind has a salty smell. Olli informs Aino that Tuomiojärvi isn't a lake any more; it has turned into a sea. There was a long article about it in the newspaper.

"I know that," Aino says. "I can hear the mermaids' song."

Olli notices that Aino's skin is a lovely brown and her physique is statuesque and beautiful. It attracts him and arouses him again. He puts his hand between her legs.

Aino stiffens and looks at the sky. "We shouldn't," she says sadly, glancing around them meaningfully. "You know why…"

"They're not here right now," Olli says. "Besides, we still have one intercourse left in our marriage. If it's all right, I'd like to use it now."

Aino hesitates. "Our son is over there. We can't do it where he can see us."

The boy's sandcastle is now several metres tall and wide. Olli realizes that it's going to be a copy of Notre-Dame cathedral in Paris. What marvellous arches and ornamentation their child has built out of sand!

Then Olli notices something in the water. A school of bare-breasted mermaids has appeared among the waves, close to the shore. They're playing with something that looks like a plastic boat.

"He can go and play for a little while with the mermaids," Olli suggests, kissing his wife's breast, which tastes like chocolate. "I saw on a nature show that they like human children and are happy to suckle them."

Aino smiles, now obviously aroused. "Well, perhaps just for a little while. But if he starts to smell like fish, then you have to scrub him with soap and a brush…"

Aino gets up and leads their son by the hand into the waves, encouraging him to go in deeper, like a good boy—the mermaids are waiting for him. He obeys and the mermaids take him with them. Aino turns and looks at Olli, and Olli becomes frightened.

Her face is chalky white and registers a bottomless sorrow. Olli feels deep horror. The weather has turned dark and cold. Snow is falling.

The mermaids escape beneath the sea. Their son is nowhere to be seen. Aino shrieks like a bird, falls into the waves, and vanishes from sight.

Olli can't move. Little by little the snow blocks his nostrils, his mouth, until his breathing finally stops.

When he woke up, Olli went to read his new instructions on Facebook.

Anne was happy to report that she had arranged for Aino to have an unpaid holiday lasting until Christmas, so Olli didn't have to worry that the school was wondering where she was.

It goes without saying that we will reimburse your wife for all the income that she loses being away from work because of our little project, and we'll pay her an executive level per diem as well. A sum has also been deposited into your account which should admirably cover any costs the project entails for you.

Anne assured Olli that he didn't need to worry about anything, and that their collaboration seemed to be going swimmingly.

Olli tried to believe her, nodding to himself reassuringly. But he started to feel faint and had to go curl up on the sofa for a while before he felt able to look through the Facebook profiles of his wife, Greta and the Blomrooses.

Aino's status said:

Aino Suominen is on holiday! Greetings to everyone in Mäki-Matti!

There was a new photo on her profile. A picture of the boy sitting on the beach building a sandcastle—though not a cathedral—and Aino rubbing suntan lotion on her legs. She was looking straight into the camera. Her mouth smiling, her eyes empty. Maybe they were feeding her tranquillizers, or maybe she was just stressed.

Olli wrote a comment under the photo:

Greetings from Jyväskylä. Don't worry, I'm taking care of everything.

He would have liked to write his wife a long letter and apologize for the way that his past had been mixed up in their present and turned her life into an incomprehensible nightmare. He felt vaguely guilty. When exactly had the Blomrooses decided to meddle in the lives of Greta and the Suominen family? Had it only been once Facebook had thrown them all together?

Clearly the Blomrooses were in control of Aino's Facebook account, and he definitely shouldn't do anything to upset Anne as long as his family was at the mercy of her whims. So he always gave brief, businesslike answers to the Blomrooses' messages and was careful what he wrote to Aino.

Greta's status said:

Play it, Sam. Play 'As Time Goes By'.

Leo and Richard's status hadn't been updated for a long time. There were a couple of mentions of "meeting old friends" in posts from months past. Anne was a more diligent

Facebook user. According to her most recent post she was "atoning for youthful sins before it was too late" and sorry for "any discomfort this is causing for those not involved."

Olli clicked the *Like* button.

For the past few weeks Olli had, with the help of some acquaintances of his, found out what Anne Blomroos had been doing over the years. It was obvious that she was a charming but dangerous sociopath. Of course, Olli knew this already from his days with the Tourula Five, and in particular from the day that the Blomrooses, led by Anne, had destroyed Greta. Anne's Facebook profile said only that she worked in "a leadership position in business".

More thorough research—mostly Googling and enquiries to friends in the business world—told him that Anne Blomroos was a senior executive and leading shareholder in a chemical company. Olli knew a Dutch publisher who had connections to the firm. According to him, the stock value of the company had been falling lately, because of rumours that Anne Blomroos had incurable cancer that had spread to her brain. A brain tumour would certainly explain many things, and make the situation even more to be feared. A person with a terminal disease had nothing to lose.

Olli returned to his wife's profile and stared at the blank picture attached to Karri Kultanen's profile. He had spent two days not daring to click on it. His testicles had gone cold when he thought about what he might see.

When he finally did look, Facebook coolly notified him:

Karri only shares some of his profile information with everyone.
If you know Karri, send him a message or add him as a friend.

He wasn't sure if he was relieved or disappointed. Probably both. *If you know Karri…* Yes, he knew Karri. Or had known him decades ago. Before the boy disappeared into the secret passages. And he did need all the information he could get. So he made himself move his mouse, and Facebook-friended Karri.

He waited for his former friend to confirm, although he wasn't sure what would happen next.

After looking at Facebook a little longer, Olli went downstairs, wrapped himself in a blanket, and started watching old movies, because he couldn't go to sleep. *Casablanca, The 400 Blows, The Bridge on the River Kwai.* At some point he closed his eyes and let the sound of the film recede behind the hum of sleep. Just before he dozed off, Colonel Saito told the men building the bridge: "*Be happy in your work.*"

The next meeting would be at the river. *Wait on the bridge at 7 p.m.*, Anne's message said.

When Greta arrives, rush up to her and kiss her. This time you have to shift the friendship to romance! That is what she hopes and expects. Be brave and make the first move. Kiss her in a way that removes all ambiguity. Read the chapter on stolen kisses in A Guide to the Cinematic Life *and you'll know what to do.*

28

THE RAIN WASHED over the river valley, which looked like an old sepia-toned photograph.

Olli stood on the bridge. He thought about his recent dream, and the dedication on the first page of Greta's book: *For the love of my life, from the girl in the pear-print dress.* The same message in millions of books sold all over the world, and no one knew that the love of Greta Kara's life was Olli Suominen, from Jyväskylä. The mystery had even been discussed in women's magazines.

Olli leant against the railing and watched the footpath that passed under the bridge. Raindrops pattered on his umbrella. He was nervous and anxious. He tried to shake off the feeling the *Guide* called slow continuum attachment—he had a task to accomplish. It was hard not to think about where his family might be right now and what Aino was thinking and feeling about all this.

Olli lit a cigarette. Over the past few days he had started smoking. Not a lot—usually just two or three cigarettes a day—but he hadn't smoked at all before. He had stopped in at the publishing house and, on a whim, pinched a cigarette from the pack on Maiju's desk and lit up when he got outside. It tasted awful and made him cough, but it also calmed his nerves. According to the *Guide*, smoking could help free you of attachment to the continuum.

*A cinematic way of life always has a certain fatalism, and what
could be more fatalistic than allowing yourself to enjoy the aesthetics of cigarette smoke?*

He focused on smoking.

Olli is playing with the smoke, losing himself in the glowing
tip of his cigarette.

That fiery dot is the only thing real in all the grey;
everything else is a dream. The smoke mixing with the wind
is like a wordless poem. According to *A Guide to the Cinematic
Life*, smoking is, at its core, a lyrical, metaphorical and med-
itative activity that can deepen the sense of meaningfulness
and dispel the sensation of ordinariness. A cinematic life
can't take away pain, but it can make it more aesthetic, make
of it a kind of wine of emotion, a music of feeling.

The walking path is between the river and a steep bluff.
The ravine is lined with trees and bushes and along the top
are houses surrounded by wooden fences. The place is cinematically beautiful. It also has drama—with enough heavy
rain the bluff could collapse and send the houses tumbling
into the river.

The path is still empty; the only movement is on the
bridge. A bicycle whizzes past behind Olli's back. Pedestrians
come and go. Each pair of shoes has its own sound, each set of
steps its own rhythm. Gazing over the valley, Olli listens and
tries to guess what kind of person each one passing might be.
A long-legged man in no hurry. An old person in pain with a
walker. A young couple intertwined. A mother with her children, in a rush. A woman in high heels, swinging her hips.

The smell of floral perfume makes Olli turn around. A Veronica Lake copy is coming onto the bridge, headed into town. Maiju?

No. She's shorter and stockier than Maiju, and she has an angry look on her face.

He sees another woman at the opposite end of the bridge in a beret and trench coat, carrying binoculars. She's pretending to use them to watch the birds in the trees along the shore, but they're actually aimed at Olli. He's been trying not to think about it, but it's obvious that the Blomrooses have been watching him and Greta.

In any case they've been watching Greta closely, no doubt through hired henchmen. Anne Blomroos has virtually unlimited resources. There could be a hundred people in Jyväskylä hired to monitor the progress of the Blomrooses' mission of atonement. Their reconnaissance must also include analysts collecting kernels of information and formulating predictions of Greta's behaviour. They have to be getting information somewhere to be able to know where Olli needs to go to run into her.

Olli pretends not to notice the woman. And who knows, she might be an innocent birdwatcher; the spies might be somewhere else, out of sight. He needs to focus on Greta anyway, and forget about other things.

Just as he's starting to suspect that the Blomrooses' information was wrong and Greta is somewhere else today, an umbrella with pears printed all over it comes into view from beneath the bridge.

Olli walks towards the downtown end of the bridge and the stairs that lead to the river. He can see the woman better now. It's Greta, in a dark suit. Olli readies himself. It's time to enact the Blomrooses' kissing scene, and finally set this romance in motion.

He's terrified. Not so much because he is acting against his morals, but because of how much he's enjoying it. Maybe it's the influence of M-particles, he thinks, not sure whether he's serious.

He braces himself to run down the wooden steps. He feels light on his feet.

She's walking down the path, taking no notice of him. Olli waves and is about to shout her name when someone grabs him by the arm.

"Suominen!…"

Olli turned around and saw three gentlemen from the Jyväskylä Club with suits and umbrellas which he recognized immediately as high-quality merchandise. They were obviously on their way to some occasion, or perhaps coming from one. One of the men coughed and said, "So, Mr Suominen, I assume you've paid your club membership?"

The other men chuckled.

Olli was surrounded, the men prodding at him as if he were a horse for sale.

"Well," a man in a hat with a moustache and a red nose said with a sigh, "we're all very busy, we all have to make a living—and luckily, for the present company at least, it's a decent living—but when a man's been elected to the parish council, he ought to have a place where he can take some time out of his day-to-day grind and spend an evening sitting and talking among equals without the riff-raff jumping on his every word, wouldn't you agree? So I'm going ask you straight out, right here before the eyes of God and these humble representatives of the Jyväskylä elite: how long do you plan to keep us waiting for you to join us and take your rightful place in the club? Or do we have to call your wife and ask permission for you to come out and play with the other boys?"

The men laughed.

Olli mumbled something about being in a hurry and smiled apologetically. When he tried to leave, they scolded him for being in such a rush and one of them laid a heavy hand on his shoulder. "Too much hurry's bad for the blood pressure. Isn't that right, boys?"

The others agreed.

Now Olli could smell the cognac on their breath. He said a firm goodbye and moved off so quickly that they made way for him.

The moustached man stumbled and would have fallen if the others hadn't grabbed him. His hat and umbrella fell on the ground and he stared after Olli in shock.

"Did he hit me?" the man asked, panting and red-faced.

"He didn't hit you," the others said, patting him. "Mr Suominen's just in a hurry and didn't feel like chatting with us, nice as we were to him."

Olli mumbled his apologies and ran down the steps. He stopped under the bridge. His temples were throbbing.

Greta was nowhere to be seen.

The gentlemen from the Jyväskylä Club watched him from above, grumbling. Olli wondered if he should go back and offer a proper apology and exchange a few pleasantries with Jyväskylä's movers and shakers.

Then he changed his mind, and started running upriver.

Still no sign of Greta. When he got to the cemetery he sat down on a bench to rest. The rain was stopping. It was warm, but Olli was shivering. He lit a cigarette, then immediately tossed it away.

Eventually he got up and headed towards home. As he started across Puistokatu he noticed that he no longer had his umbrella with him. He went back to the bench. It was empty.

A little farther down the river shore stood a scruffy-looking cocker spaniel. Unless Olli's eyes deceived him, it had his umbrella in its mouth.

He tried to approach the dog, but it turned and ran off.

It took Olli fifteen minutes to walk the two kilometres home. When he got there, he climbed to the second floor, winded, and sat down at the computer to look at Greta's Facebook status.

She had just updated it:

Greta Kara has just come from a walk through the postcard landscape along the shores of Tourujoki, continuing to get to know the old places. A pleasant walk, which nevertheless felt somehow lacking. I guess this cinematic pilgrim was hoping that since she was in the old places she might see an old friend…

Olli wrote a comment on her post, directed more at the Blomrooses than at Greta:

I saw you from the bridge and tried to run after you, but I was held up and lost sight of you. If not for that, you would indeed have seen an old friend…

A moment later Greta's answer appeared:

Olli! Were you really there? I know it sounds silly, but I was actually hoping the whole time that I would run into you. Maybe I sensed you were nearby. Judging by the past few days, it seems Jyväskylä is a surprisingly small town.

Olli thought long about his response, feverishly wondering if he dared suggest they meet that evening. Would that make up for his mistake, or would the Blomrooses be angry that he took the initiative?

While he was thinking these thoughts, a red number one appeared in the notifications slot at the top of the page. It said: *Anne Blomroos posted something on your wall.*

Olli went to his own profile.

Anne had posted a picture on his wall, a scanned image of a crayon drawing, by his son. It showed the boy himself and Aino, on the beach. They were both waving happily. At the top of the picture it said, in wobbly letters, *HI DADDY.*

Along the edges of the picture were dark, threatening-looking shapes. The post was accompanied by a message:

Hello, Olli. Your son asked his mother today when they were going to go home. She answered (beautifully!) that they would go "when these lovely holidays are over". Then he asked when the lovely holidays would be over. And she patiently explained that it would be as soon as Daddy got all his work completely done at home in Jyväskylä. The dear child (he is the sweetest thing!) thought for a moment and then started to cry a little and asked with his little chin trembling, what would happen if Daddy didn't get all his work done? What an adorable child!

Your boy really enjoys drawing! (Here's his latest for you.)

Olli stared at the screen. The hours passed. Sometimes he got up to get a drink of water or take an aspirin. He wrote several messages to Anne and Leo begging, threatening, negotiating, pleading and enquiring in many different ways what Anne meant exactly.

He didn't send any of them. It was wisest not to annoy the Blomrooses now that he'd already made his first mistake. He was sure he would receive another message if he just waited, and maybe it would offer some clarity.

He tried to pass the time by reading the Facebook profiles of his acquaintances, but at some point he let himself fall asleep.

In the dream he finds a video link on his profile and opens it with a sense of foreboding. The video was taken in a small room. The grainy, blurry image jerks. His son is sitting at a table, drawing. Aino is sitting beside him, her eyes blurred.

When the picture is finished, Aino shows it to the camera. *"Here's his last picture for you,"* she says in a crackly voice that sounds like an old gramophone.

She smooths the boy's hair, then takes hold of his wrists. *"I'm so sorry, but I don't think Daddy got his work done."*

The boy nods in resignation, his eyes downcast.

A girl of about ten years old with blonde hair walks into the picture holding a large pair of scissors. Anne Blomroos.

A cute girl, Olli notices. Like a postcard angel. No wonder he had a crush on her as a boy.

Anne looks into the camera, nods to Aino, who obediently holds down the little boy's arms, and begins to snip his fingers off.

29

OLLI'S EYES SHOT OPEN.

As he jerked his head up a series of cracks ran down his spine and he gasped for breath until it felt as if his ribcage was about to burst. It took him a moment to realize he had been dreaming. There was no video from Anne Blomroos on his Facebook profile.

But he did have a message from her in his inbox.

Olli's heart stumbled into an arrhythmic series of thumps. He took a breath and prepared for the worst.

Just as he clicked on the message, the doorbell rang. He ran downstairs. It was a delivery. "Will you sign for this?"

The parcel was about the size of a box of margarine, addressed to Aino Suominen. He carried it to the kitchen table, sat down in a chair a couple of metres away and stared at it in disbelief.

What would the Blomrooses send to him after what had happened? What could be in that package? He tried not to think of his dream. Instead he thought of Schrödinger's cat.

Finally he started to open the box, feeling like an executioner.

There were no child's fingers in the box, just a silk handkerchief with the embroidered monogram OS. His initials.

With his legs shaking beneath him, covered in a cold sweat, he returned to the computer and read the message.

Olli my friend, your family sends their greetings. They're both well. Be on Puistokatu, at the wall of the old cemetery, tomorrow at 7 p.m. Wipe your tears away and take care that your heroine gets her kiss this time. Show some passion. She's expecting it, although she's too afraid to show it.

The message ended with a quote from *A Guide to the Cinematic Life*, the chapter titled 'Stolen Kisses':

Of all the crimes one can commit, stealing a kiss may be the most forgivable. Truffaut even named a whole film after it.

Stealing a kiss doesn't mean forcing a kiss on anyone, but rather that the recipient of the kiss is surprised and has not given any verbal or nonverbal permission. When done right, however, the victim allows the kiss to happen, even if she has done nothing to initiate it, and may even reciprocate if she is not moved to resist. In either case, the kiss stealer should expect to receive a talking-to from her. If a womanly slap on the face seems too high a price to pay, he should forget the whole thing. Ideally, however, the victim's resistance quickly melts, and a kiss that was stolen to begin with quickly becomes a classic kiss of passion.

Of course, a woman can also steal a kiss from a man. In that case the situation becomes more complicated. While a man who steals a kiss and is rebuffed is a somewhat comical but at the same time romantic (and by no means ridiculous) hero, a woman thief whose kiss is refused becomes a tragically fearsome, desperate and sometimes even contemptible creature—familiar from film noir—and is condemned to ruination for her unrequited passion. On the other hand a woman whose stolen kiss is not refused is likely to succeed in wrapping her male victim around her little finger, thus becoming a femme fatale, and can then use her power over him in whatever way she wishes. (More on the rules of the femme fatale in the next chapter.)

The riskiest stolen kisses, of course, occur when both parties are of the same sex. With the exception of certain specific settings (such as a gay bar), the probability of the kiss being rejected is increased exponentially. In the best cases, the rejected homosexual kiss leads to comic embarrassment, but in many situations it is likely to end in tragedy. As a cinematic character, the male homosexual thirsting for love is one of the most tragic, at least when it comes to traditional cinema (a tradition for which the character of Jack Twist in the film Brokeback Mountain *represents a breaking point of sorts). Films with more modern values—such as Wong Kar-wai's* Happy Together, *which normalizes homosexuality—are more merciful to him.*

As with all cinematic acts, stealing kisses demands a sense of space and rhythm and an ability to influence the mood so that every aspect of the situation points to the kiss like a road sign. I hardly need add that the M-particles in magical places invariably facilitate the success of the endeavour by decreasing the slow continuum attachment of both parties.

(See next page for stills of cinema's most famous stolen kisses.)

Greta Kara opens the iron gate in front of the chapel. She hasn't yet noticed Olli and doesn't know he's watching her, but she moves with careful grace, like an actress who can hear the hum of cameras and feel the heat of the spotlight wherever she goes. Greta is radiant, but the day is cold and grey. The air holds a hint of coming rain.

Olli has a small red umbrella. It belongs to Aino. It was

the only one he could find. He's smoking a cigarette. The smoke strengthens his deep cinematic self and dispels his insecurity.

Her pale figure moves from the cemetery to the other side of the wall, the world of the living. The banging of the gate interrupts the pastor's flow of words, carried across the graveyard. *From dust you came, to dust you shall return.*

A group dressed in black is crowded around an open grave like a flock of crows. As she walks past them, Greta stands out like a protest against the transience of it all, in a conical white hat, a white dress that leaves her arms bare and a handbag of the same colour. Felliniesque. "A combination of tastelessness, sensuality and exuberant colour," as the *Guide to the Cinematic Life* put it.

Olli steps out from the shade of a maple tree, drops his cigarette and rubs it out with his foot.

Greta's face brightens. "Well hello, Olli. I suppose I should be surprised. But I'm not. I had a hunch I would see you somewhere today. This lovely hillside town is apparently so small that we can't go a day without running into each other, although I seem to have accidentally averted that fate yesterday... You aren't stalking me, are you, Mr Suominen? Following me around?... Ha. As if a busy man like you didn't have more important things to do. Conspiracy theories aside, though, I didn't mention anything about this on Facebook. It's weird and stimulating this way, don't you think? In a good way. I went out for a walk, my feet brought me here, and on a whim I thought for once that I would put some flowers on Anna's grave, since I am in Jyväskylä."

"Anna's grave?"

Greta's brow furrowed and her nose scrunched up, making her look like a cross little animal. "Olli, if you don't remember Aunt Anna, I'm going to be upset. But I refuse to believe that you are one of those horrible people who treat the past like some trivial movie they remember watching long ago, or at least partway through, but they can't recall the names of the actors or the plot, and they don't care to… *The love interest was the blonde one. Or was it the other girl?… No, it was definitely the one with the golden hair. And they met at a dance or on the beach or maybe on a carousel, I can't remember, but anyway, then something bad happened to them… or did they get to be together in the end?"*

Greta's stream of words starts light-heartedly but turns bitter at the end. Her eyes grow wet. Black streaks run down her cheeks.

She raises a hand in front of her face. "Oh no. Olli, be the gentleman I know you are and don't look at me," she sighs.

Olli hands her the handkerchief the Blomrooses sent him. She takes it, thanks him and turns half away from him.

"I can't bear it that you, of all the people in the world, should see me like this. I'm dreadful. Pitiful. Ugly. Make-up down my cheeks… You'll think I look like a dressed-up raccoon—No, don't deny it, you're absolutely right. I'm a catastrophe. I ought to pull my Donna Vinci right down over my eyes and run home, on the side streets so no one will see me. I would call a taxi but I left my phone at home. Do you have a phone with you, Olli? Please call a cab right now to take the aesthetic catastrophe known as Greta Kara where no one can look at her…"

She returns his handkerchief, stained with mascara, takes

out a mother-of-pearl compact, lets out a little cry of alarm and begins to repair her make-up. Her hands are shaking. "I can't get in a taxi looking like this," she whispers, shaking her head.

Olli senses that she's teetering on the edge of some kind of breaking point. "Of course I remember Aunt Anna," he says. "I just didn't know she was buried here."

Greta isn't listening. She's concentrated on tidying her appearance.

Olli tries not to look at her too directly so as not to distress her any more. It's obvious that his gaze is painful to her. After what happened thirty years ago—the way that their last meeting ended—it's understandable that she would want to be well groomed and cinematically beautiful when she's with him.

That's fine with Olli. He wants to see her as beautiful and as perfect as she can be, too, out of respect and fondness, and at this moment—identified as he is with the character that his deep cinematic self has created—out of a kind of love for her, because it's so terribly important to her.

"I didn't even know that Aunt Anna was dead. Though I didn't really think she was alive, either. I suppose I imagined she was still baking cookies in her kitchen in old Tourula, but those cookies were eaten up and the crumbs brushed away years ago. That place doesn't even exist any more, but that doesn't stop me from dreaming about it every night."

Olli lights another cigarette to cover the embarrassment he feels at what he's just tacitly revealed.

Greta looks past her mirror to somewhere far away, years away. "She died five years ago. Her body gave out. Drink did her in."

"How sad. I wouldn't have guessed…"

"Yeah."

Greta manoeuvres her lip-liner with frenzied motions. The funeral party in the distance has come to the part where each person takes a turn dropping sand onto the coffin. Greta gives her lips a final check, packs her make-up into her handbag and starts across the car park towards town. She walks ahead of him, her high heels clicking over the asphalt, and Olli follows in unhurried steps.

The sound of traffic on Puistokatu rises and falls like ocean waves.

The *City Guide* manuscript describes the street thus:

Puistokatu is like a lost fragment of Paris. The old cemetery is reminiscent of Paris's Cimetière du Père Lachaise, and in other ways the street has the feeling of one of Paris's side streets. In fact, viewed from certain points, there is a street near Père Lachaise that is almost identical to Jyväskylä's Puistokatu (see map).

A car arrives with another funeral party made up of five stocky men and a skinny little girl in pigtails and a black mourning dress. She curtsies to Greta as they walk past.

"Hello, child," Greta says, striving for kindness. There is a choked sound in her voice. As they move away she takes Olli's arm and whispers breathily, "Do you think her mother has died? I can't bear it…"

She looks at Olli wide-eyed, demandingly, waiting for his reply.

"I don't think so," Olli says. "Perhaps her grandmother.

Or some old relative who's been sick for a long time. After a long illness, death is a relief."

"But where is her mother, then?" Greta insists, looking back at the group and grabbing hold of his coat as if to reproach him. "Surely no woman would send her little girl alone to a funeral and stay home to wash the dishes or watch television. Oh yes, I know where her mother is. She's lying dead in her casket. That girl is about to watch as her mother is lowered into the ground in a wooden box and covered with dirt. Oh Lord. The mother of a girl that young can't be very old herself…"

Olli removes Greta's hands from his lapels and squeezes them so tightly for a moment that her eyes moisten. "These things happen," he says coldly. "Bad things happen. People die. Even children. No one can grieve for every dead person. We each have our own dead to cry over. If not today, then maybe tomorrow, if we haven't wound up under the dirt ourselves for somebody else to grieve."

He thinks of Aino and the boy, on a beach somewhere far away, waiting for him to complete his task and earn them a safe return home. *Wipe your tears away and take care that your heroine gets her kiss this time. Show some passion. She's expecting it, although she's too afraid to show it.*

Greta's make-up starts to run again and Olli loosens his grip. He takes out his handkerchief and uses it to wipe her eyes, as if she were a little child.

"Maybe she died of some illness," Greta whispers, unresisting, the tears streaming down her cheeks. "Or maybe she was in a car accident, or was run over. I hope she had time to say goodbye to her husband and daughter. Oh Olli!

It's so terribly sad when people are torn from their loved ones and don't even have a chance for a proper goodbye! What point is there in anything when everything that's beautiful can end at any moment, with no warning?"

Olli puts his handkerchief in his pocket. The worst damage is repaired now. Greta stands looking at him, sad and petulant, as if the impermanence of everything were somehow his fault, or at least his to explain.

There's nothing he can do about her fear. Words are useless. Greta has plenty of words of her own. The entire *Guide to the Cinematic Life* is an attempt to use words to answer a question that torments the author herself.

And the book's answer is that lasting happiness may be impossible and joy impermanent, but life can at least be made aesthetically beautiful.

A beautiful story has a beautiful beginning and a beautiful ending. The illusion of happiness makes the beginning beautiful, but the ending draws its beauty from pain.

Olli dispenses with words, pulls Greta close to him, looks into her eyes, lays the fingers of his left hand along the back of her slender neck and kisses her.

The red umbrella falls to the ground with a clunk. A warm wind takes hold of Greta's hat and throws it into the Puistokatu traffic.

At first she's cold and stiff in his arms, as if in the sudden grip of death. Gradually the stiffness melts. Olli feels her lips arch into a smile. She answers his kiss, shyly at first, then devouring his mouth like a hungry predator.

Her delicate frame presses tightly against him and trembles uncontrollably. It's the same greedy desire Olli remembers discovering in her years ago.

When they finally break away from each other, hot and breathless, Greta sighs and lays her head against his chest. "I can hear your heartbeat," she whispers. "It's pounding so fast. Because of me? For my sake? Silly thing. It still remembers me, after all this time. How many times will it beat before you're taken away from me again…"

Olli breathes in the gold of her hair. He is too roiled with emotion to speak. Contradictory thoughts chase and tear at each other in his mind.

His gaze falls on a pale white wall on the other side of the street. On it is a painted Goodyear tyre ad, blue letters and a tyre with wings. That sign has followed him through all these years. He points it out to Greta and they look first at the ad, then at each other, smiling in amazement. A moment from thirty years ago rises from the secret passages of memory, its colours deepening until it's all too easy to fall into.

It was when the Five were breaking up and Olli was walking down Puistokatu with Greta, and they stopped to look at this ad and kissed under the umbrella, hidden from the adults walking by. Olli remembers now that it was an unusual, domed umbrella that Aunt Anna had brought home from France. It was the same kind that Maura at the umbrella shop ordered for him.

And now here they are in the same spot, holding on to each other, Olli and his pear-print girl from Tourula. Olli touches Greta's cheek and looks into the green of her eyes, amazed, as if he has only just now understood who is in his arms.

The warm wind wraps itself around them.

For a few short breaths everything that has happened since that summer they shared fades away and drops into meaninglessness.

Then Olli remembers again that somewhere in the world, right now, a woman and child are on a beach waiting for the day when they can return home.

30

*The deep cinematic self is an artist that sees life above all as
an aesthetic construct. It is like the voice of the conscience but
instead of moralizing it leads us to make cinematic choices and
interpret our roles as well as we possibly can. It also silences
the stage fright of slow continuum attachment so that stories
can be set in motion and cinematicness can be achieved.*

GRETA KARA,
A Guide to the Cinematic Life

As Olli begins to relive a story that started and ended thirty
years before, he feels guilty because at times it is frighteningly
easy to let himself get caught up in it. Every time he meets
Greta in Jyväskylä's magical places he feels the M-particles
affecting his mood, feels parts of his life slowly but surely
shifting into new positions within his consciousness. His
whole way of thinking is gradually changing, and it terrifies
him.

But he has to surrender to the change and let his deep
cinematic self take over, for his family's sake. He has to throw
himself into the love story with Greta Kara; any superficiality
or pretending would only lead to failure, and he has never
learnt to act.

Of course the thought of his wife and son at the mercy of
the Blomroos siblings casts a shadow over every moment with
Greta, but the whole thing is steeped in a cinematic aesthetic,

turning all his conflicting feelings into an emotional work of art.

Every time he comes home from one of their meetings, his deep self falls asleep. That's when the seriousness of the situation hits him: his wife and child are being held hostage by psychopaths in some foreign country; he himself is holed up in his house, afraid to tell anyone about his predicament and having daily trysts with a woman he knew for one summer as a child.

While he waits for new instructions, Olli searches Facebook for signs that Aino and the boy are all right. And he finds new photos on Aino's profile every day. They show mother and son in various travel destinations.

Apparently they are being flown to a new location every couple of days.

The photos come from beautiful, exotic, picture-perfect places around the world. In the newest one Aino is smiling into the camera, and the boy doesn't look particularly sad, either.

They're getting used to this, too.

31

O N THE CORNER OPPOSITE the university library is the
Puistokatu cafe kiosk. Greta is sitting on the terrace.
On the table are two glasses of raspberry soda. In the glasses
are two straws.

Olli walks up, sits down across from her, leans his
umbrella against his chair and smiles.

Today Greta looks like Grace Kelly in *To Catch a Thief.*
The same pink dress with the white patterns, sleeveless, her
golden hair pulled back. The look becomes her.

Olli's dark-grey coat and trousers are enough like Cary
Grant's that they complement each other's cinematicness.

In the park below, children run squealing towards the
carousel with the boy's head on top, in the same spot as it
was decades before. That was where Olli befriended the
Blomrooses and Karri and touched Anne for the first time.
Greta searches his face and says nothing for a long time.
An unspoken greeting hangs in the air between them. Olli
continues to smile, purposely teasing her.

Finally Greta speaks. "I had strange, disturbing dreams
all night. I woke up after noon, ate breakfast, put on my
make-up, played the piano and went out half an hour ago. I
was walking downtown and on a whim I sat down here on
the terrace. I bought a bottle of soda, the same kind we used
to drink, in the same place. We used to come here because
we thought the Blomrooses might not come to this part of

town. We even kissed. We let people see that we were lovers. You said that it was like we were in some other country, so we could behave as we wished."

Olli says he can almost remember.

Greta purses her lips reproachfully. "The park has changed a little over the years, but the spirit of it is the same. There are still M-particles here. Not as many as there were then, but enough. So, today I came here and asked for two glasses and poured soda in both of them. I thought that if I just believed hard enough, you would appear somehow, like in a dream. I waited five minutes. Just as I thought I was being a silly, stupid girl, you did appear, and here you are. So have some soda, my darling."

Greta is smoking a cigarette. Olli feels like one, too. He takes a pack of menthols out of his jacket pocket and starts searching his pockets for a lighter. He's left it at home.

Greta rummages in her black handbag, takes out a gold-coloured, old-looking lighter and says, "You know, this Barlow lighter was a gift from Frank Sinatra."

"Really?"

Olli sucks the flame into his cigarette.

"Or so I was told," Greta says. "He didn't give the lighter to me, of course. It was a gift to Judy Garland. I was in Paris and feeling lonely and rich, and I wanted to treat myself. I went to an auction. I saw the lighter there and heard its story. I paid three thousand euros for it, so if they tricked me, I don't want to know about it. You see darling, once a thing is done and there's nothing I can do about it any more, if I'm offered a pleasant lie about it or a depressing truth, I'll take the lie."

She smiles and Olli secretly trembles at her exquisiteness.

Olli has been to Paris six times as an adult, every time to represent the publishing house at the March book fair. Two years ago he happened upon an exhibition at the Pompidou and stood for an entire hour looking at one painting.

It was Gustav Klimt's *Judith I*.

Olli wanted the painting for himself, although he knew he couldn't have it. Perhaps precisely because he knew he couldn't have it. There were poster reproductions of the painting at the museum shop, but they weren't what he wanted. He wanted the original. It wasn't the most beautiful painting he had ever seen, but it felt as if it belonged to him. He stood admiring it and felt an almost sexual desire for the sensuous woman in the picture.

Finally he had to make himself leave so that he wouldn't grab the painting and try to take it out of the museum before anyone could stop him.

As he gazes now at Greta transformed into Grace Kelly, he's overcome with the same need to possess her that he felt for that Klimt painting.

He finds himself writing in his mind the same description of Greta that he wrote on lined paper once when he was sixteen:

She walks quickly, her body tense, yet supple as a cat's tail, her head held high, self-assured, dropping words sometimes casually, sometimes excitedly, wrapped in mysterious scents, so that her whole way of being reaches out to the senses of the men who turn to look, and says, "Keep up with me and you just might catch me."

Greta seems to sense his thoughts or at least the feelings behind them. Her sea-green eyes flash. Her slender hand takes hold of his shovel-like one and squeezes tight and she glows as if she's just been given a gift.

32

Lounais Park is one of Jyväskylä's oldest parks. It was estab-
lished in the 1860s and is known throughout Finland for the
music festivals that have been held there since the 1880s. Over
the course of its history the park has had many different more
or less temporary bandstands and amphitheatres, including the
vaulted festival stage designed by Alvar Aalto for the upper part
of the park in 1924. The present outdoor stage was designed
by Olavi Kivimaa in 1954. On the upper edge of the park is a
kiosk cafe which was refurbished at the turn of the millennium.
The park also has a children's play area, with its peculiar old
boy's head carousel, preserved through many decades up to the
present.

Lounais Park has its own distinct atmosphere and its
meaningfulness particle radiation levels are powerful. It also
sits above numerous secret passages which rest close to the sur-
face and intersect right below the carousel.

GRETA KARA,
Magical City Guide Number One: Jyväskylä

On the kiosk cafe terrace, people come and go. Olli and
Greta remain. Their eyes plumb each other's dark depths
across the table.

Olli plays with his smoke.

Greta sucks raspberry soda through her straw, thirsty
and agitated, her green irises sparkling with girlish joy at a

situation which had seemed so hopeless and now seems to be turning to triumph.

Olli notices that he can feel their connection working again. He remembers suddenly how easy it once was for them to read each other: each knowing what the other was feeling and sometimes able to guess with frightening accuracy what thoughts were turning in the other's head. Maybe they had been peeking into each other all this time by means of their dreams.

The memory is attached to a bunch of emotional mycelia and Olli is moved when he realizes that he's never managed to create the same connection with anyone else in his life, not even his wife.

His deep self nods approval and makes some additional adjustments to his mental state.

They've been meeting almost every day for three weeks now. The fourth day was the only one when he wasn't given any orders except to rest for a while and wait. On every other day the Blomrooses have informed Olli which magical place Greta will be visiting and when, and Olli has sought her out according to their instructions.

Their relationship has remained relatively chaste, limited to kisses exchanged under his umbrella in various places around the city. Once, however, at the front gate of the paper mill, Greta's hand grazed the front of his trousers as if by accident, and she smiled, mischievously at first, then blushing. Every time they parted, they went their own ways without planning or promising anything, Greta to her unknown lodgings and Olli, as far as Greta knew, home to his family.

Coming home to an empty house has become more difficult each time.

Greta no doubt believes that these frequent encounters are due to their spiritual connection, that Olli's ability to find where she is comes from some kind of romantic intuition. This, of course, makes the whole thing that much more magical in her eyes. Or maybe she's only pretending to believe that they have some larger connection between them because of their magical cinematicness, and she secretly assumes that Olli has her under some sort of surveillance. *You see darling, once a thing is done and there's nothing I can do about it any more, if I'm offered a pleasant lie about it or a depressing truth, I'll take the lie.*

Whatever the case, when he can't reveal the truth about the Blomrooses' messages, or his family, or anything else, Olli has the paradoxical feeling of being betrayed himself.

And there are quite a few things that he would like to tell Greta, not to mention questions he would like to ask her. For instance, he's mystified at how the Blomrooses are able to know a day ahead of time where she'll go, and at what time.

The most logical explanation is that she's working with the Blomrooses. But Olli doesn't believe that. Because he can see in her eyes that she would never conspire against him. And besides, Greta hates and fears the Blomrooses after what they did to her.

Another thing that Olli hasn't asked her about is where in Jyväskylä she's staying. He has the impression that it's not a hotel but a house somewhere north of the city centre.

Each cinematic encounter is a complex dance of expressions, gestures, words, intentions, cues, sensations, actions and retreats, the *Guide to the Cinematic Life* says. And indeed, in the present situation certain things feel natural to say or do while others break the rhythm and flatten the mood. They're like errors that the two of them, caught up in the cinematic moment, instinctively avoid to the very last. It's remarkably difficult to ask questions if they don't seem to belong in the built-in script of an encounter.

When they've emptied their glasses of raspberry soda, Olli and Greta walk down the stairs that lead to Lounais Park. They find a bench sheltered by shrubbery and sit down to watch the children ride around on the carousel. The sky has gone grey. It's drizzling. A bus drives by on the street below, its chassis rattling over the cobblestones.

Greta lights a cigarette.

Olli opens his black umbrella, which is large enough to cover them both. It's the Chantal Thomass design dome umbrella, direct from France. He picked it up the day before when Maura called to tell him that his order had arrived. Greta looks at the umbrella in surprise and starts to reminisce, smiling dreamily, about the summer they shared thirty years ago.

She knows how to choose her words skilfully. Her talk brings the past closer, close enough to touch the present, like the hand of a beloved. The years that have grown up between them gradually fade until they lose their meaning completely.

His consciousness saturated with M-particles, Olli closes his eyes to listen to the waves of Greta's words and the rhythm of raindrops on the umbrella.

33

As Olli's eighth and last summer holiday in Tourula is coming to an end, it's obvious to all of them that the Tourula Five are no more.

The tart smell of autumn rises from deep in the earth and birds gather in restless flocks. It's been raining all summer. Little by little the rain is wearing the green landscape down to shades of brown, and Olli, Anne, Riku and Leo look at each other as if they were strangers. The Five have spent the whole summer without Karri, who disappeared into the secret passages the summer before.

They don't go into the secret passages any more; without Karri they don't even know how to find them. Their memories of the passageways are fading, too, like long-ago dreams.

The Blomrooses have been hanging around Aunt Anna's house and Olli has gone to see them, but even their best visits have been pitiful attempts to recapture something that no longer exists. Even Aunt Anna's treats have lost their flavour, and Anna herself is nervous and strangely brusque now, and she's often drunk.

They've tried to go on picnics like they used to, but without their expeditions in the secret passages their outings wither to listless wanderings and the heavy rains drive them back indoors. There's not much to talk about and attempts at the old banter turn into arguments. Anne in particular needles the others; it's especially hard for her to accept that Karri is gone. Riku throws tantrums, has fits of rage, breaks things—he jumped Olli once. Leo had to calm him down. Riku broke two fingers and Olli came away with a bloody nose.

Leo's usual firm patience is wearing thin, too, and his gloomy outbursts frighten the others. Once when Leo seemed particularly sullen, Anne blurted that he ought to find himself a woman, or at least go and jerk off. Leo turned pale and stood up. He had grown considerably since the previous summer and thickened up, and when he glared at Anne, a vein in his temple throbbing, she left the house.

There are still those moments when everything feels like it used to be. At those times the remaining members of the Tourula Five look at each other with their eyes shining and the colours seem to brighten. But that happens less and less often, and the moments are slipping away from them faster than the mice that used to run away from Timi.

Olli is shocked that the Blomrooses have started to seem ordinary to him, even unpleasant, just like his classmates in Koirakkala. They seem tired of his company, too. They don't seem even to enjoy being with each other. Karri is gone, and with him the magic that they shared for so many summers.

The Blomrooses have pilfered Aunt Anna's cognac a few times and tried to medicate away the tedium. Olli didn't want to touch the alcohol, at least not since the time that Anne, alone in the house, drank until she was so messed up that she was laughing like a lunatic, and broke the porcelain cat and the floor lamp, and ended up making a pass at Olli.

"You've wanted this for a long time, Olli," she purred, and

took off her shirt. Her nipples shone through her white bra. Her fingers groped at his fly.

It was true that Olli had dreamt of something like this at one time. But now Anne smelt disgusting—and Olli's heart belonged to another. So he turned his back to her and said as kindly as he could that he wasn't interested, and suggested in a fatherly way that she put her clothes on and have a cup of coffee and clean up after herself.

She wouldn't listen. She put his hand between her legs and promised that he could do whatever he wanted as long as he kept it to himself, promised she wouldn't get pregnant.

It scared him, and he jerked his hand away. It was wet and slippery and smelt weird.

They stared at each other.

Then she fell onto her hands and knees and started throwing up on the rug and Olli ran out of the house.

The next day Anne was washing the rug in the yard and acting like nothing had happened. But since then she's been colder towards him.

That was two weeks ago. In three days Olli's father will come to take him back to Koirakkala. The day after that school starts. Olli doesn't want to think about that yet. He sits at the table drinking juice and eating pastries with Leo, Riku and Anne. He's come to say his goodbyes to Aunt Anna and the Blomrooses today so that he can spend the rest of his holidays with the girl in the pear-print dress.

The clock ticks on the wall. Riku gobbles down one pastry after another. Anne sips from her coffee cup, her face tight. Leo is sunk in thought.

Olli wants to leave but can't bring himself to get up from the table. He should be polite.

The house has been different since Karri went into the secret passages. The air is hard to breathe. There's not enough light even with all the lights on. Aunt Anna doesn't feel like taking care of the house or her summer guests any more. She just talks about how much she misses her son.

The Blomrooses said a couple of days ago that they won't be coming to Tourula for the summer next year. Anne is planning a beach holiday somewhere warm.

Aunt Anna is standing at the sink. Her hands hang at her sides. She's wearing her bright-yellow summer dress, but she looks grey. Her plumpness has thinned and shrivelled.

"Oh how I miss that boy," she sighs again. She's slurring her words a bit from the cognac, although she tries to speak carefully. "One of the neighbours asked about Karri. I couldn't even begin to explain it to them. I don't understand myself what happened to my Karri."

Life returns to her a little as her temper flares. "Didn't I do everything for him? I even took him to Paris so he could get out of this little town for a while and fill his head with the fresh air of Europe. We saw the Eiffel Tower. We went to the Moulin Rouge… You raise a child for a decade and a half to be a good boy and then all of a sudden you've got a flirty little girl in his place, a complete and utter stranger."

From upstairs comes the sound of a piano beginning to play. Olli doesn't know very much about classical music but he knows that the piece is Chopin's Prelude no. 16. He can't help but admire the skilfulness of the playing.

Aunt Anna sways a little and says, "I told the neighbours

that my son moved to Sweden to live with his father, to make room for my sister's daughter. I said that she came here from Helsinki when her mother's arthritis got so bad that she had to move into a nursing home. They raised their eyebrows and said, 'Oh, is that so. And a very pretty girl you got, too. Just like a little Goldilocks in a fairy tale.'"

She thinks for a moment and adds, "Of course, Karri wasn't perfect. I'm not saying he was. He was a moody, difficult child, and I never could tell what he was thinking. He never learnt to play the piano, either, in spite of all his lessons. But I'd still trade that silly, musical girl straight across for Karri if I could."

"You're not the only one," Anne mutters, her eyes glued to the table.

The music has stopped now.

There's a squeak at the top of the stairs and everyone's neck stiffens. Olli looks towards the landing, sees a flash of the pear-print dress, and his face flushes.

Greta has avoided the Blomrooses ever since she arrived. She comes down to get something to eat when the others are outside, and when she's at home she stays in her own room, where no one else feels like going any more. She slips in and out of the house without anyone noticing. When she's not playing the piano it's easy to forget she exists, which suits Aunt Anna and the Blomrooses fine.

Olli and Greta have kept their meetings secret from everyone else. They've been thrown together a couple of times when Aunt Anna or the Blomrooses were around and smoothly pretended that they hardly noticed each other.

Now Greta appears in the kitchen in her pear-print dress.

Her golden hair is shining. Her green eyes glance at Olli shyly, as if seeking courage, then her chin lifts and her gaze sharpens. It moves around the room, stopping at each person for an excruciatingly long time. No one meets her eye. Anne turns pale and looks ill. Riku and Leo stiffen, as if waiting for a dog to attack.

Aunt Anna can't do anything but stare at the girl speechlessly.

Greta puts a radiant smile on her face, walks across the kitchen, and stands at the window. She looks outside with her head high, humming a cheerful little tune.

"*The fact that you love me, Olli, makes me like myself, too,*" she whispered yesterday as they lay side by side in their secret room. "*You know, maybe I don't want to be ashamed of myself any more.*"

"Do you think it will rain some more?" Greta wonders aloud, turning to look at them. She smiles innocently, defiantly. "I'll bet we're going to have a real downpour. Good. I like the rain."

Aunt Anna scratches her arm. The muscles of her face are working under the skin. Her cheeks redden. She bites her lower lip until a drop of blood drips down her chin. As if by agreement the Blomrooses get up from the table and march out. After a moment's hesitation Olli follows, but tries to do so in such a way that his departure can't be interpreted as a protest. Something wriggles in his belly. He has no way, and no desire, to interfere in what happens in that house. It's a matter between a mother and child. He can meet Greta later, after dark.

The Blomrooses are standing outside under the apple

tree, speaking in whispers, their eyes red, their faces hard as stone. It's starting to rain. Olli senses that they don't want his company and leaves, heads for his grandparents' house.

The thought of his girl in the pear-print dress makes his skin tingle and moves the fluttering from his belly to his chest. When the rain starts to fall harder, he breaks into a run.

34

A T THE BOTTOM of the steep ravine flows the Touru River. The house is not far from the shore. There's just a narrow strip of hilly land between, covered in meadow and leafy trees. There are secret passages there, too, if the atmosphere of the place is any indication.

You can smell the river there, and particularly could back when the paper mill used to pour its waste water into the river. Aunt Anna's house and the Blomrooses are many turns and junctions behind Olli now; he can relax. When there's a real rain the rest of the world disappears on the other side of the roaring water. At those times, this is a good place to be.

Olli and Greta always arrive separately, usually Greta first and Olli a little later. Once they're sure that no one is watching, they go into the yard and slip inside the house.

Until last winter the place was occupied by the old railway-man who got his bike back thanks to the Tourula Five. When the old man died, the house was left empty. The heirs to the place came and hauled away a truckload of his belongings, then left the rest, locked up the house and never came back.

On the very first day of the school holidays Greta leads Olli to the place. It's raining. They hide under their shared umbrella. Greta breaks a porch window, slips inside, opens the door and smiles slyly at him. Please come in, my darling. Welcome home. I've been expecting you. Did you have a nice day?

The ground floor has a high ceiling. Daylight penetrates the room through large uncurtained windows and makes everything too bare, too defenceless, so the secret lovers can't linger in the room for very long.

No furniture. No carpet. On the wall is a painting of a steam engine that the heirs didn't want for some reason. The dusty wood floor is strewn with magazines, empty bottles, books, dishes and rusty tools.

When they come to the house for the first time, Olli picks up a pair of pliers, a frame saw and a bent gimlet, and says that as the new owner he ought to get started remodelling the place. Greta laughs.

Don't bother, she says, Tourula's a dying neighbourhood. New buildings aren't allowed and renovating old places is discouraged. The young people are moving away and the old people are staying in their dilapidated houses hoping that they'll have time to finish living their lives before the city makes them leave. The gentry of Jyväskylä has plans for Tourula, and that includes destroying everything old.

Olli drops the tools. The thought of destroying Tourula makes him sad.

Greta comes to him and wraps her arms around his neck. Don't worry, she whispers in his ear. Even if everyone else leaves, we'll stay here forever.

The stairs are just off the front entry. They lead to a room that has a ceramic stove, an old piano and a bed with covers. There are thick red curtains over the window. They filter the sunshine to softness, slow the passage of time, separate their time alone together from the world outside.

They have walked together through the city, publicly, in

broad daylight, like innocent friends. They've bought ice cream from the booth on Puistokatu, slipped into the Adams or the Maxim to see a movie, sat next to the blue-bottomed fountain in the old church park, chased the pigeons in the plaza. They always have the large umbrella Aunt Anna bought in France. In the shelter of its deep, pastel-green dome they can exchange kisses without anyone knowing.

The rain is a good excuse to hide under the umbrella. It frees them to be lovers elsewhere as well, like here in this room.

What they do in the upstairs room of the abandoned house is their own business.

They talk a lot, of course. They plan their future. Daydream. In a few years we'll go to Paris and rent a room on the banks of the Seine, they vow with a kiss. We'll have coffee and cream tarts in little street cafes, drink red wine in the Latin Quarter, walk hand in hand down the Champs-Élysées, and climb up the Eiffel Tower and kiss at the top where the whole world can see us.

But what about before that? The summer holiday is almost over and we'll have to be apart…

Of course we'll see each other in the winter, too; we'll arrange it somehow. You can come here, or I'll go there. We'll have weekends and holidays, after all. We'll miss each other, sometimes terribly, but what is there to keep us apart? Nothing. Nothing at all. We'll stay together, we'll call each other, write each other letters, and then when we're of age we'll thumb our noses at the rest of the world and get married and have dozens of children…

They laugh a lot.

And then there are other times. Sometimes Greta lays

her head on Olli's breast and listens to the pounding of the rain on the roof and Olli strokes her golden hair and dark thoughts overcome her and she starts to talk about them in a low voice, the salty drops of her sadness falling on his skin.

And sometimes she asks Olli to take off his clothes and she caresses him with her mouth and her hands. At first he was too shy. As the summer passed he learnt to enjoy it more and more. What Greta does to him is so sweet, so private, that he can't even think about it afterwards. The darkness of the room makes it all unreal, like it's all half a dream.

Greta herself refuses to take off the pear-print dress. She says it's because her body isn't the way it's supposed to be. She sometimes lets Olli touch her naked body under the dress but she guides his hands, and she's tense the whole while.

Her breasts are small, quite different from Aunt Anna's, and smaller than Anne's. Olli likes them.

And he likes the slim lines of her body, the softness of her skin.

One day when Greta is lying on the bed with her eyes shut Olli lifts the hem of her dress and touches her belly, then the skin of her thighs. Her breath quickens. Her hips start to move hungrily. Her tongue licks her lips.

Olli reads these signs as an invitation, and pushes his hand into her underwear.

Then she freezes, jumps to her feet, and slaps him in the face. Don't ever do that, do you hear me? If you do I'll kill you.

Her dark fury flares, then disappears.

The familiar, playful spark lights up her eyes again. Then it, too is extinguished by bewilderment.

Hey, you're bleeding. Did I hit you? I couldn't have... Was it me? I don't understand. You know that I'd rather kill myself than hurt you? Olli, my love, please forgive me.

They lie side by side, not speaking, listening to each other's breath until the light behind the curtains starts to grow dim and the room is quite dark.

A light rain patters on the roof. Then Greta, who is only a voice now, whispers words in Olli's ear that he still doesn't completely understand.

I love you more than I love myself. You know, don't you, that I wouldn't even exist if not for you? You see darling, I was created just for you to love.

35

As the summer came to an end they enjoyed being in the throes of their fierce longing for each other. It was as if deep down they had already been separated and were groping for each other across time and space.

What did it matter that they had only just met at the end of the previous summer and now they had to part? They had always known each other and they would always know each other. They expressed this in many words and deeds. They made promises.

On the first day of summer they had met as agreed on Touru Bridge, where Greta was waiting for him under the French umbrella. They had become lovers over the winter through letters. It was raining. They took each other's hands and exchanged a kiss. After that they met every day and hid their relationship from the Blomrooses and everyone else. Before that summer Olli thought that nothing could be better than the adventures of the Tourula Five. Now he knew that it was time to move on. The spell of the secret passages belonged to childhood and he had to let it go as he let go of his childhood. In the end, love was the most exciting thing of all.

Their love wasn't mutual at first; Olli was confused and afraid. Encountering Greta for the first time in the secret passageway, he was terrified. When he got back above ground he ran away without looking back, although she called after him to stay.

When his father drove him home to Koirakkala he tried not to think about what had happened, because he didn't understand it. He didn't want to go back to Tourula ever again. The thought of it made him feel sick.

But a few weeks later he got a letter that changed everything.

Olli, you don't know me but I know you and I love you. My name is Greta. I've been secretly watching you for some time and hoping that you could like me when I was finally ready to show myself to you.

I'm sorry I scared you. That wasn't my intention.

Do you think you might like us to write to each other? Because I'm quite alone here now. I'm being blamed for Karri leaving, although he did it voluntarily, so that you and I could be together. Before he left he asked me to tell you that even though you weren't interested in knowing him better and it upset him, he always liked you more than you realized.

Olli, I'm sending a picture of myself with this letter. I hope you like it.

With love,

   Greta

The letter didn't help him understand any better what had happened. But the girl in the photo was beautiful. After looking at it for about a week, Olli answered the letter, apologized for his earlier behaviour and said that he was pretty lonely in Koirakkala, too, so he understood how she felt.

In her next letter Greta said that she was happy that Olli was willing to share his thoughts with her. Their letters went back and forth between Jyväskylä and Koirakkala every couple of days. In the fourth letter, Greta wrote, *I'm so looking forward to next summer, when we'll see each other again.*

Olli answered, *Me too.*

After he posted the letter he felt faint. The promise had been made. He would be going back to Tourula after all, even though he wasn't sure what he would find waiting for him there. Greta was one of those things that he couldn't talk about to anyone, as was the fate of Karri. The whole thing was bizarre and confusing but at the same time somehow simple: sullen Karri was gone and now this sweet girl named Greta had taken his place.

Olli spent days sitting in his room looking at the girl in the photo and trying in vain to understand. Finally he decided that maybe not everything was meant to be understood completely. Some good things in life just have to be accepted as they are without asking too many questions.

Like the secret passages.

And now Greta.

After seeing the Blomrooses for the last time and witnessing how Greta has stopped being ashamed of her existence and defied her cousins and even her mother, Olli runs back to his grandparents' house.

He tells them he's going to spend the night at Aunt Anna's.

"Now you be sure to behave so you leave them with another good memory of this summer," his grandpa says without looking up from the newspaper. His grandma turns away from the sink and tells him to have a nice visit and to give her regards to Anne, Leo and Riku. She also tells him not to forget to thank Aunt Anna for her hospitality.

Greta doesn't need to think up a story for anyone. Nobody will notice whether she's in her room or not.

That evening they meet in the secret room by the river and spend their first whole night together. The girl in the pear-print dress gives Olli pleasure in many different ways. But he still can't get her to take the dress off.

In his passion Olli makes a blustered demand: he has to be able to touch Greta the same way she touches him. After all, it's not right that only one of them has that pleasure.

He blushes; he's glad it's dark. Greta stares at him frozen, like a frightened animal.

"Don't you trust me?" Olli says.

His voice is thin with guilt. He forces himself to continue to try to persuade her.

"We don't have to… to go all the way, if you're scared. I don't think I'm ready for that, either. Greta, I just want to touch you so bad."

It's true. He's been thinking about it so much lately that he hasn't been able to sleep. Remembering, through the long hours of the night, what it felt like to touch Anne, and imagining what it would be like to do the things to Greta that Anne wanted him to do.

Finally Greta nods.

She takes off her dress and underwear and folds them in a neat stack on the chair next to the bed. Then she lies on her back next to Olli and waits there, like a sacrificial lamb.

There's not much light; all he can see is an outline, but it's enough.

"You're beautiful," he whispers.

Greta smiles, her eyes closed.

Olli strokes her cheek, feels the hot stream from her eyes, realizes she's trembling.

He suppresses his guilt, kisses her small, perfumed breasts and licks the smooth skin of her belly.

Then his hand slides down and stops between her legs.

It isn't the same as Anne's, anyway, or his own.

He lays his head on her chest, strokes her hair with his left hand, kisses her face every so often, letting the fingers of his right hand explore with gentle curiosity.

He doesn't try to picture it, figure it out, understand it. He isn't a naturalist here, just an inexperienced lover eager to learn.

So he concentrates on finding the right ways to touch, the ways to please his beloved.

Greta sighs in the dark and lifts her hips.

Olli learns.

When night finally withdraws from around the house, a dim red glow comes through the curtains.

Olli and Greta lie in bed naked, wrapped around each other, covered in nothing but a thin sleep.

Then they open their eyes and look at each other with frightened faces.

They hear footsteps on the stairway.

The door flies open.

Shouts.

Greta is yanked out of the bed and dragged down the stairs.

A clatter.

Olli sits up, bewildered. Anne is standing in the doorway. She grins at him mockingly. She's drunk.

"Good morning, lover boy," she pants. "Amazingly fine day today. The sun is shining and all that cliché shit. I have a bit of a headache. We were up all night, too, you know. But hey, come on downstairs and see what sort of freak you've been messing with."

Anne runs down the stairs. Olli pulls on his jeans and stumbles after her.

36

IT'S STARTING TO RAIN HARDER. Lounais Park is gradually surrendering to autumn. The children abandon the carousel and swings and run away.

Olli and Greta are left in the park alone.

Under the umbrella a little world has come into being, warmed by a sun from thirty years ago.

As Greta continues to reminisce, Olli watches her mouth. It's beautiful. He could kiss it, but he doesn't have the heart to stop the flow of words. The words are building a living picture of the summer they once spent together.

Nothing feels quite real any more. Maybe the secret passages under the ground are leaking the substance that dreams come from. Making the tiniest details significant, making life feel like a dangerous, mesmerizing dream where no sacrifice is too large if it can let you experience something beautiful.

To die with the blossoms, or else to live forever—those are our choices. Anything else is a waste of time.

Olli understands now what Maggie Cheung was saying in that film.

Greta speaks and the words make her skin glow. Olli finally has to reach out and touch her lips to make sure she's real.

Her talk breaks off for a moment. She looks at him in surprise, smiles and continues.

One memory follows another.

As long as she keeps remembering more details of that summer together she doesn't have to come to what happened that morning.

Remember when we climbed up the observation tower and spent the whole day there, looking out over the city? There was a thunderstorm all around us, and we kissed, and the lightning made me jump and I bit your lip so hard that it drew blood, and I licked it away, and then we started to plan exactly what kind of house we were going to live in someday. It had to have a big garden and have lots of spacious rooms, a piano so I could play for you and a greenhouse… You wanted apple trees in the garden… They had to be Finnish cinnamons…

As Greta brought that long-ago summer back one word at a time, Olli was amazed to realize how much he had forgotten.

Greta's talk, together with the M-particles, is altering his mood. His deep cinematic self is controlling what he experiences, how he feels, what he thinks.

It's scary.

Familiar things are becoming strange, forgotten things familiar. His character is coming into focus as he realizes his role in the love story. His deep self is whispering dramatically that in order to save his family, Olli must betray his family.

Cruelty, betrayal and ruthlessness can, in some situations, be aesthetically justified and even unavoidable choices, and categorically avoiding them can lead to slow continuum attachment and the death of life feeling.

He hesitates.

He's horrified that part of him is enjoying having to

step out of bounds and surrender to the power of feelings that he would normally reject. What Greta is saying is too beautiful to resist. Just as he wanted the Klimt painting at the Pompidou, he wants a life with Greta now, even though the part of him that's attached to the slow continuum is still resisting it. Its power comes from things like the familiarity of Aino's face, from the things they share, like their son's ear, so perfect it almost makes him believe in God.

Yesterday he received a message from the Blomrooses that was probably the last one for a while:

> *Hello, Olli! So far you've followed the script to the letter. Thanks! Here are your final instructions. You will meet Greta in Lounais Park on the cafe kiosk terrace at 3 p.m. After that you're on your own. Your mission: to make her completely happy. You have until the first snow. Then your family can come home, but only if you complete your mission.*
>
> *We wish all the best to you and Greta!*
> *Your friend,*
>
> > *Anne (and her pesky brothers)*

So his task is to make Greta completely happy before the first snow.

Completely happy.

How will he know when he's achieved his objective? How can the Blomrooses know? Can a person ever really be completely happy?

And when will the first snow come to Jyväskylä?

These thoughts race through his mind, until he gives up. Greta is still talking.

Her sea-green eyes glow with the light of the summer past. The memories are terribly beautiful, but the shadow of that last morning falls over them all. Olli remembers now, the footsteps on the stairs, Greta naked, dragged out of his arms and taken away.

He realizes that he has felt the hopelessness of that moment every night for all these months.

Olli presses a finger against Greta's lips and she falls silent. "What?…"

Olli holds the umbrella with one hand and presses her against him with the other. She makes a noise like a frightened animal and tries to wriggle free.

Rain splashes from the edge of the umbrella.

"I'm sorry, but I can't let you go," Olli whispers.

Greta freezes.

Then, realizing that she has got what she came to Jyväskylä for, she sinks her fingers into Olli's hair and presses against him, trembling with passion.

PART THREE

37

Jyväskylä has preserved some buildings that are particularly cinematic, of which the highest in M-particles is architect Wivi Lönn's city villa. The villa and its separate outbuildings were built in 1911.

On the southern part of the property is a large garden. The lot is bordered by rows of flower beds and birch, larch, and apple trees separated by gravel paths. On the Hämeenkatu side is a fence contiguous with the back wall of the storage barn. The fence terminates in a gate known as the Apple Gate for the decorative relief of apples that tops the rounded arch. Through it one passes into a pillared passage. The house itself is graced with such features as an attached glass conservatory with a fountain.

Many of Jyväskylä's secret passages lead to the gardens and building foundations of Wivi Lönn's villa. For this reason, the concentration of M-particles in the house reaches considerably elevated levels.

GRETA KARA,
Magical City Guide Number One: Jyväskylä

Olli sees a blonde-haired girl in a doorway.

"Good morning, lover boy," Anne says, sizing up his middle-aged nakedness with amusement. "An amazingly clear day today. But hey, come on downstairs and see what sort of freak you've been messing with."

He turns, and the dream fades.

Olli sits up, rubs his eyes and looks around.

He's alone in the room. Someone who was just sleeping beside him is gone. He can still smell the scent of another person in the bed. Confused, he scratches his hairy chest and sighs as he remembers the fresh feeling of a cool hand on his skin.

He hears a piano playing, and realizes where he is.

Not in Tourula. There is no Tourula any more, not like the place in his dream.

And not at home in Mäki-Matti.

He gets up and puts on his dressing gown. Classical high windows admit the grey autumn sky into the room. He looks at the garden and farther off at the glimmering lake, then goes downstairs to where the piano music is coming from.

The stairs curve in a graceful arch. Everything in the house is flawless to the last detail.

The piano is in front of a window. Greta is playing. Olli lays a hand on her shoulder and smells her golden hair.

In a smiling voice she wishes him a good morning, while her hands continue their skilful rendition of Chopin's Prelude no. 16.

She's still wearing the sleeveless green dress, like Maggie Cheung in the film *In the Mood for Love*.

Olli has spent three nights now at the northern edge of Jyväskylä in the house Greta is renting—Wivi Lönn's city villa.

His summer holiday ended five days ago. It only dawned on him yesterday while eating breakfast with Greta in the dining room, watching her make corrections to the manuscript of the *Magical City Guide*. Olli jerked upright and slammed his hand on the table: he had to get the book to the printers immediately! He grabbed the stack of papers from Greta, told her to send her final edits to the publisher's by email, called a taxi, got dressed and hurried to the office.

He had forgotten to look at his phone or read his email for days. Both were filled with worried enquiries and reminders.

Olli apologized profusely for his forgetfulness, gave the manuscript to Maiju and delegated a large part of his other duties to her and Antero. He explained that unfortunately he had to dedicate some time to a personal matter, but would be into the office daily to check on things.

Antero smiled sourly. "Uh-huh," he said, shooting Maiju a look which Olli took to mean *Midlife crisis. Poor devil.*

Maiju answered the look with a cold stare.

While Olli had been on holiday Maiju had traded her Felliniesque look and exaggeratedly feminine attire for the other extreme—now she was Catherine from Truffaut's *Jules and Jim*, dressed as a man in an oversized checked cap, loose turtleneck, men's trousers and leather walking shoes. She hadn't, however, drawn a moustache on her lip.

"Olli, we've seen you with this 'personal matter' of yours," Maiju said. She didn't try to hide her admiration for the cinematic turn Olli's life had taken. "You can see the park from the conference room. She's beautiful. And so cinematic that it hurts to look at her. Who is she? No, don't tell me. I don't want to know. You do what you have to do. It's none of our business. Go and live your own story. We'll keep the place standing and make sure the books get to market on time. And hey, Antero…"

Antero looked at her expectantly.

Maiju quoted Rhett Butler. "*No, I don't think I will kiss you, although you need kissing, badly. That's what's wrong with you. You should be kissed, and often, and by someone who knows how.*"

Young Antero turned red.

The Chopin prelude ends.

"That was beautiful," Olli says.

"Thank you."

"This place is beautiful," he says.

Greta, in half profile, turns to face him.

"Maybe you haven't noticed," she says, "or who knows, maybe you have—but this is the house we used to dream of in Tourula. Down to the last detail. There's even a conservatory, and a Finnish cinnamon apple tree. I found it when I was researching my book, and I pulled some strings and managed to rent it for us."

"Us?"

Greta closes her eyes, embarrassed. "From the very beginning I lived in the hope that eventually you would move in here with me," she whispered. "But since I'm a sensible girl, I knew that would never happen."

"Right," Olli says. "Never."

"You had your own life, a home, a wife and little boy—why would you up sticks and move in with me?"

"There was no way," Olli says.

Greta begins to play a new, careful piece, then stops, spins around on the piano stool, and wraps her arms around him, laying her head against his stomach.

"Oh, Olli… You could have told me earlier that you were

separated… Of course I'm sorry for the two of you, I pity your poor little boy, but at the same time I'm so immensely happy. Does that make me a bad person? It doesn't matter. I don't care if it does. I've been unhappy for so long that I just want to be happy, even if it means I have to start being an evil, twisted person…"

"You're not evil," Olli says, stroking her hair. "Just ever so slightly twisted."

Greta laughs and looks at him with damp eyes. "You know me too well, Olli. Tell your twisted girl again when your wife and son are coming home from their holidays… And when you intend to tell your wife about us. Or no, you don't have to. I know. You've told me many times. They're coming back in October or November. And you'll tell her about us when they've safely returned home, because you don't want to spoil your son's holidays by giving his mother a shock. I understand. I'm sorry I'm like this. Twisted and impatient. But I've waited so long already."

They exchange a kiss.

Then Greta continues playing. She conjures Debussy's *Clair de lune* from the keys.

Olli leans against the piano and lights a cigarette. The smoke and the music wreathe around the room in the clear light. To his surprise, Olli realizes that he's having a pleasant time. He feels cosy with Greta. He's at home. It feels like life is as it should be.

He doesn't remember the last time he felt this way.

When his son was born?

No. It was an important event, of course, and it still moves him whenever he remembers it. There's no question that the birth of his son gave him a deep, biological satisfaction. He was fulfilling the reproductive task programmed into his genes; but it was more like giving up on living his own life and avoiding the whole process than it was making cinematic meaning of his existence.

When he and Aino got married that, too, was more of a pleasant surrender, in the name of clarity and tranquillity. Of course he loved Aino, and their wedding day was beautiful. But he can see now that the main point of getting engaged and married was that it fit into the slowly progressing continuum that had been set in motion the moment they met. Olli hasn't told Greta the whole truth about his family and the Blomrooses, but the most important part is true: he has decided to divorce Aino once the kidnapping is over.

Olli has finally recognized the truth. He and Aino have no chance of continuing their marriage after everything that has happened. If telling the truth doesn't estrange them from each other, keeping it secret will.

If they were forced by attachment to the slow continuum to stay together, they might manage to be together for a few more years. But eventually the day would come for them to part. And while they waited for that day they would tear each other to pieces, and their son in the process.

Life is too short. Olli understands that there is no way he can content himself any more with an ordinary life slowly going sour, not now that he's met someone and realizes he's been pining for her for thirty years. His marriage with Aino might become just an interlude in a larger story, it seems. It's sad, but without sadness there is no beauty.

But, of course, Olli isn't stupid: he knows that his attitude towards his new cinematic life is like that of a sinner who gets religion. Like it says in the *Guide*, the grandiloquence of a romantic scene also contains an ironic distance. A person has to know how to live out his greatest emotions while simultaneously laughing at them. Olli's greatest emotions notwithstanding, it's clear that divorce may not be easy. There might be problems and arguments and a lot of tears. Aino isn't cinematic and she definitely won't immediately see the situation as Olli sees it.

After all, Aino doesn't really understand movies, not the way they're meant to be understood.

38

OLLI NEEDED TO PICK UP some things from his house in Mäki-Matti.

As he had feared, the slow continuum struck as soon as he walked in the door. It was difficult to breathe. He wanted to go upstairs, crawl under the covers and wait there for his wife and child to come home, for everything to go back to the way it was before. Then he would make sure that everything would stay the same. Preferably forever, but at the very least until he died.

With trembling hands, Olli lit a cigarette and got enough cinematic energy from it to pack a suitcase with his most important personal items and return to the taxi waiting at the gate.

39

CONTRARY TO WHAT ONE MIGHT EXPECT, their first night together at Wivi Lönn's house doesn't culminate in a passionate love scene.

Before Olli follows Greta into the house, they sit in Lounais Park under the dome umbrella in the rain and Greta talks until midnight about memories that have troubled her all these years.

Several times as she speaks, she inadvertently comes close to that summer's end. When she does, she turns pale and loses her words and only finds them again when, with Olli's prompting, she returns to those carefree days long enough ago that the Blomrooses' shadow hadn't yet been thrown over them.

When they finally take a taxi to the manor house, pass through the Apple Gate, walk through the door and climb the stairs to the bedroom, as if by unspoken agreement they perform the same ritual that they did many times in the secret room in Tourula: Greta undresses Olli, but not herself, in complete silence, lays him on his back on the bed, and caresses him with her hands and mouth until he comes.

Afterwards they lie intertwined, breathing each other's breath, Olli naked and Greta in her dress, until they fall asleep. This is repeated for six nights in a row.

On the seventh, Olli stops her. He takes hold of her shoulders and looks into her eyes.

Greta avoids his gaze and nods. Olli closes his eyes and lets his hands move over her dress.

His touch delineates her slender neck, her soft but muscular arms, firm back and narrow waist, in both their minds. Then it finds the breasts like oranges, the curve of her hip, her supple rump.

All the while Greta is trembling, her breath catching. But she allows him to continue, just as the girl she was thirty years ago did the first time.

Olli, too, is terrified. He's afraid he may break something that can't be repaired, in both of them.

When he opens his eyes he sees that she has closed hers. He kisses her lightly on the lips, slips his fingers under the shoulder straps of her dress and lets them fall. When he starts to take off the dress, Greta panics, opens her eyes and grabs his hands.

"Wait. Olli, please close your eyes. You can open them when I say it's all right."

Olli can feel her get out of the bed. He hears the rustle of fabric as she takes off her dress, bra and underwear and puts them on the chair. Then she lies down on her back on the bed. "Give me your hand."

Olli puts out his hand.

She takes hold of it and starts to move it slowly over her skin.

40

WHEN THE DRUNKEN BLOMROOS SIBLINGS break into their room on the last day of summer, Olli and Greta are naked and asleep.

Before Olli has time to wake up, Leo and Riku wrench the golden-haired girl out of the bed and out of Olli's arms and drag her down the stairs like a goat to the slaughter.

Olli would like to go to help her.

But Anne is still in the doorway, freezing him with her mocking eyes. "Good morning, lover boy," she laughs, and Olli covers his dick.

He hears shouts and banging from below.

Anne delays him for a moment longer, then beckons him down the stairs so he can get a look at the "freak" he's been messing with.

Trembling, Olli pulls on his trousers and follows her. Downstairs the morning light is flooding in through the large windows, leaving everything naked and defenceless. Most naked and defenceless of all is Greta, pinned to the floor by the Blomroos brothers. They're holding her arms and legs so that every inch of her body is bathed in light, as if she were a specimen, an object to be examined by strangers, down to its last detail.

If she struggled against her captors at first, she has given up by the time Olli bursts into the room. The damage is already done. Her green eyes peer out from under her hair, filled with shame.

Olli stands in the middle of the floor not knowing what to do. He's helpless and scared.

Anne coughs behind him and says, "Thanks to brother Riku's natural curiosity and voyeurism, we found some interesting papers in Aunt Anna's bureau drawer, a drawer we've been wondering about because it was always locked."

Anne's voice oozes cold sarcasm. There's a rustle of paper. Riku sneers.

Leo is horribly drunk. He stares at his naked cousin, filled with disgust.

"What we have here, it seems, are doctors' reports on a newborn baby," Anne says, flipping through the documents. "Very interesting. And here are some similar reports from later doctor's visits. There's a urologist and a gynaecologist and a poor, frustrated surgeon who wasn't allowed to operate because the child's pig-headed mother refused to give her consent. A lot of papers full of fine medical terms like genitalia, developmental irregularities, hormone levels…"

Anne lets out a little giggle.

"There's all kinds of interesting stuff in here. I guess we both made a serious mistake about our cute little freak of nature, Olli dear, although your mistake was obviously a little more serious than mine."

Anne starts to read aloud. The words squirm into Olli's ears and scratch around there like insects. He doesn't want to listen, but he hears her nevertheless.

Eventually he manages to say that he's going to kill them if they don't let Greta go.

Leo shakes his head in disbelief and Riku breaks into a

high-pitched laugh. Olli's slim torso and thin arms don't frighten them.

Olli growls like an animal and is about to throw himself at them when his legs unexpectedly give way beneath him and he falls on his face with a thud.

Then comes the pain.

The backs of his legs explode. He yells.

Or is it Greta who's yelling?

Olli grinds his teeth, turns his head and sees Anne strike him right on the back of his knees with a crowbar.

"Mind your own business, Olli," she mutters. "We don't have anything against you…"

But Olli tries to get up. He's concerned for Greta. The Blomrooses have gone mad; there's no telling what they might do.

The crowbar swings again and for an instant its shadow darkens the room.

Olli opens his eyes and realizes he's alone. The room is darker now. The sky has filled with clouds; there's a drizzle of rain outside.

He tries to stand up. His legs don't want to hold him, and he has to put his hands on the floor. There's a stab of pain in the back of his head. His whole skull feels tender. He squints.

On the floor where Greta was lying is a large, dark spot. With other streaks around it. Large and small streaks. The Blomrooses seem to have made quite a mess.

Even the walls have dark handprints on them. To be more precise, red handprints.

There are similar stains on the tools, which have been neatly arranged in a row after use:

A screwdriver.

Pliers.

Pincers.

A hammer.

A chisel.

A drill.

A saw.

41

OLLI FOLLOWS THE BLOODSTAINS OUTSIDE.

He feels dizzy, wants to throw up. The back of his head is throbbing. His legs hurt, too.

He stumbles around, and then he finds the Blomrooses, at the edge of the ravine.

They're standing in the drizzle, among the trees, blank-faced, spattered, staring at the ground. They see Olli, and Leo turns to look at him, like a wild animal. Leo can't speak, just makes a sound, and finally grimaces.

Riku, looking pale, points at a hole in the ground with blood around it.

"She's in there," he whispers, his eyes shining. "She gave us the slip when Leo turned chicken. Ran out here and crawled in before we could catch her. Slipped right underground. Now if we just had the guts to go in after her…"

Olli didn't know what to do or say. His brain wasn't working. He turned to look at Anne.

The rain was gradually washing the blood off her pretty face.

Smiling sadly, she wiped her brow with a hand red to the elbow. Then she sighed and said quietly, in a carefree, pensive voice, "What a mess. Say what you will but I still think that somewhere under there is my sweet Karri…"

42

G RETA IS ALL WOMAN NOW.
    But her whole body is covered in scars.

When Olli's hand, with Greta's guidance, has been everywhere, they lie down, holding each other, naked and quiet.

Finally Greta, noticing Olli's ardour rising, whispers in his ear, "Darling, I will gladly give you this body, but first you should know its whole story. So listen..."

I was born in the secret passages, right before your eyes, born among the M-particles, out of love for you.

I'm sure you know the story of how Hermaphroditus, the son of Hermes and Aphrodite, met the amorous nymph Salmacis, and they merged with one another. This created a being that was both man and woman. That happened in mythical antiquity. Another story began in Finland in the 1960s, in Jyväskylä Central Hospital, when a young woman named Anna Kultanen happened to have a baby like that.

The father had really wanted a boy. He took one look at the baby, freaked out and left. The doctors examined the child, conferred for a while and decided they wanted to make it a girl.

But the mother refused to let them touch her baby. She named it Karri, and started raising it as a boy.

The first few years passed without any major problems. Then came the Tourula Five. And little by little, unknown to everyone, I started to develop, in the mind of the boy you knew as Karri Kultanen, at the same time that he was having one adventure after another roaming through the secret passages with the Tourula Five. I came to be because of his secret, hopeless devotion to a boy he knew he could never have. That was you, of course, Olli. You probably remember how I once told you that there would be no me if not for you. That was literally true. He started watching you. He learnt to sense what you liked. Then he imagined a girl you could love, and he found the necessary parts in himself—the parts that he didn't need for being Karri.

In the darkness of the secret passages he recreated himself and hid the change under a dirty hoodie and silence.

Finally he decided that the time had come for him to step aside, and he let the girl he had created stand before you, a little nymph whose name was Greta. Her whole being was crystallized around one singular hope, the same hope that had brought her to life: that you could love her...

Now you're smiling. Why? Are you laughing at the big emotions of the little girl in the pear-print dress? I suppose they are funny. But please be kind and don't laugh. It's a sad fact, but those feelings haven't really changed in all these years. If you know me at all, you know that I am what I am. I may behave like a self-sufficient cat, but I have the heart of a faithful dog who can't help but love you. That's what I was created for. For you, Olli. You mustn't forget that.

All right, I forgive you. Of course I do.

That summer together was wonderful. But then came the last night, and the morning, and the Blomrooses...

I'm sorry.

Please hold me tighter. Otherwise I won't be able to stop shaking. Kiss me. On the lips. And one on the forehead. OK. I can continue now. Stroke my hair. Don't let go of me.

I could understand Anne, in a way. The poor crazy girl had always loved Karri as hopelessly as Karri loved you. So naturally she hated me from the moment she saw me.

One time she came into my room drunk while I was playing the piano and tried to find Karri in me. She examined me up close, exposed herself and tried to get me to touch her. She said that I still smelt like Karri under my pretty dress and my phony act. She said she wanted to show Karri all the wonderful things a girl can do for a boy.

I gave her a cheeky answer, like furious teenagers do, said I knew very well all the wonderful things a girl can do for a boy.

I still remember the look on her face. It was a combination of disgust, anger, jealousy, sadness and something I didn't recognize at first. She left without saying anything more. I thought I had won, and relished the feeling. It wasn't until later that I realized what that last look on her face was.

An epiphany.

I had given her a hint about you and me.

Olli, about that last night we had in Tourula—it was wonderful, and it was awful, and if you had known how afraid I was you wouldn't have asked me to get undressed. Because if you had recoiled in disgust, when you saw...

But that night, in that dark room, Olli, I felt myself through your touch and for the first time in my life I was able to accept myself completely.

I had never touched myself the way you touched me. That night, I had my first orgasm.

Then the morning came, and the horrible, lacerating brightness that the Blomrooses brought.

And the pain.

I'm not talking about the rusty tools. Yes, they tore my body open, but I could have lived with the pain.

The part that hurt the most happened before a drop of blood had fallen.

The most horrible part was when they dragged me into the light and made you look at me and see me the way they saw me, reading those awful papers out loud, words that destroyed all the beauty you had given me.

I didn't even know how to hate them back then. I hated myself. The Blomrooses just took away the mercy of darkness and the illusions, the beautiful lies we'd made up, and they forced me into the light of the truth. And their truth made me a freak.

No, don't try to console me... Don't touch me.

Just listen.

The last thing I remember about that house was Anne showing me the drill bit.

You were lying on the floor, quiet. I wondered if they had killed you. I hoped that you were dead. I was terrified of the thought that you would live and remember what kind of freak your girl in the pear-print dress had turned out to be. I prayed to God that both of us would die.

Then Anne made me look at that red drill bit, and everything turned dark. And I was happy.

You see, I thought it was death.

43

When I woke up, my body was bandaged and there were tubes and cords coming out of it. Pain medication pumping into me. I realized I was in the hospital. Anna sat beside my bed and cried for several days. Then she stopped and just stared at me. She kept saying, "My child," as if she were trying to reassure herself. "Karri, Greta, what does it matter? It's still my child."

She looked like a ghost. I didn't know how to think of her as my mother any more. She was Karri's mother—to me she was Anna. My aunt. She had even introduced me to the neighbours as her sister's daughter.

They told me I had been found bloody and nearly dead at the old cemetery. I must have come from the railwayman's house to the other side of the river through the secret passages, although I didn't remember it at all.

The police came to question me. Eventually I made up a story about a drunken drifter down by the river, said he had started following me and dragged me into the house, knocked me unconscious and done terrible things to me.

The police searched our room by the river. They asked if I had been there. I told them I had been there many times to play the piano and think about things, when I wanted to be alone. And I told them that other people besides me went there, too. It was obvious that the police had examined the bed and found evidence of our games. You weren't mentioned, of course.

I couldn't go to high school as planned, so it was decided that I would take a year off to recover, physically and mentally.

The doctors started examining me again, like a fascinating specimen. They prodded, measured, took pictures, peered at me, felt around my most private parts. Sometimes when the doctors were between my legs arguing over whether I was more boy or girl, I felt like I was in the hands of Anne and her brothers again. I had to break a water glass over a doctor's head before it occurred to them that I might not be that interested in listening to their medical attempts to define me.

I asked them if they could fix me and make me a real woman.

They said, in theory, yes. But Anna had already assured them that regardless of my special genitalia, I had always clearly been a boy, a boy who had simply been very mixed up and confused lately. So the doctors didn't want to rush into anything under those circumstances, and some of them thought that physically I was more a boy than a girl. I would have to see a psychiatrist and a psychologist for at least a couple of years before thinking of surgery.

Every moment that I was in the hospital I hoped and feared that you would walk through the door. I didn't really want to have anything to do with you if I couldn't show myself to you as what I was meant to be in your eyes, in bright light, without shame. But when you didn't come, I was crestfallen. I made up excuses for you, Olli; sometimes I hated you. What kind of thing is that, to know that I hated the very person I was fated to love for the rest of my life?

You sent me a letter?… I never got it. That might have been when I'd already left home. If it came earlier, Anna probably destroyed it. She sensed that Karri's change into Greta had something to do with you, so she was quite bitter towards you.

My life was unbearable. To pass time in the hospital I watched old movies on the little television in my room and planned how to kill myself.

I gave up on the idea, though, when I realized that death was easy, when you thought about it—I could kill myself later, any time I wanted. I understood that even if I did keep living I didn't have to accept the flat ordinariness that everyone was trying to drag me into—with their diagnoses and reports and measurements. That didn't have to be my reality. To their way of thinking I was nothing but a curiosity, a freak of nature, a walking developmental irregularity, Mother Nature's defective goods.

So I learnt to think cinematically.

I started to see my life as an adventure and myself as its tragic but glorious heroine, who would eventually triumph over her hard fate if she only learnt to live fearlessly. I was Natalie Wood, Kim Novak, Vivien Leigh, Grace Kelly, Ingrid Bergman, Catherine Deneuve, Jeanne Moreau, Anita Ekberg and Audrey Hepburn all rolled into one. You only have one life, so why settle for a small part?

It was winter when I got out of the hospital. Anna had saved Karri's clothes, and she offered them to me. It was like being offered the clothes of a dead person. I asked where the pear-print dress was. Anna said she couldn't find it anywhere. I cried for several days. She eventually got tired of listening to me and sewed me a new one.

As soon as I put the dress on, my mood improved and I started to think about my life going forward.

I've never been able to actually remember the things that Karri experienced. His memories are like stories someone told me, or pictures in a stranger's photo album. But I found all the information that had accumulated over the course of Karri's life within myself.

The previous autumn—the first autumn of the girl in the pear-print dress, I mean—I had gone back to school. For understandable reasons, I went to a different school from the one Karri went to. I noticed that I was a good student, better than Karri had been. All the information that had made Karri yawn was there in my mind, accessible, as if my mind were an entire library. I was, in fact, first in my class, and got a scholarship, although some of the teachers gave me some odd looks when they heard about my past.

I was thrilled when I realized I could play the piano, even though Karri had been a hopeless music student. The school music teacher encouraged me to get a proper piano teacher—she thought I might even have the talent to be a concert pianist.

Tourula started to feel oppressive; Anna thought I was an interloper. I found a job in Helsinki as a nanny. I packed my bags, left a short note for Anna telling her I'd got a job in domestic service, and hitchhiked to Helsinki. From there I went straight to Sweden, then to Amsterdam. I guess you could say that the little girl in the pear-print dress decided to go out into the wide world to find herself.

You can smile now, darling...

For a while I was working in a coffee house in the Jordaan district in Amsterdam. I shared an apartment with two Indian Hijra. We had a lot in common, and I ended up going with them to Bombay.

But before that I hired a boy prostitute. You see, I missed you terribly. I chose someone who looked and smelt a little like you. I wanted to experience the same feeling I had on that last summer night. I paid him, and then we went into a dark room. I did the same things to him that I had done to you. I explained in detail how he should touch me, and I called him Olli. I had my second orgasm.

I'm sorry, Olli. I can see that you don't want to hear this. But it's all a part of the history of my flesh, my skin, and I want you to know all of it.

Have you ever been to India? They have a book fair there, too, you know. It's in Mumbai. Although when I was there it was called Bombay.

I spent three years in the heat of that city. It smells bad and there are too many people, too many rats, too much noise, but I felt extremely

at peace there. Because there they recognize a third gender, the hijras,
who aren't men or women. My new Hijra friends welcomed me into
their community.

The hijras have their own caste. A long time ago they were considered
sacred and were respected, but then the English colonists gave India the
gift of slow continuum attachment and showed them the hijras in the light
of ordinariness, in other words as contemptible deviations from the norm.

We were hated and feared and honoured, depending on the situa-
tion. We got badly beaten up a few times, sometimes by gangs of men,
sometimes the police. But we showed up at ordinary people's weddings,
made a lot of noise and sang naughty songs until they paid us to leave.
It was a custom there.

When I'd been living in Bombay for almost three years, I learnt
that a hijra friend of mine named Heena was in love with me. We had
sought human happiness and warmth from each other and agreed that
that was all it would be. And I ended up chasing her out of my bed.
She was beautiful in her orange dress, and she was a sensitive person.
There was something like you about her, so I enjoyed being near her.

The next evening we went out to some bars and I told her all about
you. I also told her that for me she had mostly been a shadow of you. It
was cruel, but at the time I thought it was necessary.

She cried but said she understood.

On the way home, three men ambushed us and dragged us into an
alley. One held a knife to my throat while the other two violently attacked
Heena. I was silent. She screamed like an animal being slaughtered. I
knew it would be my turn next.

But a large, drunken tourist happened to walk by. He yelled some-
thing in German, waved a pistol and scared the rapists away.

The tourist and I helped the bloodied Heena to her feet and set off
to take her home.

We hadn't walked very far when a police car pulled up beside us. Two policemen in grey uniforms and caps got out. They asked us in a very intimidating tone what we were doing. I suspected that they had been watching the whole incident from a distance. The German explained that we had been the victims of an attack, but he was reluctant to get involved in the incident any further. The police ordered him to leave and threw Heena and me into their car.

In the back room of the police station, I was handcuffed to a chair and Heena was hung by her hands from a window grate. We were beaten and insulted. I still remember the words they said, although I didn't understand them. Khoja! Gandu! Ninna ammane kevya!

The police continued to defile Heena. They treated me more warily because I was a Westerner, but I got a few good thumps from them and was unconscious part of the time. It was no longer morning when the German reappeared, cleaned up and wearing a crisp white suit. He must have bribed the police because they took off our handcuffs.

But Heena slumped to the floor.

The German, who said he was a doctor, pronounced her dead. He pointed out her wounds, explaining with dry professionalism what the cause of death was. It seemed to me like he was trying to establish his authority in the eyes of the police. They listened to him blank-faced. The atmosphere was tense.

I was crying with rage and sadness. I just wanted the police to be held responsible for what they had done to Heena. The German whispered to me in English that we had better be leaving. He understood enough Marathi to know that the police would kill me as soon as he wasn't there to witness it. And he himself wasn't completely safe now that he had been a witness to the police committing a murder.

We went outside and got into a taxi. The German introduced himself as Hans Engel, a plastic surgeon with a practice in Rio de Janeiro. I told *him I was Finnish. He was delighted and suggested that I pick up my passport from my rooms and fly with him to Brazil. He wanted to give me a job as a receptionist, said that he thought Finns were reliable employees.*

Heena was dead, so I couldn't think of any reason not to accept his offer. And besides, I knew that I needed plastic surgery, so my chance meeting with Hans Engel felt like divine providence.

Olli, do you feel like hearing some more?

Good.

Tonight I'm going to tell you everything you need to know. After this we'll never talk of these things again.

I spent the next seven years of my life with Hans Engel.

He turned out to be an agreeable person. I had my own room in a lovely house where he kept his practice. It was in a prominent place on Saquarema, on the Rua Maximino Fidelis, near the beautiful beaches. I was living in a picture postcard. I quickly mastered my job as a medical receptionist. In the meantime I studied the language and served as a sort of part-time substitute daughter to Hans.

Sometimes in the evenings I would play the piano and Hans would listen. He wasn't the least bit musical, but he had an expensive piano because he thought it was a beautiful object. His younger daughter was also a promising pianist, and my playing lightened his gloom. Hans had to leave his wife and two daughters behind in East Germany several years earlier. Apparently it was due to some sort of tax difficulties. As time went by he told me more about himself, but his reason for leaving East Germany was always left unclear. I had the impression that there was something about it that even he didn't want to remember.

At some point things started to change. I became the object of Dr Engel's aesthetic ambition, a human work of art; he thought he could do what he wanted with me—and for all practical purposes, he could.

Hans was forty-one when we met. He seemed trustworthy. He was tall, and in his own way handsome. When he volunteered to be a father figure to me, of course I was more than ready to step into the daughter's role.

When we had known each other for about six months, he came into my room one night. I was sleeping in the nude. When I woke up I saw him sitting on the edge of my bed with a little light in his hand, looking at my body.

There was nothing sexual about the situation. I wasn't afraid or angry. I knew that I had invited him there myself by means of various subtle cues.

I didn't say anything. The light wandered over my hips and breasts and I spread my legs for him. I knew that he was looking at me with the eyes of a plastic surgeon, and not as a man does, and I trusted him. And he had also mentioned that he'd been impotent ever since he left East Germany.

After examining me for a time, he stroked my hair and apologized for intruding. He just wanted to confirm that he had been correct in his assessment of my situation. It would have been embarrassing for us both if he had been wrong.

I said I understood.

He told me he had guessed back in Bombay what my background was—I had been going around with the hijras, after all. But he hadn't confirmed it, and that had been worrying him. And because I reminded him of his daughters, he felt a need to help. He said he was well aware that he was a sentimental fool, but helping me made him feel closer to his daughters.

He asked me if I was content with my body.

I shook my head.

He asked how I would like it to be.

The blood started rushing in my ears and my skin tingled. I was afraid I would faint.

I thought, I want to be the kind of woman you could love, Olli.

What I said out loud was that I just wanted to be entirely a woman. An attractive woman. Like in a movie. He smiled broadly and said that if I simply trusted him and was ready to undergo some pain, a few changes could make me another Audrey Hepburn, if that was what I wanted.

44

G RETA GOES THROUGH the history of her body surgery by surgery and scar by scar.

Olli starts to feel cold. Eventually he pulls the blanket up over himself. It's painful to listen to such detailed descriptions. He would like to ask her to stop. But he can see that compared to the telling, the listening is easy.

Greta trembles as she tells the story of her flesh, lying on her side on the bed with her fists against her chest, bare and fragile, like a suffering child. Olli can't touch her—this isn't the time to console her, first she has to get the words out.

For seven years Dr Engel performed dozens, perhaps hundreds of plastic surgeries on Greta. Olli can't keep count of them, but Greta remembers every one. For the first couple of years the doctor's treatments were skilful and professional, done with careful consideration, honouring all the rules of aesthetic surgery, consulting with Greta about every operation and making sure she knew what he was going to do.

Gradually the flow of customers to the clinic dried up when a few dissatisfied patients made a fuss about Engel's alcohol consumption and the quality of his work. He used his increased free time to examine and tinker with Greta. Little by little the "beautiful little hermaphrodite", as he called her a few times when he had been drinking, became his obsession.

Eventually the phone nearly stopped ringing altogether.

Dr Engel drank, and felt sorry for himself.

Greta felt sorry for him, too.

She tried not to listen to the rumours, but the truth was that many of his treatments didn't seem to have been very successful. There was one operation that required multiple corrective surgeries. When she awoke from the anaesthesia she might find that he'd done a lot of other things besides the ones he'd told her about beforehand.

Her body was now more womanly than she had ever dared dream, for which she was grateful. But she didn't want any more surgery.

When she asked him to stop the operations, he said that she wasn't finished yet. He ought to do at least one more operation, perhaps two. A plastic surgeon's eye, after all, can see the truth. Surely Greta wanted to be sure that her secret love liked what he saw? *Ach Greta, mein Herzchen,* men can be so terribly picky about a woman's body…

After every surgery, and before every new one, he put on his doctor's coat and ordered Greta to stand naked in front of him. He examined her body from various angles, like an artist examining an unfinished work. Sometimes he made her undress, sit at the piano and play. He said that when she was in that position it was easier for him to see which parts were finished and which still needed work.

Before her scars even had time to heal properly the impatient doctor would want to perform another operation. Sometimes the scars became infected and she had to have an intravenous drip. When that happened, he would care for her with fatherly tenderness.

*

Eventually she'd had enough.

She packed her bag, marched up to Engel, thanked him for everything, resigned her post and told him she was going back to Finland.

Dr Engel ordered her to stay right where she was. He took off her clothes as if she were a doll and pored over his seven-year project with a furrowed brow. As he did this he talked to himself with studied calm, like a man soothing a skittish animal.

He could understand, of course, that Greta was tired and sometimes wanted to give up. But she didn't understand, in the impatience of her youth, how wondrously beautiful she could be if she would only let him finish his work. He said he would sooner bury Greta in the garden than let her walk out of there half-finished.

Greta looked into his eyes and realized that he was serious.

She understood that there was nothing she could do. The doctor knew best, and he would be the one to decide.

Engel's eyes shone as his unfinished masterpiece acceded to his fatherly wishes.

A couple of days later Greta was sitting naked at the piano, playing.

It was early evening. Dr Engel was sipping a whisky and walking around the piano. The setting sun outside the window blazed on the piano's polished black surface. He fiddled with the tie she'd given him for Christmas, watched the movements of her body, and wondered aloud whether the line of her neck needed augmentation or whether it would be better to concentrate on the earlobes for a while—they still had a certain roughness about them. Or perhaps he could touch up the breasts...

Greta stopped playing. She had decided to view the situation with resigned positivity. The previous Christmas Dr Engel had given her a collection of Emily Dickinson poems and pointed out one in particular that she ought to think about. It began: *The hallowing of pain, Like hallowing of Heaven, Obtains at a corporeal cost.* The ending was particularly apt: *But He who has achieved the Top—All is the price of All.*

The sound of the piano filled the room as Greta pounded out Chopin études with precision and force.

At some point she became aware that her hands felt stiff.

She found herself struggling more and more to make her fingers strike the right keys. First her playing slowed. Then she started to make mistakes, and a few wrong notes escaped. When she finally lost the notes completely, she lifted her fingers from the keyboard.

She shook her head in horror. She couldn't play any more.

"What's wrong?" Dr Engel asked, annoyed at the interruption.

"I don't know," Greta gasped.

Oh. So it's happened, she thought, only slightly afraid. I'm finally going to die!

She stood up and looked the doctor in the eye, and everything went dark.

Greta didn't die. She woke up in her own room. She was lying in bed with a blanket over her, and was no longer naked. She was wearing a dress and shoes.

It was afternoon. Of the following day. She had been asleep for eighteen hours.

Next to the bed was a packed suitcase with a plane ticket to Paris laid on top, where she would be sure to see it upon awakening.

The plane was leaving in five hours.

She was thrilled, but she didn't understand what it was about. Had Dr Engel finally got the message that what he was doing was wrong, or had he been hurt by his protégé's impatience? And why Paris in particular?

In any case, it had apparently all been arranged while she slept so that she could leave immediately. And who else could have done this for her but Hans Engel? She had no one else.

He must have wanted her to leave without saying goodbye. But she decided to find him and thank him for everything one more time.

She found him in the living room.

He was lying on his back on the floor in front of the piano, obviously stinking drunk. He stared at Greta, his eyes wide, sticking his tongue out at her like a naughty child.

It was bewildering. Greta turned to leave.

But something made her hesitate for a moment.

In spite of his clowning, the doctor didn't look like he was feeling very well; his face was an unhealthy blue and his eyes were more bloodshot than she'd ever seen them. Greta went to look closer.

Then her legs gave out.

While Greta slept, Dr Engel had strangled himself with his own tie.

A note was stuck to his chest with a scalpel. It was written in Brazilian Portuguese.

Over the previous seven years Greta had learnt enough of the language to know that it said something about unpaid debts which were "hereby paid in full". The letter also mentioned Greta's name and said sardonically, My little pet—*mimada*—it's time you were on your way, because your host—*mestre*—is now *morto*.

Greta fetched the suitcase, ran out of the house, caught a taxi to the airport and flew from Rio de Janeiro to Paris.

45

"WHAT DID YOU DO IN PARIS?" Olli asks warily.
Greta smiles. She's relaxed now, lying on the bed and stroking her stomach like a cat. Her eyes twinkle. The bad part of the story is over now.

"All the things a twenty-six-year-old woman can do in Paris. I went places. Learnt about art. Met people. Read books. Started to plan to write a book of my own. Went to the movies. Lived. I had seven years of my life to get back, after all.

"Olli, it would be sweet to say that I saved myself for you, but neither one of us is stupid. I was scared, but I wanted to experience my new body and practise sex. Often. I had many lovers, men and women. At first I did it in the dark, then in bright light. I tested myself and my ability to experience pleasure, conquest. I wanted to know if I could do it."

Greta stretched, let out a joyous laugh and looked at Olli with a mischievous grin.

"You're not jealous, are you? I hope you are, at least a little bit. You had gone on with your life and I was thinking of you. When I went to bed I always imagined what sorts of girls you might be lying with. I was tremendously jealous and I took my revenge on you for your presumed sexual adventures many times.

"I met a famous photographer couple at a party. They wanted to take pictures of me, and I let them. When I undressed in the studio, they looked at each other and I could tell that they liked what they saw. The man asked me about my scars and I said I'd been in a car accident. The woman said that I was beautiful and that the scars were beautiful, too, and she wanted to touch them. I let her. The three of us went to bed together.

"The pictures they took were wonderful; they were displayed at the Carrousel du Louvre. We had fun together. We went to concerts, to artists' cafes, bicycling, on picnics in the countryside. Then I realized that both of them had fallen in love with me. They started to compete for my attention and bicker with each other, so I left them. It was too easy to do. I wasn't able to genuinely connect as long as the thought of you was always with me in bed. Or maybe I was just afraid of intimacy and used you as an excuse. I don't know.

"I found new friends. Life was interesting and pleasant. I missed you of course, but I learnt to live with that feeling. Several times I almost got in touch with you. I looked up your number and held the telephone in my hand, found your address and wrote letters. But I always put down the receiver and burned the letters—because I didn't have the courage. I thought that you would surely have completely forgotten the girl in the pear-print dress who you loved for one short summer. I was sure that if I were to appear in front of you and tell you that I had been thinking about you all those years, you would look at me with pity and wonder. I couldn't bear that."

Greta describes how she lived in Paris for twenty years, making her living writing art reviews and articles for newspapers and travelling all around the world. Shortly after moving to Paris she officially changed her name from Greta Kultanen to Greta Kara to sever herself once and for all from Rio de Janeiro, Bombay and Jyväskylä. Every couple of years she returned to Jyväskylä to look around and think about her life.

"I walked down Puistokatu and even went to Tourula—or what was left of it—but I could never stay there for long; the magic of our summer always came too close to me eventually, and I started to change from Madame Doinel to the girl in the pear-print dress. Every time I came here it was harder to return to my family in Paris."

Olli flinches. "Madame Doinel? Family?"

Greta rolls onto her stomach, swings her feet in the air and avoids Olli's gaze. "Yeah. When I was thirty-one I met an engineer named Armand. He was twelve years older than me, a widower with a daughter. Simone was five at the time. We lived a very comfortable life as a middle-class family for six years. I didn't ever actually marry Armand, although he wanted me to, but I used his last name and introduced myself as his wife. I didn't love him, but I was faithful to him. When I felt temptation I thought, I'm practising being a faithful wife so I can live with you someday, if fate ever brings us together."

"Then what happened?"

Greta sighs. "Armand wanted more children. He wanted a son. And of course I couldn't give him a son. There were arguments. I finally moved out and after that lived on my own. I never really saw anyone. I travelled a little, went to a lot of movies, and spent many years writing a book, which came to be *A Guide to the Cinematic Life*. I sold it to a large French publisher. Everything was going beautifully.

Sometimes I felt a bit depressed, but medication and therapy helped."

Olli notices Greta growing more tense.

"Then the Facebook craze started spreading everywhere, starting in 2008, a little while after *Cinematic Life* came out," she says quietly. "I was among the first to join, out of curiosity. And besides, now that I was a writer, there were people I needed to keep in touch with. One evening I noticed that the Blomrooses had found me."

Greta grimaces, covers her face with her hands, and shouts, "*Tabarnak! Merde!* By that time I had to all intents and purposes forgotten about them. I fell apart for a little while, couldn't sleep... Oh God... can you imagine? First they tear me to pieces as if I wasn't even a person, and then the next time our paths cross they want to be friends on Facebook..."

Olli takes Greta in his arms and strokes her golden hair until she stops trembling.

"That must have been awful," he whispers.

Greta nods. "I started to have nightmares about them. That horrible morning in Tourula felt so near that I couldn't see anything else. I thought I was going crazy. I read what I wrote in my book about cinematic revenge over and over, and I decided to kill the Blomrooses."

In March of 2008 she decided to dedicate herself to revenge, and she accepted the Blomroos siblings as Facebook friends so that she could kill them.

"I thought it was meant to be. Why else would fate have thrown them in my path like that?"

She started gathering information. She found it on the Blomrooses' profiles, and from the Blomrooses themselves, of course. Although Anne had sought Greta out as a Facebook friend, she had apparently been too busy to answer Greta's brief greeting or the posts on her brothers' or Greta's walls. Riku and Leo were more eager to exchange thoughts with her. They didn't really discuss the Tourula days. Both men concentrated on talking nonsense and—once they had seen her photo—flirting with her.

Wow, I would totally do you, was Riku Blomroos's comment on her photo.

Leo, on the other hand, wrote:

I recall there was something weird about you in the Tourula days, and if I remember correctly, I think I even hated you for some reason, but hey, you certainly look OK now!

Greta was pleased. She could kill them now without any qualms.

She didn't need any added confirmation to kill Anne Blomroos. She saw Anne's leering face and bloody drill bit every night in her dreams.

Greta continued to keep in touch, and at some point Riku mentioned in a chat that the siblings were planning to get together at Anne's summer house. Anne, it seemed, didn't really stay in touch with her brothers, but now she had invited them to her place, which made Riku excited and slightly nervous.

This visit intrigued her. She found out as much as she could from Richard Blomroos and, in addition to the date, found out that the summer house in question—Anne had several—was in the south of France, in Trans-en-Provence, to be precise.

But the visit was just a week away. Greta began feverish preparations.

First she needed a gun. An old acquaintance of hers who was now a Facebook friend collected guns and had in fact tried to give her a pink designer pistol that he'd got at an auction. Greta had turned it down, because she didn't like guns. Now she called him and said that she would accept the gift after all. He was pleased, invited her over, served her dinner, and showed her how to carry and shoot the gun.

Then she rented a car to drive from slushy Paris to the other side of France.

Greta stops talking.

Olli is thoughtful for a moment and then works up the courage to ask, "Well, did you shoot them?"

Greta gives him a blank look.

"I guess you could say I did. I drove to Trans-en-Provence, found Anne's house, and walked in with the gun in my handbag. It was a cool, cloudy afternoon. I hoped there wouldn't be any security guards or dogs. Executives of large companies rarely go anywhere without bodyguards, but on this occasion Anne apparently wanted to meet her brothers without any outsiders present. She had no way of knowing that an extra guest was coming, and that it was someone she herself had summoned through Facebook."

Greta continues.

I found them in the dining room. They were sitting at the table, just the three of them, drinking red wine.

I had expected to find them having a rollicking time. But Anne was pale, thin and weak. Leo and Riku were red-faced and overweight, but they were as silent as their sister. It felt like I was walking in on a family drama, and the pistol in my bag seemed stupid. Riku and Leo looked as if Anne had just given them some bad news that they were trying to absorb. They didn't notice me even though I stood there for several minutes.

I felt a tinge of curiosity, but then I reminded myself that I was there to get revenge.

I released the safety on the pistol and walked closer to the table. They finally noticed I was there. I took aim at each of them in turn. I was trying to decide who to shoot first.

The brothers looked at me and didn't know who I was.

Anne recognized me immediately. She said my name. "Greta," she said softly.

She seemed to be expecting me. I aimed the gun at her forehead. She laughed drily, poured herself more wine, and took a drink. Unlike her brothers, she wasn't afraid.

Riku and Leo were terrified, like two Oliver Hardys, and if I hadn't hated them so much I'm sure I would have thought them endearingly silly and forgiven everything.

They asked pathetically what harm they had ever done to me, assured me that if they had somehow offended me in the past they were terribly sorry about it. They kept saying that they were sure they could make it up to me, couldn't they? Weren't we all old friends?...

Then Anne told them to shut up and they went quiet.

Anne said something like, "If you two idiots could so easily forget a thing like that then you deserve to die. I deserve to die, too, but at least I'll die knowing why."

Then she stood up, smiled with a peculiar sort of innocence and gave a little speech.

I remember it word for word.

It went like this:

"Greta, before you do what you came here to do, I just want to say that you look fantastic! I can see now that you were strong enough to survive what we did to you, and believe me when I tell you that I'm glad. Don't get the wrong idea; I don't want to offend you, but ever since I read your book, I've thought of you as a friend. I want you to know that I accept what you came here to do to us, even if these two idiots are trying to weasel out of it from sheer heartlessness and attachment to the slow continuum. We deserve to be shot. I would do it the same way myself. Cinematically. I read A Guide to the Cinematic Life *and I liked it immensely; it's very inspiring. I started planning all sorts of cinematicness for the rest of my life, but now look at me, me and my blockheaded brothers, the scoundrels in your cinematic revenge... How funny! But this is exactly how it should be. I don't imagine that asking forgiveness will make up for anything, so I won't ask forgiveness. But I will ask one thing."*

I nodded.

"Before you shoot me, I want to talk to Karri for a moment," she said.

"Talk to Karri?"

Olli sits up in bed. Greta's story started to worry him the moment the Blomrooses appeared in it, and now the story has turned considerably more worrying.

Greta nods. "That's what she said. It totally threw a spanner in the works. I don't know what happened next. I think I simply forgot what I came to do. The next thing I knew I was sitting at the table across from Anne Blomroos. Her brothers were gone. I looked at my hand, and it didn't have a gun in it any more, but a glass of wine. Half empty. Anne poured me some more."

Greta continues:

Anne said my name. It sounded like a question. I tried to pull myself together and asked what had happened. She smiled and said that she had just told me what it was that she wanted to experience more than anything before she died, and asked me what it was that I wanted.

I thought for a moment. It was a bizarre situation. A moment earlier I had wanted to shoot Anne Blomroos. Now I just wanted to answer her question.

So I told her what I wanted. Anne nodded. We looked at each other with some kind of shared understanding. But I didn't understand it at all. My bloodlust was gone. I drank the rest of my wine, got up and walked out.

I wondered what had happened to the pistol. Then, as I was getting in the car, I found it in my handbag. I guess I didn't shoot anyone after all, I thought. I was both relieved and disappointed. Then I noticed that the pistol smelt different. When I looked in the chamber, there were only two cartridges left.

Greta wriggles into Olli's arms, nibbles his neck and puts her hand between his legs.

"Please don't ask what really happened there, because I don't know and I don't want to know. And don't ask what answer I gave to Anne. You know the answer. It was you."

Olli nods. They look at each other solemnly.

"Now you know the story of my body," Greta whispers shyly. "It's yours, if you want it."

As Olli gently kisses her chin, something fierce flames up in her green eyes.

"It was made for you," she says, her voice husky. "Take it. Please. Stick your cock in it. Pound it to your heart's content. *Baise-moi, mon amour...* Fuck me, my love. Olli, please make love to me. I can't wait any longer."

46

After this they're blessed with a few sweet, unhurried summer days.

Then Jyväskylä erupts into autumn colours and the clear though diminishing light fills the house that Wivi Lönn built for herself, where they walk from room to room, sometimes hand in hand, sometimes following each other, making love on the floor, the tables, the stairs, enjoying a cigarette, reading Christina Rossetti poems to one another.

Greta often sits at the piano playing Chopin and Olli listens, thinking uneasily of the task the Blomrooses have given him: *Make her completely happy. You have until the first snow. Then your family can come home—but only if you complete your mission.* Every day as he listens to Greta play, he lights a cigarette, inhales pensively and asks with a smile, as if the question were a game, "Would you say that right now you are completely happy?"

Not lifting her fingers from the keys, she answers with something like this: "Hmm. I'm happier than I ever thought I could be... The problem is that the more I love you the more I fear losing you. I have a sort of premonition... Oh, it's so stupid, I know, but you see, Olli, the most beautiful stories always have sad endings, and our story is so beautiful. I don't know how I can be completely happy when I'm always afraid that fate will separate us somehow and then I'll die of sadness."

"Greta, remember that I love you, too," Olli assures her.

"You're my girl in the pear-print dress. No power in this world could take me away from you again."

Greta's eyes grow wet. Chopin's notes welling up from the piano grow more emphatic.

"Well, you've done it again... I just started to love you a little more," she says in a tone both sad and amused. "And now the thought of losing you only feels all the more unbearable... I'm sorry. I realize I'm being stupid and childish. I promise to stop being afraid and learn to be completely happy. I'll try, anyway. Ask me again tomorrow."

Olli takes care of the publishing business from home and only goes to the office when it's absolutely unavoidable. Book Tower has to be kept running, but he doesn't have time to actually be there.

October arrives. The first snow could come at any moment. Olli tries not to think about it too much. He has to surrender to the power of cinematic fatalism or he'll go crazy. In the end all he can do to make this work is to love Greta and proclaim his love for her for as long as it takes to begin to dispel the shadows from her mind, and hope that it happens before the first snow falls.

The *Magical City Guide* is scheduled for publication in a few weeks and Greta will be marketing it in publishing events and television appearances. At Greta's insistence, Olli will accompany her at all times. "I'm just afraid that if I leave you at home alone, I'll come back and find you gone," she says with a tense smile.

"I'm not going anywhere," he promises. They exchange a look; Greta's eyes are alight with faith and desire, but behind them there's still a touch of doubt.

After a night of frost, they walk the paths in the garden over crackling leaves, eating apples and smelling the change of seasons.

"You know what I'm really looking forward to?" Greta says suddenly, turning around so quickly that her golden hair brushes Olli's face. "Snow. And winter. And spending my first winter with you. Maybe it will be a magical winter. We can light a fire, throw our clothes in the flames and wrap ourselves up in each other. Make love and drink hot cocoa with whipped cream on top and roast sausages and marshmallows on sticks. I've never had roasted marshmallows, and I don't really like sausages. Olli, when does the first snow come to Jyväskylä?"

"Sometimes in November, once in a while even in October," Olli says, glancing at the sky.

They've reached the entrance to the colonnade. Olli presses Greta up against a column, kisses her lips and nibbles her neck, whispering, "I'll never leave you."

She wraps her arms around him. "Good. I'm happy that you say that. It's just that what a person wants, and what they promise, doesn't mean much if it's on a collision course with what's meant to be. You see, Olli, I trust you, but I fear fate."

"Fate?" Olli says. "Silly girl! Fate has no power independent of us. We create our own fate through the big decisions we make, and the small ones. Things move in their own trajectories and everything has its own weight. My grandfather used to say that there is no act so small that it can't have larger consequences, but if you're careful about even small things, I think you can make your fate whatever you want it to be. Look where our choices and actions have brought us… Here, in each other's arms. This is our fate."

"I suppose it is," Greta says, and presses more tightly against him.

Every night Olli wakes up in the wee hours. He looks at the woman sleeping beside him, tiptoes downstairs to the kitchen, turns on his computer and reads his Facebook messages.

He doesn't want to mix family matters and his life with Greta, so he updates his Facebook at night. Often, though, he comes back to bed and Greta wakes up a little while later and opens her own computer, which she keeps on the bedside table. Olli hasn't brought the matter up, but he understands that she also doesn't want to waste the time they have together on Facebook.

There are no new messages from the Blomrooses. They haven't really been updating their profiles. No doubt they're just waiting for Olli to see his task through to the end.

Olli thinks about Greta's story, how she planned to shoot the Blomrooses and instead ended up making wishes with the dying Anne Blomroos. At least now he knows what gave the Blomrooses the idea to make him a part of their insane plan for atonement and send his family on a perpetual, involuntary world tour. It's obvious that they were watching them both over Facebook, and probably by other means as well, and once he and Greta found each other they saw to it that Olli's attachment to the slow continuum didn't prevent Greta's wish from coming true. *You and Greta had a beautiful love story; we understand that now. It's time your story had a beautiful ending.*

But of course Olli can't blame Greta for what's happened,

nor does he want to. How could she have known what the wish she spoke aloud would lead to?

New photos from various parts of the world continue to appear on Aino's profile. She and the boy are doing well, except that they look exhausted.

The most recent update is from the end of September: *Aino Suominen would like to go home with her son before the first snowfall.* When Olli sees it he rubs his temples and wonders anxiously if she might know about the deadline the Blomrooses have set for him, or whether the post was written by her captors, as a reminder to him. He writes in the comments: *Aino Honey, I'm working as hard as I can so you can be home for the winter. You are in my thoughts. See you soon!*

He feels like a coward, wants to add: *P.S. Right now I'm living in the Wivi Lönn house with my lover and I want a divorce, but hey, there'll be time to sign all the papers when you get back.*

He remembers something he read in *A Guide to the Cinematic Life*:

> *A person who surrenders to cinematicness will inevitably experience shocks to reality from the change of perspective, and unfortunately those whose lot is to become less important in the scheme of things will be the casualties.*

Greta's profile is updated every day. Her prevailing mood is apparent in her posts:

> *Greta Kara and a lost summer reawakened (for a moment) under an umbrella in rainy Lounais Park.*

Greta Kara with the summer of youth sleeping beside her. Once lost, long missed, newly found.

Greta Kara made love for breakfast. Now she's combing the cornflakes out of her hair and secretly crying at all the beauty, because beauty fades.

Greta Kara wants to love! Ilsa's lines: "Kiss me. Kiss me as if it were the last time."

Greta Kara would like to be happy, but?... Oh, these awful premonitions...

Her most recent update was written a few hours earlier in the day. It says: *Greta Kara would tell you a love story, but she doesn't yet know the ending.*

Olli writes a comment on the post: *Here's looking at you, kid. I'm coming back to bed. I'll wake you up and kiss you and then we'll write another erotic scene for your story...*

When he walks up the perfect curve of the staircase, Greta is awake. She's sitting on the edge of the bed, naked, examining her body as if she's never seen it before.

Olli watches in wonder as she touches her breasts and thighs and arms. In the light of the garden lamps through the window she looks more ghost than human. As he touches the skin of her back, he feels the thin scars. The room is cool. Greta's skin is cool as well.

Greta turns and looks at Olli as if she doesn't know him, her eyes dark. Finally she breaks into a smile and whispers, "Olli... She's asleep now, but I woke up and found myself here. I was just looking at her while I waited for you. She's beautiful. I hope she pleases you. And this house. This is the one you wanted, isn't it?"

There is a peculiar expression on her face as she pulls Olli's pyjamas down, continuing to speak in such a low voice that he can just barely hear it. "She's tired and worried, poor thing. Let's not wake her. Let me do this now. I've waited so long. Don't worry. I know how to do it."

Olli doesn't like this new game of hers. There's something frightening about it, something repellent.

Then it occurs to him that it might not be a game. Greta doesn't seem to be completely awake. She's behaving like a sleepwalker.

But Olli doesn't resist when she lays him down on the bed, touches his body everywhere, wondering at it like a child with a new toy, and finally takes him inside her with her face glowing in joyous surprise.

Since moving into the Wivi Lönn house with Greta, Olli hasn't dreamt about the girl in the pear-print dress, or anything else. This seems natural to him—his life is like a dream now, so why would he have dreams?

Then, after making love to Greta in this strange state, he does have a dream that lingers troublingly in his mind.

In the dream, he wakes up to a humming sound and sits up in the bed at the Wivi Lönn house. Greta is sleeping beside him. He can see the dark autumn garden through the window. Everything is just as it is in reality, except that at the end of the bed there's a spinning wheel, and the three umbrella vendors are sitting around it.

325

The large, dark woman from Jyväs-brella is naked. She's sweating and milk is dripping from her breasts as she spins her wild, overgrown pubic hair into green yarn.

Maura with the golden hair is measuring out the yarn and checking its quality.

The woman from the Pukkala umbrella shop is smoking a cigarette, her hair in a bun, her face paler than before, her profile remarkably similar to that of the woman sleeping in the bed beside him. Olli is startled when the woman from the umbrella shop suddenly shoots him an icy stare and holds the glowing end of her cigarette near the green strand of yarn, which starts to smoulder.

Then the sleeping Greta stiffens, stops breathing and begins to go pale. The gold of her hair changes to the colour of hay after a frost.

Maura grabs the smoking woman's hand and shakes her head. *Not yet*, she seems to say. The smoking woman gives in and leaves the yarn alone.

The colour returns to Greta's face and hair and she sighs in her sleep.

The next day Greta is playing the piano again. A cold rain lashes the garden. No snow, at least not yet. Olli sits on the little sofa next to the piano reading Rossetti: *Remember me when I am gone away, Gone far away into the silent land...*

Then he puts the book aside, lights a cigarette, smokes for a while and asks: "What about today? Are you completely happy?"

Greta doesn't answer. Her face tenses as she stretches for the notes.

"These hands," she mutters.

"What about them?"

"The clumsy things don't want to play Chopin today," she says. "Maybe I should play 'Chopsticks'. Dr Engel knew how to play it. I taught it to him. Although he knew it by the name *Der Flohwalzer*—the Flea's Waltz."

She's trying to sound amused but when she stops playing and turns to look at Olli there's panic in her eyes. "I think I'm sick. This has happened several times before. I just suddenly can't control my own hands. I feel as if I'm falling into a deep, dark hole."

Olli helps her to the sofa.

"Maybe it's the flu," Olli says, surprised at how unconcerned and sensible he manages to sound.

"Yeah," Greta sighs. "Maybe I'm just coming down with something. Take me in your arms. Hold me tight. I feel cold and dizzy. Don't let me fall. Please don't let go."

A cold sweat breaks out on her forehead. It's clear that she's about to faint.

"Wait a moment," Olli says, laying her down on the sofa. "I'm going to call a taxi and get you to a doctor. Or maybe we should go straight to the hospital."

Greta grabs his sleeve and says in an urgent whisper, "No. I don't want to go to the hospital, I want to stay here. I have my own doctor. Call him. I got a letter about it. I think my French publisher hired him when he heard that I was coming to Jyväskylä. He wanted to make sure I got good care way up here in the godforsaken north. There's a phone number in the letter. It's on the night table."

Dear Miss Kara,

    Welcome to Jyväskylä! I am writing to inform you that I will be at your disposal here for the duration of your stay, should you ever need a physician. I also make house calls. My services are free of charge, and will be covered by the publishers, to whom it is important that your health is attended to. Please do call if you need me, at the number below.

    With best wishes,

        Helmer Oksanen

        General Practitioner

47

T HE DOCTOR ARRIVES an hour later. Olli goes out to the street to meet him.

Dr Oksanen is a greying, bespectacled man with warm eyes who fidgets nervously as he introduces himself. He takes a large De Boissy doctor's bag from the back seat of his Mercedes, walks through the Apple Gate and into the house, and climbs puffing up the stairs to where Greta is waiting in bed.

It takes him two hours to give Greta a complete physical examination. At her request, Olli sits the whole time on a chair next to the bed where she can see him. Dr Oksanen peers into her mouth and ears, feels her glands, draws a blood sample, makes notes, pokes her with pins, talks with her and flips through a thick file with her name on it.

"Her records," he explains to Olli, tapping the folder. "I collected them from every place she's ever been treated the moment I learnt she was to be my patient."

"Ah," Olli says.

When the doctor finishes his examination he asks if he can speak with Greta alone. Olli goes outside the door. Doctor and patient speak in low voices. Then the doctor comes out of the room. "She asked me to speak with you," he says. "Let's go downstairs."

He turns and says to Greta, "Miss Kara, you should avoid any stress and get some rest until you feel better. Goodbye, then. I'll come again in a couple of days—or sooner, if the need arises."

Olli and the doctor sit at the table across from each other. Olli has poured them coffee and put some Domino biscuits on a little tray.

Neither of them is drinking or eating. Olli wishes Dr Oksanen would at least take one biscuit. It would be a good sign.

"Mr Suominen," the doctor begins, his brow furrowed. "I'm very sorry to have to tell you this, but the fact is that Miss Kara's condition doesn't look good."

"What's the problem?" Olli asks, his hands cold as stone.

"Her nervous system," the doctor says, then pauses dramatically. "Of course, I can't make a definitive diagnosis until I see the laboratory results, but based on today's examination and her medical history, I can state with a fair certainty that she has a disorder of the central nervous system of a type that causes demyelination, the destruction of the myelin sheath surrounding the nerve axon. That is the reason for her difficulty in playing the piano, and it's probably also the cause of the diminishment in her level of consciousness which she mentioned to me as well. Basically, her central nervous system is suffering from intermittent interruptions. They're a bit like power outages in a house where mice have gnawed at the wiring, if you'll permit a clumsy analogy. Sometimes everything works smoothly, perhaps even for a long while, but little by little her nervous system will cease functioning and her lungs, heart and other organs will be paralysed, after which death will follow. It's not multiple sclerosis, which is more well known, but a rare and aggressive variant with a progress that is difficult to predict. I'm very sorry."

Olli doesn't feel anything. His body is like a mechanical doll that someone inside him is controlling with strings.

"How can it be treated?" he asks, noting the practised tone of sensibleness in his voice. "Surely there's a treatment for it?"

"Once the lab results come back, I'll send a nurse over with pre-filled syringes. She can advise you then. Injections of glatiramer have been used to slow the progress of symptoms, and they may be effective for Miss Kara. Unfortunately I can't predict with any certainty."

The doctor gets up, pats Olli on the shoulder, picks up his bag and leaves.

The next day a nurse comes over with syringes and teaches Olli to give the injections to Greta, who, luckily, is feeling better again. As he gives her a shot, she looks at him trustingly, like a child. They feel somehow closer than they ever have before. When the nurse leaves, they don't say a word, just take off their clothes and make love.

Greta wraps her legs around him and squeezes so tight that it's hard for him to move.

Her green eyes study him gravely while her body writhes in pleasure.

Not until the very end do her eyes close, and at that moment a sob escapes her lips. "*Mon amour, la petite mort…*"

48

As OCTOBER ADVANCES, the shadows darken in the Wivi Lönn house, but Olli and Greta continue their lives as before, except that they have sex more often and more fiercely than before, not really making love but fucking. They smoke so feverishly that they nearly choke themselves with coughing fits, filling the house with smoke, reading Christina Rossetti over copious quantities of wine, devouring chocolate with no regard to calories and taking long night-time walks.

They walk through the dark side streets of Jyväskylä, sometimes silent, sometimes fervently debating art and politics.

Greta believes in socialism with a human face, while Olli thinks the whole idea is an oxymoron, and proceeds from the assumption that only free markets can ensure people an opportunity to live life as they wish. And when Greta tells him she bought a Jack Vettriano painting for a large sum and hung it on her wall in Paris, Olli says she succumbed to tasteless trash and begins to fervently defend Gustav Klimt, whose work Greta finds coarse and artificial, merely decorative. When Olli praises Ellen Thesleff, Greta says that for some reason she can't stand Thesleff's work, even though the *Sleeping Girl* hung on her bedroom wall in the Tourula days.

They end up arguing, and then, when their talk comes to a sudden stop, they look at each other and Greta gets an impish gleam in her eye. They've just come to an arched courtyard entrance, and Greta pulls Olli under it, takes off her underwear, pulls up her skirt, and announces that she wants him inside her, right now.

Olli smiles in confusion, but he's ready to obey her until a police car cruises past and stops.

They laugh and head back to Hämeenkatu hand in hand. They enact Greta's wish in the colonnade at the Lönn house, oblivious to the cold wind.

Greta is playing Chopin every day again, every piece like it was her last.

Olli is amazed at how much he can enjoy Greta's playing in spite of her diagnosis. It's probably the influence of the M-particles in the house—everything seems slightly dreamy, and thus not so wounding.

"You haven't asked me that question in a while," Greta says once, without a pause in the music, shooting Olli a smile.

Olli doesn't say anything. He doesn't want Greta to see his tears. They haven't really talked about her nerve disorder because they don't want to cede to its power and spoil the moments they have together by talking about it the way you talk about important, life-changing things. They recognize its existence only at the moments when Olli gives Greta her injection of glatiramer, and even then they always make love immediately after the shot, as if to wipe it away from her bodily memory.

When they go upstairs to bed that evening, Greta takes out *A Guide to the Cinematic Life* and reads aloud from the chapter on cinematic death and renunciation:

Everything that is truly awful becomes, by its very inevitability, profoundly beautiful. We have only to learn to embrace the deep shadows of life along with its bright moments, for otherwise we won't have the courage to really live. You don't have to like the pain. It is enough to love it.

Afterwards, they cling to each other.

That night Olli awakes and realizes he's alone in bed.

It's raining.

He hears Chopin from downstairs. Sonata no. 2. He clasps his hands behind his head and listens. Forces himself to comprehend that he is listening to the music of his dying lover.

His chest begins to heave as if gripped by an earthquake. He lets the tears come, covers his face and allows himself to grieve for the first time in months. He's crying for Greta, but also for his own suffering, and that of others. Especially the others.

At the same time, no doubt due to the M-particles, he senses the beauty of his grief, allows himself to enjoy it, like a cigarette or a glass of wine or the music he's listening to at that moment. The feeling comes from deep inside, from the same place as music and literature and all art, filling every corner of his consciousness the way the organ music filled Notre-Dame as he sat in the last pew and listened.

It's just as Greta says in *Cinematic Life*—sorrow, when experienced properly, is an even more beautiful and cinematic emotion than love, though difficult to endure.

The piano plays until wrong notes creep into the composition. Olli sits up.

Silence.

There is a bang from downstairs and a cold draught flows through the house.

Olli runs to the window.

Greta is pacing back and forth in the garden, oblivious to the rain, wearing nothing but a dressing gown.

She seems to be looking for something.

Olli pulls on his pyjamas, stuffs his feet into his slippers and goes down to bring her inside.

When he gets outside he doesn't see Greta anywhere.

The rain is increasing and growing colder. The plants in the garden tremble under it. Olli shouts for Greta. The large, dark garden is filled with hiding places. He checks the storage shed, peeks into the greenhouse and goes to the Apple Gate to make sure she hasn't wandered out into the street. Then he returns to the yard and checks every inch of it, several times. He even looks in the apple trees, in case she's taken it into her head to climb one of them.

His wet pyjamas are clinging to his skin. He's shivering, but he's too worried to notice the cold. Finally he stops in the middle of the garden and stands in his striped pyjamas looking around helplessly, trying to think.

Could she have gone back inside? No, he's sure he would have seen her.

Then he notices Greta's dressing gown lying under a bush, and his heart sinks. Now she's naked, and will surely take a bad chill.

He walks over to the dressing gown. It is, of course, soaking wet and dirty, but looking more closely Olli notices that part of it has also been pulled down into some kind of hole.

An animal's burrow.

Some dirty, diseased, yellow-toothed animal, probably oozing bacteria.

Olli feels like he's going to throw up. His head is buzzing. He has a tremendous desire to forget he saw the dressing gown, to look the other way and get out of there, get away from that revolting hole.

But he makes himself stay because the feeling itself tells him what is happening. He falls on all fours and finds the narrow opening in the tall grass where Greta crawled in. He starts to tear away the grass and withered flowers and wet leaves, until the entrance to the secret passage is finally visible.

He starts to shiver harder as he looks into the darkness that waits under the ground. No person in his right mind would even put his hand in there. There could be beetles, snakes, centipedes, rotted carcasses, rats or larger, sharp-toothed animals...

All his instincts tell him to cover the hole up again.

Right now.

Before something awful happens.

He takes a deep breath, willing his pulse to level off, his stress hormones to dissipate. He empties his mind of thought and focuses, as though preparing to dive into cold water.

Then, without thinking, he sticks his hand into the hole in the ground.

Then his head.

Followed by his upper body.

The smell of earth strikes his face and he almost pulls himself out again. What in heaven's name is he doing? The only sensible thing to do is of course to run into the house and call the police, or the fire department, to come and get Greta.

Olli sobs and trembles as he forces himself farther under the ground.

Eventually his body begins to crawl, automatically, like he learnt to do as a child with the other members of the Tourula Five. He can still remember Karri's words: *Think of your body as a crawling machine. Don't think about anything else.*

You can only go into a secret passage if you learn to eliminate your natural psychological resistance.

Wet mud gets into his nostrils, his mouth, his eyes. The cold earth tears at his skin. His pyjamas are no protection. He coughs and snorts. He doesn't just fear, he *knows* that in a moment he will suffocate and die, get stuck, have a heart attack, or bleed to death when some fierce animal—a weasel, or maybe a badger—bites his face, goes for his throat.

But Olli's body remembers thirty years ago, ignores his instinct for self-preservation, and crawls ahead, deeper into the cold and the dark.

49

O LLI CRAWLS.
Once you manage to get inside a secret passage, moving forward becomes easier. Your mind stops struggling, opens up to the M-particles, and starts to move.

Then the secret passages begin to lure you deeper and deeper.

Reality becomes a Rubik's cube played with by invisible fingers. Olli starts to remember things he's forgotten, and at the same time to forget the parts of his life that he left above the ground a moment ago—or maybe hundreds of years ago. Time has no meaning here. In the secret passages, the past and the present are touching, as are what is and what simply could be. In the secret passages you can remember every choice you've ever had to make and all of those crossroads are spread out in alternative continuums. You just have to know how to listen to the music of the M-particles.

Karri once warned them that the magical feeling in the secret passages is powerful and dangerous and can rinse your mind so clean of all human connection that there is no return.

Even a short visit there always changes a person somehow.

Olli crawls. He knows he's searching for something. But what?

A girl.

Not a girl.

A woman.

The woman that the girl became.

Greta, the girl in the pear-print dress, is here somewhere. It's dark. Olli holds on to that name, and to the shadow of Greta; he can't drop them, no matter how hard the M-particles shake him.

Shadows waver in the blackness. Sometimes he thinks he sees something, but in the secret passages you can't trust your eyes. You might see all kinds of things and become so confused that you forget to crawl. And you can't stop crawling, not for more than a second, or something bad could happen.

The size of the passage varies. Sometimes it's open and he can walk in a stoop. Sometimes he can even stand up straight. Then he has to crouch again, hold his breath and wriggle forward like a snake or a lizard.

Holding on to the name, and the thought of the pear-print dress, Olli crawls and crawls.

At some point the darkness begins to flow around him like water and mermaids swim up to him. They smile sweetly and beckon him to come and play. He smiles back.

Rest a while and look at us. Are we not beautiful?

You are, he answers, not stopping, remembering the importance of crawling.

Wouldn't you like to touch us, caress our salty skin, kiss our breasts? Let us take away your burden and everything you've left behind up there. We can give you sweet forgetfulness in our arms...

Olli shakes his head.

You can have your little plastic boat back, too. Remember? Perhaps we won't need it any more once we have you... At least tell us your name. What do you say—the boat for your name?

No, Olli whispers.

The mermaids' playfulness vanishes.

Then maybe we will take your son. He likes our song so much, because he can hear the M-particles in it, and he might wade too far out at some moment when his poor mother is looking the other way...

Olli stops, flings a handful of gravel at the mermaids, and keeps crawling as they scatter into the darkness.

Then comes a tight turn.

It leads to the right and down.

He gropes at the darkness, feels the walls, twists and turns his body to make his way forward. Gravel scrapes his belly bloody. His trousers come off. A root on the ceiling tears at his face.

As he pulls himself a little farther forward a root catches at his testicles, like the cold hand of a witch, and he has to stop to keep them from being torn off.

Then a memory begins to unwrap itself in his mind, so powerful that it makes him stop where he is, his body painfully twisted.

In the memory he's in a boat on the Touru River with the Blomrooses and Karri. Three days of heavy rain has just ended a couple of hours earlier. The air is still damp. A thick mist hangs over the river, hiding the shores and making the world dim and cottony.

Leo is rowing upstream. Anne is at the rudder. Her white panties peak out from under her plaid skirt. Anne notices Olli looking at them and smiles teasingly. Karri in his hood is crouched at the bow, a grey lump, peering out at the ravine. Riku is sitting next to Olli in the middle of the boat, sourly playing with his Coca-Cola yo-yo.

Anne eventually tells him to put the yo-yo away so the boat won't rock.

The weight of the five of them makes the little boat ride dangerously low. They couldn't fit Timi in the boat, but he follows along on the shore. They can't see him, but they can hear him panting and barking through the fog, and they shout encouragement so he won't give up and wander off.

On their right, invisible on the high ridge, is the beginning of the grounds of the paper mill. On the left is thick forest. Beyond the trees the land rises up in a steep hillside with the old cemetery at the top.

When they left the house they told each other that it was a perfect day for an expedition.

Yesterday they looked at a map and saw that it was only two kilometres upstream to where the lake emptied into the Touru, and they decided to take the boat to the river's source. Aunt Anna, however, told them not to go beyond the dam at the paper mill. They lamented this for a moment, then decided that they could still explore the ravine in the boat and go ashore somewhere interesting.

Such a place seems to have just been found.

Timi starts to bark excitedly and comes to a stop somewhere in the mist.

Karri points towards the sound and Anne steers the boat in that direction.

The shore comes into view through the fog. They're headed towards it fast. Olli takes hold of the sides of the boat and prepares himself for a crash.

But they don't crash.

The boat clatters and scrapes through a wall of bushes

and branches and up a narrow bank of sludge. They come to a rocking stop in a cove just slightly larger than the boat.

Timi weaves his way towards them through the trees, then leaps into the boat, barking happily, and licks Olli's hand.

They crouch under the encroaching branches for a moment, then start pushing the limbs aside, preparing to get out and explore the riverbank.

Timi dashes between Riku and Olli to greet Leo and Karri, and the boat lists out of balance.

Then something unexpected happens.

There's a crash and a fall, as if the earth has given way beneath them. A cavern opens up and the water in the cove rushes into it, as does the bow of the boat. As the stern rises into the air, Anne falls with a scream into Olli's lap. Timi howls in panic and bites Riku's leg. Riku curses loudly. Leo orders everybody to hold on.

Someone laughs.

Karri.

The others aren't laughing. They're lying on the bottom of the boat as it slides with the sludge into the darkness.

A secret passage.

Anne squeezes Olli's arm and Olli holds the side of the boat with one hand and the girl with the other. He can feel her breast against his arm. They can't see anything, and the noise of the fall blocks all other sounds.

The trip down seems to take hours, but the powerful M-particles in the secret passages make it impossible to tell; it may all be happening in a matter of minutes. Olli's world shrinks to a clatter, a thud, a scream, darkness, sliding, tossing, falling and Anne's aching grip on his arm, until he can no longer remember there ever being anything else.

At some point the boat's side strikes a rock with a violent shake. Something soft, darker than the surrounding blackness, falls onto Olli, then climbs up him and flies away.

On many nights afterwards, at the border between waking and sleep, that moment returns to him. When it does, he tortures himself by imagining that through the noise he hears panicked barks, followed by a desperate, echoing howl.

They stop. Silence.

Then sound returns and the five children stumble to their feet. The wooden carcass of the boat creaks under their weight.

There's a dripping of water somewhere.

Olli can hear and feel Anne breathing. As the particles of light begin to collect, diluting the darkness, he sees Leo and Riku looking around, their eyes wide. Anne, in shock, completely forgets to be mocking and self-assured.

Karri is already exploring the place. In the secret passages are many wondrous things, and although the memory of them never lasts the light of day, they're still worth investigating.

If Olli can trust his eyes, they've come to some sort of underground chamber. In the passages, you can never be sure.

He sorts out his mind, which the M-particles have penetrated and muddled, and realizes that Timi is no longer with them.

He's gone.

*

343

In the secret passages, it's dangerous to stop; to keep crawling forward is life itself. The Five learnt that quickly, and as Olli becomes aware of a pain in his back and side, he realizes that he has stopped at that bend in the tunnel to gnaw on his memory like a dog on a bone, and he's started to forget himself in the process.

In the nick of time, he gets a hold of that self and starts moving again, crawling forward for a time with his head humming empty.

Eventually he finds his name, straggling somewhere behind him, more than half disconnected. He gets hold of his Olliness and continues crawling, starts to collect himself from memories scattered in the dark passageway, and put his life back together one piece at a time.

One of the memories is of one of the numerous times that the Tourula Five returned from under the ground. It follows the earlier memory, but large portions are missing.

In the memory, Olli and the others are crawling, first in the dark, then in the light, although they don't notice it at first. Finally they realize that they can let their bodies stop crawling, and they look around in stunned silence.

They're in a large fenced garden. Higher up the slope is a grand, palatial house with pillars like the Greek temples in Olli's geography book, curved, ornamented windows and some sort of glass pyramid attached to its side, with plants growing in it.

The house makes Olli tremble with excitement. He whispers that it's exactly the sort of house he wants to live in when he grows up.

Karri turns and looks at him from under his hood,

seeming to sniff at the words, trying to see the thoughts behind them.

Anne wrinkles her nose and says sure, it's a fine house, but too small and modest for her taste. Once she's rich she'll be able to buy it for a place to stay whenever she has business in Jyväskylä. But her permanent home will be in France, or maybe Spain.

Leo and Riku chuckle. They don't take their sister's plans very seriously.

Then the balcony door opens and the occupant, an old woman, appears.

The Five take to their feet.

As he runs with the others, Olli notices that Timi isn't with them.

He doesn't have time to stop and mourn because the mistress of the house is now standing at the ground-floor entrance, in front of the pillars, and next to her is a German shepherd with a booming bark.

The memory ends with them running out to the road in relief, and at the very end Olli turns back to look one more time and sees apples carved into the curved top of an arch.

Olli puts the memory aside. He has to concentrate on crawling and keeping himself together. He thinks and remembers and organizes his thoughts as he turns right and left, up and down in the twists of the passages, making his way by instinct. Some of the memories are wrong and have to be discarded, and even the correct pieces don't all fit together. But eventually he thinks he's whole enough to venture to pay attention to what's outside him.

There's space around him now.

He stops, wraps his aching arms around his bruised and bloody knees and sits naked in the dark, waiting for the light particles to begin to gather around him.

Eventually he sees something. He's in some kind of chamber. Or cave.

In the darkness he looks at his hands, his legs, his stomach, his hairy chest, his cold-bitten penis, his sad, muddy testicles and time-battered skin, and is amazed to realize how old he is, how adult, when just a moment ago he was a smooth, slim young boy.

If he could go back to the branch of the passageway he came from maybe he could reach his childhood and stay there…

But he remembers what he has to do: find the girl in the pear-print dress, the woman pianist, and bring her back.

He's tempted to forget the whole thing, but the task must be very important to him above the ground.

So he gets up and gropes his way forward—until astonishment stops him. There's a tree growing from the ceiling, upside-down, with branches sagging under a weight of pears.

He reaches out and finds he can touch them. Then his eye falls on two grey boys sitting among the branches, staring at him with pitch-black eyes.

They look at each other for a long time.

Olli recognizes them. Leo and Riku Blomroos.

Then the boys smile and point at their heads. They both have a small, black hole in the middle of their forehead, and a peculiar, thick darkness is seeping out of the holes.

The lips are moving on the one who looks like Leo, and although there's no sound, Olli understands what he's saying.

We're dead now.

When Olli turns to the ghost that looks like Riku, it nods grimly and points at something.

Look over there. Look familiar?

Farther away, Olli sees the remains of Aunt Anna's boat. He's been to this place before.

We can't eat the pears, but you can have one. Take a bite. That's what she's doing.

That's when Olli notices the naked, golden-haired woman sitting on the other side of the tree.

Greta.

She's tasting pears, which are arranged around her, taking a bite of one and then another, as if she were deciding which one is best to eat.

Her face is filled with utter pleasure.

Olli becomes curious, picks a pear from a branch and warily takes a bite.

A soft flavour spreads through his mouth and his mind fills with living images that are like memories of things that have never happened. They are clear and enthrallingly cinematic and they show him his life as it could have been if he had only made brave, cinematic choices.

He has to see more, to finish the story. He takes another bite, and another.

When he's eaten the first pear, he eats a second one, and a third. After that he takes just one or two bites from each fruit.

Every one shows him a different film version of his life.

347

He bites a bitter pear that is a tragic story of survival, filled with illness and misfortune, and spits it out. The next one is sweet and filled with success, glory, riches. Almost all of them have larger-than-life love stories. Some of them are romantic comedies, others portentous melodramas. There are many different women that he's met during his life, and others that he's never heard or dreamt of.

He goes through hundreds of lives, forgetting each one as he tastes the next, smiling in the dark. The naked, golden-haired woman is eating pears nearby, but he doesn't pay her any attention.

There are plenty of pears. The Blomroos brothers drop more for them. *What kind of life is this? Good or bad? Sadness, fear, excitement or insane, intoxicating love?*

Then, from out of the dark, a dog appears.

A cocker spaniel. It barks at him, growls and shows its teeth.

Timi, he says, testing the name.

The dog recognizes him and its tail wags joyfully, but it still approaches yapping and growling.

He realizes that the dog is looking at the bitten pear in his hand.

He throws the pear away, teeters and falls on his back. There's something leathery beneath him, something fragile that crunches. Dead birds with delicate bones, he thinks, cringing. Or bats' carcasses.

As the light particles gather around him, he sees that he was mistaken—he's lying on umbrellas. There are umbrellas everywhere; the whole floor of the cave is covered with them.

He sits up and takes hold of one of them. It's the

starry-night umbrella that he lost at Sokos department store. It's not the only one he recognizes—all the umbrellas he's ever lost seem to be here.

He remembers now that he often saw the dog at the same time that he lost an umbrella.

He shakes his head, looks at Timi for a moment, then pushes him aside and goes back to the pear tree. There are still a lot of pears to taste, regardless of what that ghost dog thinks about it.

Riku and Leo each ply him with pears, their black eyes glittering, dark puffs of air coming out of the openings in their skulls.

Have a taste of this firm little one and tell me what you see!

No, take a bite of this one first. It's got to be something amazing; look how juicy it is…

Olli chooses the pear Leo is offering. Timi comes back just as he takes a bite, and drops something at his feet.

Olli picks it up. It's the dome umbrella from thirty years ago. His skin tingles.

Aunt Anna brought this umbrella home from France, and Olli and his girl in her pear-print dress kissed under it as they walked through the streets of Jyväskylä. Their very first kiss was under this umbrella, on the bridge over the Touru, on the first day of the summer they spent together.

It gleams in the dimness with the green light of distant summer.

The ghostly Blomroos brothers grimace and climb as high into the pear tree as they can, as far as the trunk that protrudes from the ceiling of the cave.

Olli and Greta look at the green dome of the umbrella,

then at each other, and finally at the dog sitting under the tree with a look of contentment.

Then they look at each other again, and they recognize each other, and embrace.

50

H<small>E'S CRAWLING.</small>
      He has what he came for, and now he's crawling.

They're both crawling, although it would be so nice to stop and forget themselves in the dark. His body hurts and his mind wants to give in to the M-particles, but the dog is following them, forcing them to keep moving.

The mermaids return and swim around them, sparkling and dancing, and the swirling dance grabs hold of him and spins him wildly. *You're not leaving, are you? Rest here awhile in our arms... We want so badly to kiss you all over... You can't know how good we can be for you...*

He smiles at them but then the dog chases them away. They recoil from the green umbrella he has in his mouth.

The darkness turns to light.

Olli's battered, dazzled body crawls out into the bright cold, dragging Greta with it.

Gradually their minds and eyes adjust to the world above the ground. They stumble towards the house. It's a cold morning. The ground is frozen but there's no snow yet; the garden is still filled with autumn colours. They're naked and filthy and covered in cuts, scrapes and gashes. They're shaking uncontrollably. Their arms and legs jerk like clumsy marionettes; their bodies want to keep on crawling.

Olli thinks he hears something, and turns to look. At the

place where they've come out of the ground stands a black and white cocker spaniel. It seems to have a green umbrella in its mouth. Olli rubs his eyes and looks again, and the dog is gone.

Everything that happened in the secret passage quickly fades and disappears. He knows he followed Greta into the passageway, and that they came back out together. All sorts of vague things linger at the edge of his consciousness. There's a dog, for example, who has something to do with what happened down there.

Timi?

Olli strains his memory, then gives up and turns to Greta. She's staring blankly at her dirty feet.

Inside the house Olli fills a hot bath and they clamber into it. When they've stopped shaking, he asks her why she went into the secret passageway.

She answers glumly, guiltily, that she has no idea, and asks him to forgive her. "All I remember is that I went downstairs to see if I could still play. Then we were there in the garden and it was horribly cold."

"Crazy girl," Olli sighs.

They look at each other for a long time without speaking.

"I wish we could remember what happened down there," Olli says. "We were there for a long time. And the M-particles were... How do you feel? Any different?"

Greta shrugs.

Silence.

Finally they get out of the bath, dry each other off, go up the stairs and climb under the covers to sleep off their weariness.

"Olli, don't go to sleep just yet," Greta says. "Let's make love first."

Olli is tired, but he nods, takes her in his arms and kisses her. Then he realizes she's snuffling, fast asleep.

When he wakes up, it's evening.

Greta is awake. She's lying beside him on her back, facing the ceiling, looking at him from a strange angle, out of the corner of her eye.

"What's wrong?" he asks with a smile from under the blanket, laying his arm across her belly. It's warm. "Is there a spider on the ceiling?"

Greta tries to smile.

"It's just that I…" she says in a whisper. "I don't seem to be able to move."

51

AFTER EXAMINING GRETA, Dr Oksanen gives her an injection in the arm, strokes her hair, and leads Olli out into the hallway.

Greta watches them, her face peaceful.

"The exposure to cold has worsened Miss Kara's condition. It's a shame that it's come to this," the doctor mutters. "But mental confusion is a symptom of this illness, and there's no telling what a patient may do when a spell like this comes over her. Some of her ability to move has returned and she's calm now, but she's experiencing arrhythmia and difficulty breathing and her internal organs are beginning to fail. And unfortunately all of these things indicate that her central nervous system seems to be entering its final paralysis. Her condition may change for the better temporarily, but it may also collapse completely at any moment. All I can do is alleviate her pain. I just gave her some morphine. She has a few hours, perhaps a day, or two at most. I'm very sorry."

Olli bows his head and struggles to understand. "I'm sorry," he laughs, "but this can't be how it goes. Why don't I take her to a hospital? Surely they can help her there?"

Dr Oksanen lays a hand on Olli's shoulder and looks at him closely, right in the eye, to be sure that he hears and understands.

"Mr Suominen," he says emphatically. "Believe me when I say that nothing can be done. Nothing. The end is near, and the only thing left open is what happens before that. Yes, we could take Miss Kara to a hospital, but the strain of that would, I fear, only hasten her end. At least here the two of you can say goodbye to each other in peace. I'll leave you now and go home. I live just fifteen minutes away, and my phone is always on. Call me if it seems necessary, and I'll come. But I must tell you again that I can't do anything for this patient but give her more pain medication if she needs it. There is no hope for her, but there's enough of life left that while she is alive, something beautiful could still happen."

When the doctor is gone, Olli goes back to Greta. She beckons him closer. "It doesn't hurt any more," she says quietly, and smiles.

"Good," Olli says. "That's very good."

"I heard what the doctor said. We don't have much more time."

"No, we don't."

Olli can't bear to look into her eyes.

Greta snorts, grabs his head and turns his face towards her. "My sweet fool," she whispers. "Look at me while you still can! Let's get all we can out of the time we have left. To start with, help me get out of this ridiculous nightgown. It's like some sort of horrible shroud, and I don't intend to be a corpse until the doctor pronounces me dead. Take off your clothes. Come lie beside me. Touch me. Let's hold on to each other."

Olli gets undressed and crawls in next to her, under the covers. Her skin feels cool.

"You're so warm," she whispers.

She's pale and exhausted and her voice is like a fragile

instrument, but the green in her eyes begins to burn with frightening power.

"Please kiss me, my darling. And don't hold back. I won't break. Kiss me for all the years we should have had together."

Olli presses his lips against hers.

As they kiss, the M-particles in the house wrap around them, seep into their skin and flow through their veins.

Kisses are an important part of a cinematic way of life.

A kiss can be playful, light, rough, violent, stolen, gentle, cold, sensual, deceitful, treacherous, cavalier, forbidden, sinful, loving or lustful—and combinations of these can also be very interesting—but a kiss is always a kiss. The touching of lips is a basic unit of erotic contact. Like a cigarette, a kiss can be used to express thoughts and feelings too complex, or too straightforward, to put into words.

The most interesting cinematic kisses are always alive, and can contain the contextual contrasts of detachment and desire, faith and betrayal, love and hate, approach and separation. What could be more cinematic in feeling than a goodbye kiss, combining sensual joy and pleasure with the pain of renunciation?

(Kissing stills on following page: Robert Taylor and Vivien Leigh in Waterloo Bridge. *Humphrey Bogart and Mary Astor in* The Maltese Falcon. *Errol Flynn and Olivia de Havilland in* They Died with Their Boots On. *Humphrey Bogart and Ingrid Bergman in* Casablanca. *Gary Cooper and Ingrid Bergman in* For Whom the Bell Tolls. *Nino Castelnuovo and Catherine Deneuve in* The Umbrellas of Cherbourg. *Gregory Peck and Jennifer Jones in* Duel in the Sun. *John Garfield and Lana Turner in* The Postman Always Rings

Twice. *Heath Ledger and Jake Gyllenhaal in* Brokeback Mountain.*)*

GRETA KARA,
A Guide to the Cinematic Life

When they finish their kiss, Greta wipes the tears away, first from Olli's face, then from her own, and smiles, and whispers, "Well, that certainly won't kill me, now will it? And darling, I'm so glad that I still turn you on. And you do me, too. Now lie on top of me, Olli. Make love to me."

Olli hesitates.

"I can't."

Greta scowls and slaps his face.

He yelps, rubs his cheek and looks at her in amazement.

"I'm sorry, darling, but don't be an idiot. I don't have time for it," Greta pants, taking him in her limp arms. "It won't hurt me. Can't you see I'm still alive? I love you now more than I will when I'm dead. Take me now, so I can feel it... And hold me, hold me so tight that I scream... You see, there's one thought that comforts me: that when I'm dead and cold and they come to take my body away, it will have your smell on it, and the traces of your love."

52

AFTER THEY MAKE LOVE they are overcome with a weariness as big as the universe. Greta is falling asleep. Olli's still awake.

At some point Greta lets go of his neck, turns and sighs. She is pale but calm. Her breath is fairly steady now, though shallow and quick. The marks of Olli's teeth are distinct on her pale skin, just as she wanted. Olli, too, has deep, bloody scratches on his back and sides. *I hope that at my funeral the marks of my fingernails will remind you of one thing: the most important part of our love story won't be that I died, but that I lived, through you, and for you...*

Greta smiles in her sleep. Olli smiles at the sleeping woman. For a little while everything is all right.

After a moment's hesitation, he puts on his slippers and goes downstairs. He uses the toilet, drinks a glass of mineral water, eats a pear, sits down at the dining-room table and turns on the computer. He can spend a few minutes on Facebook while Greta gets some rest.

Aino's profile has a new travel photo. Aino and the boy look straight into the camera, sunburnt and exhausted. Their eyes ask: *Why can't we come home?*

The M-particles ease Olli's guilt. They show him in a filmic light. Enthralled to the mission he's been given by the kidnappers, Olli Suominen may be a selfish cinematic character, in some sense even a traitor, but it's all for the sake of a larger-than-life love, and there's nothing a cinematic person can do about a sequence of dramatic events once it's set in motion. All's fair in love and war.

Then he notices that he has a new Facebook alert:

Karri has confirmed you as a friend on Facebook.

A chill goes through him. His hands feel numb and he sits there for a moment. He goes to light a cigarette, takes a drag and goes back to the computer to look at Karri Kultanen's profile.

The profile photo is a sculpture of a naked youth. Olli remembers seeing it in person when he was at the Louvre. It's called *Sleeping Hermaphroditus*. It was sculpted by Bernini sometime in the 1600s, on a commission from a cardinal. The sculpted figure had a woman's breasts and a penis. When Olli noticed this at the Louvre it gave him a start, which made the French publishers and the Swedish literary agent he was with burst into laughter.

Olli looks at Karri's information, which doesn't mention his birthday, gender or hometown. All that's there is his favourite quote, which Olli recognizes. It's from Ovid's *Metamorphoses*:

> *The restless boy still obstinately strove*
> *To free himself, and still refused her love.*
> *Amidst his limbs she kept her limbs intwined,*
> *"And why, coy youth," she cries, "why thus unkind!*
> *Oh may the Gods thus keep us ever joined!*
> *Oh may we never, never part again!"*
> *So prayed the nymph, nor did she pray in vain:*
> *For now she finds him, as his limbs she pressed,*

Grow nearer still, and nearer to her breast;
Till, piercing each the other's flesh, they run
Together, and incorporate in one:
Last in one face are both their faces joined,
As when the stock and grafted twig combined
Shoot up the same, and wear a common rind:
Both bodies in a single body mix,
A single body with a double sex.

Karri's profile has a few status updates, though not many comments. But then he only has five Facebook friends: Olli, Aino and the Blomrooses. The most recent post is from a week ago, written at night:

Karri Kultanen just woke up and is trying not to wake the man beside him and his little nymph.

Underneath it says:

Anne Blomroos likes this.

The next most recent post is from more than a year earlier, in the spring:

Karri Kultanen took two jacks out of the game, but spared the blonde Queen of Spades.

Under that one it says:

Anne Blomroos and 2 others like this.

The two others are Riku and Leo Blomroos.

There's also a comment from Anne:

I don't think my dear brothers would mind my bringing them along on this little cinematic project of ours (which I think of as a romantic comedy, although it does perhaps have hints of black). It'll make them look a little less small-minded than they really were, in at least one person's eyes.

Olli's cigarette has fallen on the table. He picks it up, brushes the ashes onto the floor and takes a long drag, trying to comprehend it all.

Now a little chat window with a tiny image of the sleeping Hermaphroditus and Karri Kultanen's name opens up at the bottom of the screen; Olli is so frightened that he shouts a curse.

Of course, he's aware that it's possible to chat through Facebook. He's just never had any reason to try it. Email is modern enough for him.

The message in the box says: *Hello, friend.*

Olli feels like screaming. And turning off the computer. But instead he writes: *Karri?*

Answer: *Yes. We should talk.*

Olli shakes his head. No, no, no, he really doesn't want to talk; he doesn't want to know anything about Karri. With trembling fingers, however, he writes: *Where are you?*

Then, answering his own question, he mutters aloud, "Where do you think, Sherlock?"

He shivers. His ears ring. He feels like he's going to vomit. A moment passes. Olli imagines his correspondent putting his thoughts in order.

Finally, text appears on the screen:

Olli my friend, I'm so sorry, but it's nearly time for the closing scene.

53

WHEN OLLI WALKS into the bedroom, Greta is slumped on the edge of the bed. Her arms hang at her sides and her whole body is trembling. The laptop on the night table is open and the screen illuminates her pale face. "I guess I turned on the computer in my sleep," she says quietly. "I must have wanted to look at Facebook. But I can't. I feel numb. My feet are frozen."

There's no green in her eyes now, just the dark of October.

Olli helps her to lie down on the bed and puts the covers over her. Her breath is laboured and her pulse erratic.

"I can rub your feet to warm them," Olli says, and looks out the window. "But first let's put the computer away…"

The approaching winter grips the house tight. According to the weather reports the first snow could come at any time.

Greta takes hold of Olli's hand and whispers, "No, leave it on. I need Facebook… Please don't think me silly, darling, but I want to leave a goodbye message for all the people I know around the world, when I feel the end is at hand… I still have to think of what to write. Would you help me with that, Olli?"

Olli strokes her golden hair and nods, because he can't speak. It feels as if his chest is trying to tear itself open. But for Greta's sake he'll hold himself together until the end. For Greta, and for his family, of course.

"All right," he finally whispers. "But that's not something

that has to be done tonight. Not at all. There'll be time tomorrow. Let's wait until morning, together."

Death is justly considered the high point of a cinematic life. It is a strong ending for any story that has been lived truly, and also serves as a dramatic element, if not the critical turning point, in the lives of those who know the dying person.

Depending on the context and point of view, death can be emotional and melodramatic, coolly laconic and expressionless, courageous, happy, symbolic, senseless, terrifying, sickening, ironic, tragic, even comic, but whatever the tone, it gives ultimate meaning to everything that has come before it. If at all possible, a cinematic person should pay particular attention to his or her death, in order to make it elegant and cinematically meaningful.

(See following page, death scenes: Max Schreck in Nosferatu; *Lew Ayres in* All Quiet on the Western Front; *Helen Hayes in* A Farewell to Arms; *James Cagney in* Angels with Dirty Faces; *Gregory Peck and Jennifer Jones in* Duel in the Sun; *Ali MacGraw and Ryan O'Neal in* Love Story.*)*

GRETA KARA,
A Guide to the Cinematic Life

The windows brighten. They lie under the covers, holding each other. The house is heavy with silence. The doctor, whom Olli summoned at six o'clock, is making no sound downstairs. He's probably reading the book he brought with him, some kind of play.

Olli's hand is on Greta's left breast. His index finger is laid across her nipple, his thumb gently pressing the side of her breast. He feels a scar stretching under his hand and thinks that it's there because of him. The thought floods him with an overwhelming tenderness.

His face is pressed against Greta's neck. He breathes through her golden hair and seems to smell the scent of a warm hillside. It fills the room and carries him back to a meadow where they had a picnic a few days after they lay together in Wivi Lönn's house for the first time. Autumn was postponed for a day and summer blazed up one last time before the coming winter.

They sat in the tall grass to eat, and ended up having sex. It was more ritual than unbridled passion. Without a word, Greta put her half-eaten tomato sandwich back in the basket, unzipped Olli's trousers, took her panties off under her dress and sat on his lap.

As they merged, the M-particles sang to them from deep in the earth, and for one moment Olli sensed all the secret passages in Jyväskylä, their locations, their routes, as if he were viewing a map drawn on his soul.

Naturally, their meadow is mentioned in the *Magical City Guide*. Olli wonders if a lot of people will go there now that the book is available and the first printing is virtually sold out. Maiju at the office has told him that next summer the Jyväskylä tourist office is planning to sell guided tours to all the magical places where his love for Greta Kara was reborn. The thought of it makes Olli sad, although it is good news for the business.

He lies at the edge of sleep and imagines them first at the meadow and then in Tourula, in the house on the bank of the river. He is startled when Greta makes a sound.

His left knee has been tucked between her thighs for a

long time. His leg is starting to go to sleep, but he can't bring himself to move it because he doesn't want to disturb her.

Greta turns, points at the computer and breathes a request. Olli picks it up, puts it in her lap and helps her hands to the keyboard. She writes her last status update, closes the computer, and looks up at Olli.

Before she falls into another sleep, he thinks he sees the sun reflected in the green of her eyes. He turns to the window and is surprised to see that the sky is an impenetrable grey.

He puts away the computer, gets dressed and sits in the chair next to the bed, watching the life fade from the golden-haired woman. He holds her hand and looks at her red-painted fingernails. Her fingers grow cold; her face turns waxen; her breath slows and stumbles. Olli isn't sure if he knows how to feel for a pulse, but it feels weak and irregular and sometimes disappears altogether.

Hours pass.

Olli sits, waits and makes observations. They fall like drops somewhere inside him, waiting to be pondered later.

Greta has been silent and still for a long time. Olli bends closer. Then her lips part and smile weakly.

She whispers, "Olli, ask me now..."

Her voice is like the rustle of dead leaves. It takes a moment for him to understand what she means, and another moment to collect himself.

Finally, he asks her the question. But Greta is already gone.

The End

AFTER PRONOUNCING GRETA KARA DEAD, Dr Oksanen sighs and pulls the blanket up over the face of the deceased. The blanket is covered in white satin, and the effect is impeccably cinematic.

Olli feels cold. He and the doctor stand next to the bed in their suits, stiff and serious, their arms at their sides, both wearing ties. Greta lies naked under the blanket, the marks of Olli's teeth still on her skin.

"My condolences," the doctor says. "It's obvious how much the two of you meant to each other. I sense a great love. I hope that you were able to say goodbye to each other and nothing was left unresolved between you. As a physician, I see all sorts of things. Many kinds of deaths. Sad ends. Bitterness. Inability to put away pride and ask for forgiveness even when faced with eternal separation. This is so very sad, but I hope I don't offend you if I venture to say, Mr Suominen, that your love story had a very beautiful ending."

Olli nods. He's numb, and the situation is unreal, right down to the drama-reading Dr Oksanen's brief speech.

They go downstairs and shake hands. The doctor prepares to leave. He promises to take care of the requisite notifications relevant to Greta's death, which he says "falls to him in his role as physician". He also says that someone will come soon for Greta's body, and the owner of the house will come to take care of everything connected with terminating the rental contract. Olli needn't worry about anything. He can "walk out of this house of sorrow and close the door behind him and focus on grieving".

They look at each other. The doctor seems to remember something. "Ah, yes. I nearly forgot something in the bedroom..."

He goes upstairs and remains there for several minutes. Returning with his bag, he avoids eye contact, bows quickly and leaves.

After the doctor left, Olli packed up the things he'd brought with him to the house. There wasn't much. He put the suitcase by the front door. Then he sat down at the dining-room table, poured himself a cup of thick, bitter coffee, turned on the computer and opened Facebook.

Greta's last status update said:

Greta Kara is completely happy.

Olli stared at the text for a long time.

Finally, he closed the computer. He knew that he was supposed to leave so that everything could progress as it was meant to. His part of the story was over. His life would continue elsewhere, more or less attached to the slow continuum. He had many things to take care of.

But he wanted to see what happened after the credits rolled, so he stayed to watch.

Roll Credits

55

S OME TIME PASSED, and then Olli heard sounds from the bedroom. First the squeak of the bed. Then coughing.

He didn't go to look, just poured himself some more bad coffee. He could imagine what was happening upstairs. Karri had briefly described what would happen by chat, saying that he didn't want to give Olli a scare or mislead him unnecessarily. But certain things had to happen in a preordained manner.

In spite of his curiosity, Olli didn't think it wise to go and look as the body of the one he had loved more than he had ever loved anyone opened its eyes and emerged from under the covers as a different person.

The medicine he had given to Greta was a substance that slowed the vital functions, and the doctor had gone upstairs just before he left to give the faux deceased an antidote.

Someone opened the front door with a key. Olli heard people talking. A white coffin was carried in. Two men set it down in the middle of the floor, glanced at Olli and walked out again.

A bustling, well-groomed woman came in after them. Olli guessed that she was a beautician. She had a garment bag over one arm and some kind of tool satchel in the other. She greeted Olli and pointed at the stairway.

"Up there?"

Olli nodded.

She smiled gratefully and climbed the stairs.

About an hour passed. The woman came back downstairs, waved at Olli and left.

Olli looked up at the staircase.

On the top step stood an androgynous figure with black, shoulder-length hair, a white dress shirt, grey trousers and a black waistcoat with shiny buttons.

Karri smiled, descended the staircase, looked at the coffin with a furrowed brow and sat down across from Olli.

"My hairdresser told me that there was a stylish gentleman down here drinking coffee," Karri said light-heartedly, in a voice only partly familiar. "The plan was for you to leave before I arrived, but I'm glad you waited. So, Greta Kara's funeral is in three weeks. She'll be buried—or at least her pear-print dress will—in the old Jyväskylä cemetery, near to you and to all the places where she was happy. It was her last wish. Of course, you'll be expected at the funeral, both as a grieving lover and as a grieving publisher."

Olli lit a cigarette and offered it to Karri. He shook his head. "Thanks, but I don't smoke. That was Greta's vice, not mine."

Olli looked at Karri's neck, where his teeth marks were still visible, and sighed.

Karri smiled. "I'm sorry. I know that this is all strange to you. No doubt you won't be able to get it into your head that Greta is gone, and that this is Karri sitting in front of you. My hair is short and black now, I'm wearing different clothes, the red is gone from my fingernails, but…"

"Yeah," Olli muttered.

Karri shrugged and said, "Actually, Karri is no more real than Greta. He'll have to step aside soon, too. Greta was created in a bombardment of M-particles to be a girl that you could love. I gave her all my love for you and it became her defining characteristic. Karri, on the other hand, was a boy, like his mother wanted. Both are only half the truth. I'm going to find myself a new name in the secret passages, but for now you can call me Karri."

Olli looked at the graceful creature sitting across from him and said, "But I loved Greta."

It sounded like an accusation, and it was something like it.

Karri took his hand, looked at him thoughtfully, and said, "And Greta loved you, Olli. That was what she was created for. As a matter of fact, she loved you a thousand times more than you could ever love her back. The years spent without you were torture to her.

"She could only bear it because she believed that in the end the two of you would get to be together, one way or another. And you did. We arranged it. I arranged it, for Greta. But I knew Greta better than anyone did. She expected a lot from your love. She expected too much. Over these past few weeks you learnt to love her so much that it was just barely enough for her, and in the end she dared to be happy. But in a year, or two at most, your feelings would inevitably start to fade, while she was destined to love you more and more as time went by. Do you understand what that would have done to her?"

Olli nodded, but he didn't understand completely. Although in his chat last night Karri had tried to explain what was happening and why.

He patted Olli's hand now and explained gently, as if to a child: "You read her book. Every story has a beginning, a middle and an end. We thought that a beautiful ending would be the right thing to do for you, and…"

"You said *we*," Olli interrupted. "Who's we?"

"Us," Karri said, confused. "Me and Anne Blomroos. Didn't I mention her? Greta went to shoot the Blomrooses—she was always so dramatic in her cinematicness—but she was also too weak to carry out what she came to do. That was why I had to free her from that horrible Dr Engel, and take care of the situation with the Blomrooses."

"My Greta is not a murderer," Olli said stiffly.

Karri's eyes flashed and an expression came over his face that Olli could never have imagined on Greta's face. "Well, she certainly would have shot Anne, who tortured her thirty years ago, without batting an eyelid, but she probably would have decided to take pity on those foolish brothers and got herself into a lot of trouble. That's why I pushed her aside, shot Riku and Leo, and made a deal with Anne."

"A deal?"

"Yes. Anne would use her resources to arrange it so that Greta's greatest wish, her one and only hope in this world, would come true, and she could spend the rest of her life with you and experience complete happiness and love. Then, after the beautiful ending, and preferably before Anne herself died, I would step in to fulfil Anne's dearest hope."

Olli walked through the Apple Gate onto Hämeenkatu. A taxi was waiting. Snow had started to fall. A scooter pulled up in front of the house. A gaunt but cinematically elegant blonde woman dismounted—the same woman Olli had talked with at the film club.

Anne Blomroos.

"Well, if it isn't Olli," she said. "My dear old friend. You're still here. I thought the show was already over. The heroine died completely happy and so on. Mission accomplished, and just in the nick of time. Olli, you should be at home now. I'm sure you don't want your family to come home to an empty house."

Olli didn't say anything. Anne gave him a peck on the cheek and whispered, "Now don't be a sourpuss. Guess who's on her way to the secret passages?"

For a moment Anne Blomroos looked like the young girl who years ago happened to take a ride on the same carousel as Olli. She flashed him another smile and went into the house, where the person Olli had known first as Karri, then as Greta, the person who had now become someone else, was waiting for her.

Olli watched the snowflakes fall, got into the taxi and rode to Mäki-Matti. He went into the house, climbed the stairs, turned on the computer and looked at his wife's Facebook profile.

Aino Suominen and her son are on their way home.

Then he opened his own page. His status was empty.
What's on your mind? Facebook asked.

Post Credits:
Alternative Ending

52

A FTER THEY MAKE LOVE they are overcome with a weariness as big as the universe. Greta is falling asleep. Olli's still awake.

At some point Greta lets go of his neck, turns and sighs. She is pale but calm. Her breath is fairly steady now, though shallow and quick. The marks of Olli's teeth are distinct on her pale skin, just as she wanted. Olli, too, has deep, bloody scratches on his back and sides. *I hope that at my funeral the marks of my fingernails will remind you of one thing: the most important part of our love story won't be that I died, but that I lived, through you, and for you…*

Greta smiles in her sleep. Olli smiles at the sleeping woman. For a little while everything is all right.

After a moment's hesitation, he puts on his slippers and goes downstairs. He uses the toilet, drinks a glass of mineral water, eats a pear, sits down at the dining room table and turns on the computer. He can spend a few minutes on Facebook while Greta gets some rest.

Aino's profile has a new travel photo. Aino and the boy look straight into the camera, sunburnt and exhausted. Their eyes ask: *Why can't we come home?*

The M-particles ease Olli's guilt. They show him in a filmic light. Enthralled to the mission he's been given by the kidnappers, Olli Suominen may be a selfish cinematic character, in some sense even a traitor, but it's all for the sake of a larger-than-life love, and there's nothing a cinematic person

can do about a sequence of dramatic events once it's set in
motion. All's fair in love and war.

Then he notices that he has a new Facebook alert:

Karri has confirmed you as a friend on Facebook.

A chill goes through him. His hands feel numb and he sits
there for a moment. He goes to light a cigarette, takes a drag
and goes back to the computer to look at Karri Kultanen's
profile.

The profile photo is a sculpture of a naked youth. Olli
remembers seeing it in person when he was at the Louvre.
It's called *Sleeping Hermaphroditus*. It was sculpted by Bernini
sometime in the 1600s, on a commission from a cardinal.
The sculpted figure had a woman's breasts and a penis.
When Olli noticed this at the Louvre it gave him a start,
which made the French publishers and the Swedish literary
agent he was with burst into laughter.

Olli looks at Karri's information, which doesn't mention his
birthday, gender or hometown. All that's there is his favourite
quote, which Olli recognizes. It's from Ovid's *Metamorphoses*:

> *The restless boy still obstinately strove*
> *To free himself, and still refused her love.*
> *Amidst his limbs she kept her limbs intwined,*
> *"And why, coy youth," she cries, "why thus unkind!*
> *Oh may the Gods thus keep us ever joined!*
> *Oh may we never, never part again!"*
> *So prayed the nymph, nor did she pray in vain:*
> *For now she finds him, as his limbs she pressed,*

Grow nearer still, and nearer to her breast;
Till, piercing each the other's flesh, they run
Together, and incorporate in one:
Last in one face are both their faces joined,
As when the stock and grafted twig combined
Shoot up the same, and wear a common rind:
Both bodies in a single body mix,
A single body with a double sex.

Karri's profile has a few status updates, though not many comments. But then he only has five Facebook friends: Olli, Aino and the Blomrooses. The most recent post is from a week ago, written at night:

Karri Kultanen just woke up and is trying not to wake the man beside him and his little nymph.

Underneath it says:

Anne Blomroos likes this.

The next most recent post is from more than a year earlier, in the spring:

Karri Kultanen took two jacks out of the game, but spared the blonde Queen of Spades.

Under that one it says:

Anne Blomroos and 2 others like this.

383

The two others are Riku and Leo Blomroos.

There's also a comment from Anne:

I don't think my dear brothers would mind my bringing them along on this little cinematic project of ours (which I think of as a romantic comedy, although it does perhaps have hints of black). It'll make them look a little less small-minded than they really were, in at least one person's eyes.

Olli's cigarette has fallen on the table. He picks it up, brushes the ashes onto the floor and takes a long drag, trying to comprehend it all.

Now a little chat window with a tiny image of the sleeping Hermaphroditus and Karri Kultanen's name opens up at the bottom of the screen; Olli is so frightened that he shouts a curse.

Of course, he's aware that it's possible to chat through Facebook. He's just never had any reason to try it. Email is modern enough for him.

The message in the box says: *Hello, friend.*

Olli feels like screaming. And turning off the computer. But instead he writes: *Karri?*

Answer: *Yes. We should talk.*

Olli shakes his head. No, no, no, he really doesn't want to talk; he doesn't want to know anything about Karri. With trembling fingers, however, he writes: *Where are you?*

Then, answering his own question, he mutters aloud, "Where do you think, Sherlock?"

Without waiting for an answer, he gets up from the computer, runs up the stairs and bursts into the bedroom.

Greta is sitting on the edge of the bed, in the dark. She's naked. The laptop is open on the bedside table. The screen illuminates her pale face.

She looks at Olli and says, "My dear old friend, it's just about time for the closing scene."

The voice doesn't sound like Greta. The posture and gaze are wrong, too. There is something in the eyes that is both strange and distantly familiar.

Olli feels sick.

53

OLLI FLINGS A ROBE into Karri's lap and tells him he could at least cover the woman's body that he's had the nerve to hijack. Then he ushers him downstairs—he doesn't want to spend any more time in this room.

Karri has difficulty walking on Greta's feet; they're still stiff and numb. Olli has to help him down the stairs. It feels awkward. He's grateful for the powerful M-particles in the house that make the situation feel at least slightly less insane than it really is.

They sit across from each other at one of the downstairs tables. The room is dim; just one small light shines on the wall. Wind blasts the rain against the black window. Olli lights a cigarette and offers one to Karri.

He shakes his head and says, "Thanks, but I don't smoke. That's Greta's vice, not mine."

Olli blows smoke across the table.

"I guess it doesn't matter any more," he says quietly. "Greta's sick. The woman I love will live for maybe a few more days, then she's going to die. I wish I could say I'm glad to see you, Karri, but you're a ghost. We left you behind thirty years ago in the secret passages, me and Greta. What are you doing here now? Couldn't you show just a little respect and let us say goodbye in peace?"

"I'm sorry," Karri says in a conciliatory tone, with Greta's mouth. "Greta really is dying. She's dying tomorrow at sunrise, to be precise. She'll take her last breath in your arms and die completely happy, because she'll no longer have to fear living her whole life without you. A beautiful cinematic ending. It's my gift to her."

"How magnanimous of you," Olli whispers, horrified. "Were you planning to give something to me, too?"

The golden-haired creature across from him smiles diffidently, seeming not to notice his hostility.

Olli tries to see Karri through Greta, and when he can't, averts his eyes.

"Yes, I was," Karri says. "For the sake of our old friendship, and because I respect you, I'm going to tell you what's going to happen. I'm sure it will help you bear the sad ending more easily. There's no reason to deceive you any longer. It was only for Greta's sake that this whole performance was written and produced."

Olli must not look terribly appreciative, because Karri's eyes grow moist.

"Oh, Olli," he sighs, pressing the back of his hand against his mouth. "You make me feel like the villain in this movie, revealing his dastardly plan to the hero just before he carries it out. Greta is very important to me. I created her, after all, from myself, for you. Luckily there was still something left of me, whispering in the background. Greta thought I was her deep cinematic self. If it weren't for me, she would have remained just a plaything in Rio de Janeiro and eventually died on the operating table. And when she went to Anne Blomroos's villa, I had no choice but to step out and rescue her from her impossible revenge plan."

"Greta isn't a murderer," Olli says.

Karri is quiet for a moment, then turns serious. "Actually, your innocent little Greta would have shot Anne Blomroos without batting an eyelid. And she would have spared those foolish brothers, so she would have got caught. She would have been convicted of murder and sent to prison for the rest of her life. I couldn't allow that. So I pushed her aside, shot Riku and Leo, and made a deal with Anne."

"A deal?"

Karri nods. His eyes brighten. "For a long time I wanted to somehow make Greta's greatest dream come true. And I saw that I had the opportunity to do it. Anne and I agreed that she would use the power she had to arrange things so that Greta could spend the end of her life with you and experience complete happiness and love. And after the beautiful cinematic ending—"

Olli doesn't want to hear any more. "Well, thank you, Karri, for coming to prepare me for the death of the one I love," he snarls, shaking his head, "but I'm sure you understand that right now I really want to—"

Karri leans towards him, touches his hand, and says, "Olli, you can call me Karri—I don't mind—but Karri is no more real than Greta is. Greta was created in the secret passages to be a talented, wonderful girl that you could love. Karri, on the other hand, was the inhibited, shy boy Anna Kultanen raised for herself. Each of them is less than half of the whole truth that they both have to make way for."

Olli looks at Karri, not able to really listen to what he's saying. There is still some of this night left, but the morning is a bright front rolling towards them from the east. He lights another cigarette and wipes the tears from his cheeks as Karri whispers what is to come.

"So. Greta's condition will collapse sometime in the morning, and when you've said your goodbyes, she'll release her hold on life and pass away. Dr Oksanen will arrive, pronounce her dead and cover her with a sheet, like in the movies—we both know that Greta would appreciate that. Then the doctor will say his lines. They're sentimental and corny, but let him have them. For a respected chemist he's a surprisingly enthusiastic amateur actor, and working for Anne Blomroos, he rarely gets a shot at drama. Then you'll leave the house, and your part of the story will be over. And while the credits are rolling—if you'll pardon the expression—our doctor will give the patient the antidote, and—"

Olli grabs Karri's hand and looks hard at him. "Antidote?"

Karri avoids looking him in the eye and pulls his hand away. "Yes. The shots you've been giving her are real compounds that weaken the nervous system and slow the functions of internal organs, until they eventually nearly cease." He adds, almost in passing, "When the antidote has revived her system, Greta will be gone and I'll carry on from there."

Olli stares at him.

Karri draws himself up and continues brightly, "I'm sure you and I will see each other again, in two weeks' time, at Greta Kara's funeral in the old Jyväskylä cemetery. We can think of it as a sort of epilogue. I'll look different then. I was thinking I would cut my hair and dye it black."

"But I love Greta," Olli murmurs.

"And Greta loves you," Karri says, his eyes glowing.

"That's what she was created for. She loves you with more passion than you could possibly imagine. And over these past few weeks, with the shadow of separation looming, you have loved her so strongly that it was enough to make her happy. But in a year, or two at most, your feelings would inevitably start to fade, while her love would burn just as strongly as before… It would kill her spirit."

The resolute, passionate note in Karri's voice reminds Olli of the final scene in *Casablanca*, when Humphrey Bogart convinces Ingrid Bergman to give up their love and get on the plane with her husband.

Karri is silent for a moment, then says, "You must understand now why everything has to happen according to the script."

Olli tries to think.

They look at each other. Karri is waiting for his approval.

Olli stubs out his cigarette and shakes his head.

Karri looks confused.

Olli has had enough of this unwelcome presence. He gets up, takes a breath, grabs the golden-haired creature and drags him to the piano. Karri resists, but Olli is stronger. "Play," he growls, his hands pressed on slender shoulders.

Karri looks up at him angrily from under yellow curls. "Don't be a fool, Olli. We still have things to talk about. I haven't told you everything. We should let Greta sleep while we prepare for her last, great scene."

Olli wraps his fingers around the slender neck, presses his thumbs against the vertebrae and squeezes. "Play Chopin for me," he whispers. "Or else this whole thing will be over right now, and there won't be anybody getting up when the credits roll."

Karri starts striking the keys with a mocking grin, making no attempt at music.

Olli tightens his grip.

The lovely face reddens, the breath wheezing. Karri tries harder now.

With tears in his eyes, Olli squeezes still tighter.

"Play."

Gradually the tinkling begins to sound like music. At first there are just a few notes that sound right. Then a few stuttering passages of notes.

When the room finally fills with one of Greta's favourite nocturnes, Olli loosens his hold and lets his hands rest on her shoulders.

"How did I get here?" Greta says, hoarse and sputtering—but continuing to play.

"The main thing is that you are here," Olli says, kissing her neck and picking up the telephone. "Please keep playing. More than anything right now, I want to hear Chopin. I'm going to call Dr Oksanen. He has to come over right away. Darling, I think he may be able to cure you after all."

The End

54

THE WINDOWS BRIGHTEN. They wake at the same
time, lightly make love and lie for a long time under
the covers, holding each other.

Olli's hand is on Greta's left breast. His index finger is laid
across her nipple, his thumb gently pressing the side of her
breast. He feels a scar stretching under his hand and thinks
that it's there because of him. The thought floods him with
an overwhelming tenderness.

His face is pressed against Greta's neck. He breathes
through her golden hair and seems to smell the scent of a
warm hillside. It fills the room and carries him back to a
meadow where they had a picnic a few days after they lay
together in Wivi Lönn's house for the first time. Autumn was
postponed for a day and summer blazed up one last time
before the coming winter.

They sat in the tall grass to eat, and ended up having sex.
It was more ritual than unbridled passion. Without a word,
Greta put her half-eaten tomato sandwich back in the basket,
unzipped Olli's trousers, took her panties off under her dress
and sat on his lap.

As they merged, the M-particles sang to them from deep
in the earth, and for one moment Olli sensed all the secret
passages in Jyväskylä, their locations, their routes, as if he
were viewing a map drawn on his soul.

Naturally, their meadow is mentioned in the *Magical City*

Guide. Olli wonders if a lot of people will go there now that the book is available and the first printing is virtually sold out. Maiju at the office has told him that next summer the Jyväskylä tourist office is planning to sell guided tours to all the magical places where his love for Greta Kara was reborn.

The thought of it makes Olli sad, although it is good news for the business.

Greta sits up in bed, stretches, glows for him, wraps her arms around his neck and gives him a kiss. Then she turns on her computer and updates her Facebook status.

Greta Kara is completely happy today!

Two days earlier, Greta experienced a miraculous recovery from the neurological disease that had been pronounced terminal.

When Olli called Dr Oksanen and told him that Greta was lying in bed, not breathing, the chemist hurried over to perform the deathbed scene and help Karri rise from the dead.

The moment he walked in the door, the doctor discovered that there had been a last-minute rewrite.

Olli forced him to inject Greta with the antidote and declare that the patient would have a complete recovery. "My dear Mr Suominen, I don't know what to say," he mumbled as Olli shoved him out through the Apple Gate onto the rainy street.

Olli had no intention of telling Greta about Karri's plans. If Karri came back to haunt Greta's body, Olli was ready to do whatever the situation demanded.

Now that Greta was well again, Olli could consider what to do about his wife and son.

He felt that he had completed the task that Anne Blomroos had given him, and before the first snow, too. Karri could say what he liked, but Greta had said—on her Facebook status, no less—that she was completely happy. It was official.

That night Olli tiptoed downstairs to the computer and opened Aino's Facebook profile. The status was a relief. But it also meant that he had a lot of explaining to do to his family.

Aino Suominen and son are on their way home.

The Blomrooses' Facebook profiles had disappeared from Olli's friends list. He pondered this for a while and decided that it meant he had seen the matter to its conclusion, and there was no need to continue their connection.

He also checked to make sure there were no new posts on Karri's profile.

When he went back to the bedroom, he noticed light peeping out from Greta's laptop. It had been left open a crack.

Greta was asleep, so he pushed the computer closed and crawled into bed.

It's Sunday, so although Olli has to stop in at Book Tower to take care of some marketing plans for the *Magical City Guide*, he and Greta have the rest of the day to themselves. Greta's legs are still a little stiff, and the weather is cold. But she announces that she wants to go out and walk hand in hand through the city.

Olli is glad.

They eat breakfast. Afterwards Olli smokes a cigarette and stares out the bay window. Greta plays Chopin. Waltz no. 7.

She gets up, comes to stand behind him, and wraps her arms around him.

"Olli," she says hesitantly, "do you think we'll always love each other as much as we do now?"

Olli blows smoke at the window and tries not to think of what Karri said to him. Snowflakes are starting to fall in the garden.

Greta is waiting for an answer.

"Darling, I am sure that we will be happy for the rest of our lives," he says, suddenly filled with certainty. "And when the moment of death finally comes, we'll go together."

Death is justly considered the high point of a cinematic life. It is a strong ending for any story that has been lived truly, and also serves as a dramatic element, if not the critical turning point, in the lives of those who know the dying person.

Depending on the context and point of view, death can be emotional and melodramatic, coolly laconic and expressionless, courageous, happy, symbolic, senseless, terrifying, sickening, ironic, tragic, even comic, but whatever the tone, it gives ultimate meaning to everything that has come before it. If at all possible, a cinematic person should pay particular attention to his or her death, in order to make it elegant and cinematically meaningful.

(See following page, death scenes: Max Schreck in Nosferatu; *Lew Ayres in* All Quiet on the Western Front; *Helen Hayes in* A Farewell to Arms; *James Cagney in* Angels with Dirty Faces; *Gregory Peck and Jennifer Jones in* Duel in the Sun; *Ali MacGraw and Ryan O'Neal in* Love Story.*)*

Roll Credits

55

As they leave the publishing house, Greta takes his hand and tugs him towards Harju Ridge.

"Come on! I want to climb the steps!" she whispers, and Olli follows with a smile.

They cross the street and start up the stone staircase. Frost covers the ground. The sparse snow starts to fall thicker, turning the hillsides white.

Greta glows.

"It's winter, so we ought to go to the observation tower and drink hot cocoa with whipped cream on top. Oh, Olli, I've always hated the cold, but I love this snow! We've had two summers, but this will be our first winter. The best winter ever!"

She hangs on his arm, chattering happily.

Olli grows winded. His heart is light, but beating fast. His feet feel heavy.

Through the falling snow he sees a large, black car stop at the top of the steps. A door opens and two women and a child get out of the back seat. The first woman points at them. The other starts down the steps with the child.

"Maybe after this we can go have hot cocoa every Sunday," Greta says. "We can do it every year after the first snow and stop when the snow is melted... What's the matter?"

Olli has frozen. Greta lets out a laugh and teases him for being out of shape.

Aino and the boy have stopped a few steps above them. They're both suntanned. Her face looks tired. The boy sees his father and smiles.

They stare at each other.

Greta tightens her grip on Olli's arm.

He waits.

The other woman has started down the stairs. A pale blonde—the same woman Olli had a brief dialogue with at the film club. The one with the scooter. His feet stumble on the steps.

Anne Blomroos.

She's dying, but she is still cinematically elegant. As she comes closer she smiles wearily, one arm hanging heavily at her side.

Aino looks at Greta unconcerned and says to Olli, "Well, we're finally here. It was quite a trip. She's brought us, but she seems disappointed. She said to tell you something about how you were supposed to follow a script and apparently you didn't."

"Daddy ate the pear and he forgot," the child mumbles, his brow furrowed.

Olli turns cold.

Aino strokes the boy's head. "Yes, that's what the nice lady said," she murmurs. "She said that the second part of some previous agreement wasn't carried out and so that changes your agreement... But I guess it doesn't have anything to do with me. Whew! What a trip! We can talk about all of it later. Right now we just want to go straight home and have a shower. What do you say, Olli? Are you coming home for dinner, or do you still have work to do?"

Olli shrugs. He glances at Greta.

She looks back at him questioningly and squeezes his arm.

The falling snow fades the world around them to invisibility. Everything else is gone; all that's left are the five of them and the massive Nero's Steps, and even those are being covered little by little in a blanket of white.

Anne Blomroos is standing a few steps above. She raises both arms in front of her. Olli barely has time to think that the black thing she's holding looks a bit like a pistol, when a bang closes up his ears.

His son falls face-down on the steps as if he's been shoved, and tumbles head over heels to Olli's feet.

"Oopsy-daisy," Olli says.

The second bang makes Aino flinch, as if she's just remembered that she left the stove on. She spreads her arms, bends over and throws herself at Olli's feet, taking hold of his left shoe.

Olli looks down in surprise, first at Aino, then at his shoe. His ears are ringing. Anne's voice sounds like it's coming from somewhere very far away.

"After the beautiful ending Karri was supposed to come and take me back into the secret passages," Anne says. "It was my one and only wish in all this world. Oh, Olli. You should have known that you can't take away a girl's one and only wish."

A third bang.

Greta sighs and falls on her side, still holding Olli's hand. Her green eyes stare up at him, her pupils dilating, her mouth gulping for air.

Something red starts to mingle with the new-fallen snow on the stones.

Olli turns and looks at Anne.

She looks back at him, pistol raised, tears in her eyes. The snow falls thicker and thicker.

It is quite a cinematic moment.

SCANDINAVIAN BOOKS
FROM PUSHKIN PRESS

MIRROR, SHOULDER, SIGNAL
Dorthe Nors

Translated by Misha Hoekstra

'Sonja is a thoroughly modern heroine… nothing at all like Bridget Jones. Comical and clever, with a knife-twist of uneasiness'

The Times

KARATE CHOP
Dorthe Nors

Translated by Martin Aitken

'Beautiful, faceted, haunting stories… Dorthe Nors is fantastic!'

Junot Díaz

MINNA NEEDS REHEARSAL SPACE
Dorthe Nors

Translated by Misha Hoekstra

'Darkly funny and incisive'

FT

MY CAT YUGOSLAVIA
Pajtim Statovci

Translated by David Hackston

'A strange, haunting, and utterly original exploration of displacement and desire… a marvel, a remarkable achievement'

The New York Times Book Review

THE STOCKHOLM TRILOGY

1. CLINCH

2. DOWN FOR THE COUNT

3. SLUGGER

Martin Holmén

Translated by Henning Koch

'Ferociously noir… If Chandler and Hammett had truly
walked on the wild side, it would read like *Clinch*'

Val McDermid

A WORLD GONE MAD

The Wartime Diaries of Astrid Lindgren, Author of Pippi Longstocking

Translated by Sarah Death

'Lindgren recounts the commotions of the grand theatres of
war alongside the domestic dramas playing out in her life. Her
empathy for and insight into the horrors of war is striking'

Observer

BUTTERFLIES IN NOVEMBER

Auður Ava Ólafsdóttir

Translated by Brian FitzGibbon

'Funny and wistful… very moving, layered and optimistic'

Financial Times

THE RABBIT BACK LITERATURE SOCIETY

Pasi Ilmari Jääskeläinen

Translated by Lola Rogers

'Wonderfully knotty… a very grown-up fantasy masquerading as quirky fable. Unexpected, thrilling and absurd'

Sunday Telegraph

31901063832119